THE
Gold Eaters

Books by Ronald Wright

THE
Gold Eaters

RONALD WRIGHT

RIVERHEAD BOOKS

New York

2015

RIVERHEAD BOOKS
An imprint of Penguin Random House LLC
375 Hudson Street
New York, New York 10014

Library of Congress Cataloging-in-Publication Data

Wright, Ronald, date.
The gold eaters / Ronald Wright.
p.   cm.
ISBN 978-1-59463-462-8
1. Incas—Fiction.   2. Culture conflict—Fiction.   3. Conquerors—Peru—Fiction.   4. Explorers—
South America—Fiction.   5. Pizarro, Francisco, ca. 1475–1541—Fiction.   6. Insurgency—South
America—History—16th century—Fiction.   7. Peru—History—Conquest, 1522–1548—Fiction.
8. South America—History—16th century—Fiction.   9. South America—Discovery and
exploration—Spanish—Fiction.   I. Title.
PR9199.3.W75G65   2015   2015014720
813'.54—dc23

Printed in the United States of America
1   3   5   7   9   10   8   6   4   2

BOOK DESIGN BY NICOLE LAROCHE

MAP BY MEIGHAN CAVANAUGH

For Deborah

O Peru, land of metal and of melancholy!

—FEDERICO GARCÍA LORCA

❧

And my forebears there in Cusco . . . called themselves lords of Tawantinsuyu, which is to say the Four Parts of the World, for they thought there could surely be no other world than this.

—TITU KUSI YUPANKI

THE INCA EMPIRE ca. 1525

MAJOR ROADS ⌇
CITIES • ■

Kitu (Quito)

Tumipampa (Cuenca)

Tumpis (Tumbes)

Qashamarka (Cajamarca)

Wanuku (Huanuco)

Hatun Shawsha
(Xauxa)

Willkapampa

Rimaq (Lima)   Vitcos   Tampu (Ollantaytambo)

Machu Piqchu

QOSQO (CUSCO)

Willkaswaman

Lake Titicaca

Hatunqolla

Chuqiyapu (La Paz)

Qochapampa
(Cochabamba)

Pacific Ocean

Panama

SOUTH
AMERICA

Tukuman

Mawli

© 2015 Meighan Cavanaugh

Not until a generation after they reached the Caribbean islands in 1492 did Spaniards begin to invade the thickly peopled mainland of the Americas, which many still believed to be a part of Asia.

They achieved no major conquest until smallpox—a mass killer new to the New World—opened the way, enabling Hernán Cortés to recover from his 1520 defeat by the Aztecs and return to take their capital, the city of Mexico, by siege in 1521.

Meanwhile, Vasco Núñez de Balboa had crossed the Isthmus of Panama and waded knee-deep into an ocean new to Europeans. This he named the South Sea. In 1519 the Spaniards began building an outpost on its shore at Panama, a base from which to explore, subdue local "Indians," and plunder seafaring traders who plied the Pacific coast.

From such traders came tales of a great empire where people lived in stone cities, kept animals resembling humpless camels, and ate from plates of gold.

Far to the south, beyond the jungle, where the trees gave way to dunes and snow-capped mountains, lay the realm of the Incas. Running more than three thousand miles from southern Colombia to central Chile and western Argentina, the Inca Empire was then the second largest on Earth (after China) and the last great civilization unknown to the outside world.

In 1526, Francisco Pizarro, a founder and mayor of Panama, formed a company to find and conquer this golden land.

ONE

Northern Peru

1526-27

{ I }

He is first on the beach, as he loves to be, alone in the foredawn light where the dunes fall down to the flump of the sea and the rippled foam gleams dimly at its edge. Only pelicans are there, dark shapes along the tideline gazing seaward, hunched against the morning chill, awaiting light enough to show the glint of fish. The breeze wafting listlessly ashore is salty on his lips. Later the sun will give it strength as the desert warms, drawing it onto the land.

The boy is happy with thoughts of an easy paddle to deep water, filled nets, a freshening wind to bring him home by noon. He walks to the boats—fifty slender shapes, sharp prows in the air, flat sterns on the dry sand—a row of fangs against the sky. Today, for the first time ever, one of them is *his*.

A few weeks ago his grandfather told him to gather tall reeds from the irrigation canals. "That boat of your father's is sitting too low," he said. "Rot at the heart. I can smell it. I doubt she'll last till he gets back. Whenever *that* may be." The old man spat gloomily onto a pile of sweepings in the sunbaked yard. "For now, you're the man of this house. You're big enough to need a boat of your own. Bring me the makings and I'll build it. New britches, new boat— that's what I say." He smiled and gave a little sniff, a sudden uptake of breath, his sign he was done speaking. The boy ran to a canal right away, coming back in a sweat with the first of many loads, spreading them in the sun. Every day he watched his grandfather's old hands stook and trim and bind the dry reeds into a sturdy, unsinkable craft.

It is there, waiting for him, its pale new body standing out from others in the gloom. As he grasps it by the waist and lifts—so light!— he breathes in sun and earth. Smells of the land not the sea. How long will it take, he wonders, to become a sea-thing of salt and fish.

The dawn begins to show behind the highland wall beyond the desert, silhouetting the dark rim of the lower range and blushing the snowfields far above. He turns his back to the light, takes off his clothes—a plain cotton shirt and the new breechclout—grown-up wear to go with his grown-up name. Waman. Like his grandfather. It still sounds too big for him, a name he must learn to make his own. He folds the breechclout carefully, smoothing the soft white fabric, admiring the even weave and elegant design—bands of blue cormorants and red fishes along each border—done by his mother's hands. Sometimes he saw his cousin Tika take a turn. A deft weaver too. He thinks of her slender fingers working the mysteries of the loom.

A less happy thought clouds his mind: Is Tika becoming so accomplished that her weaving might take her away? They are almost the same age, he older by six months. Since he now has his manly name, she will soon be grown enough to follow the womanly arts at a House of the Chosen in some distant city, to weave and sing and brew for the Empire, for its temples, its lords. Not long ago they spoke of this. "Why not?" she said. "I don't want to stay in this village forever. I want to see the cities, the highlands, the jungle. Don't you? And"—her voice faltered and the exuberance drained from her face—"and I want to see where I lived before. Before I came here. That will be hard, I know, but one day I must."

Waman asked her how she could go there, go anywhere, if she became cloistered with the Chosen women. "Oh, they let you out now and then," Tika said brightly, recovering her spirit, as if she'd looked into it. "And if I were to do well there, and tend my looks"—she cocked her head, running a finger along the edge of her jaw—"I might marry a great man."

An old man, more like, Waman answered tartly, burning with jealousy and a sense of his youth, his rustic simplicity.

He sighs, leaving the clothes under a stone. He carries boat, paddle, and net down to the ocean, wet sand spreading his toes.

Besides a gourd of drinking water and a small bag of toasted corn which Mother and Tika give him every morning, for this special day he has brought a small pot of his grandfather's beer. Filling his mouth with the yeasty drink (he is still too young to like it, though he wants to) he purses his lips, spraying boat, sea, and the first bulge of sun rousing from its sleep under the earth.

Father Sun, Mother Sea, he says aloud, may this be a good day. The first of many. Let it be so.

One by one the pelicans take flight.

The new craft rides lively and high between his legs, cresting the swells, tossing its prow, gliding into the troughs. Like a dolphin. Or like Drum, the big old dog he used to ride over the fields when he was little, named for the taut hide on her back, her deep bark. A good name for a boat.

Far out to sea he fastens the paddle and lets himself drift, casting the net, watching it sink, hauling it in, casting, scarcely feeling the sun on his chest and the chill of the deep around his feet. The fishing is good, though he has to drive off gulls who swoop in with fierce cries whenever he stows a catch in the keep-net under the boat. At mid-morning he stops to chew some corn and drink from the gourd. His mind lifts from sea to land. The sun is nosing into a thin overcast that builds above the desert at this time of year, robbing the sands of contrast. The mountains seem to have drawn back, mere suggestions of bulk behind a dusty scrim. Up there somewhere is his father, toiling in the thin air and hard light of the highlands. Making the Emperor's roads, perhaps, or building houses in the Emperor's great cities of stone. Or fighting in his wars on the northern edge of the World.

That is the worst, the fighting.

The boy looks at the water again and becomes aware of his smooth brown legs astride the neatly woven reeds, salt drying on his thighs, shiny black whiskers sprouting above his cock. He is changing, becoming a man. Fighting is a manly thing. But these wars are not our wars, his father used to say. What need do we have of roads and empires? Here we have the sea and good earth, the green valley to grow corn for food and beer, cotton for cloth and nets. We travel by sea. We eat from the sea. And when we eat from the fields it is the fish buried with the seed that makes the land bear. We are blessed. Never forget that. And never forget the mountains. Like the sea, the mountains give water and life. Though at a price. For the highland lords come down and meddle in our lives. They hold the strings of the World.

His mother, Chaska, would laugh at such talk whenever she heard it. "Come, now, Mallki. I'm a highlander myself. It didn't seem to bother you too much when we were younger." And she'd wink at the boy and the girl. And Grandfather would smile and give his little snort.

Something out on the horizon. One, two, three . . . seven sails. Two pairs and three alone. Five ships, then: three small and two big freighters with twin masts. All hull-down, showing only the rig, their deckhouses hidden by the curve of the seaworld. Heading north to lands beyond the Empire? Or following the current until they stand westward twenty days to the Tortoise Islands?

The sight always stirs him. This is what he will do as soon as he's old enough. He will go to sea, where there are no emperors, no wars. Where he can become a man, and a man can become what he may. Soon.

The sun is still high when he carries his boat up the beach, sets it on end, and heads home with a full net over his shoulder. The path winds between dunes and rocky hillocks; soon the valley is below him, the crops a startling green under the arid hills, fields fanning out from the river between silver threads of channelled water. In thanks for a good day's work, Waman adds a stone to the cairn that marks the highest point on his way. The town comes into view—Little River, the only place he knows—its flat-roofed houses the hue of the desert from which they are made, brightened by red and yellow awnings over doors and patios, by striped blankets draped on washing lines, and some by a band of ochre paint where the walls rise above the rooftops. Here and there are seated figures of women in white shifts, weaving at back-strap looms tied to posts or fruit trees. The wind brings children's voices, bird and animal cries. The family dog—one of old Drum's puppies—runs to greet him, sniffing the swollen net. Tika gets up from her work, clasps his shoulders and congratulates him on the haul. The neighbours' little ones are playing outside, chasing ducks in the narrow canal that runs along the street. His mother puts steamed corn and soup with avocado before him, leaving him to eat on the bench below the awning while she and Tika sort the fish into those they will cook, those they will salt, and small bony ones to set aside with the offal for feeding the land.

Having eaten, he lies down on the cushioned bench and drowses until the heat relents. He feels too tired to go to the little schoolroom on the square, where a teacher gives lessons in the Empire's general language, in counting, and in the related art of the quipu, by which numbers and words are tied on strings. Waman finds the system hard to grasp; so far he has learnt the knots for one to a hundred and his own name, nothing more. Today his mother does not press him. She seems weary herself, overcome by a sadness that settles on her sometimes. For the first time, he has seen a white hair in her braid, and spidery lines beneath her eyes. The girl's face, though, is clear and lovely. Tika catches him staring and frowns, fluttering a hand as one does at a bee. Waman looks away. He is shy and dares not look that way at other girls. But why should Tika mind?

She came to Little River not long after his eighth birthday. There was a postal runner, announcing an urgent message with a trumpet blast. There was also a woman, older than his mother, a Chosen lady of importance, who came to the door leading Tika by the hand. Surely the runner must have come before the lady, weeks before? Yet in his memory it's as if they arrived together on that day. The terrible news, his mother wailing and pounding the wall, crying for her lost sister; and the silent, bruised survivor, the thin, shrinking child—like a little fish herself. He had never met his cousin or her parents. They had lived far away, more than a month's journey over many high mountains, somewhere in a province called Huanuco. There had also been another child, a younger brother. Tika seldom speaks of them, even now, and when she does she becomes tearful and withdrawn. Later Waman's mother told him how Tika came to be here, speaking in whispers after she'd regained composure by busying herself with the poor girl's care. The Earth had stirred in her sleep one night, Chaska said, burying people in their homes, drowning others in a flood of ice and clay that swept down from a mountain lake with a roar that could be heard in the next province. She called it a *pachakuti*—a word new to him—an earthquake, a catastrophe, the world turned upside down. The Empire's men came quickly in teams with llama trains and spades and crowbars. They set up tents, kitchens, and they dug and dug. One corner of Tika's house had not fallen, and there in freezing mud they found her, blue and barely alive. "That's how Tika was born to us," Chaska concluded, "pulled like a baby from the womb of Mother Earth."

An odd way to put it, Waman thought, but his mother has always had a way with words. And he recalls that she'd lost a baby girl of her own a year or two before, stillborn and unnamed, a small mummy wrapped and taken to the Town of the Dead in the desert beyond the fields.

He watches his mother and his cousin talking softly as they sort and clean the catch. Never has Tika seemed so dear to him, so lovely. There is grace in her upright back and the deft movement of her fingers as she slits and guts a fish. He will marry her. They will be together always. After all, she's a cousin not a sister (though often she seems like one). Only an emperor can take a sister for a wife. But anyone may wed a cousin.

The boy's father, Mallki, comes home, unharmed yet changed. He will not be called up again for five years, having paid his work-tax to the Empire. And he has been honoured, made some kind of officer while away, in charge of a hundred men, with a hint that he may become the village leader when the incumbent retires. The family is also rewarded with bolts of cloth and bags of grain from government warehouses. Mallki is full of new tales—of fellowship, foreign ways, fighting for the Empire. And a new loyalty towards the Emperor, an awed affection that the boy mistrusts. "Why do you like the Emperor now," Waman asks, "when you didn't before? He's a haughty, meddling highlander. I've heard you say so. Those very words."

A shadow darkens Father's face. His hand whips out—the surprise worse than the blow. His father never used to hit him. Not like that, for something so small.

"I come home after a few months and find you a man, eh?" Mallki says. "Grown-up britches and all. A man's mouth too. Don't forget, *Master* Waman, that you're half highlander yourself. Your mother lived in the highlands until the Empire settled her family here on the coast when she was little. The Empire's language was her own."

Mallki falls silent, eyes on his son, scowling, but Waman can tell he regrets losing control. Then:

"I've brought you something. From the mountains." His father opens the plain cotton bag that hangs from his shoulder and takes out another, this one of wool and brightly coloured. "Open it." Inside Waman finds a small, slim-necked gourd with a rubber stopper and some dried leaves wrapped in a square vicuña cloth. Coca and lime. A man's gift! The boy grins happily and throws his arms around his father.

"Let's sit over there under the tree," Mallki says. "Let's chew."

He shows his son how to lay out the leaves on the cloth, how to pick five of the best and fan them out in his hand. He does the same himself. He then takes all ten leaves, lifts his face to the sunlight filtering through the pepper tree, and blows over them gently. Adding lime from the bottle, he makes up two small quids. They chew without speaking for a while. Waman feels a numbness in his cheek, a warmth flowing into his chest, an inner power.

"I'm not sure I understood the Empire until now," his father says at last. "And of course I'd never met the Emperor himself. People like us seldom do. You're right that I used to grumble. The Empire makes demands. We must work for it, till its fields, pay taxes with our time, even risk our lives, as I've been obliged to do. The World is changing fast. When your granddad was born—in this house, just as I was—there was no Empire. Not down here. In those days we had our own kings and queens. They lived by the sea, as we do. They spoke our language. Everyone in Little River spoke only Tallan. There was no Quechua here then, except a little for trade."

Waman has heard much of this before. He is bursting with thoughts of his own. Brilliant thoughts. He wants to cut in, to answer, to argue. What is his father's point? But, grateful for the fine woollen bag, for the honour of being allowed to chew, he holds his tongue by listening to voices in the street and the sounds of the yard, wind in the branches above them, the *cuy-cuy* of guinea pigs scuffling for scraps.

"The Empire," his father goes on, the coca making him talkative, "we have to do things for it, but in return the Empire does things for us. It builds new canals, new fields, new roads. When we have a bad harvest, the Empire feeds us from its granaries. If there's an emergency, it sends help. Your cousin Tika, for example—Tika lives with us because the Empire rescued her and found her next of kin."

"But the Emperor makes war all the time," Waman says, unable to keep quiet any longer. His father stops chewing, stares fixedly. As a llama does when about to spit in your eye.

"Not all the time, Waman. Many provinces joined of their own free will. Some in fear of the Empire's might, to be sure. But others welcomed an end to their own squabbles. I did see some fighting in Quito Province, yet only to secure the northern border. Mostly we were building roads and bridges. The Emperor has announced that these wars will be the end of war. The boundary is now fixed at the Blue River; the World is big enough."

Mallki chews on thoughtfully for a while. He wipes a little leafy spittle from his lip and moves the quid to his cheek, where it makes a small bulge. "Some doubt it. But I believe the Emperor meant what he said. Ask anyone in the highlands what they think of him and they'll tell you he's a good king. Open-handed with everybody, great and small—as those who hold power should always be. And affable. Twice while I was there he threw a big feast and drank with his troops. He could outdrink any of us—yet we never saw him drunk. His enemies fear him with good reason. But he's a great friend to the weak. He opened the storehouses to the wounded and the widows— on both sides—after our victories."

Waman thinks: *our* victories?

Weeks later, in the cool time of mists and sea fog, when grass greens the desert like mould, a line of stakes appears across the sands. Then come imperial workers, teams of men who dress and speak strangely—in several different tongues. Waman knows only Tallan and Quechua. Now he hears languages for which he has no name. The workers build a bridge across the river, a great hammock of thick cables slung between stone piers. Through the dunes they cut a highway—with flagstones, walls, and a canal beside it—stringing the small valley like an emerald onto the great coast road, which it's said will link all the seaports in the World. The road brings new sights, new sounds: the clicking toes of llama trains, the slap of many sandals on pavement, laughter and beery singing from a barracks outside the town.

A time of fullness. The mountain snowmelt is heavy, the fields are well watered, the river runs fast under the hanging bridge. Now it is his father who takes the new boat to sea and comes back laden with fish. Waman is sent to school most days and given humbler tasks: weeding, clearing ditches, feeding ducks and llamas, scaring birds from the young corn with his sling. As if he were still a boy. But his voice is cracked and deepening. He's had enough of children's work.

His daydreams follow the ships on the horizon. Above all he misses the sea.

"Why won't you let me take the boat out?" he asks his father one day, as he has many times. "No more of that!" Mallki snaps. "Do as you're told."

Waman sees that mood on his father again, the mood brought home from the wars. He opens his mouth. Says nothing.

"If you're such a man, Waman, you'd better speak up like one. Out with it."

"Granddad made that boat for me."

"I'll hear no *me* in this family!"

Next morning, while the house is still asleep, Waman packs water and food in his woollen bag as if heading to the fields. Tika comes into the kitchen to light the fire, gathering dry stalks from under a bench, scattering the guinea pigs who live there. He worries their squeaks will wake his parents before he can talk to her alone. Tika knows of his daydreams—the dreams of many a youth. She has her own dream of becoming a Chosen. And she has ears. Waman is sure she will help, or at least understand. Crouching beside her as she tends the flame, whispering his news, he fails to see the flare of anger in her eyes.

"You can't mean it."

"I do. I must."

"When?"

"Today. Say nothing. Not until I'm well away. You're clever, you'll know what to do. And what not to."

She is on him like a watchdog. He is knocked on his back, stunned by the strength of her blow. She holds him down, his wrists locked in her wiry hands, her long hair tenting his head. No, she hisses. No! The words are loud in his ear though her voice is low, her nose touching his, her tears running into his eyes, mingling with tears of his own. He bites her chin, frees one hand as she rears, tries to push her off. His hand connects with the softness under her shawl. He pinches hard. She hits him in the eye and pins his hand again. But still she has not yelled.

Her face, warm and salty, is against his. She strokes his nose with hers. She draws his lower lip into her mouth. She lets his lip go and kisses him firmly, spreading his mouth. The way he has heard that grown women kiss their men. "You can't go," she says. "Stay longer. Then we can plan things. We can go together." Still astride him, she sits up and pulls her shift over her head. He sees her small breasts in the firelight, her upturned nipples, the deep blush from his pinch.

Often he has thought of this, longed for it, pictured how this moment might be. But he finds to his dismay that desire has left him like a tide. He is trembling, a strange fear stranding him on the earthen floor, a voice in his head saying he is unworthy and this is all too much, too soon. His mind is a welter, his face hot, pulse quaking in his ears. He must go, and think, be alone.

"I will come back for you," he whispers. "We'll be together. But not now. Now I must get away."

She releases him, wipes her mouth. "You're mad."

They listen to the house. It is still, except for snores. Mother, Father, Grandfather were drinking beer up on the roof last night. She stands, pulls on her shift and a shawl. "All right," she whispers. "You've got what you want."

"What?"

"I want you gone. We'll see how you do out there." She scoops a guinea pig off the floor and wrings its neck. He hears the crack, a small, sad sound.

"This hurts," she says.

Waman says nothing, burning with shame.

"Oh, I don't mean you," she adds. "You can't hurt me. It just hurts each time I take one of these little lives."

She presses the warm furred body and a bag of toasted corn into his hands. "We can't have you getting hungry and slinking home tomorrow like a dog."

Now Waman is glad of the Emperor's new road. He had pondered taking the boat—which he still regards as his—and paddling north till he reached the big port where the ships come and go. Three days with luck, maybe four. But that would make him a thief. Even if he wasn't caught and jailed by the authorities, his father and mother would never forgive him.

He moves quickly as the morning lightens, at a trot on the stone flags. He pushes hard, as if wanting to wear himself out, test himself, make himself stronger. Older. How can he turn back now? He must go on, and to sea, if only for a month or two.

Twice he hears running feet, but they belong to postmen who streak by in their checkered uniforms without a glance, intent on handing their messages to the next relay.

His mind runs over what happened in the kitchen, and what did not. To keep going takes all the will he can muster. If Tika had not shamed him—*dared* him—with her parting words, he might turn back. But then there'd also be Grandfather Waman to face, a bold man who went to sea in much the same way when he himself was young. And who has given him his name. The boy fortifies himself by recalling the elder Waman's tales of twenty-day voyages west over deep water, with no sight of land until the Tortoise Islands, where he caught the giant in whose shell he brews his beer. And onward many more days, to the place called the Fire Islands where the Sea People live, those who skim the waves like flying fish in boats with tall sails and twin hulls of hollowed trees. And the long coastal runs up north to the hotlands where the desert ends and a thick jungle runs down to the surf—a land of wild beasts and cannibals. And yet further to other kingdoms with wooden towns on stilts, strange people eager to trade.

Anywhere. I will go anywhere.

The road leaves the sea and cuts through low hills, taking the shortest way to Tumbes, northernmost port of the Empire. He rests that afternoon in a gully shaded by tall cactus and a carob tree. Others have just been there; he is able to breathe life into the embers of their campfire and grill the guinea pig before it spoils. A sad meal, the last he will receive from Tika in . . . how long? *I want you gone.*

On the second day the country begins to change, scattered bushes thickening into dry woods in the folds of the hills. That night, he sleeps by the roadside in a cutting, glad of retaining walls between himself and the trackless bush. The darkness is alive with cries of foxes, monkeys, parrots, owls, and other things he doesn't know and tries not to imagine. Once or twice he stirs at the quick feet and breath of an imperial runner, but they never stop between relays. There are no other travellers, no fires in the night, nothing but the new highway and the woods. He has never felt so alone.

On the third day the road drops down from the foothills to rejoin the desert. He sees a wide river, fields and canals spread like green wings over the tawny land. The sea beyond. And a great town on a rise, buildings blazing in the sun.

Waman has never seen a city before, nor such a throng: farmers and fishermen in plain cotton like those at home; lofty officials of the

Empire with checkered tunics and gold earspools; lords or wealthy traders in multicoloured cloaks and turbans; splendid ladies in long gowns, hair braided and studded with gems. He is dismayed by the human din, not the drowsy murmur of a village but a flurry of cries and tongues—his own, spoken here with a slight accent, others he has never heard, and the crisp mountain speech of the Empire, which all must learn or at least understand.

It is about midday. The boy passes fruit and vegetable stalls shaded by awnings, and an inn where people are drinking beer and palm wine. The place is smoky with cooking. Smells of seared meat, steamed maize, and spices torment him—he finished all but a handful of his corn at first light and has nothing to give for a meal. Nor is it a weekend, when the Empire lays on a public feast in every town.

He goes on towards the centre, which he must cross to reach the docks. At home he would be greeted by passersby, but here no one pays any mind to a fisherboy. Parts of the town are old and plain, of mud brick and poured adobe like Little River, but around the square are newer, grander buildings. One, filling a whole block, is startling— its façade painted with whales, birds, conches, and swordfish, in red and black on ochre walls. Uniformed sentries stand outside, and Waman guesses this must be the famed hall of the city's Governor: a great lady, he has heard.

A few townsfolk are sitting drowsily in the middle of the square, on the edge of a low dais with a trickling fountain. He joins them to take a drink and eat the last of his grain. His eyes roam over the city sights, particularly a strange and even larger building opposite the painted palace. He strolls by for a closer look on his way out. This must be a temple of the Empire, for its roof is steeply pitched—not flat like the others—and trimmed with sheets of gold. The doorway, twice his height, is made of smooth masonry, the work so massive and precise it looks impossible, as if stone blocks had magically been

17

rendered soft as clay and pressed together in a perfect fit. A crimson curtain hides the mysteries beyond the threshold. In the heat, his hunger, his light-headedness, the boy feels a little of his father's awe for the highland emperors who can build such things—who long ago, when Grandfather was young, swept down from their city in the clouds to rule the World.

It's a tiring walk to the docks, longer than expected, though Waman is cheered by the familiar sight of fishing craft upended along the shore. There is little business at this hour. Most people are indoors or under trees and shelters, resting after lunch.

Three big ships are tied at a jetty that bends into deep water. Men and women are working by the furthest, stowing freight briskly as if aiming to catch the tide. Delicious smells of pineapple, coconut, sweet potato, peppers, and jerked meat waft from the ship's stores, contending with the burnt sharpness of pitch from timbers and ropes. Bales of cotton and wool are being slung aboard and fastened on deck beneath oiled tarpaulins. In charge is a burly man wearing nothing but a white cloth tied up around his loins, a red turban on his head, and a tattooed band of pelicans marching in faded blue across his chest. He is bent over a tangle of rigging, sweating heavily, cursing to himself.

"Are you the owner?" Waman asks.

"Owner? If it's the owners you want, you won't find them here. They're fifteen days south, and that's the way I like it."

"But this is your ship?"

"I'm her skipper. And I'm busy."

"Do you need men?"

"Men, maybe. Boys, no."

"I can paddle, steer, and fish. I'm strong . . . I've sailed to the Tortoise Islands."

"How so?" The captain looks the boy up and down for the first time.

"With my grandfather."

"Why aren't you sailing with him now, then? What's his name? Has he got one? I know every skipper from here to Chincha." Seeing that his lie is about to unravel, Waman glances aside, to where several ships are moored abreast in the channel. The serpents-and-rainbow flag of the Empire hangs limply from each masthead. Soldiers are dozing against a deckhouse.

"The Emperor took his ship. For the wars. But not him—he's too old."

The captain looks up from his work again, a sly grin on his face.

"I'll say one thing for you, boy. You're quick-witted. Get loading there. We'll see what kind of worker you are."

"I ask nothing. Only food."

A single cough of mirth from the tattooed chest.

"Food is all you'll get."

At the dock, in Tumbes, the ship had seemed huge—thirty paces in length, eight in beam, made of giant balsa logs cunningly notched and lashed, with a raised deck of slatted timber and a long split-cane deckhouse between the masts. But alone on the heaving vastness of the sea, the craft has shrunk in Waman's eyes to a floating cage. They are twenty-three on board: ten crew, himself, and a dozen traders, men and women who between them have more than thirty tons of cargo. At first the boy is entrusted only with tending the cook fire, fishing on calm days, tightening lashings over the freight whenever seas are high. But he is quick to learn the ship's ways—how to spread and reef a sail, how to raise and lower the centreboards that make her tack into the wind.

They are eleven days out, in a region where twice a year the noonday sun stands straight overhead, when the lookout spies another sail. A ship is approaching from the north, running before the wind as if homeward bound to the Empire. The merchants get angry with the captain: he should have told them others had sailed this way already. Their goods will fetch less. The choicest products of the hotlands—the best gems, chocolate, conches, corals—will have been snapped up. The captain glares at them, makes no reply. He climbs the foremast and stays aloft at the crosstree for a long time, staring, gripping the perch with his knees, roofing his eyes with both hands.

"Rigged like us," he says, upon regaining the deck. "But I don't recognize that ship." He stands by the foremast, arms folded, waiting. When all the traders have gathered and calmed themselves, he speaks with the air of someone who knows more than he will say.

"That ship isn't one of ours—though it's rigged like ours. It looks as big as we are. It is sailing swiftly. There's a strange emblem on the sail. You should worry less about your prices and more about your skins."

They are far out on the open sea, the white cusp of a mountain the only trace of the World in sight. He orders the crew to fall off and make for land.

The strange ship matches the change of course. It will catch them. The captain knows this. As the vessel draws near he sees it is indeed the new thing he has heard about from other seafarers, the thing he dreads.

❦ 2 ❧

Francisco Pizarro is sick of salt horse. "Horseflesh is for riding, not eating," the Commander growls at the cookboy as they all sit down to another meal of the same foul stew in the caravel's sterncastle.

Pizarro stares at the hollow faces, mangy beards, and dull eyes around the table. A skeleton crew—eight lads and a brace of old men, counting himself and Pilot Ruiz—and beginning to look like skeletons too. The Commander tests the slackness of his belly with a clutch. It was firm when the expedition sailed from Panama in such hope and pride: two ships, two hundred men, three dozen horses, and enough stores to feed them all (so he gambled) until they reached the golden kingdom of the south.

Pizarro's belief in this rich land—*Perú*, as some call it—is still unshaken. The rumours have been many and consistent. But in Christ's name, how much further can it be? He asks himself this every day. How can native traders reach such a far country with their clumsy craft, while his ships meet only headwinds, squalls, tempests, eerie becalmings, thwarting currents? To say nothing of the shipworm, who never sleep, gnawing their little tunnels through the hull.

Sometimes he wonders if Pilot Ruiz has missed Peru somehow, overshot it in fog or darkness. But the kingdom sounds too big for that—a vast country of dry sands stretching forever along the shore, a land without trees except where rivers run down to the South Sea from ranges of snow-capped mountains. They have seen no hint of anything like this. Quite the contrary. Nothing but gloomy jungles, impenetrable mangroves, endless rains, snakes that can swallow a man whole, and enough mosquitoes to bleed the hordes of the Great Turk dry. And the few open spots where Christians might rest, might even settle and live—all teeming with cannibals and sodomites who fight like tigers, unfazed by horses and guns.

The Commander keeps these musings to himself. Outwardly he is confident, as the leader of any pack must be lest his fellows tear him down. Thank God his irascible partner, Almagro, isn't aboard. He'd be making mischief by now, to be sure. It is all too clear to Pizarro, and doubtless to others, that this southerly reconnaissance is the last hand he has to play, its opening provided by a lucky change of wind two weeks ago. Months before, with supplies exhausted and his men on the brink of mutiny, he had no choice but to halt and make camp on a small island. Until conditions improved. They did not, though costly raids on the mainland for corn, meat, women, and whatever gold could be sacked from Indian towns and villages bought him a little time. Almagro, the other ship, and the bulk of the force are waiting back on that island, barely one hundred men all told—reduced to half strength by hunger, illness, wild beasts, and poisoned arrows, one of which took out Almagro's eye. *Half strength!* he thinks ruefully, scratching his ribs. He could say that of himself. His shirt sags loose, his belt has been shortened, and in the looking glass his cheeks hang like rags.

Pizarro seldom allows himself to feel his years, though he's old enough to be the father or even the grandfather of his shipmates, all in their late teens and early twenties. All except for Pilot Ruiz, the gaunt fellow of forty or so presiding self-importantly in the captain's chair. The Pilot, too, might be the father of this lot. Not that there's anything fatherly about him. A master shipman without doubt, but what a pious, humourless, ascetic stickler. The Commander sighs, releasing a foul gust. Every one of his fifty years, it seems lately, weighs upon him like an incubus.

The Commander's dislike for the Pilot is reciprocated. Ruiz has not forgotten that Pizarro was among the betrayers of poor Balboa, beheaded on false charges. Eight years ago now. Long enough to be set aside in mutual interest, maybe. Not long enough to forgive.

What does Pizarro know about horseflesh anyway? Ruiz asks himself on hearing the growled complaint. Our leader he may be, but everyone laughs behind his back whenever he's fool enough to get on a horse. The man rides like a drunk on a donkey.

The Pilot also glumly scans the men around the *Santa Elena*'s table. And these the best: the fittest from the base camp. What a relief to have left the rest of that mob behind! Better at sea with ten starving men than ashore among a hundred. If the damned Indians hadn't killed so many horses, there wouldn't even be this filthy meat. And if so many Christians hadn't died, there'd be even more mouths to feed. Mouths willing to eat rats, dogs, seagulls, perhaps even their own dead—a thing he's seen more than once in thirty years at sea. A feast for the Devil.

The Pilot notes several men drooling as the miserable fare is ladled into their bowls, especially the Greek Candía, Pizarro's gunner and the tallest aboard. They can barely wait for the grace. Time to put matters before them all, once we've eaten. Time to give up before we die, one by one, and slide into the sea. Although Ruiz is master of this ship, the decision to turn round cannot be his alone—once back in Panama (God willing), Pizarro would gladly make him the scapegoat for yet another failed expedition. Rotten wood sinks, the Pilot says to himself, but rotten men tend to float above their betters.

He raps his pewter mug on the table.

"Commander Pizarro. Gentlemen. Two weeks have now passed since we left Gallo Island and our comrades. The stores"—the Pilot waves his hand at the cleaned-out bowls—"well, we've barely enough left for another fortnight. Furthermore, it has pleased God to keep the wind behind us until now. Unless He turns His winds around when we do, they'll be against us heading back.

"By my reckoning"—the Pilot pauses theatrically, straightening in his chair to give the listeners time to reflect that Bartolomé Ruiz is the best pilot in the Indies, his navigation not to be doubted—"by my reckoning we've made four degrees of latitude since Gallo: a little under three hundred miles, give or take. Land miles, that is." His eyes settle on the Commander to underline Pizarro's ignorance of seamanship. "The astrolabe tells me we are now upon the equator. No Christian has ever sailed so far into the great South Sea. Yet what have we seen of the southern kingdom we seek? Have we come to a desert land where people ride camels, where they dwell in stone cities, where gold is common as iron?"

The Pilot searches the faces to gauge the effect of his rhetoric. "It is true the forest savages have some gold and emeralds on them," he adds, to forestall any argument on those grounds. "But only enough to lure us on, to make us hazard our God-given souls."

Murmurs and nods around the table. Pilot Ruiz's frustration is widely shared.

Commander Pizarro sits rigidly upright, glaring like an eagle over their heads. Without a glance at the Pilot, or any sign he's even listened, he speaks at last.

"We'll hold our course. I have no doubt the golden land draws near. And we must cross the equatorial line decisively so none can deny that ours is the first Christian ship to do so. This honour is within our grasp. Let us seize it for King Charles!"

He gets up from the table abruptly and goes on deck, into a moonless night.

Has my luck forsaken me at last? Francisco Pizarro asks himself, clutching the rail and staring towards the distant shore which lies like a black whale basking under the stars.

He conjures a boyhood memory from Spain, an inner talisman he summons whenever he's especially low. A spring evening in the year his whiskers sprouted. The church of Santa María in Trujillo. He was praying to the Virgin for good fortune, kneeling on a floor paved with the gravestones of dead Pizarros. Often he came here to greet their bones and beseech their souls to help him, since the living Pizarros never did.

As he left the church, his sleeve was plucked. A ragged man stood there, a cripple with an arm hanging like the writhen stem of a dead vine. *For Holy Mary touch this shrivelled arm, young man,* the beggar said. *For God's love give me a coin and I shall tell you all. One day you shall be great!* Francisco looked into eyes like boiled onions framed by a filthy hood. The man was blind. Yet the sightless gaze had some unearthly hold, the gaze of a seer. Pizarro had two *maravedís* in his pocket. He gave one, and did not shrink from tapping the handless arm, for somehow the words seemed more than beggar's lies. *Your sword-arm shall be as mighty as this arm of mine is weak. You shall win wars in a far land. You'll be the greatest warrior since Alexander. You'll become the richest conqueror in the world!*

When, old man, and where? Granada? Italy? Tell me!

But the beggar slid away, saying nothing more except to turn his head towards the west and hiss, *The sea, the Ocean Sea.*

So not Granada, the infidels' last nest in Spain. Nor Naples, where his father had gone to war. Did the beggar mean the Canaries, the Azores? Even a boy knew those islands had no riches.

Young Francisco walked on in a trance, stopping beside the chapel of Santiago, Slayer of Moors. There, watching the daylight flare and fade behind the Moorish castle on the height, he thought of the great sea that swallows the sun. He had to give his last coin and hear more! He ran back through narrow streets and thickening shadows to where the fellow had accosted him. But nobody was there. The evensong worshippers had left for home, the iron-bound doors were locked. Only swallows scything the sky, stray dogs regarding him with shifty eyes, storks on the bell tower clacking their bills like doleful castanets.

For weeks Pizarro sought the man, roaming all Trujillo, accosting monks and shopkeepers, even searching shepherds' huts in rocky outcrops where the hills break up in a stony surf on the Extremadura plain.

A beggar! people said, laughing. You seek a beggar? Look in any doorway. And Pizarro, given to daydreams born of hunger and solitude, eventually came to doubt the meeting had ever happened; even to fear he'd been tempted by a minion of the Devil.

Then, just two or three years later, Admiral Columbus found the islands of the Indies across the Ocean Sea. When the Admiral sought men for a second voyage, Francisco Pizarro was on board.

The following day, about mid-morning, a lookout sings from the crosstree. He has spied a sail—another caravel—beating towards them from the south. The Pilot orders the man down and goes aloft himself, hoisting his worn body up the shrouds, no easy task for an underfed man of his years. Ruiz has been scrupulous in giving the same rations to all, making no exception for himself—nor for the

Commander, however much that mastiff growls. He stays aloft half an hour, until certain the lookout is not mistaken. The unknown ship is still hull-down, but her rig and twin masts must be a caravel's.

The Pilot regains the deck in a fury. Not only have they failed in their errand to find the golden land, but the consolation prize of being first to sail these waters has been snatched away. What has he, a devout man, done to so anger the Lord? And who in God's name could those seafarers be? One of Magellan's long-lost ships? Some other navigator sent round the Horn by King Charles? Or a Portuguese from the Spice Islands, blown here by storms or—worse—daring to trespass on realms the Pope has given by treaty to the King of Spain?

He draws the Commander aside, out of earshot from the rest, who might well look on this unwelcome surprise as a deliverance. Pizarro shares the Pilot's thoughts.

Their misgivings sharpen when the other ship goes about and falls off, as if to avoid them and run for land. But she is slower. Soon the two close to half a mile, and the sharp-eyed Pilot—again at the crosstree—is more baffled than ever. Though rigged like a caravel, the other ship is long and low on the water, with a house amidships. Unlike any vessel he has seen.

Drawing nearer, Ruiz sees she is built of buoyant timber like the rafts made by Indians along the coast. But this is far bigger, with two masts, and her sails are indeed as tall and shapely as his own. There are stacks of freight or provisions and some twenty people on deck, watching him as he watches them. What can they be but survivors of some shipwreck—most likely a Spanish wreck—who have made a craft from local timber and their salvaged rig? Yet the striped pennant at her masthead bears no sign of a cross. And the folk aboard are outlandishly dressed in turbans and bright tunics, as if they were Moors or Jews.

The Pilot runs alongside and hails the strange craft, calling in Spanish and Portuguese to the only figure now on deck—a bear of a man, half naked, at the helm of a long steering oar. This must be the master, for he ordered his shipmates into the deckhouse. Ruiz then tries a few words of the Mexican language, words used both by Indian and Spanish traders on the Isthmus.

Getting no answer, Ruiz has grappling hooks thrown and winched. The tied ships begin a slow, ungainly dance to the harsh music of scraped wood and clapping sailcloth.

The Commander takes over from the Pilot, ordering Candía the Greek to man the swivel gun on the foredeck. He picks out a boarding party: García, good with a blade; Molina, who speaks Arabic; and four others.

"*Salaam aleikum!*" says Molina, forcing a smile—more a foxy grin—as his feet touch the slatted deck of the unknown ship. "*Kaliméra!*" Candía shouts from the caravel, more warmly, more persuasively.

Candía should lead the boarding party, Ruiz tells Pizarro. The big Greek is the only man equal in build to the strange helmsman. He is also a friendly fellow by nature, a sunny, carefree soul. Candía would be the best ambassador. The Commander ignores him. This fool would take the gunner off the gun?

The bronze helmsman with the blue tattoos neither moves nor speaks. Molina strides up and prods the man's chest lightly with his sword. Stow that! Ruiz calls from the caravel, but his words are lost on the wind. Molina pokes harder; a trickle of red runs over the band of blue.

"*Imatan munanki?*" the man says at last.

The words mean nothing. But the tone is clear. Outraged, imperious. As one might say, *How dare you!*

The deckhouse light is dim, filtering through the wicker walls in pinpricks like a starry sky. Waman is afraid, and thankful others cannot see his fear. The room has a comforting smell of wool and cotton, oiled wood, grass mats, buckets of pitch. But there is no comfort now. They all watched the approach of the foreign vessel riding high on the waves like a wooden tub. They all heard the skipper's warning, followed his order to go inside: "Stay there till I call you. Strip off your jewellery. Hide it in the cotton. If you have weapons, keep them out of sight, but keep them handy. Defend yourselves if it comes to a fight, but above all do not start one." At this, several traders protested, saying they'd take their own chances and would not hide from thieves.

"Listen," the captain answered. "Now I'll tell you what I know. Last season one of our ships returned from northern waters beyond the Empire—not far from the region for which we're bound. When they put in to trade at a place they knew, they found it burnt and abandoned. In the streets and fields were many dead, mere bones by the time they got there. From a few survivors they learnt that a new kind of barbarian had appeared in strange ships. From a distance the hotlanders had mistaken the ships for ours. But the men on board— they were all men, no women, no children—were short and very hairy, with long beards and pale skin, pale as maggots. They looked sickly, and when they came ashore some of them rode like sick men on big llamas. The hotlanders thought they might be the dead, returning from the underworld. But they had the appetites of living men. They seized food, drink, gold, women. They killed anyone who tried to stop them. They killed easily but were hard to kill.

"For your lives' sake, do as I say. Go into the house. Stay there until I give word. That is all."

For a long time, it seems to Waman, nothing happens. There is only the fear, the blood throbbing in his ears. Something strikes the ship. Shouts on the wind. Heavy footfalls on deck. More shouts in a strange tongue, and the captain demanding, "What do you want?"

The deckhouse door is torn open. Sunlight blinds him. But he can hear and smell. Cries, strange laughter, women shrieking, knives ripping into bales, the breaking of jars, a reek of sweat and blood. A hand. Leather fingers closing on his throat.

Could the day's work have gone another way? the Pilot asks himself, preparing to write up his log that night. Perhaps bloodshed might have been avoided. He should have been more forceful with Pizarro. They should have acted more slowly, with restraint. Would that have exposed them to any higher risk?

On the Commander's orders, the helmsman was seized and tied to his own mast. The others were rousted from the deckhouse. There were men, women, an unconscious boy, limp yet breathing. The Commander ordered the boy brought aboard the caravel at once. Youngsters learn fast.

Then one man—a tall fellow, middle-aged, richly dressed— flourished a weapon, a kind of knife or axe, of bronze or gold. This he held out in his right hand while reaching slowly with his left for García's sword, holding the young Spaniard's eye. From where the Pilot stood, it looked like an offer to trade. But García thought otherwise. With a single blow he struck off the stranger's hand. He insisted afterwards that he was threatened, would do the same again without a moment's dither. Who knew what weapons those Indians had hidden in their clothes?

At that, some of the Indians—if such they be—leapt overboard and swam for their lives. They swam well, but the man with the bleeding stump was soon overtaken by sharks. So were others. The sea boiled red. Meanwhile the boarding party killed several more before Ruiz could cross to the foreign ship and stop them. Pizarro stayed where he was, looking on from the caravel's rail, absorbed yet indifferent, as if watching a second-rate cockfight.

The Pilot cannot quell the scenes before his eyes. The women's shrieks and tears, the futile valour of men armed only with small blades. And the worst: an old man, his belly opened by a sword, cradling his innards in his arms, spilling them in panic, snaring his feet with his own guts and toppling into the sea.

The worst was done when he himself boarded the craft, though he found three swordsmen ploughing a woman—in truth a mere girl—on a bale in the deckhouse. Strange how the act of death spurs the act of love. How love—if for decency's sake one may call it that—becomes a thing of war. Upon being freed, the young girl took to the sea, wild-eyed as a mad horse. And bleeding. The sharks ended her ordeal. Ruiz crosses himself. How easily Christians become savages.

Alone in his cabin, the Pilot still smells the gore, still hears the screams. He's seen his share of mayhem in the Indies. And in Spain. He has killed, but only when he had to. He is not among those who delight in it. Killing pains Our Lord. Even the killing of heathens. Ruiz crosses himself again. He shuts his eyes. But the scenes are not darkened. They play on in the theatre of his mind.

The Pilot struggles with his conscience until the candle gutters.

What of this day to set down in the log? From the other side of a thin partition in the sterncastle come rhythmic snores like the sound of sawyers ripping oak. Pizarro! How does such a man sleep soundly after that? The answer, Ruiz concludes, is *because* he is such a man.

"Be sure to make a list of the loot," the Commander told him before retiring. "Be sure to write it in your log, including the gold and silver. In broad terms only, mind. Don't burden yourself with details like weight and purity. We can't know what we have until it's assayed."

As your grace commands, Ruiz said to himself. *Let's see you check my list!* The Commander can't read or write a word beyond his name. Though that doesn't make him a fool. One-fifth of all treasure found in the Indies belongs to the King. Royal tax gatherers will be sure to inspect the ship's hold—and the ship's log—when the *Santa Elena* puts in at a Spanish settlement. No wonder Pizarro wants to keep things vague.

It is the blood, not the gold, that worries the Pilot. What can be said? What must be left unsaid? On the advice of learned churchmen, His Catholic Majesty the King has forbidden his subjects from staining his royal soul with innocent blood. Even the blood of infidels. It is therefore unlawful to attack new-found peoples unless they first harm Christians. Unlawful, that is, without due warning. Before the boarding party was dispatched, Ruiz should have read the strangers the Requirement, offering the chance to yield in peace to King and Cross. A mere formality, perhaps—especially when there's no interpreter. But the King's law should have been followed to the letter.

The Pilot allows himself a cup of vinegary wine from the last bottle in his sea-chest. Thus fortified, he concludes that all things are known to God. But not all need be known to men.

December 16, 1526
The Santa Elena
Pilot Ruiz

*About the middle of the forenoon watch we spied a strange
vessel carrying more than twenty souls and thirty tons of
freight. The ship was of a size and quality never seen before
among the natives of the Indies, having masts of fine
woodwork and sails like our own.*

*They were bringing goods for trade: mirrors, plates,
and drinking cups of burnished silver; crowns, pendants,
bracelets, armour, greaves, and breastplates, all made of
gold; tweezers, bells, crystals, and boxes of small copper axe
heads in three sizes like those the Indians of the Isthmus use
for coin; many mantles of wool and cotton; shirts, tunics, and
other clothing like that of the Moors—some fine as silk and
everything richly coloured and adorned. And they had
weights and scales for weighing gold, like those of Roman
workmanship.*

*They also carried much food and good water, cotton bales,
strong ropes, bronze crowbars, and barrels of pitch (of which
we are in great need against the shipworm).*

*We were unable to learn where they had come from and
where all these wonderful things were made. We took as much
of the freight as we could stow aboard the* Santa Elena. *We
also took fruit, vegetables, corn, potatoes, and other supplies.
In return we left axes, pig iron, and glass beads. Lastly, we
took on board a boy, that he may come with us to our camp
and learn our tongue. In due course, if it pleases God, he will
guide us to his home port and marvellous land.*

The Pilot stops writing and strokes his ear with the quill. He sighs. A long exhalation of guilt. He wipes his face with a kerchief. Nothing he has set down is untrue. And at least we left iron, he thinks. We were not thieves. Though iron is cheap to us, the natives of the Indies esteem it more highly than gold. He consoles himself that soon after the *Santa Elena* cast off and headed north for Gallo, he saw survivors climb back onto the drifting ship, freeing her captain from the mast.

Pilot Ruiz shuts the log. He prays. He goes to his bunk.

❄ 3 ❄

Waman awakes in darkness. Is he awake? Or mired in that other world his spirit wanders while his body sleeps? His head feels thick. The air, too, is thick; close, yet also chilly and damp. He is panting and his tongue is dry. He must be in the deck-house, surfacing from a bad dream. As his breathing becomes more regular he notices the smell: foul, smothering, with the fetor of turned meat, as if he were trying to catch a condor, lying in wait under a rotting deerskin, ready to seize the bird's feet as it alights. Soreness, heaviness, about his ankle. Cold metal. It is he who has been caught. Shackled and chained.

Now memory wells up, a flood of terror. Men like ghosts or fiends, bursting in, seizing him, a cadaverous hand at his throat. Waman begins to tremble. They are *runa mikhuq*, eaters of men, and they have thrown him in their larder. The dead and dying from Tumbes must be with him in the dark. His breathing races but his lungs can't fill. He blacks out.

Waman is roused by a strange vibration, a purring sound, as if a puma were with him in the reeking darkness, very near. Of course! He is trussed here as food for wild beasts as well as wild men. He imagines bodies all around him, half devoured. Next, he feels soft fur against his cheek and the purr loud in his ear. He cries out and flails against the beast, but it's too quick. He lies rigid a long time, straining to hear the cat's stealthy movements above the roaring in his temples. But if it moves, it makes no sound. He drowses fitfully until awakened by another touch of fur, this time against his shackled leg. The creature is still. Slowly he understands that it has crept beside him for warmth in the dank hold. Too small to harm him, only a youngster, a puma kitten purring in its sleep.

Footsteps on the roof above. Words he can't understand. Then the barbarian ship falls silent except for groans of timber and rope, the *clop* of waves against the wooden wall to which he's chained. Later there comes a strange sound, drifting, keening, as if from bowstrings; weirdly beautiful.

He comes fully awake to a shaft of sunlight. A door in the roof slides open and someone descends into the wooden cave: a youth not much older than himself, bringing a tray. The youth smiles broadly, makes a beckoning gesture, sets food and water within reach. Still dazzled, Waman takes some time to notice that his visitor is painted black from head to foot. As his eyes adjust he scans the recesses of his prison, fearful of what may lie around him. There are barrels and bales, seemingly from his own ship, and dirty straw, and shackles and cinches for tying down large animals. But he sees no corpses, no other captives, no big carnivores. The young man leaves, and so does the little cat. Not a puma kitten, but some other kind, striped, tame, bounding like a puppy up the ladder.

Two of the ghost men from yesterday come to take him up on deck. His hands are tied behind his back and the heavy iron is left around his ankle. He looks for signs of his people, his ship, but there is nothing. No sail, no land, no others from the World. The open sea rolls all around, empty but for the distant feather of a whale spout. He drinks the fresh air deeply, tries to calm his mind. They seem to be heading northwards now, hauled to the wind, tacking to wherever it is they came from.

He is taken to a low wooden house at the stern, made of planks, lit dimly by small round windows filled with crystal. Four barbarians are seated at a high board in the middle of this room: two old, two younger, all lean and watchful as stray hounds. They wear leather caps, tight britches, loose cotton shirts. Their strange clothes are torn and dirty. Vermin roam in their hair and beards. No wonder the hotlanders took them for the dead: all have a deathly pallor, young and old; their mouths are blistered, their teeth rotten or missing. The stench that pervades the ship is coming from *them*—their bodies and their breath.

More enter, making eight. One has reddish hair, others black or brown, and the red one has eyes like the sky. Their skins are of all shades: pink, wan, grey, and one much the same hue as himself. The youth comes in, sets a bowl and a jug of water on the dining board. This one is indeed dyed black, except for the palms of his hands.

The oldest begins speaking from a mouth like a sea anemone, toothless and red, sunk in a grizzled beard. Waman cannot hear the words. It's as if he is deaf, yet he can hear the ship and the water and a mewling of gulls from the door. He gives silent thanks to Mother Sea that he's alive. And thanks that Tika did not run with him, into this. His thoughts fill with her, with everyone at home. Tears spring in his eyes.

The barbarians are speaking again and still he cannot hear them. He wants to ask many things. Where are his shipmates? Are they alive? Why is he the only one here? What do they want with him? But when he opens his mouth they are as deaf to his tongue as he to theirs.

After the fifth night they unbolt the iron from his foot and let him walk the ship by day. They have not harmed him, and he is growing used to their looks and ways. He has counted ten on board including the barbarians' leader and the captain, who are much older than the rest. There is also the black one, their cook and helper, who treats him kindly yet still locks him in the hold at night.

The unearthly keening he heard the first night is no longer a mystery. On evenings without rain two or three gather on the foredeck, where they sing and play an instrument with strings and a round belly made of wooden strips like the hull of their ship. Waman has always loved music. Sometimes in Little River he would play his flute at weddings, and he was a good singer until his voice began to fray. He hates these barbarians who must have slaughtered many, perhaps all, of his shipmates. He is ashamed that he blacked out and did not see what happened. He vows in his heart to kill them, as many and as soon as he can. Yet he can't help becoming drawn to their weird music. Surely men who can make such beauty must have had some goodness in them once, if only when they were children?

So many other wonders: the abundance of iron in the ship's fittings, the great knives they wear; also iron helmets and armour, all cunningly wrought and riveted. They have stacks of white leaves between leather covers, the leaves painted with marks like rows of black ants, which the captain can read as easily as the Emperor's men read quipu strings. On the walls of the wooden deckhouse hang strange gods or spirits: a dead man nailed to a scaffold, a lady in blue with a baby, another dead man porcupined with arrows. One morning they all gathered at the stern and listened to words read from the white leaves, after which they knelt and shut their eyes and sang. They brought Waman to listen, showing him their gods and gesturing that he should do as they did, kneeling, shutting his eyes, tracing the four quarters of the Earth with a finger in the air.

They are teaching him words or names. The nailed god is Tius or perhaps Hisús. The skipper who runs the ship is called Luwis. The small panther who prowls the ship is Ilqatu. The oldest barbarian, who Waman can see is more feared than trusted by the others, has several names or titles, as leaders often do. Waman can say Pisaru with some difficulty, but he dubs this one Machu. The Old One.

Several times the boy has tapped his lips and told them his own name, but they shake their heads and laugh and stab their fingers at his chest, saying *Pilipillu*. Whenever they want him, they yell out *Pilipillu!*

The Empire is far behind, and Waman fears he will never see home again. By his reckoning tied on a loose thread of his shirt, six more days and nights go by before the ship makes landfall and the lookout begins scanning the shore, as if watching for a port or anchorage. The winds have been contrary, and the barbarian craft tacks badly because it has no centreboards. Strange, he thinks, that a ship so cleverly made should be lacking in this way. It is mainly a strong current that carries them against the wind.

Pilot Ruiz's noon sighting reveals he is near the second parallel above the equator. Aside from the unhelpful wind, the weather is fair. A white jaw of great peaks gnaws the eastern sky, and the skirts of the land below are verdant in the sun—dark forest broken by lighter green wherever the Indians have their fields and towns. Savages we deem these natives, Ruiz reflects, yet they've bested us too many times. Even when we fought on horseback.

At least one town that was whole when he left has been burnt to the ground during the month the *Santa Elena* has been gone. Wondering if this is the work of Pizarro's partner and deputy, Almagro, the Pilot keeps within sight of land in case the Christians have moved camp.

Ruiz thanks God for the current bearing the *Santa Elena* northward like a river. He also gives thanks for the gift of the Indian ship. Were it not for that prize well stocked with food—worth more to him just now than all her gold—he might have lost some men. He looks with satisfaction at the improvement in everyone's health, not least his own. Mouth sores are healing, breath is no longer quite so foul. Though there's nothing to be done for teeth lost to scurvy.

The captive boy has proved an able fishermen, casting a small net they took from the Indian ship. The Pilot orders the last of the salt horse, alive with grubs, heaved over the side. Not even sharks will touch it.

On the following day the lookout spies a ship's masts by a small island with a comb of trees. This is the one they named Gallo, the Cock. But is that a caravel, or another Indian ship? Before they get near enough to settle the matter, a dandelion of smoke lifts from the crest. The bark of a cannon follows. Almagro and the men are still here.

Waman is taken ashore in the ship's boat by the Old One and four men pulling on long oars. How oddly the barbarians paddle: sitting backwards so they can't see where they're going.

He has become used to the men on the ship, has begun to think of them as individuals. But here he beholds many more—perhaps eighty—waiting on the island's foreshore to greet their lord. The sight is both frightening and pitiful, for what he sees is a throng of starvelings, ragged, filthy, hairy—like drowned men draped in seaweed. As he draws nearer he sees that most of these skeletal figures are only a few years older than himself. The midday light shows up particularities: a weak chin under a thin beard, grey skin spotted with moles, thighs little more than bone beneath torn britches and peeling skin. Men in such straits should be easy to kill when he gets the chance.

Now an even odder sight: behind the crowd is the bobbing head of a man borne aloft as if on others' shoulders. He seems to be wearing a close-fitted skullcap, shiny and red. As the crowd parts to let this man through, Waman sees that he is sitting on a beast—tall as a llama but with a thicker neck and build.

His eyes return to the rider's head. What he took for a red hat is the barbarian's scalp—shiny, sunburnt, bald as a gourd. The face below, furrowed and liver-spotted, wears a short white beard like the muzzle of an old dog, but its outstanding feature is a lone blue eye swivelling up and down, back and forth, scanning around warily. The other is merely an empty socket, rough-healed, puckered like an anus.

The man climbs down from the animal's back, showing himself to be much shorter than the Old One, whom he approaches with arms spread in welcome. The two embrace, smiling and clapping each other on the back. The Old One breaks free first and snaps his fingers at the boatmen. Some pieces of loot—gold cups and dishes—are brought forth in a strongbox and shown to the one-eyed man, who inspects them closely, turning them in the sunlight, weighing them in his hands, even biting the metal and uttering cries of delight. Waman is shocked. He has never seen men of importance show feelings publicly. In the World, as his father and mother taught him, people of rank carry themselves with reserve. And lesser folk do well to follow their example.

The half-starved rabble comes suddenly alive, thrusting in on all sides, elbowing, fighting for a sight of gold. Not until the Old One draws his sword and waves it above his head does the clamour begin to die down.

Once the onlookers have been driven back and the gold returned to the boat, the Old One grasps Waman by the shoulder, pushing him towards the one-eyed man. He feels a tap on his chest, hears himself called *Pilipillu.* Then the Old One puts a whiskery mouth to Waman's ear, points to the other and says a word that sounds like *amaru.* But Waman has already named the bald rider: Sapa Ñawi, One-Eye.

The Commander rations out food taken from the Indian freighter. As soon as the men are somewhat stronger he has them careen his ships, hauling the vessels from sea to sand with a windlass and long hawsers at high tide. The wormy hulls are scraped, caulked, given a coat of stolen tar. This done, he sends his partner to forage on the mainland. Almagro is always keen to raid Indians, especially these hotlanders, for it was one of their arrows that took his eye.

Pizarro installs Waman in a back room of his own quarters, a strong timber-framed house that survived the fighting when he took the island. Recalling that many of the natives escaped by swimming, he keeps the boy chained to a post. Few of us Christians know the art of swimming, Pizarro muses, but the Indians on this coast are eels.

To teach his prisoner Spanish, he picks out men who got to know the boy on Ruiz's ship: Molina, a hothead but good talker; Tomás the cookboy; and Candía, the genial Greek gunner. Having two languages each, these men are well suited to the task. True, Candía speaks with a thick accent, and the cookboy's first tongue is Arabic, but their Castilian is good enough. And though Molina also knows Arabic—may indeed be half Moor or even a full-blood passing as a Christian—his Spanish is as good as the Commander's own. Maybe better, Pizarro thinks sourly, recalling his unschooled youth in Trujillo.

Within a fortnight the prisoner suddenly falls ill, racked by sweats and chills, babbling deliriously, his life running from every pore and orifice. Each day he is thinner and weaker. The Commander begins to fear he won't pull through. How easily these Indians die! Everywhere Spaniards have been in the Indies—the Caribbean, Mexico, Panama—it's as though the mere smell of a Christian is enough to kill the natives. Measles, mumps, chickenpox, even a cold, cut healthy men and women down like babes. To say nothing of smallpox, the deadliest plague of all, but luckily Felipillo does not seem to have that.

"Well, Father?" Pizarro asks the camp's priest, who has spent much time on this expedition ministering to the sick. "What's wrong with my interpreter? Will he live? If he won't, give him the rites. But first baptise him. Christen him Felipe."

"Why Felipe, Commander? We're nowhere near Saint Philip's Day."

Pizarro shoots a withering glance at the weedy, black-frocked young churchman—how dare he question an order—then relents.

"He's been called Felipillo ever since we found him. He may as well come by the name honestly. And mind you pray well for his life—for your sake as much as his. Christen him now."

Waman slowly crawls back from the borderland of death. All his life he has enjoyed good health. Now he knows what it is to feel old, to be weak and worn, to be sucked like a drowning dog into the underworld. Sometimes he woke from his delirium to moonlight falling from a window, burning his eyes like the sun no matter how tightly he shut them. His skin was on fire. His hands looked unfamiliar, like another's; or some animal's claw, a bear's, a crab's. He willed them to leap at his throat but they wouldn't stir. He begged Mother Moon to take him: *Mama Killa, yanarimuway, wañuchirimuway. Hina kachun.* Please help me, please kill me. May it be so.

Now he is glad Lady Moon didn't heed his prayers, that he lives after all, in rekindled hope of going home, of killing these barbarians or at least escaping before they make him lead them back to the World. Dimly he recalls one in a black gown like a widow coming to his bedside, uttering long incantations, sprinkling him with water, saying *Pilipi.* A sorcerer? Is that what brought him back to life?

The Old One was there too. *¿Cómo te llamas?* he kept saying. Why was he speaking of llamas? They have none.

But now he knows.

Wamanmi sutiy. My name is Waman.

¡No! The Old One again. A curse, a cuff on the head. *¿Cómo te llamas?*

Pi-li-pi my name.

Better. Say it better, Felipillo!

I am called Felipe.

To himself he adds, *Qanllarayku.* Only by you.

The lessons resume with Candía, the big man with the thicket of raven beard, and with Tomás the cookboy. Molina sometimes comes too, good-humouredly correcting their pronunciation. Soon Waman has a smattering of the barbarian tongue. His first words are questions. Where are his shipmates? What happened after he blacked out? His teachers try to be evasive, but the Greek and the Spaniard are talkative by nature. Little by little Waman learns something of that day.

He is healthier now, built up with extra rations. But when the Old One at last unbolts the chain and lets him walk outside—unsteady on weak legs, yet still with a heavy shackle on one ankle—Waman sees that most of the barbarians look as underfed as they did when he got here. One-Eye still raids the mainland if the winds are fair, but each time he comes back with less food. And with fewer men and horses.

On the island itself there is nothing to eat but crabs and limpets and mangrove nuts, a seal if they are lucky, or a thin broth of barnacles and seaweed. Waman is set to work digging shellfish or casting his net from the small boat, chained to a thwart and rowed out to likely spots. But the weather is seldom good enough to go to sea. For weeks they are stranded by thunderstorms and drenching rains, by great waves crashing on reefs and headlands. The days crawl as if the sun were slowing in the sky. Men die—three or four taken each week by fever, scurvy, knife fights, festered wounds. Waman hopes some of these deaths are his own work, for when he can he befouls the food he brings them, adding seal dung, even his own filth, and bad herbs that he has seen the horses never touch. Once, he believes, he killed in a manly way—hurling a stone at the head of one foraging in a pool among the rocks. Waman did not linger to make sure, but he heard a sound like the cracking of an egg, saw the man pitch forward into the water. With that deed he has begun to fulfill his vow.

Even though the Old One allows himself more food than his men, Pizarro is growing hollow-faced and sickly, the whites of his eyes almost as yellow as the irises, the beard sparser and greyer. How old can he be: fifty? sixty? Waman can't easily tell, and those he asks don't seem to know. Certainly much older than all except Almagro, who has about the same years. But One-Eye seems more vigorous, as if feeding on his anger. The Old One is withdrawn by nature, stern, saying little, watching all. At first Waman took him to be better bred—a man in command of himself, as those who lead must be. But now Pizarro's temper is no better than Almagro's. The two leaders snap at each other like hounds, slapping the hilts of their great knives, shouting torrents of harsh words.

In desperation, for it is risky on many counts, Pizarro sends one ship back to Panama with Almagro and Pilot Ruiz to resupply and recruit fresh men.

They are gone more than a month.

Sight of the returning sail sparks jubilation in the camp. All rush to the beach to greet them, even the lame and sick. But once Almagro lands, the Commander hears his news in wrath and disbelief. The ship brings food, but no reinforcements, no new men, no horses. Worst, Almagro comes with strict orders from the Governor of Panama: all who wish to leave Pizarro's failing enterprise must be allowed to sail home without delay.

Home? Not mine, Waman thinks. Now the barbarians don't need him, they will kill him. Or maroon him here to starve. His parents will never know what befell him, or even where to find his bones. And he will never be able to make amends to them and Tika.

He wishes he had killed the Commander before things came to this, had crushed the Old One's head with a stone in the night.

Two days later, at dawn, Pizarro summons the men to the bay where both ships ride at anchor. When all have assembled—what a sorry lot in rags and rust!—he draws his sword and holds it high, the risen sun flashing from its blade into the sunken eyes around.

"Friends and comrades. In His mercy the Lord God has looked kindly on us, and His weather smiles at last. You have all suffered. And I no less than you." Hearing a snort, a guffaw, Pizarro halts and searches the faces like a bird of prey. "We have *all* suffered," he goes on. "But our suffering is not in vain. You have seen the wealth we took from the Indian ship—gold, silver, silk, plump bags of jewels. Such goods and riches have never been seen in the Indies before, not even in Mexico. The Indian boy Felipillo can now speak. He tells of a southern kingdom with many ships, much gold, great cities, and strange camels like those on the drawings we saw years ago in Panama. What else can this be but the golden kingdom of Peru? That land still has her maidenhead. Let us go there and take it!"

Another murmur from the men. Sounds of doubt, unrest.

Enough! some call. *No more of your dreams, Pizarro.*

The Commander lowers his sword and scratches a line on the beach. Then shakes his blade at the north.

"That way, men, lies Panama. Panama—and poverty."

He turns to the south and strides across his line.

"This way lies risk—and riches. One ship will go north. The other south. Let each man choose. I choose Peru."

Pilot Ruiz is first to join him. Not because he trusts the Commander—far from it—but because he believes most firmly that the golden land is there. He will not let the honour of finding it fall to another. Candía and Molina follow (even though Felipe has said less about his homeland than Pizarro claims). Several more break from their fellows and shuffle, almost apologetically, across the line. All but a few are men who were on the *Santa Elena* when she met the trading vessel, men who not only have seen pieces of gold and silver produced from a strongbox but who saw in that strange ship, as big as their own, a sighting of Peru.

Pizarro waits in silence. No others come. With small nods he counts them. Only a dozen. Too few to fight. But enough to explore.

{ 4 }

The *Santa Elena* runs fleeter than before, cleaving the waves with a hull newly scraped and tarred. And this time there's enough to eat on board, a share of the food from Panama.

Late one afternoon about a month out from Gallo Island, Waman sees a familiar smudge of land beneath the white crest of the highlands floating on the haze. That night he smells the World on the wind. In the morning he guides Pilot Ruiz up a mangroved channel, into the harbour from which he ran to sea. The caravel drops anchor, away from any freighters and the Empire's troopships.

So strange to be home, thinks Waman. And home so strange. On the rise are the buildings of Tumbes, layered streets and houses crowned by the great temple with its steep roof flashing golden in the sun. Only months ago he left this place, walked its streets, yet each month seems a year. Tumbes was never his city. But this is his land, his *country*—a notion new to him. The smells of home are overwhelming now: tarred ships, dunged fields, cooking fires, baked fish, steamed corn. And sounds. A crowd has gathered on beach and jetty and rooftops; above the din of voices drifts the music he most loves—flutes, drums, tambourines, and the breathy rasp of great pan-pipes as long as the men who play them.

Could anyone he knows be here? Only by chance. Little River is three days away and the *Santa Elena* could not have been sighted until yesterday. Yet Waman cups his eyes and scans the onlookers until clothes and faces all begin to seem the same, till he doubts he can remember what his parents and his cousin even look like. Mother, Father, Tika, Grandfather . . . have they forgiven him? And will they know him after all he's done and seen? The Old One has dressed him in Spanish clothes, in a loose white shirt, green velvet cap, leather britches buttoned down the side. But it is more than a matter of clothing. Perhaps, Waman fears, the new growth in him contains too much of these barbarians. He knows them now. He can speak their tongue, if badly. He can even play a little of their music. A few he has come to regard as friends. Candía the Greek, Tomás the slave, Molina. How is that possible when he has also killed some of them, or tried to? It's as if he was some other youth back then when he last saw Tumbes, someone who shares his body and his boyhood but is no longer himself.

Waman or Felipe? First he received his grown-up name from his grandfather. Now he has become Felipe also, a name that has something to do with their god. A god perhaps as mighty as they say, for this Tius has given them many fine things. Yet also a cruel god, for he makes them suffer so. Waman has grown used to his Christian name, though it took him a long time to pronounce it. He only wishes they would call him that and nothing more. It is Felipillo he detests—Little Philip—as if he were still a child.

Waman is a man's name. Hawk. Nothing little about that.

He takes off his cap and waves it. He searches the crowd again. A few wave back, but not as if they know him.

Tomás comes up, sheepish, holding shackle and chain. "The Commander thinks you might be tempted by a swim." Indeed. Waman hasn't changed so much he wouldn't run from the bearded ones at the first chance. Before sinking into the dank hold, he looks around once more at the painted houses, the busy streets, the Emperor's great buildings—the stone bulk of the fortress, the gilded temple. His dread of what might happen next is as strong now as his joy at coming home.

Commander Pizarro casts a sour eye over his dozen men. Hotheads and rogues. Mere youngsters with nanny-goat beards. And these the best, the quickest: those bold enough to turn their backs on Panama and their eyes to Peru. His first move, he decides, is to send one man ashore with gifts for the ruler of the city: a red velvet cap, a Venetian goblet, a pair of trussed hogs. He picks Molina for this task. Not the most dependable fellow, but the most expendable.

Molina is gone for some hours. His shipmates wait uneasily on deck, Candía at the guns, a small brazier on hand to light the matchcords if need be. It is mid-afternoon before they see Molina shouting and waving from the beach, then wading out to the ship like a madman in a lather until chest deep in soupy water.

"Lower the tender," Pizarro orders, "and fish out that fool before he drowns."

Molina comes aboard like Neptune, trailing weed and foam, raving of the comeliness of the women, the friendliness of the men, the wealth of a "mosque" he has seen—adorned with gold, silver, precious stones.

Before he can be calmed and questioned thoroughly, there is movement on the water. A raft is punting out to the ship, a raft with a white awning and a man seated in its shade.

"Tomás," Pizarro calls, "bring up Felipillo. Mind you put that heavy doublet on him, the one with the weights sewn in."

Waman emerges from below, blinking in the light, sweating from sudden heat and heavy clothes. The Old One inspects him, checking the jacket is tightly fastened. "That stays on whenever you're on deck," Pizarro warns. "You jump, you sink."

The raft is alongside now, and Waman sees it is laden with mouthwatering things from home: fruit, vegetables, a heap of roasted meat steaming on a salver. Under the canopy sits a high official of the Empire, wearing a tightly wound red turban, golden discs covering his ears, and a splendid tunic of many-coloured frets.

Accepting Pizarro's outstretched hand, the official climbs nimbly aboard the *Santa Elena*. He is in middle years, finely lined about the eyes, his chin furrowed and freshly tweezered; about the same height as the Old One, yet stockier, more strongly built, with the barrel chest of a highlander. The short haircut of the Empire's lords shows grey at his temples below the headcloth.

Candía keeps an arquebus trained on the visitor from the poop deck. Pizarro seems ill at ease, stroking his beard, probing an ear with his finger.

"Little Philip! Greet this Indian warmly. Welcome him aboard. Tell him I come to kiss the hands of his king. If he's the king himself, I'll kiss them now."

When the official hears the boy—whom he took from his clothing to be one of the outlanders—addressing him in the Empire's language, surprise ripples the mask of his face. The ripple is instantly smoothed, the mask restored. He leans in closely to Waman.

"So you know their tongue?"

The interpreter nods, struggling to find voice before this nobleman, fighting a tightness in his chest at the first words from home he's heard in months.

"Good. You will tell me everything they say. Exactly as they say it. But everything I say, on the other hand, you will convey with the greatest courtesy their barbarous tongue allows. You will speak sweetly. If I ask when they'll be going back where they came from, you will say, for example, 'How long will our esteemed visitors have the kindness to favour us with their presence.' Always like that."

Waman does his best, unsure whom he fears more: the Old One

or this Emperor's man. He knows his Castilian is still flawed. And his Quechua leaves much to be desired, lacking the polish and crisp accent of this highland lord. Still, he speaks it better than most in Little River, because his mother and Tika, having come from the highlands, sometimes spoke it at home—especially when they didn't want him to overhear.

The official thanks Pizarro for the gifts sent with Molina, then strides casually about the deck of the strange ship, beguiling the foreigners with an easy manner, asking about her construction and her gear like one seaman to another. He is also curious about the animals, the swine, the ship's cat—the only Spanish animal not eaten on the island—who is sunning herself on the rail. Are there bigger animals below, creatures like llamas on which, he's heard, these idlers ride?

Waman says he saw such beasts at the barbarian camp in the hot-lands but they all died and there are none on board.

So much is impossible to render. How to translate *compass, cannon?* Even *hog* and *cat* aren't easy. Eventually he recalls words for the wild swine and small spotted cats of the jungle.

After a long inspection, the Emperor's man comes to the point. "Three things. Where have these vagabonds come from? Why are they here? What do they want? Be sure to ask sweetly."

"This lord asks from what land the esteemed Christians hail. To what end do they favour his humble city with their visit? And in what way can he best fulfill their needs?"

"Tell him we come in friendship," Pizarro replies. "We bring him greetings from King Charles, the greatest prince in the world, and we bring him good news of the True Faith, so his soul may live forever."

At this, Pilot Ruiz steps forward, tapping Pizarro on the shoulder. "Let's not forget the Requirement, Don Francisco. We must read it to him now. Before . . . anything happens. Anything that might stain the blessed soul of His Majesty. To say nothing of your soul and mine. I'll fetch it." Ruiz goes briskly to his cabin.

"Now, Felipillo," Pizarro says. "Ask this Indian where we are and who he is. What rank does he hold? Is he a king? What land is this? Have we reached Peru?"

Waman has never been able to answer them about their imaginary land of Peru. He knows the name of his hometown and of this port. Also the capital, the great city of Cusco—far to the south and high in the mountains—and a few other places he's heard his family and others speak of. But he has never heard of anywhere called Peru. Or even that his country *has* a name. As far as he knows, it is simply the Empire. Or the World.

He is no clearer about his captors' geography. Do they come from *Panama, Castile, Spain, Rome, Europe*? He has heard them speak of all these, and more. But are they one kingdom or many?

"This port is Tumbes, as I said before, sir."

"Never mind what you've said. Tell me what *he* says. And what sort of man he is. Is he the king?"

The official chuckles politely at the question and gives a long answer. Waman feels the steam of Pizarro's impatience at his side.

"He says he is not a king. He is only the Emperor's man in Tumbes. An official of the Empire. The Emperor lives far away, beyond the great snows, in his royal city. This lord here is . . . he says he is"— Waman wrestles with the title the highlander has told him, *Tukuy-Rikuq*—"one who sees everything. He looks into all things that concern the Emperor in this province. You could say he is the All-Seer. He asks what you mean by *Perú*."

"Tell him that Indian traders I questioned some years ago said they came from a place called Peru. A land of gold and camels, like those over there"—Pizarro points to a llama train being unloaded on the jetty—"and great sands without trees, as I see beyond the city."

Waman does as he is told. The All-Seer taps an earspool, looks around, points with his chin to the south as he replies.

"He says he knows a town and valley called Wiru, a port down the coast about three hundred miles. He says the seafarers you speak of might have come from there. It's a place of small importance."

"Then what is this land?"

"It's the World."

"Don't answer me yourself, boy! I know you don't know. Ask him."

The All-Seer weighs the question. His duty is to watch, to listen. Not to reveal. The breeze has died. Again he becomes aware of the barbarian ship's foul smell. Like death. And the barbarians themselves look like men on the way to death. He knows of their piracy some months ago. He has also heard reports of their hardships and losses up the coast beyond the Empire. The people there called them vagabonds, thieves, and *wiraqocha*—scum of the sea. A fair assessment. Yet where is the harm in answering this question?

"He says the World is called Tawantinsuyu."

"A mouthful, boy. Is it just a name, like Spain? Or does it mean something?"

"It means . . . the World, sir." Waman flinches, afraid Pizarro will hit him, as he has many times. "The World in four parts, as all things are . . . East and West, North and South. Four in one. J-joined together . . ." He hears himself stammer. "You could say the Four Quarters or . . . the United Quarters of the World."

Pilot Ruiz returns with a sheet of paper written closely on both sides. He hands it to Pizarro, knowing Pizarro can't read. Let him be shamed, Ruiz tells himself with pleasure. He may have to obey the

Commander, but he's not obliged to like the man. He thinks again of Pizarro's shabby role in the death of Balboa.

The Commander hands the document back without looking at Pilot or paper. His face has reddened. He nods stiffly.

The All-Seer watches this exchange. "What is that leaf?" he asks the boy. "A gift? An offering?"

"They have something to say. Those black marks serve them as the knots serve us."

"Why don't they just say it, then? Are their memories so weak?"

The Pilot begins to read aloud, a tremble in his voice. Pizarro tells the interpreter to hold his tongue.

> *I, Commander Francisco Pizarro, vassal and envoy of the high and mighty Kings of Castile and León, conquerors of barbarous nations, hereby inform you that God Our Lord, One and Eternal, created Heaven and Earth and a man and a woman from whom you and I and all the world's people are descended. And God set one called Saint Peter in the holy city of Rome to reign over the Earth as High Priest and Pope, to govern and judge all peoples.*
>
> *And the heir of Saint Peter, who is, as I have said, the Papa, the High Priest of the Earth, has given all these lands to the Catholic Kings of Castile.*
>
> *And so I request and require you to recognize God's Holy Church as Mistress and Governess of the whole world, and in Her name to obey His Majesty King Charles as your Ruler and Lord King. You must allow the Fathers of the Church to instruct and preach to you. And if you do this, all will be well. And His Majesty—and I in his name— will welcome you with love and charity. But if you do not do this—*

"Stop there, Ruiz!" Pizarro cuts in. "If he hears the rest we'll all be dead by sunset." He raises a whiskery eyebrow to the warships, the crowd at the waterside. "If that lot turn against us, not even God can save us Christians. Keep it for next time." The Old One has a far-away look in his eyes, which stray from those beside him to the channel and the sea beyond. "Next time, Pilot Ruiz," he repeats, with a sly pout of his lips. "When we come back with an army big enough to take this land."

Ruiz is used to hearing blasphemy from Pizarro, and he knows that the Requirement—often read without translation—is a farce. Still, the form must be followed. The Commander has no right to send them all to Hell.

"In the name of God and His Majesty let me finish, Don Francisco. The Indian hasn't a word of Spanish. How much the boy renders to him is for you and your conscience to decide. But as master of this ship and chaplain—there being no priest aboard—it's my duty to read out every word of this writ as the King commands." He resumes before Pizarro can reply.

If you do not do this, with the help of God I shall come mightily against you, and I shall make war on you. I shall bend you to the yoke and obedience of the Church and His Majesty; and I shall seize your women and children and make them slaves, to sell and dispose as His Majesty commands; and I shall do all the evil and damage to you that I can. And I insist that the death and destruction will be your own fault.

"It is too much at once, sir," Waman says nervously. "Please ask Pilot Ruiz to repeat it slowly, in bits . . . little by little."

"No need for that, Felipillo. Tell the Indian no more than what I said at the beginning—about our King, our friendship, and Our

Lord. Keep it short, or I'll rip that pink tongue from your dusky head."

Waman turns to the All-Seer, nerves failing him. The Emperor's man may not understand a word of Castilian, yet he can surely tell a short speech from a long one. The boy feels giddy, on the edge of tears.

"My lord All-Seer. The bearded ones say they worship a god who made everything in the world, our forebears and theirs. This god has a high priest . . . somewhere in the land they come from. The priest's name is the Papa . . . and this Papa . . ." Suddenly the boy feels laughter rising inside him like vomit, for in the Empire's language *papa* means potato. He stares at his feet, fighting to keep a straight face. If he catches his countryman's eye he will be done for. "This . . . this priest has given the whole world to their king called Carlos, who they say is the greatest ruler on Earth. And this king sends the Old One here to tell your lordship of his love and friendship, and to bring news of their god. That is all I could follow, my lord."

The official stands perfectly still, his face unreadable. It is Pizarro who breaks the silence, beckoning to Ruiz, grinning at the visitor.

"Hand it to him, Pilot. Let the Indian keep the Requirement." A mocking laugh. "Let him study it."

The All-Seer accepts the paper and folds it carefully like a kerchief, putting it in a vicuña bag that hangs at his belt. He turns to hail his boatman on the raft.

"Tell him not to leave yet," Pizarro says quickly, smiling at the All-Seer. "He must dine with us before he goes."

The Emperor's man accepts.

"Extraordinary! Quite extraordinary." The All-Seer releases Tomás's arm. The African continues round the cabin table with the wine flask. He has grown used to such inspections in the Indies.

"It won't rub off, my lord," Waman explains. "The colour is natural to them." Though still uneasy at speaking with the lofty official, he feels emboldened by his standing as his captors' *lengua*, their lone interpreter. Indispensable; therefore safe. At least until others learn. For now, nobody will break the *chaka*, the bridge between worlds.

"Apparently so," the All-Seer replies. "But what an extraordinary coincidence! In our language we use the same word for anything black and for those who serve and help us. For no reason anyone remembers—it just happens to be the same word. And now these barbarians show up with a helper who really *is* black. It's the oddest thing I've seen since they arrived. Do their women give birth out of colour sometimes, like llamas?"

"What says the savage?" Pizarro asks. "Does he want to buy Tomás? What's his bid?"

Making as if he hasn't heard, Waman continues speaking to the All-Seer. "The black ones come from another faraway land, beyond the country of the pale ones. They are the pale ones' prisoners."

"So there are many more like this?"

The interpreter explains he has been gone from the Empire only a few months and after his capture was in the barbarians' island camp. He has seen only a hundred of the outlanders, all told. No women, no children. Of the hundred, four or five were black.

Pizarro has Waman by the ear, rough beard against smooth cheek. "Enough of that babble! Tell him I'll take the black's weight in gold." The boy shrinks from the bristly touch and winy breath. "Go on. Tell him that!"

"What is the Old One saying?"

"He wants to know if you would like to buy the black man."

"In return for what?"

"For his weight in gold."

The All-Seer laughs politely, without mirth. A diplomat's laugh, left hanging while he thinks up a reply.

"The brand is easily changed," Pizarro adds, misreading the hesitation.

"What now?" the All-Seer asks Waman. "Don't forget what I said earlier. You're to tell me everything. Exactly as they say it."

"He says he can change the black man's mark."

"His mark?"

"They wear signs . . . like marks on bricks or pots. Burnt into the skin to show who is their lord."

"I will see this."

Waman plucks Tomás's arm as the African glides around the table with the wine. Tomás is his jailer, but a kindly one. It was he who taught him his first words of the barbarians' language, and how to behave among them. "Tomás. Show him your back. Your brand."

The African turns, white shirt dropping from black shoulders, revealing the Commander's monogram.

"Mother Earth!"

"We can burn a new one over that," Pizarro cuts in, worried the All-Seer might think he's being offered damaged goods. "Go on! Tell him. Any device he wants."

Waman does as told. His ear, at last, is released.

"The black man is certainly a fine cook," the official replies smoothly. "I have eaten well at my hosts' table. One of the best meals in memory. And this drink is splendid. It warms the belly so much better than our beer. Say all that to the Old One. Give him my highest compliments. But say with regret that I am not authorized to trade with him. Besides, the Emperor has many cooks and helpers. And I think there may be more important matters to discuss." The All-Seer looks Waman in the eye, the first time he has done so, and lowers his voice. "What is it with them about gold? I see their hunger for it. As if they would snatch the spools from my own ears. *Qorita-chu mikhunku?* Do they *eat* gold?"

"What's he saying, Felipillo? I want it all. Every word that popin-jay utters."

"He asks whether Christians eat gold."

Now it is Francisco Pizarro who laughs, pale eyes sparkling in their sunburnt wells. "Did you hear that, gentlemen? This savage lord's a fool. Or he's drunk too much wine and dares make fools of us."

"I've spent longer with him than anyone, Commander," Molina volunteers. "He was with me the whole time I was ashore. Of course, we couldn't talk except by signs. Not without Felipe there. I know some of you doubt the wonders I saw—their mosque full of gold. Call me a liar if you like. You'll find out the truth soon enough. But think how this lord inspected the ship. All his questions—and his silences. He asks many things. He tells little. What did he say, Don Francisco, when we spoke of our True Faith, our friendship, and King Charles?" Molina looks around the table, pleased to see he has his shipmates' attention. "Nothing. Not one word. I say he's no fool."

Candía claps his hands, nodding vigorously. "Well said, Molina, well said. I think as you do." The Greek turns to Pizarro. "As you put it so well yourself, Don Francisco, when you picked out us goats from those sheep who went back to Panama. To be poor is to be nothing. To be poor is to starve. So, yes. Yes! The Indian's right. We live on gold."

Waman to the Emperor's man: *"Arí, nispa. Qoritam mikhunku.* Yes, they are saying. They do eat gold."

That night, in the ship's belly, the boy can't rest. At times he reaches the foreshore of sleep, his mind sinking into nonsense. But each time, the cat appears, butting him under the chin with a bony head, kneading his chest with her paws, filling his ears with a loud, insistent purr. The day's events parade before him, all the brighter and more grotesque for the darkness in which he lies chained. The All-Seer left after a show of cordiality, begging the strangers to come ashore next morning to see the city. The official also said certain things privately to Waman, asking him his birthplace, his name, his parents' names; as much as telling him that they are kinsmen, coming down from the time the Empire took this coast and settled highlanders among the locals. The great man spoke like an uncle, and spoke well, implying—it was an assumption really—that Waman has come home after a terrible ordeal. That he will leave the bearded ones when they go ashore tomorrow. That his family will be sent for, brought to the city, where he can greet them as a young man of substance. For he will now be working for the Emperor.

At last the boy falls asleep, cat by his side.

Francisco Pizarro also has a restless night, a rarity for him. Over and over he weighs the benefits and risks of going ashore. One should never show fear to natives. Nor to one's own men. Yet the Peruvian official's shrewd demeanor has rattled him. The man's invitation to see his city is likely a trap. It would be folly to play into his hands.

He decides to send only two: Candía the Greek, veteran of many wars, a chatterbox but a sounder fellow than Molina, and the slave Tomás—mainly to watch Candía's back but also because of the impression his colour always makes on Indians. (Besides, the Peruvian might change his mind and buy the black after all.) Felipillo he keeps below in shackles, so he can neither flee nor be taken easily if the natives make an attempt on the ship. The others stay on deck, weapons at the ready, Pilot Ruiz standing by to hoist sail at the first alarm.

The All-Seer of Tumbes Province is feeling a little unwell from the barbarians' food. Or more likely their drink. After all, the food was wholesome—mostly what he gave them himself. The spies he has watching their ship tell him the outlanders are wary, which means they are afraid. He is therefore hardly surprised, if disappointed, to see only two barbarians come ashore this time, neither of them the leader.

One yesterday, two today. At this rate it will take some time to lure them into custody—assuming that is what the Emperor directs. The All-Seer has already dictated a report, marking it urgent with an orange mastercord, watching the knotkeeper's fingers weave his words into threads. He has sent this to the city of Tumipampa in the Quito highlands, where the Emperor resides while fighting northern wars.

From his roof terrace the All-Seer watched the pair of runners take off like antelope along the great north road, first link in the chain of relays who will bear his message more than two hundred miles over sand and snow in a single day and night. How lucky the court is only one day's mail away at present, instead of five to the capital. Soon the barbarians will not be his burden alone.

Candía is dressed to dazzle—striding along the jetty in shining helmet and chainmail, arquebus over his shoulder, Toledo sword at his belt, his beard oiled and glossy as sable. Tomás follows, bare-chested, wearing only a pair of white cotton britches and heavy brass rings in nose and ears. Onlookers swarm them as they walk up from the haven towards the middle of town, where the temple's golden roof rises steeply above the flat-topped buildings. Women come from their doors, laughing and smiling, stroking the Greek's beard, patting the African's springy hair, exclaiming at the white skin and the black, especially the latter with its cruel brand. One girl gives Candía's hairy cheek a pinch, and giggles. By God he could use a woman! But the Greek has travelled and fought in many lands. He knows better than to form hasty notions about the ways of foreigners.

"Some pretty ones, eh, Tomás? What do you think? Do they want to be our friends or our lovers?" Tomás grins in reply, white teeth splitting the darkness of his face. Pizarro claims that the youth lacks reason—like all Africans, according to the Church, which makes them lawful slaves. But Candía thinks the black is merely a lad of few words; when he does have something to say it's often worth hearing.

Before they have gone far, four men in red helmets and tunics of black-and-yellow squares come to escort them to the plaza, taking them to the great hall whose front is covered in bold paintings of whales, birds, and fish. Sentries flank the doorway and others stand at attention in tall niches along the building's façade, all in the same uniform, heavy pikes with bronze blades in hand.

Candía and Tomás are led into a courtyard and seated on stools beneath a cotton awning. The escort withdraws, leaving the visitors to themselves. Water is flowing from a fountain in the middle—a large eight-sided basin carved from a single stone. The water crosses the courtyard by a channel and runs under a wall into the building. Around the patio are earthenware pots with flowering shrubs. The only sounds are the purl of water and the quarrelsome buzz of hummingbirds making their way from bloom to bloom, their tiny bodies iridescent in the sun.

Door curtains are drawn aside and a man and woman enter from right and left, both middle-aged. Recognizing the All-Seer, Candía rises to greet him but is pressed firmly back onto his stool by an attendant. Lord and lady sit down calmly, saying nothing. Who is she? the Greek wonders, admiring her ankle-length dress of some silky green fabric with embroidered borders, pinned at her chest with a brooch like a chased silver spoon. His wife? Or the ruler? Felipe said something about Tumbes being governed by a woman. Maybe she's a queen—a Peruvian Cleopatra—and this lord her Antony. Candía chuckles privately within his beard.

Uniformed servants spread a cloth on a low dining board and set out food and drink. Everything is served in vessels of gold or silver, beginning with tall beakers of corn beer. The lord and lady's tankards are in the shape of a human pair, naked, sexes visible. A gold Adam, thinks Candía, a silver Eve.

"*Kunan,*" says the lady, hoisting her beer in both hands and nodding at the foreigners. "*Pachamamapaq.*" She tips a few drops on the ground. Candía understands not a word, but knows the gesture—Felipe used to do this on the island until the priest forbade it. Mother Earth drinks first. A damned heathen custom, though not without charm. He does the same.

A feast of smiling, miming, watching, aping. Candía wishes Pizarro had sent Felipe along, though he sees the wisdom in keeping him on the ship. The All-Seer, too, understands the boy's absence. The interpreter is a weapon. With two edges. Whoever wields him skilfully has the advantage, the initiative. For now, until he hears the Emperor's wishes, he must do these barbarians honour and weave a spell of friendship that will charm them off their boat. Especially the Old One, the leader, with yellow eyes like a dog.

He is pleased that Lady Sian, the Tumbes Governor, has offered to hold this meeting at her official residence. The arrival of the barbarians concerns her province as much as it does the Empire, possibly more. He will be glad of her advice. Over the years they have worked together, he has found her to be shrewd and experienced in many things. No one reads men better.

As the imperial inspector for Tumbes, a highlander and member of the royal kindred, the All-Seer knows he is sometimes seen as a meddling outsider. Indeed, his relations with Lady Sian have occasionally been delicate, especially in their early days, requiring tact. She is a well-born lowlander, a descendant of the old kings and queens of Chimor, who controlled the seaboard before their kingdom was annexed to the World. (Without bloodshed, the All-Seer reflects proudly; though it is true that highland forces persuasively diverted the headwaters of Chimor canals, to show what war would bring.) That was a long time ago now, when the Emperor's father was young. It has since become imperial policy to govern the coast through its old nobility, and to allow local customs to continue, not least the appointing of women to high office whenever they are abler than their male kin.

The All-Seer's eyes settle fondly on Lady Sian, noting a rime of beer on the fine pleating of her upper lip. They have grown to trust and respect each other. Not only professionally but personally, he believes.

Restored by the meal, the All-Seer thinks over what he has learnt about the outlanders so far. Their interpreter is one weapon— unfortunate the boy's not here—but there are other weapons to investigate. The Governor has suggested they get the tall blackbeard to demonstrate the iron blowpipe he carries on his shoulder. It would be wise to do that out of town. But first these two should be shown the sights that made such a deep impression on the one who came yesterday with gifts. Sights to draw their leader from his floating lair.

Candía and Tomás are taken across the square to the great building with the golden roof that crowns the city skyline, the temple Molina called a "mosque." They pass through an outer doorway, plain and unadorned except for the perfect fit of its massive stonework. Candía inspects the work closely. No mortar has been used. He can't imagine how it was done, even if the stone were soft—not granite—and the masons had good steel. Can there be iron in this land, he wonders, or some other metal equal to it? Perhaps steel is kept for special use, as rare in Peru as gold in Spain. The Emperor's official looked glad to receive Pizarro's parting gift of a Toledo axe head yesterday. Glad, but not amazed. Nothing seems to surprise the man.

The temple is cool, dark, empty. As if the priests have been forewarned to hide themselves and any evidence of their heathen rites. There is no sign of the idols or bloody sacrifices he expected from tales of Mexico. The place is simply a great house—four halls around a courtyard, like the house where they ate, though grander and smelling of incense and lamp oil. Each hall they are shown is devoted to a power of nature. One has a rainbow painted on the wall; one an image of the stars, skilfully done with an array of gems on a jet background; the third holds a large silver disc of the moon.

The fourth hall is unlike the others, being longer and half round in plan. A mass of bedrock, carved with small basins and ledges, rises through the floor like a miniature mountain. A tall eastern window faces the sunrise over the icefields, and on the wall across from this hangs a sun—a great wheel of heavy gold a man's height in diameter.

Incense twists lazily from a brazier below.

"God's blood, Tomás! For once Molina told us the bare truth. If that sun is as solid as it looks"—Candía moves to touch the great disc but feels the Governor's hand on his arm—"it would buy a pair of ships and outfit a hundred cavalry!"

The All-Seer moves to the window, beckoning palm-down in the Peruvian way, fluttering his fingers. Candía sees the lady shoot him a dark look, as if to object. What does she want them not to see?

Below is a walled garden crisscrossed with water channels. Among trimmed fruit trees and a stand of maize are statues—men, women, and Indian camels. All life-size. All made of precious metal: the men gold, the women silver, the strange beasts of gold with silver fleeces on their backs and necks.

"Am I bewitched?" Candía breathes, after a long silence. "Do you see it too, Tomás? They say gold can make a man lose his wits." He grips the youth's elbow. "Tell me! Tell me everything you see down there."

The African begins to confirm what the Greek beholds, but before he can finish they hear girlish laughter. In shade on the far side of the garden is an open building, a kind of cloister, filled with women. Some are seated at looms, weaving brightly coloured cloth. All are young, save for two or three older ones in charge. There are no men.

One looks up from her work. She shrieks; stifles her cry with a hand. All eyes follow hers to the strange sight in the window of the Sun. The white man and the black man wave. Most of the maidens lower their eyes; a few wave back.

The lady speaks to the lord sharply (it seems to Candía) and the party returns through the temple courtyard to the square. They are then led out of town in the opposite direction from the ship, crossing the river by a long wood-decked bridge hung from stout cables between stone piers. Candía is intrigued by this ingenious structure, but uppermost in his mind is that the Peruvians may be about to play some trick. Good thing he brought the arquebus. Then he realizes he forgot his flint and steel: no way to light the matchcord.

The All-Seer, too, is thinking about this weapon: like a blowpipe, yet heavy as a crowbar. Time to see what it can do. Once they reach open fields, he orders a wooden board set up on the wall of a government granary a hundred paces off. A good slingsman or archer could hit that. The right range, he guesses, for a test.

It takes Candía some time to understand he's being asked to fire the gun. He is lost in the sights of this new land: the watered fields spread like green carpets on the desert, the purple foothills beyond— range behind range—and, far above these, the fleshy bulk of great snow-crowned mountains. And the works of the people: the road with its canal, side walls, flagstones; runners and pack trains plying between distant cities; and the bridge suspended over the river— such a clever idea, a thing never seen in all his travels. But will the horses cross it?

Some crops are young; others are being reaped by teams of farm folk, singing as they go. The stubble is given over to Indian camels, who raise their long necks to watch him with the same feminine lashes and disdainful eye of camels he recalls from his Turkish war. These are only half the size, but they must be akin, as a spaniel is to a bulldog. How can there be camels here yet none in Mexico or Panama? What *is* this southern land?

A small throng of onlookers has gathered from houses and fields, their eyes upon Candía when he sees what the All-Seer wants and sets to work. He taps powder into the muzzle, rams down wad and ball, primes the pan, cocks the lock. He has trouble miming his need of a light for the matchcord. Eventually a live coal is brought from a nearby kitchen.

Candía did not much like the yeasty beer served at lunch, but had to drink with the others. The arquebus feels heavier than usual, the target dances in the heat. He takes a sight. Unsteady, and he hasn't a gun-rest. "Tomás, lend me your shoulder. Stand still as a post. Stop your ears."

He lays the barrel on the lad's dark shoulder.

The smouldering cord pecks the touch-hole.

Thunder and lightning in the desert sun.

All-Seer and Governor keep their composure, but many onlookers drop to the ground, hands over ears. Others rush up to Candía and jostle for a look at the weapon. The All-Seer tells his guards to keep order.

Candía has missed narrowly, making a small crater in the granary's adobe wall. He must swab and reload. Every move, he notes, is watched closely by the All-Seer. Is the man counting how long it takes? Maybe so.

This time the Greek shoots well, splitting the board in two.

The All-Seer sniffs the gunsmoke. Sulphurous, like a volcanic vent. He sends a man to fetch target and balls for further study. The iron blowpipe does not seem much more effective than a war sling in good hands, but there's no doubt of its power to startle.

"Extraordinary!" he observes to the Governor. "Such smoke, such stink. Such noise. But you kept your head."

"And you. As always."

The All-Seer accepts the compliment (if that's what it is) with a bow.

"What do you make of them?" he says, with a jut of his chin at the strangers. "What brings them here? Are they lost?"

The lady of Tumbes tilts her head to one side as she thinks, a winning gesture. "They're men like any others. I see how they look at women, especially that white one. They've been away from their homes a long time. As if they are lost." She straightens her head and looks him hard in the eye. "But I don't think they are."

In her view, she adds, these barbarians are likely the same as some who raided the eastern border of the Empire two years ago, coming up the Pillkumayu from the great jungle with a force of Chunchu bowmen. "They too had beards and metal pipes and helmets. The local garrison killed all the bearded ones and drove the Chunchus back into the forest. A pipe and a barbarian skin were brought to the capital and put on show in the Roundhouse. I saw them myself last time I was in Cusco. The pipe was just like this one."

"Was the skin pale or dark?"

"Couldn't tell. It was dry, withered. Brown hair on the chest. Like a monkey." She laughs; then frowns. "Think what this may mean: that these new people are coming from both seas. From both sides of the World. These may be only the first of many, only the scouts."

The All-Seer nods appreciatively. Time with Lady Sian is always well spent. Tonight they will dine together and go over every detail of the day. Everything must be entered on a quipu and sent to the Emperor.

The sun is sinking by the time they get back to the square. There's a faint chill on the salt breeze. Time, Candía mimes, to leave for the ship. Their hosts bid them farewell with a few words and hands raised high, like a benediction. Four guards escort them to the haven.

"Don Pedro," Tomás says, as they are punted out to the caravel (Candía likes the sound of the title, all the more because he has no right to it), "if you decide to stay here, I should like to stay here too."

"Why so, Tomás? Are you bewitched by the gold like that rogue Molina? Or is it the girls? Also like Molina, come to that."

"Among Christians I'm a slave. Before that I was a slave in Morocco. Here I was treated as a man. I see no slaves in this land. No beggars either. Everyone has good clothes. Everyone has a good house. And the houses have no locks. Their doors are only curtains. Did you ever see the like, Don Pedro, in your travels? To me this is a new thing."

"To me too, Tomás. Peru must be the richest land on Earth. But we mustn't let ourselves be charmed like witless unicorns by women and gold. Make no mistake, Tomás—if we stay here they'll kill us. Sooner or later."

Waman has been chained below all day, his mind feverish with longing to set foot in his homeland, or just be allowed on deck to watch the folk in the port. He feels deeply wronged he wasn't sent along to interpret for Candía, though he admits to himself that the Old One's suspicions are right. He would gladly have fled, have done whatever the All-Seer required. Or would he—if it led to the deaths of Tomás and Candía, who have treated him kindly? He wrestles with this, tells himself the decision was made when he killed that man on the island. How he rues not killing Pizarro too! He must put his family first. Even if to go home is to risk the lives of his new friends.

Waman's only visitor has been Molina, who came down into the hold with food and water, and many questions. Molina has made the day both better and worse. Better, by filling some empty hours below deck. Worse, by tormenting him with talk of the wonders he saw in Tumbes yesterday.

To be fair, Molina has also been kind, telling Waman that once the Commander hears what Candía has to say, he will surely want to see the city for himself, probably tomorrow, and will need his interpreter at his side.

"But don't start thinking he'll give you the slightest chance to slip away, Felipe. No. He'll keep you trussed like those hogs I took ashore."

Candía's nose picks up the stink of the caravel wafting towards him on the water. Funny how one never smells it when aboard. He forgets it as soon as wine is flowing around the cabin table and he begins to relate the marvels he has seen, keeping for last the best: the golden temple. First he describes the city, mentioning the lack of doors. "The only strong door I saw in the whole place was at the fortress. It has a big gate, with a jaguar and cougar painted on the bastions. I couldn't get near enough to see in, but there's a heavy wooden ramp that can be pulled up like a drawbridge."

"Show me," says Pizarro, going on deck and peering at the silhouette of Tumbes against an evening sky the colour of dried blood. It's already too dark to see details, but the Greek points out the three-tiered bulk of the fort on a hill outside the town.

"If, as you say, Candía . . ." Pizarro asks thoughtfully, "if there's no hunger or want in Peru, if even the lowest have enough, how do the lords get anyone to work?"

The Greek gives a Greek shrug. They return to the cabin table.

"No poor?" says the Pilot. "You must be mistaken. Such a thing can't be. It's unheard of—whether in Christendom or Turkey or anywhere. Including the Indies. Those who saw the city of Mexico before we conquered it say the poor begged from the rich in the streets, just as they do in Seville. 'Ye have the poor with you always,' said Our Lord. Poverty makes charity. Without the needy, how would we give alms to open our souls' way into Heaven?"

"I thought Our Lord told the rich to sell all their stuff and give it away," Molina cuts in cheekily. "Maybe here they've done it." He enjoys needling the tiresomely pious Pilot. And, like Candía and Tomás, he has been seduced by his glimpse of Peru.

Ruiz slams a pewter mug down on the table. "In every country on Earth I've seen or heard of, God raises the wealthy because they've earned it. The poor are here to serve the rich and test their generosity—especially when it's time to make their wills. A land without poverty is blasphemy."

Ruiz refills his mug, glaring at Candía with the eye of a horse who has smelt fire. "This temple you saw. Incense, fonts, holy statues—even a nunnery! What can it be but Satan amusing himself in this faraway land by mocking our True Faith? No, it's for God and the Church to care for the poor, Candía. Not some heathen king. If things are as you say, it's because the Devil coddles these Indians to make them worship him.

"Or perhaps, gentlemen," he adds more softly, looking around the table, "we ourselves have strayed too far from God. Has any man here ever asked himself why the Bible makes no mention of these lands? Lands unknown to Jew or Christian, though surely known to their Creator. By my reckoning, we're now as far from the Holy Land as one can get on this round Earth. Think on that. Perhaps, gentlemen, we're blundering into the kingdom of the Antichrist."

"Enough of this friars' flaptrap!" It's Pizarro who raps the table now. "Everyone knows pagan lands are the Devil's playground. What *I* want to know is how big this kingdom is. How rich. How well defended." The Commander hoists himself from his chair.

"Pilot Ruiz, we sail on the morning tide. We'll follow the coast southwards and see what else we find. But I want one man to stay here in this city and learn their ways. We'll pick him up when we come back in a few weeks. Any takers?"

"Me!" Molina's hand shoots up like a schoolboy's. "I'll stay, Don Francisco."

"Why you?"

"I like it here."

The suspicion native to Pizarro's face widens into a grin. "Not sure I can spare you, Molina. Fine fellow like you. But if you insist—"

"Because he likes the whores!" Candía barks, sorry he wasn't quicker to volunteer himself. "You know they'll kill you, Molina? Wasn't it you drew first blood on the Indian ship? The survivors probably came back here. They won't have forgotten."

"I only tickled that big fellow's tattoo! Anyway, they can't know which of us did what. To them we're all alike."

With nightfall Tomás is allowed to bring Waman on deck—so long as he is laced into the weighted jacket and never left alone. A fingernail of moon has risen over the desert. The boy goes to the side and swallows great draughts of air. The African tells of his day ashore, adding that Pizarro has surprised everyone by deciding to sail next morning. Hopes crushed, the interpreter bends over the rail and weeps into black water.

Tomás's hand on his shoulder. "Don't worry, Felipe. The ship goes south. Maybe the Commander will put in at your home village. Anyway, he must come back here soon." Waman listens in dismay to the news that Molina will be left in Tumbes, alone. He had not foreseen this: a rival interpreter so quickly. "Mama Killa," he prays silently to the slim crescent, "let the ship stop where I can flee. May it be so."

It is late now. Only the brightest stars can be seen in a sky fogged by dust and moonglow. Here and there a few lights sparkle on the dark skin of land and city. There is a smell of fish and doused fires. Phosphorescence blooms in the water wherever a wave licks a mooring or the piles of the dock.

The Spaniards are leaving Ruiz's cabin, heading for hammocks and berths. Molina is suddenly beside him at the rail.

"How now, Felipe!"

"I hear we sail tomorrow," Waman replies bleakly. "And I hear you're staying ashore."

Molina grunts.

"Tell Pizarro you have to take me with you!"

"I'd like that. But he won't. You know it as well as I do."

"If you get a chance," the boy goes on, "would you do one thing for me? Would you go and see my family? Tell them I live, that I'm well. Tell them I'm not free, but will come to them soon as I can. Above all, tell them I love them. And say I'm sorry."

"Sorry? What for?"

"Not now. When we're back."

"I can't make promises . . ." Molina's voice dies away. He stares a long time at the dark city, as if beginning to regret his choice. "Anything might happen over there."

"If you can't go yourself, have the goodness to ask the All-Seer to send a message. Will you do that?"

"How can I? I don't speak a word of the language."

"I've already taught you a few."

"What! *Yes* and *no* and *what's your name?*"

"They live in a village called Little River," Waman persists. "Huchuy Mayu, we say. It's about twenty *tupu* south by the new road—under a hundred miles. You can count the marker stones." Saying this, giving these directions, makes the plan seem less unlikely. Almost as if Waman could be making the journey himself.

"If you're careful," he adds, "all will go well for you over there. This is a good place."

"I think so too, Felipe." The Spaniard pats the interpreter's head. "I'll do what you ask, if I can."

That night, chained in the hold, Waman pulls some threads from his breechclout, the new one his mother made. He twists them together, splicing the ends to make a string. Each sound in the language has a knot. He ties the only ones he knows, for *W* and *M* and *N*. Waman: Hawk: himself.

In the morning, in the farewell flurry as Molina is embraced by his fellows, blessed by Ruiz, and makes ready to go ashore, Waman presses this tiny quipu into his hand.

"Give this when you find my family in Little River. With this they will know you. They will treat you well. Like one of them."

{ 5 }

"What better way to learn a language than in bed?" Lady Sian observes to the All-Seer in his private quarters, where they have met to review the progress of the barbarian left behind last month. The All-Seer's orders from the Emperor are to treat the man as a guest and make sure he learns some Quechua quickly. That done, he will be sent to Tumipampa, or even Cusco, for questioning. To this end, the Governor has found Molina lodgings with a young widow.

"Imagine," she adds. "That hairy monkey in her arms."

The All-Seer chuckles. These lowlanders are always so earthy. Always joking about love. And the rest of the time they're doing it. Anything one can think of, to judge from their erotic pots. He looks up at the niches on the far wall of the room, each filled with a good piece from his own collection. All startling. And some quite old. From a world before this World.

"I hear the barbarian's looking more human now," the All-Seer says. "They tell me she's plucked out all his whiskers. This work for the Empire seems to be taking her mind off her loss. I gather she's . . . applying herself."

The All-Seer offers the Governor some more grilled tuna and re-fills their tankards himself. His helpers have been given the night off.

He is simply dressed, showing her his private face: warm, confiding, thoughtful, the taut skin over his cheekbones creased in mirth.

Perhaps, she thinks, he still has hopes of her. Let him. It's no bad thing to be admired by a Yupanki, a member of the Empire's ruling clan. She knows better than to let him catch her.

"No wonder she's bathing that creature so well! Although . . ." The Governor lets the thought drop.

"What? You know you can speak freely."

"The Empire is a great thing," Lady Sian continues. "But—between ourselves—I'm not sure it has a place in people's bedrooms."

"Maybe not." The All-Seer gives her a stiff bow. "But it was the widow's own idea to become more than the barbarian's landlady."

"What if she grows too fond of him? She might take his side and fail to report as she should."

"The woman is reliable. Some traders on that ship the barbarians attacked were kin of hers. Anyway, her main task is to teach him the language. Whatever we fail to learn here the Emperor's men will get out of him later."

The Governor nods, wishing she had been less outspoken. "What will you do if his shipmates come back for him too soon?"

"They won't. They've sailed a long way down the coast. Last I heard they were nearly at Chincha. Our people there have been told to keep them entertained as long as possible."

Molina, too, is in no hurry to see his shipmates. Here in Tumbes he's a new man, a somebody, an *hidalgo*. Respect and long looks wherever he goes. Especially from women. And what luck to be taken on by this one!

One of the things Molina likes about Peru is that the custom of siesta is observed. He and his hostess, whose name is Yutu, are sharing a double hammock strung between the avocado trees that shade her patio. She is fast asleep, her chest swelling and falling rhythmically beneath thin cotton. He looks on her fondly and uncuriously, as men do with a woman whose body they've explored. His eyes linger on her upturned nose. *Yutu*—some sort of bird, no? A partridge? Something pretty. He likes her birdlike eyes, black and shiny. And her skin: bronze, sleek, hairless. Yet such a lovely head of hair, straight and glossy as the tail of a fine black mare. He loves how it sweeps his chest when she throws him on his back and rides him. So many things she's taught him! Things that would send a lesser man to the confessional. Or to the stocks.

Fine house too. Living like a wealthy Moor, waited on by servants, eating fish or meat every day. Picking up the lingo. Even starting to like the beer—a sure sign a man's settling in. And all this scrubbing and plucking. Each hair tweezered from his hide by Yutu until, with his *moreno* looks and the tunic she's lent him, he just about passes for a local. He can't have been this clean since a midwife wiped him down when he came into the world.

A cold sea-breath lops into the courtyard, chattering the leaves, chilling Molina's bare chest. His mind strays to Castilian winters, to the freezing orphanage where his mother left him the night she ran away. Away with whom? His father? He doubts she even knew who his father was. Some randy knave no doubt, as quick with his prick as with his knife. Some knave like him.

Free of all but memories. At least, he feels free here, though Yutu's no fool, never letting him wander far. Still, it's a great thing to be her lover instead of a footslogger for that piss-eyed bully Pizarro. Not for the first time Molina asks himself why he crossed the line on Gallo

Island. Ah, yes: gambling debts in Panama, and several husbands and fathers who would see him flayed.

"Badluck Molina," they used to call him in Spain. But no one knows that in Peru. Three months here now, the best of his life. Pizarro can take his time.

Molina and Yutu are strolling through the streets one evening when they hear a loud noise in the air. A howl of lamentation like a thousand lonely dogs.

Molina's first thought is that Pizarro must have come back for him at last and committed some outrage—some slaughter on the beach. Yutu grasps his hand and pulls him along, listening, saying nothing, heading for the square. The two have a hard time getting through the throng.

In the middle of the plaza imperial guardsmen have formed a ring, holding the crowd back with small shields and pikes. Inside the ring, sitting on a stone seat by the fountain, is an old man with long white hair. In his hands is a message of coloured strings hanging from a thick black cord.

"This means death," Yutu says in Molina's ear.

"*¡Vámonos!*" he shouts in hers, suspecting his shipmates and fearing for his life. "*Haku!*" Let's be gone.

She laces her fingers into his, tightening her grip. "We stay. And I listen."

"The news will be repeated," guards are calling. "The news will be repeated. Those who have heard should leave and make room for others."

The old man gathers himself for yet another reading, calling out in a voice of surprising strength and authority:

"*Uyariwaychik*. All hear me. This is now made known. Our Emperor Wayna Qhapaq has died, suddenly, in the thirty-fourth year of his reign." He pauses, while another howl of mourning fills the square; then resumes running his fingers over the knots.

Molina can't follow much. Where has their king died? And how? Could it be the work of Pizarro? Some other Spaniards?

Yutu repeats everything slowly and simply for him back at her house. The Emperor—the Sapa Inka, or Only King—fell ill from a plague without name, a sickness never seen before. This pestilence first appeared in mountain towns on the Empire's northern border a few weeks ago, spreading quickly through Quito Province to the city of Tumipampa, where the Emperor was residing. Of twelve thousand high officials, army commanders, lords, ladies, retainers, and royal children in the palace at the time, ten thousand fell ill. More than six thousand have died.

It was hoped Wayna Qhapaq might be saved by isolation—alone in a small house in the palace gardens. But after ten days condors began alighting on the roof. Then the people knew their Only King was dead.

The Emperor is to be embalmed and taken to Cusco, where he will live forever in the house of his father, the Sun.

Molina knows at once what it is: the smallpox.

They came for him the next day, two big soldiers at Yutu's door. Next thing he knew he was frogmarched from the house—toes barely scraping the ground—and thrown in jail.

He sighs and scratches the stubble in his armpits. He should have known his luck wouldn't last. Sooner or later the fates always empty a pail of shit on Badluck Molina's head. Daylight begins to show in the cell's high window. A window barely big enough for a cat, but a highway for the sodding mosquitoes, who have given him another sleepless night. The light taunts him. What is daylight without freedom? Only a change of torments: mosquitoes by night; flies by day.

He is kept in solitary. Each morning cornbread is slid under the door and water trickles into a jar from a spout in the wall. Eventually a jailer comes to clean the cell, a masked man wreathed in incense from a small brazier worn on his chest as a precaution.

Sometimes this man rouses him in the night for questioning by the All-Seer—a disembodied voice from behind a sheet. *Here for your own protection.* Ha! If that's the reason, why is the old buzzard grilling him with endless questions, expecting him to speak their lingo perfectly? I can curse in it, eat in it, and fuck in it. That's about all Yutu got into my head.

He tracks the days with scratches on his wall. He listens to the unseen street beyond the window. Why hasn't Yutu come? He misses her, finds it painful to think of her, of the good days at her house. Sometimes he hears a woman's voice in the street that might be hers. But he can never make out words.

His hairiness grows back, his beard and a dark pelt on chest and thighs. His skin turns grey for want of sunlight. Loneliness and despair settle on him like ash. Molina fears nothing from the plague himself. Smallpox visited the orphanage when he was five or six, as it did every few years. Same with measles, mumps, chickenpox. Many children died, but the rest never caught those things again.

His mind often returns to Spain, awake and in dreams. What he would give to see his shipmates now! He yearns to hear Castilian, a lute, for a taste of wine, a card game with Candía—one of the few he got along with. He even prays, a thing he does only when hope forsakes him. He tallies up his scratches on the wall. More than a month now. More than four since Pizarro sailed away. A long time. Maybe they too are in a Peruvian jail, rotting in a hole like this somewhere down the coast.

The All-Seer seems to believe that the arrival of the new sickness and the Spaniards is no coincidence. Molina has denied this, pointing out there was no plague on his ship and it did not begin in Tumbes. But to himself he admits it might well have made its way south from Mexico or Panama, through hotlands and highlands until it burst into the Peruvian Empire.

Molina gathers that the pestilence still rages, despite all efforts to contain it. The authorities have given it a name, the spotted death, and described its early symptoms. Movement on the highways has been forbidden. No ships are allowed to sail. The postal service is suspended, except for imperial business at the highest level.

Yet already the smallpox has spread south through the highlands to the distant capital. It can't be long before it sweeps down into each coastal valley, even though this land is so vast, so rugged. Molina recalls asking Yutu how long it would take to walk to Cusco. She said people in no hurry allow a month and a half, but the postmen can get there in five days. That seemed impossible. Now he knows better. Perhaps that's how it spread so quickly, with the mail.

For some days he hears bustle in the street beyond his window: the slap of many sandals, the shouts of soldiers, the soft tread and clicking toes of llamas.

Then no more. Only dogs howling by night. Only a hiss and flutter of big wings by day. And on the air a stink of death.

His captors have died or fled, leaving him here like a rat in a jar.

His cell door is a sturdy affair of hard timber, fastened outside by a thick metal bar through stone rings. No hope there. His only chance is to dig through the adobe wall, which he judges from the window opening to be about three feet thick. Molina snaps the rim off his water pot. With the shard he scrapes away a patch of plaster, exposing brickwork—big adobes of mud and gravel, laid with clay. He manages to dislodge a sharp stone the shape of a mango pit. With this he works at the joint. By nightfall he has loosened one brick, pulled it free with bleeding fingers. The work goes better the following day. The bricklayers were sparing with mortar in the core. By sundown he's wrenched out a dozen bricks, leaving only the street side undisturbed. When he kicks those away he will be free.

Molina breaks out in the thick of night, lit by a thief's moon, enough to see without being seen. He is tempted to raid a house for food, but shrinks from the reek at every door. And there are dogs, growling in gutters or sloping along behind him, lost and searching for their owners. He slips a hand into a pocket of his jerkin, checking for the tiny string with three knots given him by Felipe. Still there. Thank Christ the All-Seer let him keep his clothes, though his boots were taken and he has only rags to bind his feet. He will go south by the great road to Huchuy Mayu and look for the boy's family. If they haven't died or fled like the citizens of Tumbes. Little River sounds like a small place, out of the way, fanned by sea winds. Perhaps they have been spared.

Once well beyond the fields Molina feels safe enough to slake his thirst at the roadside canal and eat from trees planted along the Emperor's highway. The low fruit is gone—in all the world it's always so!—but he knocks down some avocados with a stick. Also a custard apple and carob pods filled with a pith like sherbet.

He is in foothills now, in thorny scrub above the watered valley. He slips over a side wall and naps on the soft screef, awakening to mad laughter: parrots. For a while he makes his way laboriously through the bush, but soon abandons this precaution. There are no other wayfarers. Even the posthouses every few miles are unmanned.

Around noon on the third day, he spots movement far ahead on a shining shield of heat. Travellers? Troops? Or a trick of the light?

It is a flock of vultures, hopping and tearing at the bodies of a man and woman. He hurls stones at the big birds, who draw back insolently, without taking to the air. The elderly couple are side by side, face down, their dead lips sunk in the cool water of the roadside channel. They have not been there long, perhaps only two days. Molina lifts the man's tunic, sees the craterous pustules that erupted from the flesh like a thousand tiny volcanoes.

He searches the bodies, finding a bag of toasted corn and slices of dried sweet potato. He pops the earspools from the man's stretched lobes—small ones of gold alloy. Worth having all the same. As are the beads in the woman's braids. Unwinding his foot rags, he tries on the dead man's shoes. They fit.

Chaska hears shouts on the breeze, though she can't see anybody from where she is weeding the beans. A cold rill of fear runs through her, though the day is already hot. Some trouble on the highway, which brings so many troubles. She takes up her swaddled baby, glances around for a place to hide him. Just you and me, she says with a smile to calm the small pinched face. More shouts. She lays him down behind a pile of cornstalks. Good thing he just had a feed. With luck he'll make no noise.

Only him and me now, she thinks again bleakly, kneeling between the bean rows. Without little Atuq—the last gift of her husband Mallki—she doesn't know what she would do. What would be the point of anything, with all the others gone? It's still possible Waman is alive at sea somewhere. And Tika just might have survived, away in a House of the Chosen. But as the months wear on without word of either, she finds this harder to believe.

Little River stands, but most of the buildings are empty. The canals run, but overflow the sluices. The fields are going to weeds and brush and sand. Llamas and dogs roam loose. And the highway brings desperate folk: dazed, hungry, dangerous.

It all began with the Emperor's death. There was public sorrow, much of it genuine, mingled with dread at what might follow. Then, quite a long time later, when many in Little River were beginning to think they might be spared, the spotted death came upon them. The elder Waman was the first to go. He had become withdrawn and listless after his grandson left, perhaps because he blamed himself for filling the boy's head with sea tales. He sickened and died in two weeks. Within another week Mallki was stricken, his suffering so hideous that at the end she *wanted* him to die.

She tries not to think of what they went through. Yet the memories are too vivid to quell: the raging fever; their cries for water; their skin bubbling like the back of a toad, seething, sticking to the sheets and sloughing off in patches as if it had been cooked. How can it be, she wonders, that I am here, untouched? She blows thanks to Father Sun for her life and for little Atuq, born only weeks before the plague.

The shouts are louder, nearer. She thinks she can hear someone calling her name. *Mama Chaska. Mama Chaska.* Could this be the news she is waiting for, news of Waman? Tika?

She gets up and shades her eyes with a hand. Two figures dancing in the heat. Two men lugging a heavy sack between them. The sack becomes a dead man, strangely wrapped. She knows the young men carrying him—a pair of idlers who fled into the desert before the plague arrived. How is it that good men die yet wastrels like these live on?

"Lady Chaska, help us!"

"So it's Lady Chaska now, is it? Last time, you called me something else. I've dead of my own to bury. On your way."

"He's not dead."

"Then he's dead drunk. You as well, let me guess."

"He's not one of us. He's not from here at all. We found him on the road, up there." The older one lifts his head to the new highway. "He said a few words before he passed out. He says he knows Waman."

"How dare you speak my son's name! On your way. And take your drunken friend."

"Lady Chaska," the youth says in a humble tone. "I am no longer what you think. Neither is my friend here. Not now. If we ever offended you, we're truly sorry." The friend nods gormlessly, as if incapable of speech. "I beg you, Lady Chaska, take a look for yourself. We don't know what this man is. We've never seen anything like him. Perhaps you can wake him up again. Please."

The unconscious man looks to Chaska like nothing so much as an old sea turtle dying on a beach. His breath is quick and shallow, his lips cracked, his torso encased in a stiff close-fitting leather shell. Pus-filled blisters cover his neck and hands. She steps back in fear of plague—instinctively, for if the spotted death could touch her she would surely be dead by now. She looks more closely. The blisters are big and soft as turtle eggs. Only a bad sunburn.

"Undo that coat. It's killing him."

The youths obey, working at the strange buttons and laces. From the leather shell emerges a young man's body. Very hairy. Unwashed. Chaska moves further upwind.

"Look. He's carrying this." The youth hands her a tiny knotted string of cotton thread. Thread she has seen before. Thread she spun herself and wove into Waman's breechclout.

"*That's why* I call you Turtle. You looked just like an old leather-back. And from your shell came word of my Hawk."

Chaska keeps the bearded one (who calls himself *Mulina*) in Ti-ka's old room at the back of the house, where it is dark and cool. Every day she rinses his burns with seawater, feeding him baby food—fruit juice, mashed squash, avocado—until his appetite comes back and his cracked mouth can take corn, sweet potato, peanuts, fish. Such rotten teeth. Half the back ones gone, the rest like charred stumps, but at least the front ones are whole, if none too straight. In other respects a good-looking man. Strong, well made. His face pleases her: shrewd, foxy, but wit in its foxiness. It reminds her of the expression on her baby's face, for which she named him Atuq. She tells Molina this when he's well enough to be plucked. The less foreign he looks the better.

"There can't be two Foxes in one house, so Turtle you'll be, like it or not."

"*¡Por Dios!*" says Molina as Chaska works on his chin with tweezers. "Weakly, weakly! Skin sore."

"*Gently, gently,*" she corrects. "*My* skin *is* still sore." His knowledge of the language, rough though it is, is a wonderful surprise. She has plied him with a hundred questions about Waman and the outlandish seafarers who took him away. My boy lives! At least he did when they sailed. She can only hope that the plague didn't reach him, wherever he went. That the ship did not sink. That the barbarians haven't killed him. That the Empire's troops haven't killed them all.

But her guest's tale is reassuring. If they took Waman to be their interpreter, surely they will treat him well?

How lucky that this land of gold is also a land of widows! Molina has begun to notice his rescuer: not quite as young or pretty as Yutu in Tumbes, but a fine woman all the same. Good figure and good teeth, shown off so well when her mouth widens in a smile, which it does more often now. If he plays his cards well, he might become her man. He could stay here. Long as he likes. At least till the Spaniards come back. Maybe forever, depending on how that goes.

Right now, a hundred Christians could take Peru with hardly a shot fired. The government, the army, the chain of command, the general population—all must be in ruins. But if we'd tried to conquer this land as it was before, we could never have done it, Molina reckons, not even with a thousand horse. What if the Peruvians have time to recover before Pizarro comes back with an army? The card of surprise has been played. So has the card of smallpox.

No, he decides. He will lie low in Little River until it's clear what fate intends.

First thing: woo the widow.

As his strength returns Molina helps with farm work, mending ditches, turning sod with a foot-plough while Chaska follows with her hoe, singing to herself as she buries each kernel of corn with a fish to give it a good start. He learns how to ride her small boat, an odd banana-shaped craft made of bound reeds; yet swift, light, unsinkable, bucking and nodding beneath him like a pony on the waves. The other fishermen—so few of them left, so many boats rotting on the shore—teach him how to paddle, to cast, to find the best spots. He spends days on the sea, as Felipe and his father used to do, wearing a straw hat and an old cotton shirt against the sun. A dead man's shirt. Her husband's? He doesn't ask, less from tact than superstition.

Soon he is bringing in anchovies every morning, with squid and tuna when they come his way. Once he caught a young turtle, bearing it home proudly, its flippers rowing in the net. But Chaska's face became a thundercloud. Bad luck! Bad luck! she yelled. Put it back now! She followed him to the beach and watched angrily until it swam away.

Late that evening, drinking beer on the flat roof of the house, he asked, "Why not eat turtle? Others catch them. I've seen them do it."

"They should have told you. Or I should have. A man must never kill his namesake. Atuq will never kill a fox. You must never kill a turtle. Turtle is your helper, your brother."

A fart for her infidel ways, Molina thought, and nearly said so. No wooing her like that.

"Before you fish again," she persisted, "you must fast three days. Then you'll take beer and corn to Mother Sea at dawn. You will tell her you are sorry. That you did not know our ways. That you will never harm a turtle again in your life. And you must thank her for all she yields to your net."

Months go by. Months almost as good as Molina's time in Tumbes, though tinged with melancholy here, with so many friends and family emptied from the homes of Huchuy Mayu. After dinner they spend most evenings on the roof terrace. Chaska brings a jug of beer or palm wine, and they sit up there in the coolness watching sunsets over the ocean and the stars come out above dark mountains and magenta icefields glowing high beyond the desert.

Often she tells him about her old life with Felipe (whom she calls Waman) and her niece Tika, who he gathers left home several months before the plague to join a nunnery somewhere in the highlands, in a great stone city of the Empire. When things settle down she wants Molina to go there with her to look for the girl, or at least find out her fate.

One evening, long after the turtle-catching incident is laid to rest, he asks Chaska about *her* name. What does it mean? What is it she must never harm? The day is a faint memory above the darkening pewter of the sea. A breeze flows over the desert from the water, yet the sun's warmth lingers in the plaster of the roof, rising agreeably through a soft blanket under their backs.

She laughs, high-pitched, like a girl.

"No one can kill my namesake. Look. Look up." She lifts an arm and spreads her fingers. "I am Star. Like the lights in the sky."

"So lovely! I not see such sky before."

"Have never seen." She touches his bare arm lightly with her fingertips.

"Your language is too hard. And I am too thick. Still I not speak right." He sighs, remembering how the nuns tried to beat grammar and a good accent into him at the orphanage. He longs to tell her he's a simple man. No scholar, no gentleman. A rough warrior, a man of deeds, not words. But such a speech is beyond him. And better she think him a big man in his country.

The moonless night is dark now and unusually clear, and the stars seem to hover near the Earth, layer upon layer, great and small. And some fine as flour, a dusting of light on black velvet.

Ever since he can remember, Molina has loved the night sky. As a small boy in that orphanage at Molina de Aragón, he would slip from his dormitory, careful not to wake the others, sliding on his belly along cold flags like a snake and up the outdoor stairs to the rooftop. There he would stretch on his back and scan the mystery of the stars. All those tiny jewels, so bright and blue and cold and far, the light of Heaven leaking through a million pores in the dark bowl of the firmament. The eyes of angels, the nuns said. But how could angels be one-eyed? Angels or not, the stars bestowed awe and consolation. No matter how friendless he felt, how sharp his woes, how cruel and unfair the beatings he received (though in truth he brought many on himself, with his tongue, his temper, his midnight raids on the kitchen for a wizened apple), his sorrows would wash away under the greatness of the stars. And later, when he left Spain for the Indies, he would haunt the deck of the caravel at night as it made its lonely way across the Ocean Sea, gazing at constellations like old friends. And as he sailed with Ruiz into this unknown South Sea, he saw new stars rising into place, pricking new patterns on the skin of the night, from below the rim of a new world.

Molina returns the touch on her arm, says softly, *"Mira, Chaska. Tantas estrellas, y tú eres la más bella."*

"What are you saying? I like the sound."

"I say stars are many. Are lovely. And you most lovely of all."

"I don't believe a word of it, Mulina!" But she is laughing. And he likes the way she says his real name. He doesn't much like Turtle. A slow and harmless creature. He is neither.

Chaska takes his hand in hers and sweeps it like a painter's brush over the sky, tracing the figures and patterns the Peruvians see. Some are familiar: Qollqa the Granary, their name for the Pleiades; Chakana the Crossbeams, which Pilot Ruiz called the Southern Cross. But there are others for which he has no match: Kuntur the Condor and Amaru the Anaconda, rearranging in his mind the stars of Scorpio. Strangest of all are the dark formations the Peruvians

recognize—ink spills on the misty whiteness of the Milky Way—
Atuq the Fox, Machaqway the Snake, Yana Llama the Black Camel,
with the twin stars of Centaurus for its eyes.

Molina does well at this, or so it seems after another drink. His
faith in his mind's agility returns. By my sins! he thinks, I'm not
doing so badly in the Peruvian tongue for only a few months. I can
curse and eat and make love in it. And now I'm learning the heavens.

They have drawn close together on the blanket. He feels the
stretched length of her beside him.

"And all that," she says, her fingers sweeping the Milky Way, so
much broader and brighter down here than in the northern world,
"that is Hatun Mayu, the Great River. We live in Little River. Up
there is the big one, greatest of all."

Molina grunts, his interest in the heavens waning as a familiar
ache in his lower body grows.

"*La Vía Láctea*," he answers dreamily.

"*Llaqta*? Which meaning, city or nation?"

"No. In my language, it's the Way of . . . *Leche*."

"What is *lichi*?"

"I don't know . . ." How to explain milk in a country where milk
is unknown? But of course, that isn't so.

"It is the drink from a mother. For feeding baby." With this he
lightly brushes the side of her breast, where there is wetness on her
dress. Chaska laughs; flirtatiously, it seems to him. His cock is tenting his tunic.

"For us it is a man's milk," she says. "A god's. The Great River is
the gushed seed of Pachakamaq, Maker of the World. Maker of all
Space and Time."

Emboldened by this, Molina grabs her hand and plants it on
his tent.

She snatches free, leaps up and strikes him hard across the face.

The blow lands like a cudgel in the fog of his lust. He sits up, feels blood running from his nose, tastes iron.

"Don't you dare do that," she is shouting. "With my husband not dead a year! His child unweaned."

Molina flees to his room—stumbling down the stairs and across the courtyard—as surprised by his own reaction as by the fury of Chaska's rebuff. What's he doing, putting up with *that*? He never takes shit from a wench. When he wants one, he has one. Can it be that this savage widow has unmanned him? Bewitched him? He must go back up and take her. A good fight makes a good fuck. Then be gone from this godforsaken town.

The pain worsens as the drink wears off. Slowly Molina calms down, begins to reflect on where he is. And on her angry words, parsing them over and over. If he heard and understood aright, her objection was not, maybe, to the move itself. Perhaps it was only too soon.

No. In the morning he will ask to be forgiven. If she lets him, he will stay. He will bide his time. They need each other. With time he may yet win this widow.

TWO

Spain

1528-29

❊ 6 ❊

Waman awakes, runs a hand along a wasted body. He pinches thigh, chest. Feels the pinch.

Alive.

A lick of air on his face. A smell of land, earth, blooms, fire. Drowned by the stink of bilge.

His eyes are sewn up like a purse.

Blind?

He lifts a hand to his face, picks at crusted lids. Sore, not stitched. Light floods his mind.

The sky is square.

He lies in stench and darkness, fixed on the blue square which slowly he understands to be an open hatch. *Aboard, then, within scent of land.* He tries to get up, can only bend a knee. He calls out, voice weak as his limbs. Nobody comes.

A touch on his cheek, very soft. A purr. All these ships have cats. And the cats always come to him. But which cat, which ship? Which sea?

Something is new.

The ship no longer heaves.

No. There. He feels it. Gentle. No pitch, no yaw. Only small answers to the wind.

Slowly he assembles details—some real, others perhaps from delirium, from dreams. They were on the Other Sea at last, the one the Christians call the Ocean Sea, which reaches all the way to Spain. In a ship bigger than Ruiz's. A better ship. Built in Spain not Panama, of Spanish wood.

There were others from the World. A girl, named Qoyllur, a little older, too highborn to notice him. And two youths, her helpers—all taken on board by the Old One during his southerly reconnaissance along the Empire's shore. Also six llamas and other gifts from ports of call.

Those people, those animals: did they die? Am I the only living creature from the World?

He sinks into a doze and a face comes before him: hard, wrathful, bald as a cannonball. A lone blue eye, scanning mistrustfully. The eye of Almagro, the Commander's partner. Dreaming again: One-Eye can't be on this ship. He was left behind in Panama. Waman's mind casts back to landing there after leaving Peru and sailing north past the hotlands. Almagro came down to the beach to greet Pizarro, as he had on Gallo Island. A great show of welcome, the two old men embracing like boys, like brothers. One-Eye plunging into the hold to see—and count—the new things from Peru. His whoops at every scrap of gold.

Waman was disappointed to find the barbarian outpost to be nothing but a straggle of huts and muddy alleys between the fore-shore and the jungle. A shipyard. A few hundred whites, a few dozen blacks, many Indian slaves and half-breed children, among them One-Eye's small son by a woman of Panama. They were there about a month, he recalls, all four from the World kept in cells beside the church: the only building made of stone.

One day the Old One came, fetched them out into steaming sunlight, had them chained behind a train of mules. Pizarro bade farewell to One-Eye with friendly words. But no warmth in his expression. Suspicion as usual in Almagro's lonely eye.

For days they followed a muddy track across the Isthmus, through a high forest to the Other Sea. There they boarded this ship bound for a place called Seville—the greatest city, Candía said, in Spain.

But did they reach it?

He hopes they did not.

Two faces in the blue square: one black, one brown. Tomás and Qoyllur, the haughty southern girl.

"Welcome back, Waman."

Why is she here, speaking to him? "You live!" he says. "The others . . . where are—"

"No talk. Drink." She lifts his head, swabs his face with soft wet cotton. Tomás holds a cup of water to his lips. Fresh water, sweet and cool.

"Have we gone back?" he asks.

He counted thirty-three days on the Other Sea, tying them on a thread. Then he fell ill, sweating in his hammock, not knowing night from day, nor caring, wanting death. How small the ship. How vast the Ocean Sea. How little food. And what food. Stinking pork, weevily corn, water like saliva, cheese that walked the board on legs of worms.

For every one of those days until he lost his wits, Waman yearned for the ship to turn back. Back from its mad fight with endless storms on an endless sea. Back to land, to life. He prayed for this to every god he knew, his and theirs. He swore he would run into the great woods the moment his feet touched the Isthmus of Panama, run all the way home to the World.

"Did we go back?"

"It's over now. Rest. We're there."

"Where?"

"The Great River." Tomás's voice. "The Wad-al-Kibir. I can see the towers of Seville."

"Ispañapim kanchik!" Qoyllur's voice. "We're in Spain!"

Waman dozes and more faces come before him: the girl, her helpers. Where are those boys? And the llamas, his special charges, whose sufferings he tried to ease until he couldn't leave his hammock.

He remembers Tomás appearing like a spirit in the fires of delirium, making him swallow thin broth, stale water. And Candía, his great beard dull and wilted. And Pizarro, telling him to trust in God.

Then a jaundiced priest with candle, book, and oil. And that was the last.

Until now. This breath of wind, this box of sky.

Again he sleeps, waking to the dankness of a tidal river, to bells and cries, human voices, the *tock* of horseshoes. A sudden clatter of armed men coming aboard. One climbs down the ladder, casts around, holds a kerchief to his mouth, climbs back into the light.

Waman does not see them arrest the Commander, but he hears of it soon enough. Francisco Pizarro has been taken to jail.

Why? Because the Old One never put in at Tumbes for Molina? Pizarro blamed winds and currents, he recalls, but Candía did not believe him. Neither did others. They whispered that Molina was marooned by the Commander's impatience, his drive to get to Panama and on to Spain, to lose no time in petitioning the King.

Next morning the Greek comes down and tells Waman what he

has learnt: Pizarro is being held for all the debts run up by Panama, because he served as the settlement's mayor and is its first official to show his face in Spain. Debts? Waman asks himself. He knows the word, but has never quite grasped its implications. They put many things down to debt. Isn't it some kind of *ayni*, a favour to be returned, reciprocated? How and when does it become a crime?

They are kept on the ship several days, forbidden to go ashore. He hears feet and heavy sounds on the deck above. Tomás and Qoyllur visit him two or three times daily, bringing food and water. He sees how changed they are. The black's skin is grey, the whites of his eyes yellow in a ravaged face. More teeth are gone. Qoyllur still has her teeth, but her mouth is a wound, her long hair dry and listless, her touch cracked and coarse on his brow.

At last she tells him: all from the World are dead except he and she and three llamas.

The llamas. Who would have cared for them after he fell ill? They are not in the hold, nor does he hear their tread on deck. The last thing he remembers is seeing them bound under nets during terrible storms, their knees and bellies rubbed raw by the reeling ship, each lying in a pool of blood and waste despite the straw he tried to spread beneath them. Fear in their soft eyes. He tried to soothe them, hugging their woolly necks, telling them one day this would be over and their feet would touch dry land. He went to the chaplain and brought them holy water, to make them Christians. Perhaps if they drank it they might survive this Christian ship. But each day the necks rose more weakly to greet him. One neck, then another, did not rise. Poor suffering beasts. Of the six, only three.

And of the four of us, only Qoyllur and myself. Qoyllur, the grand one, humbled and changed. Until now she'd made it clear she deemed him beneath her. She was not a captive. She came of her own will and curiosity, or at the behest of her parents. Or perhaps of the Empire, as a spy. She came in style, well dressed, helpers carrying her belongings.

We are the only two left. So that's why Qoyllur's being so good to me. She can talk to nobody else.

As soon as Seville's authorities give permission to unload the ship, Waman is lodged at a wine merchant's house, in servants' quarters on a back patio, with Tomás to sleep across his door. For protection, Waman wonders, or to stop him stowing away on the next ship bound for the Indies as soon as he can walk? The building has high walls, no windows except on the inside, and a single door to the street, iron-bound. Qoyllur, less valuable to Pizarro and therefore freer, stays with a seamstress not far away, below the walls and towers of Seville.

Little by little, fresh water, fresh air, fresh fruit—above all the miraculous orange, a great gift of the Christians' god—rebuild his health. He sees it in Qoyllur too, her healed gums, the gloss returning to her hair.

She treats him as a brother now, calling him *tura*, stroking his head, bringing food. As Tika used to do. Whenever Waman thinks of Tika and home he feels cloven in two like an avocado, and the hard stone that is his heart falls out.

Echoed footsteps on flagstone. Getting nearer. The chime of heavy keys.

"I piss on God!" Pizarro swears into the darkness. What a homecoming after twenty-seven years in the New World! Hauled away before Spain is steady beneath his feet. Thrown in a dungeon. And for other men's debts—not even his own. For the debts of every fool in Panama, merely because some years ago he was its mayor.

The door opens. A welcome glow. A lantern in the hand of a brute like a fairground bear.

"Curse God all you like," the jailer mutters, as if to himself, tossing some straw in a corner, setting a plate of old bread and mildewed olives on the floor. "He won't hear you. He doesn't listen to bores. Luckily for you."

"You speaking to me, man?"

"Why would I do that? You debtors are all bores. Nobodies." The jailer farts, following this with an odd, shrill giggle. "Give me a murderer. Give me a rapist. A heretic. A backsliding Jew. A Moor. Interesting work, squeezing out their lies. But scum like you . . . It's not worth oiling a thumbscrew to hear what you have to say." The jailer hawks and spits on the floor, inches from the food. He regards Pizarro, hand on hip. "Let me guess. You're a drunk? You stink at cards? You throw money at every pair of tits?

"Good night, Lord Nobody. Until tomorrow. And tomorrow." Another giggle, a slam, the old lock tumbling; echoed footfalls fading down a corridor.

I'll throw that whoreson to the dogs, Pizarro vows.

But how? How, when a lifetime in the Indies ends in this? He curses that charlatan of a beggar by the church in Trujillo, preying on the dreamy youth he used to be. Nearly forty years ago now. Might things be different if he'd been more open-handed, given both coins, not one? Better he'd never left Spain at all, better he still wandered Trujillo's hills behind a drove of swine.

The Commander sighs, eats. Rotten food, fit only for rats and cockroaches, though no worse than what was left on the ship. Self-consolation slowly cools his rage. Most men of his years are long dead. Most men of his birth would be proud to have done what he has done. In the Caribbean with the great Columbus. Discovering the South Sea with Balboa. Founding Panama. That city's mayor. Those aren't the deeds of a nobody!

But it's never enough, is it? There's a worm in him that gnaws. The worm speaks up: You call Panama a city? You call that enough? Enough, when you've glimpsed the golden cities of Peru?

On the river not a mile from this cell he has the proof of it. Gold, silver, fine silks, strange beasts. A Peruvian boy and girl. Enough—despite the dead heaved over the side, the gold already mortgaged—to turn the heads of King and Queen and make him great. And enough, by God, to bleach the stain of bastardy. They still sting, those tales: left by his unwed mother on a doorstep; unschooled, unloved; a mere swineherd on the lands of a father who never acknowledged him. None of it true . . . well, some of it, God knows. All of it murmured in drinking dens and whorehouses, even by his own men. Sweet Christ!

Pizarro kneels on the straw in the driest corner, crosses himself, asks God to forgive his blasphemous tongue. He feels better. Candía will get him out—just a matter of time, of bending the right ears, finding the right palms to grease.

"Good morning, Commander. Did Your Worship sleep well? Did the little angels send him a good night?" This not only sardonic but with a gloating tone. "Sold you short, didn't I? A would-be conqueror, eh? Less boring than I thought." A sigh of mock regret. "If only Seville wasn't crawling with conquerors just now."

Pizarro has been here a fortnight, with no visitors but Candía (who came yesterday with oranges) and this loathsome jailer. When jailers are cheerful, the news is always bad. Is he condemned to the galleys, to die at an oar?

"Such timing you have, my penniless friend." The brute sets down bread and water, then gleefully relates the news. Hernán Cortés, Conqueror of Mexico, has just landed, returning in pomp with a treasure unseen since the triumphs of ancient Rome.

"Your Worship staggers home from the Indies with a few long-necked sheep and not enough coin to pay a whore. And now comes this other man—younger than you, and a real conqueror, this one—with gold enough to buy Seville."

Hernán Cortés! The man Francisco Pizarro most wants to be. Cortés is a kinsman, a cousin of some kind, better born. But the blood tie is thin. And it's twenty years since the two met, just once, on the island of Cuba. In a Santiago tavern, where they quarrelled and drew knives. Over what? Pizarro asks himself. A slight, a woman . . . Or was it cards? He can't recall. He hopes Cortés, who was then a magistrate in Cuba, doesn't remember that night.

The jailer runs on, telling how everyone in Seville will turn out to watch the Conqueror ride a white stallion at the head of his parade tomorrow, followed by standard-bearers, slaves, women, Mexican lions and tigers, wagons piled high with gold and silver and strange idols.

Pizarro has no trouble picturing the scene, embroidered by his envy. That should be me, he thinks. That *shall* be me. He curses his luck, the timing. At best, Cortés puts him in the shade. At worst, he'll catch wind of Peru and take it for himself.

The jailer gone, the Commander's mood begins to lift, coaxed by a lick of sunshine from an arrow slit. He reflects that word of Peru is out already; that there's no shortage of potential rivals, in both the Indies and in Spain. Cortés himself might be the least of his worries: a man at the peak of fortune, a man who has everything he could possibly want. *Unless my cousin shares my worm.*

Why not send word to his lofty kinsman through Candía? The

Greek will know how to charm the hero of Mexico. With smooth words and God's help, he might enlist the Conqueror's support.

A gamble, yes. But merely the latest of a thousand.

Strength is returning to Waman's limbs, beginning with short walks around the wine merchant's yard on the arm of Tomás or Qoyllur.

Qoyllur turns up one morning in great excitement. She explains that a high lord has come back from the Indies, from the empire of Mexico, which he conquered a few years ago. Everyone is going to watch him parade through the streets.

"They say he's brought many Mexican things and people, even some lords and ladies. We must go!"

"You know I can't go. Tomás has orders not to let me step outside this house."

"That's been settled. Candía is coming here to take us." She doesn't tell the boy, from kindness, that no one is worried, that he's still far too weak to run away.

Waman has never seen so many people, not even in Tumbes. And it is odd to see barbarians, whom he knows as fighting men, thronging the streets in all kinds: fit and lame, fat and thin, women, children, and blacks like Tomás holding sunshades over their owners' heads. The noise is deafening, the Spaniards are not soft speakers and their little ones love to shriek. He smells cheese, sweat, unwashed bodies, rosewater, sewage, animal dung. Soldiers march up and down, cracking horsewhips to keep onlookers from blocking the way.

The wait is long and hot. Waman feels light-headed. If nothing happens soon, he will have to go and rest.

Then a trumpet blast. A hush. A shining form in the distance, coming slowly up the avenue of bright clothing and craned necks.

It is a barbarian in full armour and plumed helmet on a great white horse. The Conqueror of Mexico himself, Waman gathers from the whispering around him. The rider waves at the crowd, occasionally doffing his helm and making small bows to grandees on balconies along his way. He is grizzled, though younger than the Old One; plumper, his beard trimmed, his face ruddy and full-fleshed, except below the eyes, where his cheeks sag like hammocks. Despite this, he looks too well to have come straight from the Ocean Sea; he and his retinue must have restored themselves some-where.

Standard-bearers follow on foot. And men with parrots on their shoulders, birds who can pray and curse in Castilian. Then a dozen garlanded wagons pulled by oxen, piled high with marvellous things. Shields of turquoise and gold. A golden sun-wheel, richly embossed. Coiled serpents of polished stone with rearing heads, some smooth or scaled, others feathered as if they were half bird. Statues as ornate and brightly painted as the Christians' saints. A death god whose limbs are bones and whose head is a crystal skull. Mexican books, opened like fans, covered in images and symbols. Also weapons, fine pottery, robes of cotton and fur, obsidian mirrors.

Behind the wagons come dancers, jugglers, contortionists, acro-bats, naked except for body paint and knotted loincloths, some walk-ing on their hands while their feet roll logs in the air. The sight of these fills Waman with homesickness, for they look like his own people.

At a safe distance come two big cats, one plain and tawny, one boldly spotted—a puma and an *uturunku*, a *lion* and a *tiger* as Span-iards say. They are leashed with gold chains and pulled along by handlers wearing quilted cotton and rubber armour. Their hind legs are hobbled, their eyes filled with fury and fear.

Last come twenty lords from Mexico, striding along in feathered cloaks and headdresses, their cheeks tattooed and pierced with jewels, their eyes held high and straight ahead, as if still fixed on their faraway land. On their shoulders they bear a palanquin, a vehicle like those Waman used to see passing through Little River on the royal highway. The palanquin is shaded but open, so all can see the young lady and lord whose names are called out by a crier:

¡Doña Isabel Moctezuma!

¡Don Pedro Aculan Moctezuma!

A gale of applause.

"Who are they?" Waman asks Candía.

"All Seville knows who they are," the Greek says. "What you see there, Waman, are a son and daughter of the Emperor of the Mexicans."

Qoyllur speaks in Waman's ear. "Their father is murdered and their country is called New Spain. What does that tell you?"

"What the barbarians plan for us."

Waman feels patronized, a little hurt. He has known this much longer than she has, ever since he began to understand Castilian. Though it's true he's avoided discussing the implications.

"I'm going to kill the Old One," he blurts, trying to impress her, striving to believe his own boast. "I should have done it back on the island. It would have been easy then." He nearly tells her about that man on Gallo, the fulfilling crunch of bone and revenge.

"Think again, Brother. Think what might happen to you—and me." Qoyllur frowns into his eyes. "I'd like to kill him too. But not yet. And certainly not here in Spain. Make sure you never speak like that to anyone. Let them think us harmless, cowed, mere children. Mere leaves blown by the wind."

The day after the parade Candía sends word to Cortés to arrange a meeting as the Commander has ordered. Meanwhile he oversees the building of a camp on a meadow beside the Guadalquivir, where the llamas have been put to graze. There, Pizarro's men—those who have not drifted away since his arrest—are living like castaways in shanties of sticks, planks, old spars and sails. Soon the camp takes better shape, equipped with a cook tent, night watchmen, a strong armoury of oak timbers in which to keep the guns and the things from Peru—all save the gold and silver, locked in a vault beneath a banker's house.

One evening, when darkness and fog have fallen over the marshy meadow, a lowly foot soldier slips in among the tents. He is challenged by the watch and answers that he seeks the Commander in hope of signing on. Try the city jail, says the sentry, who is the worse for drink. And while you're there, ask that old swindler when we'll see our pay!

The visitor carries on, hidden in mist, stealthily observing the Indian camels—so strange—and the Peruvian capes and woollen hats worn over shabby jerkins and rusted armour by men around a campfire. Keeping to fog and shadows, he inspects a stack of earthenware storage jars, some big enough to hold a quartered ox. Behind this is a strongroom. He peers through chinks in its rough door. Two men within are playing cards by candlelight; they do not feel his gaze as it roams over guns, hatchets, pikes of polished bronze, stacks of cloth in many hues and patterns. And more pottery—smaller pieces, modelled and painted, realistic—animals, vegetables, even miniature buildings, and vessels with the faces of Indian lords so lifelike and expressive they might be portraits. Behind these are figurines showing sexual acts and giant members.

Extraordinary.

The spy slips away, on fire with what he's seen. He is Hernán Cortés.

On the following day, no longer disguised and saying nothing of the night before, the Conqueror returns and asks for Pedro de Candía. This fellow—a big Greek, voluble, with a winning smile—shows him around, then takes him into the city to see Pizarro's gold and silver in a crypt.

Only a small hoard, a mere sampling. But what weight and workmanship. Enough for Cortés to know his jailed cousin is not beguiling him.

These Panama vagabonds have found another Mexico!

What course to take, Cortés ponders. His standing in Spain is ticklish. Though many deem him a hero, by law he is a rebel, having sailed to Mexico from Cuba against orders. Years ago now. The King may be ready to forgive. But he knows there are key men at court who still suspect him of treason, of seizing the jaguar throne of Mexico less for the Crown than for himself. An old story: after the war the weapon must be locked away.

This is why he has brought Moctezuma's children and other Mexican lords to Spain: so that he and they swear fealty to King Charles in person, and are seen doing so by all at court. The procession in Seville went well, but it was merely a dress rehearsal. Will this play end in triumph or disaster?

Murders, also, have been laid at the Conqueror's feet. Of his wife, Catalina, found dead after a row over his Mexican mistress. Of a tiresome judge who died eating bacon at his table. Worst of all, the high crime of regicide: the murder of Moctezuma while in his personal custody.

Cortés has his explanations. Catalina dropped from apoplexy brought on by her wild temper. The judge's bacon was ill-cured. Moctezuma was stoned by a Mexican mob enraged at his appeasement of the Spaniards. Yet suspicions linger. No one else died from that bacon. And Moctezuma's body was unmarked—except for a long internal stabbing through the anus, which could only have been done by a Spanish sword.

His thoughts return to his jailed kinsman and the golden land of Peru. He's younger, wiser, and better bred than that rough bastard from Trujillo. He could sail away and snatch the prize himself. Why not? A man might do anything down there in the South Sea, so far from Spain and God. A man might make himself a king.

But that *would* be treason. He may elude the charge this time. But he would not be forgiven twice. Sooner or later the Crown would seek him out and break him. For the example alone.

He decides, instead, to help his uncouth kinsman. Let the King worry more about Francisco Pizarro—and less about Hernán Cortés.

❴ 7 ❵

Qoyllur and Waman are sitting on a stone bench under the fig tree in the front patio of his billet, eating bread, ham, green olives. She visits him most days, bringing food and whatever news she can glean with her few words of Castilian.

"I'm not sure I've understood, Waman. You must ask and tell me what you hear. But I think they're saying the Old One will soon be set free."

Candía later confirms what Qoyllur has guessed. The Panama debts are lifted; Pizarro should be out any day. Furthermore, he is summoned to court—along with his leading men, his Peruvians and llamas, his hoard of artefacts and treasure. There is money for the journey and new clothes. Money sent by Hernán Cortés, whose own audience with the King and Queen went well. Fruits of the conquest of Mexico will seed the conquest of Peru.

"You heard right," Waman tells Qoyllur when she comes the next day. "The Old One *is* getting out. This means we'll soon be on the road. To see their Inca and Qoya, wherever they may be."

"And then we'll be going home!" Qoyllur yells, her happiness chiming from the patio walls. She clutches his hand and squeezes it in a way she hasn't done before. "Remember what I said, Waman. Don't try to kill the Old One now." She slaps his knee and laughs. "First we get home. To our families. To that girl you talk about."

Waman looks at her. She is handsome rather than pretty. A strong broad face with high cheekbones, a stocky frame. A highlander. A trace of Tika in her features. And her manner.

"Agreed," he says, in what he hopes is a manly way. "Though I *have* been thinking about how to go about it—once we get home. A poisoned arrow, perhaps. Or"—he tunnels his hands around his lips, fills his lungs, releases an explosive gust of breath—"a poison dart from a blowpipe. Like the jungle folk use on monkeys."

"Monkeys!" She laughs again. Waman basks in her attention. He is already a little in love with her. Yet also a little ashamed. He should keep his love for Tika.

Head in hands, he stares at the patio cobbles, stirs moss and breadcrumbs with his feet. He wants nothing more in the world than to go home, yet the journey appalls him. First the long voyage across the Ocean Sea. Two months maybe. Then who knows how long in Panama, that feverish hole where One-Eye lurks like a spider, a deadly *apasanka*. Then the second voyage down the hotlands to Tumbes, another month at least.

It all seems insuperable. Will he survive it? Will she? Yet there's no choice. They're not free. Qoyllur may have chosen to come aboard Ruiz's ship. But they are both Pizarro's captives now.

"I know it's very far," she says, reading his mind. "I know things will be bad on the ship, like last time. But at least we know what to expect. We must ready ourselves as best we can, that's all.

"Here's what," she adds, in her patrician tone. "You will teach me the barbarian tongue, starting today. I will help you master the language of the Empire. You may think you know it, but really you don't. You're like all lowlanders. You say *Lima* for Rimaq and *Tumbes* for Tumpis. You can't tell *pacha* from *p'acha*. That won't do."

Waman steers crumbs with his foot to a pigeon; he looks up into the dark foliage of the fig. "One of the odd things in their language," he says, brightening, "is the way they give every word a sex. Women are *she*, and men are *he*. They also do this with anything. A word's sex can change the meaning. I still get it wrong." He picks up an orange she has brought. "This is *naranja*. It's female. But if you say *naranjo*, the male form, it means an orange tree."

"Easy," she says, her eyes lighting up. "Logical!"

"Unfortunately it isn't. Not always. The two forms of what seems like the same word often have no connection whatever." He glances at the bird pecking boldly around their feet. "Take *papa*. In Castilian it's a word for father, also the great father of their church, a man-god who lives in a holy place called Rome. Yet *papo* means the crop of a bird."

"All right," she says briskly. "Every day we'll do a few of those. And I'll teach you not to mix up things like *pacha* and *p'acha*. I also need useful phrases, greetings, little songs and poems, things easy to learn by heart."

Waman tells her he likes to sing, that he sang often at home, has picked up a few Spanish tunes. He falls silent again. Then breaks into a sailor's song he used to sing for Tika.

> *Wampulla chayamuptinqa*
> *Noqallayqa ripukusaqmi.*
> *Chay chay yana ñawiyki,*
> *Chay chay suny chukchayki,*
> *Sunqoyta suwallawashan.*

> When the ship comes
> Then I must leave.
> Oh, those dark eyes of yours,
> And that sleek hair,
> Are stealing my heart away.

Qoyllur laughs off his flirtation (or perhaps the joke is his accent) and cuffs him on the ear. Hard enough that she must think him well.

They travel slowly, Waman, Qoyllur, and the llamas, walking day after day in open country behind the Commander's jaded horses and creaking oxcarts, on the way to see the Christian Emperor. So good, Waman thinks, to leave Seville behind, to look down from the hills on the hammered silver of the sea. Mother Sea soothes him, sends him the thought that all great waters in the world are one, that the same salt waves ride the deep from this world to his own. If he could build a boat and take a net, with the help of all the gods he might make his own way home. He is nearly sixteen now— old enough to know such a voyage would be impossible. Still, the thought consoles him.

He looks with tenderness and satisfaction at the llamas, how their condition is improving on the spring grass and upland air of Castile. He and Qoyllur nursed them as best they could before leaving Seville, gathering plants, seeds, and roots to see what they would eat. Everything is different here, even the grass. No *llullu*, no *ichu*, no potato skins or quinoa greens. But the llamas aren't fussy, eating anything horses eat and more besides, like goats.

The only female to survive is dark brown, the younger male is pure black, the other has a white body with charcoal neck and legs. They have names, bestowed by Qoyllur. The she-llama has become Our Lady, in mockery (Waman suspects) of the Christian goddess. The black one is simply Blacky, Yanasapa in their language. And the old white-and-grey male, who rules the others with bites and hisses— him they call Pizarro.

———

So many strange and baffling things on the long trek to find the King and Queen. These Christians who can build temples with stone roofs held aloft by magic like the sky have no roads between their towns—nothing but dusty tracks and rutted wallows across their pampas, and scars little better than streambeds through the hills. In the mountain passes Waman sees broken carts and wheels, men levering wagons over potholes, crushing their hands and cursing their gods. Yet the mountains of Spain are puny! Why has their King built no highways? And why does the kingdom have no head city, no seat of government? At first he thought Seville must be the capital. But Candía says the court is always on the move, because no city is rich enough to house and feed it for long. This must be right: several times along the way he hears Pizarro asking travellers where to find the King and Queen: in Barcelona, Zaragoza, Salamanca, Toledo?

Here and there Waman has seen fine stone bridges and stretches of paved road, but ancient and worn by countless years. These works, he is told, were made by a vanished race who ruled Spain from the great city of Rome long ago. But is not King Charles also the Emperor of Rome? Why doesn't he rule from there?

They find the court in Toledo, nearest of the likely places. The Old One and his entourage take lodgings around the town while they await a royal audience. Waman and Candía share a room on the upper floor of a hillside tavern. He likes the Greek, as everyone does, though at times he has feared the gunner might have designs on Qoyllur and be trying to use him as a go-between. Waman is relieved to hear that Qoyllur is lodged in a convent, which he gathers is like a House of the Chosen, no men allowed. She has been with the nuns a fortnight now. He misses her keenly. Her absence sharpens a much longer and greater absence: Tika. Waman remembers how his cousin used to dream of joining the Chosen, if only for the thrill of moving to some highland city. Did she do so?

For a few hours each day the tavern below their room is loud with tanners who come from the dye pits after work, hands green or red or indigo, stinking of guano and acid used to cure the hides. Candía spends a lot of time downstairs, drinking, playing chess or cards, teasing the tavern girls. Although disgusted by the flies, the fleas, the ingrained stench of wine and puke, Waman finds himself drawn by Candía's jovial company, and by blind musicians who sing for coins and leftovers, lutes wailing with Andalusian love songs and the mournful glissandos of the Moors.

He listens closely, trying to pick up songs for Qoyllur. Since the court is in town the inn is filled with men from all over Spain, and beyond. He hears other languages of this new world—Portuguese, Basque, French, Arabic—and Candía sometimes tries to teach some words of Greek. He longs to hear the sound of Quechua, of home, on Qoyllur's lips.

"If you can't ride the horse you love, Felipe," Candía says, wiping his mouth in its nest of beard with the back of his hand, "love the one you can. That one over there now." The Greek gives him a nudge and juts a bushy eyebrow. "I think she likes the look of you. Her name's Manuela." Waman has also noticed this Manuela, an outgoing redhead about his own age who sometimes brings extra helpings of food and drink. Her green eyes, like a cat's, are often upon him. And sometimes a pat on his arm.

Candía signals for more wine, looks down Manuela's front as she sets it on the table. He bids her refill their cups, repaying the girl with a wink.

"Health and wealth," Waman says. A Spanish toast he has learnt.

"And time to enjoy them!" the Greek answers. The two drain their cups together in one long draft, Peruvian style.

"I love your land, Felipe. I can't wait to go back there. But admit it—this wine beats that murky camel piss your people drink, hands down. So much hotter in the blood. You'll find the same is true of Spanish girls. Not like that Qoyllur. She's a frosty one." The gunner raises his cup, forgetting it is empty. "Here's to good times ahead, lad. Here's to us two tomcats among the doves of the court."

"Doves?" Unsure he's decoded the Greek's peculiar Spanish, Waman leans in, chin cupped in his hands.

"Kitchen wenches, chambermaids, ladies-in-waiting"—Candía elaborates, raising a suggestive finger for each category—"wild daughters, young widows, bored wives." He calls for more drink, for ham, cheese, a loaf.

Waman is sick of Spanish food. Bread like cotton, rice like sawdust, meat like boiled dog. Then there's cheese. In the early days on Ruiz's ship he devoured it thankfully, not knowing what it was. But ever since he found out how it is made—squeezed from the teats of mother animals, left to curdle into a rancid lump—it has disgusted him. The stink of it was everywhere: in the ship's stores, the alleys of Panama, the sour odour of the Christians themselves. For months he wouldn't touch cheese at all. Now he can swallow it if he must—the easiest being a good *manchego*—so long as he doesn't allow his mind to dwell on what it is.

"The only trouble with Spanish women," Candía goes on, "is that a lot of them are hairy. Especially the bluebloods. Moustaches. Stray bristles on their dugs." He clutches his chest with both hands. "Did you bring any tweezers?"

"Tweezers?"

"What they want above all else from the Indies, I've found, is a pair of Peruvian tweezers. Nothing better for their whiskers. Wish I'd brought back a sackful." He chuckles rakishly, leans close across the table with a sidelong glance at Manuela. "Always treat a whore like a lady, Felipe. And a lady like a whore."

Waman, Felipe (who is he today?), is still puzzled by the notion of *whores*. Treat a whore like a lady seems good advice. But what can the Greek mean about treating a lady like a whore? Should he offer money? To a lady? Waman frowns. Everything comes down to money among Christians.

"What now, lad? Don't tell me you're getting too churchy for the bints?"

"I was thinking about money."

"Don't you worry about that. This is all on the Commander. Or Cortés. Anyhow, you're earning your keep. Without you, those little camels would be dead."

While Waman is outside at the loathsome jakes, Candía hands Manuela a coin, thrice her usual fee. "The young dark lad. Needs growing up. This makes you his for two nights. The extra's because he's from the Indies. They're ungodly fastidious over there, so have a good scrub beforehand. Splash on the rosewater." He pats her rump. "No offence, my love. *I* like you just as you are."

The Greek is amused, in due course, to see Waman's cocky strut and the looks and touches that pass between him and the wench.

"How was she, my friend?"

"Is it so obvious?"

Candía laughs, lifts his glass, winks across the top of it.

Not until they've eaten does the interpreter say anything. Then:

"I've never touched such skin. So pink, so pale. Her veins are like tiny blue streams." Waman doesn't want to say more. But his friend, unusually, stays quiet, and the boy can't help filling the void with his excitement, his need to speak her name. "Manuela came fresh from her bath, like a bride. The first night she smelt of roses. The second night of herself. But the third night was not good. She came to me . . . wet."

"She must like you, lad."

"I mean from another man. I could tell."

"Hmm. Already so worldly wise? It's no use getting jealous over the likes of her. If that was Tuesday night, it may even have been me who paved the way. No harm there. What's a buttered bun between comrades?"

Waman hurls the dregs of his wine in Candía's face. "You filthy rogue. Must you have every girl? Can't you leave mine alone?"

"*Yours?*" Candía mops his beard and brow with a kerchief, rolling his big dark eyes. He goes perfectly still for a while, mastering anger. Then takes a coin from his pocket, holds it up between thumb and forefinger. "One of these, Felipe, and she's anybody's."

The Greek shakes his head, beard sweeping the table like a broom.

The audience is held in the gardens of a hilltop palace not far outside the city. King Charles and Queen Isabel sit side by side in ornate high-backed chairs on a broad terrace giving onto a lawn and orange grove. It is a fine June day with a fresh breeze.

The Commander rides up at the head of his procession, only two wagons, two Peruvians, three llamas. Outwardly he seems confident, but the Queen detects the swagger of a coarse man unsure of himself among grandees. He sits awkwardly on his horse, which is more a dray than a charger. The wagons he has are no better than his steed. Their cracked boards are masked by colourful Peruvian textiles, but the frames creak and the axles wail all the same.

Pizarro is unable to hide the stiffness in his joints as he dismounts. A month in prison did his old bones no good, no good at all.

So young, he thinks, as he kneels before them; His Catholic Majesty, Emperor of Rome, King of Spain and Naples, Count of Flanders, Duke of Burgundy, must still be in his twenties. Barely half his own years. The grizzled Commander reads the royal face: handsome, clean-shaven, girlish. Unmarked by the cares of the world. And the Queen's a looker, by Christ: so slight, such dainty feet, and a wide-eyed expression that makes her all the more fetching.

Charles and Isabel are chatting *sotto voce*, he smiling and jesting, she chuckling at his words. The morning sun flashes on their finery, the breeze fluttering their robes. The King wears a rich doublet with puffed sleeves, fine burgundy leather and wood-green velvet embroidered with golden threads and sequins. On his head is no crown; only a wide velvet cap, full and plush as a cushion. The Queen is in a gown of olive silk, her face framed by lace flowing from a head-tire and long earrings of silver and pearls. Pizarro takes this in with crafty glances; his head he keeps bowed, seldom daring to stray from those dainty feet, displayed as if on sale by open shoes.

A small crouching figure shades her with a parasol. A child? No, it is hunched and wizened. A dwarf. When the parasol sways and the sun strikes her cheek, the Queen kicks the dwarf discreetly with her heel.

"Don Francisco," His Majesty says at last, "we trust you've recovered from the travail of coming to see us." Not a question, exactly.

Pizarro launches into the speech he's had written by a scribe and has committed to memory, telling of gallanter hardships than the hail-swept passes of Castile.

"Highest Lord and Lady! In Your Majesties' service my men and I wandered years along the wild shores of the great South Sea, often without sight of the sun, and through endless storms. Assailed by poisoned arrows, giant snakes, ravening crocodiles. Three years of discovery in the service of Christ and for the greatness of your Holy Empire.

"And at last, when many had lost all hope, it pleased God that we found the fabled land we sought—the mighty southern kingdom of Peru, which exceeded all our dreams with its great size, its riches, its cities, its teeming citizens and mosques full of gold.

"By then we Christians were a mere thirteen. We could take only what the natives gave us. These few things I bring are therefore no more than a foretaste of what awaits you, should it please Your Majesties to grant what my heart craves—to win Peru for God and Crown."

Isabel and Charles hear many speeches of this kind. Spain seethes with would-be conquerors—ever since Cortés sent letters from Mexico and a first haul of treasure some years ago. Most are worthless dreamers, but a few receive a royal licence to conquer in their name. As Pizarro's small procession rolls across the lawn, the King and Queen ask many questions, less from curiosity than to get the measure of this man. What do the Peruvians keep in those great jars? How do they wear those silks? Are the symbols on it their writing or their heraldry? Can that bird speak, like those of Mexico?

It is in fact one of the same birds, borrowed by Pizarro from his kinsman so as to be less outdone.

"Indeed, Majesties. Many Indian tongues. But all nonsense, lacking reason."

"Let me hear," the King says. "I have a few tongues myself. I speak Spanish to God, Italian to women, and German to my horse!" He looks around, beaming. Courtiers chuckle loyally at the threadbare joke. "Bring the bird nearer."

Pizarro beckons the man who has the parrot in a cage, rueing his impulse to bring the creature at all. He—and the sharper ears at court—can already hear a raucous avian voice uttering something much like *hijo de puta*, son of a whore, punctuated by wolf whistles. The courtiers' laughter now is genuine.

"It is nothing, my lord." Pizarro raises his voice above the parrot's, coughing loudly, signalling with a clenched hand behind his back for the bird to be throttled at once. "Nothing at all. Mere nonsense in some Indian tongue. I know not what."

A small sound like a walnut underfoot. A flap of wings. Silence.

"Majesties," Pizarro continues, still on his knees, "allow me to present two young Peruvians. The boy, I've taught to speak. The girl is learning. The lad has become a Christian, baptised Felipe. He speaks Castilian well."

"We trust, Don Francisco, that he does," Isabel says, thinking of the parrot and prodding her husband's heel with a toe.

Qoyllur carries herself elegantly in fine fabrics of her land: a sweeping sky-blue skirt embroidered sparely with red and yellow flowers, a shawl woven with black and orange frets pinned across her chest by a long silver brooch like a spoon, and a narrow vermilion cloth folded crisply on her head and flowing down her back, beneath which her hair, plaited with gold beads, swings at her rump in a glossy braid with an orange bow.

Waman is wearing the best vicuña tunic on hand—one taken by Ruiz from the Peruvian ship. He is uneasy, like Pizarro. He slept fitfully at the inn, awaking from a nightmare of Gallo Island to singing below and cries of love from the room next door.

"Felipillo here will answer any question you may wish to put to him, Your Highnesses. But first, I have told him to render homage in the manner of his nation. They're a gentle and obedient race."

Waman takes up a thick roll of red cloth, holding it across his shoulders like a shepherd carrying a sheep. Stooped beneath this burden, he approaches shyly, lowering himself with each step until stretched at the royal feet like a Moor at prayer.

The wagons have halted, and in the stillness the interpreter's words can just be heard.

"*Sapa Inka, Sapa Qoya, Tumpismantam kani. Wamanmi sutiy, yanaykichik.*"

"Don Francisco," the Queen says to Pizarro wearily, "have him kneel properly and say it again. In Castilian."

Waman's eyes make a sidelong glance at the Commander. An impatient nod.

"Only King, Only Queen, I come from Tumbes. I am your servant Waman—as I'm called in my own land. That is what I said, Catholic Majesties."

"The savage speaks well!" The King grins at his courtiers. "And that's not a bad title, *Only King.*" He bends to Waman. "Who is the man that wears it in your country, boy? How big is the kingdom of this 'only king'?"

Waman begins by saying the Peruvian Empire is very great, though he has seen only a little of it himself. "In our tongue it is called Tawantinsuyu, the United Quarters of the World—"

"Greater than all Europe," Pizarro cuts in. "More than three thousand miles from end to end! We sailed its coast through fifteen degrees of latitude, and did not see the half of it."

The King ignores him, turns again to the boy.

"This 'only king'? Has he a name?"

"He is called Wayna Qhapaq, Majesty."

"Meaning what?"

"In our language this says Young Lord."

"A youngster, then. How long on his throne?"

"I . . . I don't know, Majesty." Waman looks beseechingly at Qoyllur, on his right.

"Machu Apu hina," she says to him, shooting her brow at Pizarro: like the Old Commander. She adds that Wayna Qhapaq has ruled the World since her parents were children.

"He is a man of about Commander Pizarro's years, Your Majesty. The Emperor has had the name Young Lord since he was young. Before he ruled the World, which he has done more than thirty years."

Charles laughs theatrically, for all to hear. "The vanity of savages! There's only one world and one Emperor. You kneel before him here."

"Have you any Latin?" the Queen asks. "Can you pray? Do you confess?"

Waman produces his rosary and recites a Hail Mary.

"Good. Good. He and the girl may go."

It is time to fetch the llamas. Waman has combed and clipped them, leaving the wool short on the back and neck, but thick on the flanks, with a fringe hanging forward between their upright ears. From the pierced tip of each ear hangs a scarlet ribbon.

"These are the beasts of the new southern land, Your Majesties," Pizarro says. "I brought many more to give you, and more Indians too, but they sickened and did not outlast the voyage."

"Are they small camels or big sheep, Don Francisco?" Isabel says. "What do the natives use them for—do they ride them, eat them, or shear them?"

"All three, my lady. Above all, they use them like pack mules in great caravans. To carry gold and silver from their countless mines." He pauses to let the abundance of mines sink in. "A strong one can carry as much as an ass. But the Peruvians seldom ride them, only the old, the sick, and the young. Their soldiers do not."

"Nearer," says the King. "Bring them nearer."

"As you command. But I beg leave to warn Your Highness that

they are like camels in their ways, unruly by nature, given to spitting." It would be disastrous if a well-aimed cud of alfalfa struck the royal eye.

The King inspects the llamas warily, noting their haughty faces, coquettish eyelashes, and the way they chew, the jaw sliding to one side then the other, pausing in the middle, velvet lips curled in a sneer.

"Indeed like camels. That will do."

Waman leads the animals a safe distance away and unloads a heavy swag of striped black-and-yellow cloth from the first. He returns with this to the terrace and unrolls it like a rug at the royal feet, removing cotton padding from the things inside.

First to emerge is a funeral mask of beaten gold, a stiff human face with teardrop eyes. Then two gold beakers, a foot high, plain except for jade chevrons inlaid below the lip. Next are ceremonial weapons: a gold battle-axe with blade and handle cast in a single piece, a mace with a silver head, and two knives with silver blades shaped like half-moons and gold figurines for handles. There is a golden breastplate and a set of greaves, and a pair of serving dishes, one gold, one silver, each with a lifelike hummingbird perched on the rim. Lastly, two llama statuettes, a male in solid gold and a silver female.

The King and Queen say nothing. Pizarro has great difficulty keeping silent. And keeping still; he is growing acutely uncomfortable on his knees. Do these things seem fine to them? Is it enough? He regrets the pieces sold, the ones left with his partner Almagro, and especially those he gave to the Governor of Panama in a vain attempt to get that ass's backing. Thank God he had wits enough to withhold these—the best—to go over the Governor's head and bring his suit to Spain.

He can hold his tongue no longer.

"Doubtless these things seem few and small to Your Highnesses after the marvels brought by my illustrious cousin, the Marquis Cortés, from New Spain. But I beg your leave to point out that he had already taken that land and therefore could bring you the very best it contains, whereas I have but a sample of the wonders that await us in Peru—a land richer in gold by far. If you will grant me leave to conquer it, why, in two or three years, with God's help, I shall again stand before you with such treasure that no prince in Christendom—"

"Your point does not escape us, Don Francisco. Hand us that golden beast and . . . that dish."

Charles and Isabel turn the pieces in their hands. The artefacts are plainer than the work from Mexico, but their heft—the weight of metal in them—suggests that this fellow's boasts of Peruvian wealth may not be overblown.

For some time the royal pair are silent, a glister of fascination in their eyes. "We should summon that goldsmith again to take a look," the King says to the Queen. "The Netherlander, the one who paints. Forget the name . . ."

"Albrecht," Isabel supplies. "Albrecht Dürer. I think he may have died. A vain man, anyway. He painted too many portraits of himself."

"Quite so. But a sound judge of quality." The King turns to Pizarro. "We sent that fellow to see the first haul of treasure to arrive from Mexico, some years ago. Fellow came back raving! Nothing he'd seen in all his days, said he, gladdened his heart like those arts and wonders from another world. We took his word for it and had them melted down."

"To further our holy wars," the Queen adds primly. "Against the Lutherans and Turks."

"The worthiest cause," Pizarro interjects. "What better work for heathen gold than to afflict the foes of God?

"All these are my gifts to Your Majesties," he adds expansively.

"The livestock and the girl as well, should it please you to keep her at court. As soon as she learns to speak she'll be able to tell you more—much more—about her nation."

The royal countenance begins to sour. The King is tired of this jumped-up peasant's gift for stating the obvious. Indeed, almost telling him what to do.

"Don Francisco, your audience is at an end. You shall have word in due course."

The would-be conqueror, the monarchs agree in their bedchamber that night, is ill mannered and ill dressed. A bad horseman too. Certainly no Hernán Cortés. But he seems fearless, driven, dogged, a man who by all accounts has withstood hardship and setbacks that might have defeated many nobler men. Yet his new land is so far away that its importance is unclear. Does he need another Mexico? the young King wonders. Cortés's New Spain already presents so many problems of conversion and control. Why reach even further overseas when so many troubles beset his realms in Europe? Chief among these the Turks, now threatening Vienna. Also the Lutheran heresy in the Netherlands; uprisings in Spain itself; and the treachery of the French, egged on by the insufferable Pope, who, like his predecessors, deems himself the true Emperor of Rome.

The royal advisers fall into two camps. Some share the King's misgivings, see little to be gained in unleashing more conquistadors to run amok at the rim of the known world. What if this land is too strong to subdue, as Mexico so nearly was? They remind him the Mexicans defeated Cortés at first, that his conquest would have failed without the smallpox sent so timely by the Lord. What if this Peru turns out to be a province of some mighty Asian empire, of fabled Cipangu or Cathay? Or even, as some who saw the place are saying, the kingdom of the Antichrist? What *then*?

Others, less wary, less superstitious, argue that the dangers are few and the prize enormous. If this ruffian Pizarro fails, it will be merely his own loss, not Spain's. The Crown, on the other hand, stands to gain a realm of great wealth at little risk. Furthermore, it is the Catholic Emperor's sacred task to bring the whole world into the fold of Christendom. Surely God has set this golden land in Spain's path for that very purpose. Its wealth will humble France, make England tremble, quell the heretic, and drive the Turk across the Bosphorus.

From this flows the last and most compelling argument. If Spain does not take Peru, others will.

The King's decision is to make no decision—not until he has heard the view of the Council of the Indies, his board of trade in Seville. Pizarro must go back to that city and make his case there.

❧ 8 ❧

The summer heat of Seville gives way to autumn gales. The wheat is scythed and stooked; leaves carpet the fig and olive groves; snow steals down from the high sierras, which seem to draw nearer as the air clarifies with cold. Pizarro tries all means to sway the Council of the Indies, making theological arguments to the pious, mercenary ones to the greedy, displaying the few bits of treasure left him by the King. And to those on the council susceptible to temptations of the flesh, which is not a few, he stealthily exposes some things withheld from Charles and Isabel; namely a chest of lewd Peruvian pots, an astounding show of erotica, proof to some of savagery, and to others of civilization, in that new-found land.

The Commander's men begin to drift away from the muddy camp beside the Guadalquivir—to sea, to war, to hometowns unseen in years—promising to come back when he receives his royal licence.

Waman's old life drifts further and further into the past, though his mind reaches yearningly across the Ocean Sea. The worst, in Spain, is the loss of Qoyllur, whom the Queen has added like a lapdog to her retinue. Now Waman is marooned in his own tongue, exiled from the World he cannot hear or share.

The sight of Spanish families—going to church, sitting under trees in the squares, children running and laughing, the elderly resting on their canes—fills him with homesickness and envy. And remorse for running to sea.

No longer treated as a prisoner, he finds irregular work on a fishing boat, a small craft that comes and goes with the tide. In this way he earns a little money. Slowly, a new life, lived in the Spanish language, fills some of the void where his old life used to be.

From time to time, when especially downcast, Waman goes to Seville's cathedral to plead with the gods who are worshipped there—above all the Holy Virgin, to him a counterpart of Mother Earth. In the great building, breathing its candlewax, damp mortar, stale incense, gazing up at windows as gorgeous as butterfly wings and the roof of lofted stone, he loses himself in storms of music blowing from ranks of mighty pan-pipes hung like stalactites above the choir. Often he kneels there until dusk, begging the Mother of God to look on him, to give some intimation of his fate. But the holy doll stares pale and unmoved.

Midwinter comes, and still no word from the Council of the Indies or the King. The snows spill lower down the hills. One morning Waman emerges from his lodging, a small room at the back of a mean patio, to find roofs and streets all white. Strange that he has looked on snowfields all his life but has never felt the touch of snow till now, in Spain. Sea and river are too rough for fishing. He feels the bite of cold, of hunger; and everywhere sees want and suffering among the Spaniards. Here there are no weekly banquets hosted by the state, no gifts of cloth and corn. Why such poverty amid such wealth and wonders? Why does the Spanish Emperor shame himself by not relieving it?

Sickness comes to the city. Children are taken by fevers, fluxes, colds. And one of the fevers is smallpox.

"Candía," the Commander asks, "you've had the pox, no?" The Greek nods, saying he caught it when eight or nine, on Crete. "Then go to the house where Felipe is. Take food and drink, enough to last all in that household for a month." He counts gold into the Greek's large hand. "The place must be sealed tight as a cask until the pox has left Seville. Stay there and watch over him. That boy must live. If he dies, it'll be on your blaspheming soul."

These precautions do no good: Waman comes down with a fever in a week. At first it seems like what he had on Gallo Island, which he remembers more vividly than his illness on the ship to Spain. Candía brings him broth and bread and stewed apples. The only thing Waman wants is water, and water runs from him at every pore.

The Greek pays a girl in the house to help nurse the lad. He takes a room on the same patio, spends each day at the Peruvian's bedside, busying himself by whittling a set of chessmen from some scraps of wood. Felipe was beginning to show an interest in the game, watching him play in Toledo and here in Seville. Candía has told the lad the set will be his as soon as he's well—to give him something to look forward to. As he whittles, he prays silently in old Greek to Christ Pantocrator: *Lord God let this be only a fever, nothing more.*

Before his friend has finished shaping the pawns, Waman feels pimples in his throat, burning like acid. Within days the rash spreads to his cheek and hands.

Soon he is delirious—crying out and rambling in his language—a mercy, Candía hopes, for perhaps an unhinged mind feels less of the body's pain. He thinks it too risky to send for a physician, even if one could be found, for in his view Spanish doctors often carry more evils than they cure. Besides, there's no room for doubt. Felipe has *viruela*, the smallpox, for which the only cure is prayer. Now all that can be hoped is that the boy is strong and has a mild strain. A forlorn hope. In Mexico—Candía has heard—the Indians died in heaps like bedbugs; barely one in three survived.

Waman's pustules fill and swell, growing to the size of small grapes. A foul liquid flows from them for several days. Then, slowly, they begin to dry and scab. The Greek has never been devout—he's a practical fellow, at home with things he can touch, the things of this world not the next. He knows how to cast a bronze gun, ream a bore, make powder and shot. But there in the poor lad's stinking sickroom Candía gets down on his knees, recites every prayer he knows (which are only two or three), and gives joyous thanks to all the great icons of Byzantium. For Felipe, it seems, is on the mend.

"They are done, my friend! Your smallpox, and your chess set."

Waman smiles up at him weakly, a smile marred by hideous pitting on his cheeks, more the left one than the right. Good thing there's no looking glass in here, Candía thinks. Felipe has won his life but lost his looks.

A few days later, when Waman is well enough to sit up, to take some broth and a few steps, Candía sets out the wooden pieces on a painted checkerboard. He says nothing, drawing the lad into a game by placing his fingers on the men and walking him through the opening moves.

"I thank you for this." Waman is hoarse, his voice almost too low to hear. Each word tears at his throat. "And for my life. Without you I would be dead."

"Nonsense!" Candía answers. "It was your luck. Or my God. Most likely both. You had me praying like a monk."

At first, Waman takes a childish delight in the pieces—in the men, horseheads, tiny buildings like forts or shrines—well carved and stained, half with lampblack, half with lime. But once he has the moves and opening gambits down by heart, he becomes mesmerized by the endless complexity within simplicity, by the game's uncanny power to play out the fates of kings and kingdoms, as if it were a kind of divination.

Spring sun chases the snow up the hills. Scents of blossom: apple, orange, cherry. There are strawberries to eat. Chess has become an obsession, tied in his mind to his recovery, a rite that saved him. By May he is good enough to beat Candía, though usually when the gunner has been drinking.

One evening over chessboard and wine in a tavern that reminds Waman of their time in Toledo, he asks the Greek why Pizarro seems to have no family. Surely not all his kindred can be dead, even after so many years abroad?

"Oh, he's got family. A half-dozen brothers and sisters. By several mothers and two fathers, so they say."

"Why hasn't he been to see them? He hasn't gone home once. In a whole year. Is Trujillo so far—as far as Toledo?"

"It's not that he *can't* go, Felipe. He won't. Not until the King has made a decision. And not then, if things don't go his way."

"Is he afraid of something there?"

"That man fears nothing but the Devil and himself." The Greek grooms his beard with a mutton-greasy hand, popping nits between his nails. "No. It's pride, my friend. We Christians suffer from the sin of pride. A deadly sin, because it kills our love. Only God knows the whole of it with Don Francisco, but I'll lay gold that it's his pride. Or his shame, if you like—which comes to the same thing. You've heard the stories. Sired on a serving wench. Cast out to mind the pigs. Many are like that, many of us have things to hide. I haven't been back to Crete myself in more years than I remember"—he sighs, puzzles over his turn; moves a knight recklessly—"but Crete's a long way, further than Rome. Trujillo's only four or five days from here. Even for a shitty rider like Pizarro." The gunner winks and taps the side of his nose.

Waman is the first to call *Checkmate!*

"It would be seemlier," says his friend mock-sternly, "if you didn't yell out checkmate quite so fast. Or so—how shall I say?—so gleefully. Sometimes you're wrong. I still have a move. And even when you're right—as you often are—it's wiser to let your opponent come to the sorry conclusion himself." Candía topples his king, looks Waman in the eye. "Like so. Let him resign." He pats Waman on the shoulder. "I'm a Greek and I can take it. But Spaniards . . . When they're beaten, let them find out for themselves."

In June, the Commander, Candía, and a few others leave Seville abruptly one dawn without a word. They are gone for some weeks, and the news makes its way back before they do. The King has decided to endorse Pizarro's enterprise.

Men unseen for months begin drifting back to the boggy camp on the meadow. Half abandoned all winter, the place fills with life and expectation like a fairground. Tents go up, sea-chests are delivered, the grass is trampled and fouled. By day blacksmiths and armourers set up shop; at night cooks, moneylenders, bootleggers, whores, and card sharps make their rounds among the tents and campfires.

"What days in Toledo!" Candía tells Waman. "Don Francisco got everything he asked for—a licence, a coat of arms, and governorship of 'New Castile.' That's what they plan to call your land. Even some money towards ships and weapons. And horses and war-dogs when we get to Panama. Here's to us. To you, the royal interpreter. We're on our way!"

"Has Qoyllur come back too?" Waman asks.

"No. No, she hasn't. Not yet." A pause. "But I saw her. She asked after you, said to wish you well and *buen viaje*. She speaks Castilian now." A sweet lie, to spare the lad. Candía hopes that others won't expose it.

"Almagro got nothing," he adds quickly. "Nothing worth having. It's all in Pizarro's hands." The two partners, he explains, had agreed in Panama to share command. One-Eye has been bilked.

Waman has never understood the Spaniards' politics. Men seem to rise and sink in a moment, like carp in a pond. And devour one another like carp, too.

"That Pizarro." Candía shakes his head, beard brushing chest. "What a bastard! Oh, I forgot. We can't call him that anymore—the King legitimized him."

Now Pizarro goes home to Trujillo, to the little lion-hued town of granite towers on its sunburnt hilltop overlooking the treeless plain. It is his first visit in more than half his life. And it will be his last. He takes Waman, Candía—all his officers—and an entourage of servants befitting the big man he has suddenly become.

The celebrations last for days. Waman watches in amazement as the would-be conqueror presides from a high oak chair beneath an awning by a church. The Old One has shed years. Overnight he has changed from a brigand into a lord.

Wine flows and hogs are roasted—descendants, perhaps, of the bristle-back swine Pizarro herded as a boy. But no one speaks of such things now. All are eager to add their breath to the wind of promise in his sail. A scribe sits at a table, enlisting the hopeful and the reckless. A painter sets up an easel to immortalize the new hidalgo posing with his coat of arms: a twin-headed eagle between two columns, wings spread over the city of Tumbes, over its ships and camels, its fortress with a lion and tiger rampant at the gate.

"Say lion and tiger in Peruvian," someone asks. Waman is an object of great curiosity, treated like a rare beast, asked to open his mouth and give these barbarians a sound from his land.

"For lion we say *puma*. And *uturunku* for tiger, though the hotlanders call it *jaguar*."

"And gate. Say gate and castle and city!" It is a girl no older than himself, laughter in her eyes.

"*Punku* is gate. Castle is *pukara*. And for city we say *llaqta*."

"Look after that tongue of yours, Felipillo," remarks one of Pizarro's lesser officers, a self-important man named Torres, passing by. "It's the only one we've got."

"No, two. Once Qoyllur gets here. Her Castilian must be good by now." He longs to see Qoyllur. Yet he fears what she may think of him, his ruined face. Will she ignore him again, as she did at the beginning?

"Has no one told you?"

"Told what?"

"You'd better ask your friend the gunner."

Waman stares at the man walking off. He looks around wildly, guessing the worst. No sign of Candía. He runs along the crooked street, threads his way down alleys to the plaza. There, predictably, he finds the Greek in a tavern. Waman bursts in, not even seeing the others at the table.

"Get up! Outside! You have to tell me everything. Right now."

"What?" The shock on his friend's face is genuine. But Waman sees it change to understanding as Candía lowers his big eyes.

"You lied to me!" Waman shouts, tears running down his scarry cheek. "You lied! Qoyllur's dead, isn't she?"

"Come here, lad," the Greek says quietly. "Let's go somewhere we can talk alone." He tries laying an arm on the boy's shoulder. Waman shrugs it off, his breath frantic, whooping in gasps and gusts.

"The truth is," Candía says, when he has succeeded in calming Waman and drawing him to a quiet corner of the square, "the truth is that Qoyllur caught the pox as you did. In the winter. I don't know exactly when. None of us knew until we went with the Commander to get the royal licence. Yes, I lied when I came back. I lied for you. To spare you while you were still so weak yourself. And yes, I should have told you by now." Candía sighs, rests a hand on Waman's shoulder. "The time never seemed right. For a thing so sad, Felipe, there's never a right time.

"One thing we can do," he adds after a long pause. "We go into that church over there. We go in and we light a candle for Qoyllur, a tall one. And we think of her and nothing else."

At some point Candía leaves, but Waman doesn't notice. Nor does he feel the passing hours. He is there until nightfall, when a sexton comes to lock the church. He walks away spent, unsteady, reeling down streets lit only by tongues of candlelight from open doors.

Among the conditions of Pizarro's licence are these: he must take royal officials with him to collect one-fifth of all treasure for the King, and friars to convert the Indians; he must raise an army of three hundred; none can be New Christians, former Jews and Moors, lest the New World be tainted by the falsehoods of the Old.

The Commander gives not a turd for such minutiae. His first reaction to any order or entreaty is always to say no, or to ignore. How can he be expected to know what lurks in others' souls?

He takes his recruiting desk to all the likeliest towns in the hard province of Extremadura—to the medieval warren of Cáceres, the Roman streets of Mérida, the border town of Badajoz, and lastly the holy village of Guadalupe, high in the wooded hills beyond Trujillo.

There in the Gothic shrine Pizarro lights a field of candles and gets down on his stiff knees before the tiny Virgin, with all his leading men around.

They pray, but Waman does not hear their words.

He stares a long time at the holy face darkened by centuries of smoke and piety. It seems to look at him, draw near, become a face he knows. She smiles. She *winks*. Then a hurricane of sound, a blinding rainbow, a smothering breath of roses and gardenias. Or is it the flowers that roar, the music that dazzles, the light that smells so sweet?

He looks again.

It is Qoyllur.

Again.

The face of Tika.

THREE

Northern Peru

1531-33

{ 9 }

Molina comes back from fishing to a feast laid out in Chaska's patio. Along with squash and sweet potatoes, there is highland quinoa, which reminds him of rice, though nuttier and more toothsome. Best of all: a steaming heap of roast llama, dug from a *pachamanka* filled with hot stones and aromatic leaves. Some neighbours are already there, three fishermen with their wives, and several children playing with little Atuq. From the slack grins on one or two faces he guesses the jug on the dining board has already made a few rounds.

"What thing?" he asks, in his fluent though still uneven Quechua.

"You can't guess?" says Chaska. "How long have you been living here?"

"Oh, maybe three years or so . . ."

"Yes. And two years to the day since you and I were wed."

Two years already! Lucky she doesn't expect him to know the Peruvian calendar; a Spanish wife would be offended.

He raises the beaker she hands him, toasts Mother Earth and the guests. "Here's to all of us. Above all to my Star. Hard times these may be in Little River, but for me the best in my life." Chaska glows. He's said the right thing, which isn't always so.

After the meal, Atuq is taken to bed and the other children left to play downstairs while their elders go up on the roof for a last drink under the night. As often these days, the talk turns from banter and gossip to remembrance of the dead and how things used to be before the pestilence.

Little River was forgotten for months after the Great Death, as people call it now. Runners and knotkeepers no longer came. The Empire made no demands, nor issued any supplies. The shrunken community struggled on as best it could.

Those who'd escaped the sickness by fleeing into the wilds slowly trickled back, rebuilding on the wreckage of their former lives. But even now most houses are still empty, most fields gone to brush.

Not long before he died, Waman's father, Mallki, had been appointed town headman, known as the Hundred-Leader, since Little River then had about that many households. His duties were to make sure each family received its correct share of the common land; to settle disputes over water and grazing rights; to oversee the public feast in the plaza on weekends; and to report to the Thousand-Leader, the next rung on the ladder that reached all the way to the Apu of Chinchaysuyu—earl of this quarter of the Empire—who answered only to the Sapa Inka.

Around the time that Chaska and Molina married, government was restored and a new Emperor proclaimed, a young prince named Waskhar. Nobody in Little River had heard of him. He was merely one of Wayna Qhapaq's surviving sons in Cusco, picked by the imperial clan to replace the designated heir, who had been taken by smallpox only a week after his father. One of Inca Waskhar's first decrees was to assess the catastrophe, province by province. Overseers of a thousand reported to those of ten thousand, and so on up the ranks until a full census was gathered in the capital's archive, a great library of thread where row upon row of quipus hung like wigs on racks and walls. There the Empire's head accountants made the final reckoning, and made it known. Of some twenty-one million citizens before the Great Death, only nine million still draw breath. More than half the World has died.

Little River suffered rather worse, along with Tumbes Province. Despite returned refugees and new births, the town is barely a fourth of its old strength.

Besides her new husband, Chaska has two consolations: little Atuq, now a sturdy three-year-old; and the wonderful news, when the posts ran again, that her niece Tika escaped the plague in the highlands.

"So," Molina's wife says in bed, once the guests have left and the house is quiet except for the rasp of crickets, the scurry of guinea pigs, and Atuq's steady breathing. He knows the tone: something weighty on her mind. "So," she says again, "this summer it'll be four years since your shipmates kidnapped my Waman in the hotlands. Do you still think they're coming back?"

She has asked this many times. Molina looks through the window at the stars and a sliver of new moon. With an inner smile he recalls that night on the roof when she drove him off her. Ah, Chaska. A tough nut to crack. But so sweet within the shell. Enough to make a man forsake the land of his birth. Even his faith, such as it was. He dresses as a Peruvian, greets the Sun with a blown kiss, and never takes a drink without first pouring a drop for the Earth. I'm a heathen now, he thinks, and so be it. What did the God of Spain ever do for Badluck Molina? All the best in life has come to him here, on the far side of the world.

"Who knows, my love? They could land in Tumbes tomorrow. Or it might be ten years."

He sees her eyes moisten with longing for her son. Chaska cannot truly rest until she learns what happened to Waman.

"Don't spare me, Husband," she persists, with a sharp nudge from her knee. "Tell what you really think. Even if it's *never.*"

What does he think? What can he? He's heard nothing of the world beyond Peru.

"If I know them, they'll be back. Sooner or later. Even if the Old One has died, others will follow his lead." He explains that his countrymen won't have been hit nearly so hard by the smallpox.

"My land was crowded and poor," he adds. "No doubt it still is. Your land is rich. And badly weakened now. To them it's a ripe orchard and the farmer who guards it has been crippled. Some day they will come. Especially if they hear about the plague. And when they do, they'll come in force."

She says nothing more, reaches for him. They make love fiercely yet quietly, careful not to wake the boy. Soon Molina is fast asleep, wheezing like a seal. But Chaska's mind runs on. What is there to keep them in Little River? Isn't it foolish to linger here, so near the port of Tumbes and the royal highway? The longer she waits, the more she asks herself this. She would like to stay put for Waman's sake, so he can find her quickly when he returns. And because her dead are here. But she must think of the living. Being here when the barbarians return would put them all at high risk. There are also other barbarians—nearby—hotlanders just beyond the frontier who may well try to raid the stricken Empire. The old Emperor needed ships and garrisons to keep them out. There's the new Emperor to consider, too; his people might come looking for Molina. No, she decides, they must move to the highlands, far from any invaders or officials who might suddenly appear. Somewhere off the main roads, yet near enough to Tika at her House of the Chosen in Huanuco.

She remembers when the examiner came to Little River, a stout lady with a wattled chin, asking to see any promising girls who had had their first monthlies and wanted to join the order. Only the most accomplished and best-looking were considered. It was a great honour. But Chaska found it hard to let her niece sit the exams, especially so soon after Waman's disappearance. She privately hoped the girl would be found lacking in some way. But Tika did well, especially in weaving and singing. When she was offered the one thing she requested—a place with the Chosen in the city of Huanuco Pampa, not far from where she had lived before the earthquake orphaned her—Chaska could hardly object. Especially as Chaska herself had come from that same village when she was little. Yaruwillka, it was called. A lovely name.

Yaruwillka, she says beside Molina, startling herself from the threshold of sleep with her own voice.

Chaska decided she would accompany her niece to Huanuco and take the opportunity to see their birthplace. She also hoped some kin of theirs, however distant, might still be living in the region. Huanuco would be too far from Little River for Tika to get home for holidays, so it would be a great comfort if they could find people nearby whom the girl could visit.

The journey was indeed long, almost a month, the first half by ship down the coast. When they disembarked they were met by a Mother from the House with two other new girls in tow and some llamas to carry their things. Then came a long trek from one way station to the next, up and up into the mountains, over staircase roads and snowy passes, across misty gorges spanned by hanging bridges. She remembers their escort (a rather pompous woman) officiously waving a small quipu at the bridgekeepers, exempting the party from tolls.

Before going on to the city of Huanuco, Chaska and Tika left the others and took some days to find their childhood home. The road to Yaruwillka, overgrown as they drew near, was swallowed at the landslide's edge, running on through an underworld, a village of the dead. Where terraced fields and farmhouses had climbed the lower slopes, there was only a scree of gravel and boulders dotted with cactus. They found nothing else, not even the corner of Tika's house that had saved her. Perhaps an aftershock had toppled it.

There, where the house might have stood, they knelt and made offerings of coca leaves and seashells. They wept and sang a stately *harawi*, the lament's high tones cleaving the burdened air. But neither spoke except to pray to the Earth, the Sun—even, in scolding and propitiation, to the icebound peak who had smothered the people in his charge.

Not until evening, beside a fire in the nearest way station, did Tika speak of the memories unfurling in her mind. Her parents tall as trees above her. The hideouts she made with her brother in the standing corn; the two of them scaring birds from seeded fields, fleeing wasps and bees through shoulder-high wildflowers. The old house with its sheltering eaves and smoky warmth. Then nothing.

It was thirty years since Chaska had lived there, yet her own recollections were vivid as Tika's, if not more so with the burnish of age and nostalgia. The highlands were still lovely to her. The pure skies and racing clouds, the wandering herders in bright clothes, the llamas and alpacas in heavy fleece. But Yaruwillka itself was only a scar. It was as if her early life must have happened somewhere else, near yet unreachable. Save for the outline of that baleful mountain shouldering the sky, she did not recognize the place at all.

Upon Chaska's request next morning, an old knotkeeper at the way station went to work on records from the time of the earthquake. He seemed glad of something to do, pulling dusty quipus from earthenware jars, humming to himself, scratching his chin. They found one family related to Tika on her father's side, second cousins, she thought. These lived in Lower Huanuco, in a remote hamlet of coca growers called Puma Hill. Not a long trip for a condor, the knotkeeper said, but a tough one on foot, for the path was narrow and steep, winding down into the lush eastern flanks of the Andes, halfway to the great rainforest.

Chaska recalls the welcome they were given there, after walking for two days. A big feast outdoors. A warm, clear evening. They all sat on a terrace above the coca fields, watching the shadows of the Andes lengthen across a mossy sea of treetops spread below.

With this memory Chaska falls asleep at last.

Some days later, when Molina seems in a receptive mood, she raises the matter of moving. He says what she thought he might. The only real home he's ever had is Little River. He fishes and farms, he has friends. He's happy here. And are the highlands really so much safer?

"In my land there's a saying, Chaska: better the devil you know."

"Just think on it," she says. "Take your time. I'm not suggesting we leave tomorrow. But if your people come back to Tumbes, what's the first thing they're going to do?"

"I think," he answers dryly, "that you're about to tell me."

"Won't it be to look for you, so they can find out everything that's happened since they left? And they'll take you away, to have two interpreters. Is that what you want?"

For a while he makes no reply. Then: "You know I don't want that. I want to be with you always. But what about Waman? If we move so far, how will he ever find us?"

"Look." She lifts her index finger. "Waman is one." She spreads her whole hand. "The rest of us are four, counting Tika. I must think of what's best for us all, especially Atuq. No matter where we are, Waman can find us safely only if he gets away from his captors. Assuming he wants to. He was a child when he left. He'll have grown into a man. We can't know what he might have become. I have to face up to that. But of course I'd leave word here for him somehow."

She lets it drop for now, lets Molina get used to the idea. If he digs in his heels she'll suggest a compromise. Not a move but a visit. So he can meet Tika in Huanuco Pampa and her kindred at Puma Hill. Once there, she is sure, he'll come around. He'll see it's a far better refuge than Little River. With ways of escape into the great jungle, where the only towns are made of leaves and the only roads of water.

❊ 10 ❊

Waman smells land: spices, blossom, guano; a wet bonfire reek of cleared fields. The World on the wind.

How long has it been, this time?

More than a quarter of his life.

Mother and Father, Tika, Grandfather. His mind is already with them in Little River. They will slaughter a llama and roast it in the earth with hot stones and fragrant leaves, with peppers, cassava, sweet potatoes. Beer and palm toddy will flow. A banquet for everyone in town.

These anticipations are undercrept by doubt, by dread. Will they forgive him? Will they even know him, dressed as a Christian now? Doublet and hose, tan boots, red velvet cap. Even a black goatee, sparse though it is, which he grows to draw the eye from his scars. Perhaps, he thinks, I smell like a Christian too. What will Tika make of him? Will his worldliness, his outlandishness, impress her? Tika will be a woman now. She might have a husband, even a child. Foolish to think everything here will have stayed the same, awaiting his return as if time had stopped when he left.

And how will he get away to Little River, away from these men who mean to seize his homeland. The Old One has two ships now; two hundred men, not thirteen. With seventy horses and three dozen war-dogs. If I run, they will run me down.

The nightmares have been many. Blood, death, armoured men, armoured horses and mastiffs, trampling, tearing. Spaniards flensing helpless people with their swords, as when they captured him five years ago. He has spoken to no one of these fears, not even Candía. Nor has he been able to think them through with a clear mind. To face such things is to face himself, to probe his own soul with steel and fire like an inquisitor. Waman or Felipe? Which is he? Has he become a *converso*, an *indio ladino*? There are no words for such a being in his language, which in the years since he last saw Qoyllur has become an abandoned garden, overgrown, half forgotten, avoided for the thorns it holds. The only words that seem to fit are *iskay sunqo*—a man of two hearts. And the Castilian for that is *traitor.*

He stares across the whaleback sea at the growing smudge of land. What am I doing here? What will I bring down upon all those I love?

The distant settlement whose outline staggers in the haze seems squat, drab. This can't be Tumbes. Pilot Ruiz must have made some navigational mistake. Or is it simply a Tumbes diminished by the new eyes he brings after so many years, so many wonders and strange sights? Yet the Commander is frowning too.

Unable to clamber to the crosstrees himself, the Old One sends up man after man, every sharp-eyed lookout aboard. "Do you see it?" he shouts. "Do you see the golden temple on the hill?" Pizarro has been worn out by the slow voyage down the seaboard of the hotlands, once again fighting currents, headwinds, warriors. And before that by the months in Panama, wrangling with officials and investors; above all with his partner One-Eye.

Waman watched the two arguing—shouting, shoving, even drawing swords—on the day the Old One reached Panama. Everyone knows the reason. The King's licence to conquer Peru denied Almagro the thing he most craved: shared command. All he got is to be Mayor of Tumbes, the vague title of Adelantado, and the promise of any realms he may find beyond those granted to Pizarro. He is also outnumbered now. The Old One has brought three half brothers, all young enough to be his sons: Hernando, the grandest, the only Pizarro born in wedlock, a plump fellow in his thirties with fleshy lips and a strawberry nose bloated by drink; Juan, the boldest, though barely twenty, always the first in a fight; and Gonzalo, the youngest and most unruly, the best-looking, cruel with women.

Waman shrinks at the thought of One-Eye's gaze: ice-blue, reptilian, the ball swivelling like a lizard's in the bald orb of his head. At least that eye is an hour astern, aboard the other ship.

A hand alights on his shoulder. Candía, with the lute. On the voyage he has played often, and given lessons to Waman.

They go to the foredeck, where the Greek checks the swivel gun, then sits on his haunches, strumming a few chords. Still a lovely sound to Waman's ears; still unearthly, especially here. He watches the fretwork, hoping one day to become so deft himself.

"Here." Candía hands him the instrument. "Play something. From home, your home." He glances landward. "Go on. Let's hear Peru."

"I'm sorry . . ." The interpreter looks down at the sun-warped planking by his feet. "I can't remember."

"Nonsense. What about those songs you used to sing, that flute you played?"

"I remember nothing."

Candía pats his shoulder. "Anything. A nursery rhyme will do. All right?"

"I'll have to change your tuning."

"Change it."

"I'll have to sing along. I'm not much good . . ."
"Sing!"

Munankichu willanayta
Maymantachus kanichayta?

Do you want me to tell you
Where I come from?

Waman stops, disheartened, makes to hand back the lute. He shakes his head, saying it's a song his mother used to sing for him when he was little. A mountain song.
"Go on! It's lovely. Start again."

Munankichu willanayta
Maymantachus kanichayta?
Haqay urqo qhipanmanta,
Sachakuna qhipanmanta,
Tikakuna chawpinmanta.

Do you want me to tell you
Where I come from?
From behind that hill,
Beyond the woods,
Amid the flowers.

Amid the flowers. Waman thrusts the lute fiercely into Candía's hand. He runs to the rail and empties his guts into the sea. Tika, a girl named Flower.

Now they are near enough for a clear sight from deck. There's no

longer any doubt. The commanding feature of the Tumbes skyline—
the lofty roof of the Sun's House with its golden crest—has gone.
Pizarro, tight-jawed, sucking cheeks, says nothing.

Terse commands from Pilot Ruiz as the ship enters the channel
through the mangroves. A taut flutter of reefed sail, shouts from a
man taking soundings at the prow.

The platinum light of noon pours down on emptiness. No ships in
the haven, no fleet with the rainbow pennant at the masts. Only old
fishing smacks and sun-bleached rafts strewn haphazard on the
beach. The long jetty where Waman talked his way onto the traders'
ship is nothing but a row of stumps, burnt to the waterline. The
shops and eating houses along the waterfront are wrecked. Not a
person to be seen, not a dog.

When both ships have moored, Commander Pizarro leads a hundred men through broken streets to the middle of the city. Still no
word escapes him. They move with a clatter of weapons, creaking
armour, hoofbeats, and murmuring from the men like the buzz of an
uneasy hive.

Tumbes has been sacked. The fortress is empty, its gate thrown
down. The temple walls stand open to the sky, rafters burnt, images
and treasures torn away. The only grand building spared by the fires
is the Governor's house, which stands whole, though looted, its
colourful murals defaced with cuts, soot, lewd scribbles. Filth and
broken pottery are strewn through the rooms, and in the courtyard
bodies lie—skeletons torn apart by dogs and vultures. Almagro
draws his sword, pokes furiously through rags of clothing, carcasses,
nests of human hair.

The Old One barks at his men to clean the place, toss out the bones. He assigns rooms, orders stores brought ashore. He sends Almagro and a dozen horse along the road for a look at the hinterland (and to be rid of One-Eye for the afternoon).

Waman and Candía he sends into the streets on a search for survivors. It takes them an hour to find anyone besides some wild-haired children, who shriek and run as if from fiends. Eventually they come upon two elderly women hiding in a courtyard. One, who seems from her dress to be a highborn lady, regards Candía fixedly. She approaches, studies his face, rubs a finger on his steel breastplate, even lightly strokes his beard. *Qollqi runa!* she exclaims, the silver man. She tells her companion she recognizes him from years ago, when she was Mother of the Chosen who lived beside the temple. She saw this silver man, or one just like him, in the Sun's window, eyeing her girls. She also walked out to the fields that day and heard the thunder of his blowpipe.

"*Mamakuna,*" Waman asks respectfully, surprising the women with his Quechua, "there was another bearded one who stayed behind in Tumbes. Molina by name. Have you seen or heard anything of him?"

"*Mulina?*" She looks at her companion. Both shake their heads in the local way: a single side-to-side with the eyes half shut and raised to the sky. He had forgotten the gesture. It makes him homesick as a child.

They hear angry voices from the Governor's house as they draw near, bringing the women. Another row between the Commander and One-Eye, already back from his excursion: ". . . lies, Pizarro. More of your damned lies! Where's your great kingdom? Where are your temples filled with gold? Even the bridge is down. This land's already sacked. By whom, I wonder. Answer me that. God's blood! By whom?"

Waman despairs. What can such men accomplish? How can he escape them? Candía returns his glum look as they go inside. "At it again," the Greek says, rolling his big dark eyes.

"How should I know what's happened?" the Old One is saying. "But it doesn't matter, does it? It's obviously just Indians against Indians. And the fewer of them left the better. The gold is here somewhere. Can't you smell it?" He sniffs the air. "You'll get your gold, Don Diego. Even if we have to dig it from the ruins of every city in Peru. Upon my honour." He makes to clasp his partner by the forearm.

"Your *honour*?" One-Eye twists away. He drives a fist into the wall, dislodging a scab of plaster. "I'd sooner trust a Moor!"

The two women look at each other in dismay. Waman recalls the ways of his country. Great men do not show anger; they are feared most when they smile.

"Is this the best you can do, lads?" Pizarro calls, glad of the interruption. "A pair of old whores?"

"Don Francisco," Candía says, "these are worthy ladies, fallen on hard times. This is the Mother Superior of their convent, the very one I saw five years ago. She remembers me!"

"What about Molina? What of the Emperor's man? The lady Governor? What in God's name has happened here?"

The Mother Superior says nothing while Waman relays these questions. Then she unleashes a torrent, keening like a mourner. Many times she repeats *hatun unqoy*, *hatun wañuy*, great sickness, great death. And *hatun auqay*, a great war. He has trouble following—so long since he's heard the language—and it's impossible to slow the woman and render her words phrase by phrase. But he gets the gist.

"She says a terrible pestilence ravaged the Empire from Quito to Chile, Commander. Two-thirds of the people have died. Among the first was the Emperor Wayna Qhapaq. His chosen heir died too. Dead before his father's body was embalmed."

Waman feels the ground tilt. A storm breaks in his mind. If Tumbes is like this, and all the World, what horrors will he find in Little River? The floor drops from under him. He falls, and falls.

While Waman is being helped to his feet and revived with a swig of wine, five men, men of importance, are escorted in by the Commander's guard.

"Ah," says Pizarro, glaring at Almagro. "Now we can get some real information."

The leader, who wears a red turban, big earspools of gold, and a striped blue-and-yellow tunic, enters as confidently as if he met Spaniards every day. He has a lazy eye, and his young face is pitted like a rusty cannonball. One like me, Waman thinks, one who caught the pox yet lived. He tells Waman he is Chillimasa, Governor of Tumbes, son of Lady Sian, the former Governor who died in the Great Death. He was there as his mother's attendant when Candía dined with the All-Seer years ago. Asking Waman to point out the bearded ones' leader, he strides up to Pizarro, claps him on the shoulder and bids him welcome to his house.

"His house!" Almagro shouts. "Is that what he calls this place? Look at it. Is this my consolation prize, Pizarro: a burnt city with no citizens? No doubt you think this walleyed Indian's godforsaken fief is enough for a one-eyed fool."

"Don Diego, you know very well I did my best for you in Spain. I was your loudest advocate for joint command. Ask any who were there. It was the King himself insisted I be sole Commander. He thought it would avoid disputes. Let's be sure it does. We are two hundred in a land that still has millions. We must think of our lives, not titles." He smiles wolfishly. "Peru is big enough for both of us.

And His Catholic Majesty is very far away. We must obey, but we needn't comply. In due course—when we know what we've found—you and I will come to an arrangement of our own."

Almagro turns aside, his face a bludgeon.

Governor Chillimasa has watched this exchange closely. He asks Waman what the barbarians know of the troubles in his province.

"Only what they've seen today, my lord."

"What's that?" Pizarro grasps Waman's ear. "Every word, Felipillo. Upon your life. He—and you—must tell everything."

After the Great Death waned, the young Governor offers warily, it was his task to oversee resettlement of Tumbes. But just as things were returning to normal, war broke out between two of the late Emperor's sons, sons by different mothers: Waskhar, ruling most of the Empire from Cusco; and Atawallpa, based in the northern highlands, at Tumipampa in Quito Province. The Tumbes garrison was ordered to the mountains. Raiders from beyond the Empire—wild men from the hotlands—took advantage of this. It was they who sacked the city, only two months ago.

"Is the war between the brothers over?" Almagro cuts in. "If so, which one has it? And which side is this Indian on?"

Chillimasa is evasive on both points, saying only that the war is a dynastic matter for highlanders to resolve. His priority is to bring order to his province, to mop up any raiders he can find. To this end, he is willing to work with the bearded ones. He will reward them well with land, houses, servants, gold. And women, naturally, since they seem to have none of their own.

"The Lord God must first be served, Don Francisco." A lean man with sallow cheeks and a fixed expression of displeasure has trundled silently into the room as if without the use of feet. In the white habit and black cloak of a Dominican, Friar Vicente Valverde is the one chosen by King Charles to be Protector of Indians and Bishop of Peru. "This Indian must agree to let our churchmen preach here. His people must be taught the Holy Faith."

"One thing at a time, Father. You won't get much preaching done if they kill us in our beds tonight." Pizarro turns back to Waman. "Ask about Molina."

The Governor's divergent eyes cast about as if following two wasps. Then: "Just before my mother died, she did mention a barbarian had stayed behind. Some say he died in the pestilence. Others that he fled the city. I think there was also a tale he was killed in a fight. Perhaps over a woman."

"That sounds like Molina, all right." Candía laughs. Pizarro shuts him up with a glare.

Weeks go by, armed Christians riding out with the Governor's small force. Meanwhile the hanging bridge is rebuilt with new cables. Llama trains come and go, bringing food, wares, wooden beams, cane for roofing. From the port comes the crunch of piles being driven into mud. Bustle and chatter slowly return to the streets.

The horses are hobbled and set to graze, objects of curiosity to local farmers. Objects of outrage, too, when they trample and eat the crops. The Christians' hogs—a drove of several dozen—wallow in ditches and uproot sweet potatoes. And the war-hounds, the great spotted, half-crazed mastiffs, are another curse, chasing down the citizens' own dogs, their livestock, even their children.

Pizarro stations most of his men in the fortress, keeping a guard of fifty at the Governor's palace.

With Chillimasa's reluctant assent—or acquiescence—Valverde's friars take over the temple, drafting men to re-roof the hall of the Sun. It is soon whitewashed and adorned with a pair of painted statues: the Mother of God; and the father of war, Santiago Matamoros, Slayer of Moors.

On the wall where the golden sun-wheel greeted the dawn there now hangs a crucifix, given to Pizarro by Queen Isabel. Some argued it should hang on the east wall, not the west, but Valverde overruled them. "Our Lord must take the place of *their* lord. From this day forth, Christ is the Sun who shines on Peru."

{ II }

A tawallpa gazes on a bleached afternoon framed by the dark stonework of his bedroom window. His hand absently strokes a favourite trophy: a dried head, the brow glossy as fine leather from his frequent attentions. It is the head of Hanku, his brother Waskhar's general. Waskhar's best.

Only months ago the Cusco army overran Tumipampa and imprisoned Atawallpa here in his own quarters. But loyal servants made his jailers drunk on beer spiked with vision juice. He could hear them outside the door, singing, raving, puking. Soon they were sleeping like snakes in winter, and he slipped away. Once free, he routed his brother's troops and returned in triumph.

Atawallpa smiles at the recent throws of fate. If no Great Death, no dead father. And no dead heir. If no dead father and heir, no opportunity. If no opportunity, no war. If no war, no victory. And no victory if Waskhar had been wiser and killed him when he had the chance.

Atawallpa takes up a silver mirror and interrogates his face, as he does more than once every day. An overnight tarnish from the breath of a volcano gilds his youthful looks agreeably. He juts his chin, pulls a face, wags his head slowly side to side. Good: the scarred earlobe, spliced roughly years ago, stays hidden behind its golden spool and screen of straight black hair. He sets the mirror down and fondles the trophy again, ruffling its short brush cut, the latest style in the capital. Ugly. And no good for hiding torn earlobes. Again he smiles.

The news could hardly be better. Atawallpa's generals—formerly his father's generals—have taken city after city on their southward march along the Empire's highland backbone. They have reached the Cusco valley, are poised to take the capital at last.

Best, it is Waskhar who's the prisoner now.

Soon Atawallpa will make his way to Cusco—slowly and in splendour, sweeping all doubt and disorder before him as inexorably as a mountain glacier—and there be crowned with his father's crimson fringe across his brow. Then he will become by law what he already is in deed: Sapa Inka, Only King, supreme ruler of the World.

If nothing goes wrong.

But what can? Waskhar is caged like a puma in the army base at Huanuco. He has no sympathizers there. The only thing left to decide is when to kill him. And how.

Atawallpa toys with the idea of turning his brother's hide into a man-drum. The other day some of his troops made rather a good one, the belly stretched over a wooden frame, the dried forearms still attached by their sinews to serve as drumsticks. Amusing. But unfortunately he can't do that to a fellow Inca. Man-drums are for rebels and barbarians.

Waskhar is certainly no barbarian—much too effete. And if there's a rebel in the family, he thinks, it's a moot point which of us it is. My brother attacked me first. Though admittedly that was after I refused to pay him fealty in Cusco. But why should I?

Before beginning his long progress to the south, Atawallpa deems it wise to make offerings at the finest temple in Quito Province. No better place to don the mantle of a Sunchild than at the solar monument his father built near Tumipampa. Though not as grand as the temples of Cusco, this one is unique in its design. All others in the Empire have a curved wall on one side to represent the sun's path through the year. But this alone has a curve at both ends—facing north and south. His father's surveyors determined that through this building runs the midline of the Earth. From here the sun travels in each direction half a year.

Atawallpa recalls his father explaining these cosmic mysteries when they went to see the building work. He was still a boy then, and the occasion was the arrival of the temple's main gate from Cusco, where it had been cut and fitted by the Empire's master masons: many tons of polished stone, the lintel alone weighing ten, brought north on sleds and rollers, a task that took two thousand men six months.

They were standing on a hilltop, watching work teams unload the porphyry blocks, take off the packing straw, set them out in order on the ground like pieces of a puzzle. Wouldn't it have been easier, the boy asked, to bring the masons north and make the gate here?

His father answered that the point was not ease, but difficulty. Our power, he said, is proclaimed in two things: in people and in stone. In our command of stone—our great buildings, bridges, waterworks, farming terraces—and in the work-tax we raise by turns throughout Tawantinsuyu, labour which grows ever more abundant as the people thrive. So I have to build more each year. And since each new city is another Cusco, it must contain a wonder from the first.

"Do you see the meaning of this place?" the Emperor added, before supplying the answer. "This is the Sun's favoured haunt on Earth. I can see why, can't you? So much warmer than the capital. Lusher. More trees. More flowers. I've grown to like it better here myself."

"And because I'm here!" Atawallpa put in quickly—too quickly—wishing his father had said it. "And Mother . . . You love us more than anyone in Cusco, don't you?"

The Emperor Wayna Qhapaq, then in his thirties—about the age Atawallpa is now—laughed heartily and hugged the boy. But there were courtiers within earshot and he didn't say a word. So many sons; too many to count. Atawallpa, born to a lesser wife, a lady of Quito, would not be in the running to succeed him. Some years later the Only King named his ablest son by the Qoya, his sister-queen in Cusco, to be the heir. At the time this had seemed a mere formality, for the Inca was in his prime.

As he still was until the Great Death fell upon the World.

So many of his children gone, yet *I* survive, thinks Atawallpa, offering corn and beer in the stillness of his father's monument. So many rivals dead. Though not all.

Waskhar is no longer a threat. The half brothers who most worry him now are Manku and Pawllu. Only in their teens, mere nits. But nits become lice. Atawallpa sends the order to his generals at Cusco: occupy the city without delay; search house-to-house until every potential rival has been purged.

Those half brothers are weaklings, sapped by the capital's soft life, its endless feasts and pageants. Atawallpa's duty, his destiny, is to finish the plague's work: to kill them all and cleanse the World.

The Inca orders his army and court to prepare for the triumphal march to Cusco, a journey of a thousand miles by the great highland road. But only a week or two before everything is ready, a runner arrives, his sweat steaming the dawn air. He brings news from the coast: the hairy barbarians seen in Tumbes five years ago have come back.

Atawallpa refuses to receive the messenger until he has had breakfast and composed himself. He is not an early riser.

"The bearded ones from overseas are back, Sapa Inka," the runner says on his knees. "And in much greater numbers than before. Two ships. Two hundred men. Sixty or seventy strange animals, like big llamas, on which some of them ride. Their leader has been warmly received by Chillimasa, who became Governor of Tumbes after his mother's death."

Atawallpa recalls how that province took Waskhar's side in the war. They will not love him there.

Still. Only two hundred. Such a tiny force can be nothing more than a nuisance. Why lose time on this distraction now? The affairs of Tumbes can be dealt with later, after he is crowned in Cusco.

At dinner that evening he is approached by his high council of five advisers—headed by Wayta Yupanki, a white-haired uncle who served his father well for many years. This august figure reminds him how the old Emperor had these strangers closely watched, gathering intelligence of their behaviour at every port they touched. How he warned against them, ordering that the one left behind in Tumbes be arrested and interrogated.

"Your father's orders came to nothing with his tragic and untimely death," Wayta Yupanki adds. "But he was wise in this matter, as in all things. The strangers are few. But they may be more dangerous than they seem. First ten. Then thirteen. Now two hundred. Many more could be lurking in the hotlands. Also, let us not forget that others—much like these—raided Qollasuyu eight years ago, coming up rivers from the Other Sea—"

"My father stopped those easily enough," Atawallpa snaps. "I shall stop these when I please."

Inwardly the uncle frowns. He has never much liked this nephew, and trusts him less. Why did the spotted death pass over *him*—he with a broken earlobe, which all know is unlucky? Moreover, he's a sot, the kind who drinks alone and can't hold it. Unlike his father, who could outdrink anyone yet never become drunk. And such a liar. A bad liar too, which is worse, because it shows failure to judge others' wits.

Wayta Yupanki has not forgotten the day when Atawallpa, then eighteen or so, appeared in his father's dining hall with a bloody bandage on his ear, claiming a boil had burst, breaking the stretched ring of flesh. But the truth was already out: the young prince had forced himself on a girl; in the struggle she'd hooked a finger in his lobe and snapped it. It is this that gives him his air of gravity, for he sits very still, head to one side, making sure his hair drapes the shameful scar and the rubber band that bears the weight of his earspool.

The uncle allows none of these disagreeable thoughts to show. We're all stuck with Atawallpa now, he thinks. Our duty is to serve him as we served his father, if only for his father's sake. And ours.

"Of course, Only King. In good time, as you say. But with respect, we think this time should be sooner, not later. As you know, these strangers may well have brought the Great Death that killed your father—my dear brother—and so many millions. Who knows what evils they may carry with them now?"

The Inca goes on eating without a word, taking food and drink from the slim hands of two young women who kneel on either side of his cushioned stool. A possible link between the barbarians and the plague does not worry him. If the strangers brought the Great Death, then it is they who set off the upheaval that shook the World and made him King.

"*Who knows . . . who knows . . .*" the Inca, mouth full, mocks his uncle. "What exactly *do* you know?"

"Only the reports we gathered five years ago—and in the last few weeks. We have gone over this information thoroughly. Although some of it may be garbled, arising from the fear and credulity of simple lowlanders, much of it seems useful."

Atawallpa has just begun the soup course when the spoon slips in his hand. A few drops fall on the velvet-like fabric of his robe, a favourite one, sewn as if seamlessly from the skins of vampire bats. He leaps to his feet and hurries from the room.

"That was made for his father, you know," Wayta Yupanki remarks to his fellow advisers while the Inca is changing. "He used to order a new one every year—his way of getting the forest folk to thin those pests."

The Inca returns in a clean tunic of white vicuña. Once he seems calm, his advisers summarize their information. The barbarians vary widely in appearance. Their skins are of every shade from white to black. Some have dark hair, others have red or yellow. Their faces are covered in wool, showing only the eyes, also of many colours. They wear tight clothing they seldom take off, even to sleep. They crawl with lice and smell like corpses. Over their own hands they wear other hands of leather—possibly the hands of men they have skinned.

"This we think broadly reliable," says Wayta Yupanki. "It comes from several sources. Then there are those who say the intruders are sorcerers, that they can hurl thunder and lightning, that they *eat* silver and gold. But we think these are the tales of simple folk frightened by the strange beasts and fire-shooters. The latter appear to be the same as an iron blowpipe the late Emperor's men took from the bearded ones who raided Qollasuyu. The All-Seer of Tumbes—a good servant of the Empire—sent your father a full report on the weapon brought ashore by the barbarians last time they came."

"Very well," says Atawallpa absently. He is tired of hearing how wise his father was. "Let me know if more arrive. And if they make any move beyond where they are now."

The new Inca begins making his way south from Tumipampa in his father's palanquin, so heavy with gold that eighty uniformed men— all of high rank—are needed to shoulder its long poles of mahogany and silver. Travelling behind him, in smaller litters, are lords and ladies of the northern court, along with Atawallpa's wives and concubines. Ahead of the procession march fifty thousand troops, preparing way stations and pitching tents at each halt.

Not ten days out from Tumipampa, more news comes from the seaboard. The invaders have been plundering houses, farms, and shrines. They have raided state warehouses, taking food, clothing, footwear. They have broken into a Chosen House and raped the girls. They have also taken many prisoners, whom they keep in collars and chains. Any captives who sicken are fed to their dogs.

In response to these outrages the local people attacked, killing three barbarians and one of their big animals. The barbarians' protector Chillimasa then fled, but the invaders regained the upper hand by terror, seizing a dozen lords and burning them alive.

Atawallpa's advisers renew their call for action. But the Inca thinks only of Cusco, of his triumph, of rounding up his brothers and crushing Waskhar's faction.

At last comes such worrying news that Wayta Yupanki is able to catch his nephew's attention.

"The barbarians are on the move, Sapa Inka. You told me to warn you should this happen. They have advanced south from Tumbes to the Chira valley, which was emptied by plague and war. There they have dared to start building houses, using their prisoners and blacks. Meanwhile one of their ships has sailed north. It left empty except for the crew and some gold. It also carried a barbarian leader the lowlanders call One-Eye. We believe he may have gone for reinforcements. Lastly, my lord, they have expressed a wish to come and see you. In friendship, so they say."

Atawallpa lifts a beringed hand for silence while he thinks seriously about the intruders for the first time. They can't be ignored much longer, if only because he would look indecisive.

"Have them investigated thoroughly. I want to know everything they've done since they got here. How many men they've killed. How many women they've assaulted. Everything they've taken from government stores and private houses. What they eat and drink. Their height, their girth. Their ages. Same with these big llamas of theirs. I need a man to spend time with them, to make a thorough report. Who have we got down there? Who's the All-Seer?"

"The All-Seer of Tumbes died in the plague, Only King, at the time the city was evacuated. He has yet to be replaced."

"What happened to the barbarian left behind years ago, the prisoner?"

"Nobody knows. Some say he died in jail when the Great Death came. Others say he escaped into the hills."

"Find out."

That night Atawallpa wakes from an uneasy sleep. His eyes stare at the moonlight filtering through the cotton of his field tent. These barbarians: whom to send? His cousin Maytawillka comes to mind, one of old Wayta Yupanki's sons. Atawallpa has known him since they both were small. An annoying fellow at times, but a clever one. A joker, a charmer. The sort everyone likes right away. A loud dresser too: earspools with fussy inlay, gold sequins on his shirt and cape, on his bag. A follower of fashion—that ugly short hair, like a brush. And no headband; only a jaunty little hat like a pie. He will amuse the invaders, swim among them like a gaudy fish.

After breakfast the Inca watches with satisfaction as Mayta-willka—normally so familiar—enters his field tent carrying a burden of red cloth, humbling himself at the royal feet. Atawallpa makes him stay there longer than is proper, especially for kin. Let him learn his place! Not so long ago this cousin dared tease Atawallpa, flirting with his women to his face, yet somehow with such wit and lightness it was impossible to show offence. A joke, of course: Maytawillka likes women but not in that way.

"At ease, Cousin," Atawallpa says at last. "Get up and sit over here. We will chew together. We'll talk." From a bag at his waist, the Inca takes some coca leaves and fans them out in his palm. Blowing over them gently in the four directions, he recites the names of the highest peaks around the camp. Then he takes lime from a little golden flask with a dropper, and makes up a quid. Maytawillka does the same. The two exchange quids. For a while they chew in silence.

Maybe my cousin's not so bad after all, thinks Maytawillka. Maybe he'll grow into his new office. Maybe power will bring confidence, in others and in himself.

When the inward warmth of the coca has spread throughout his being, Atawallpa comes to the point.

"You've heard of the bearded invaders on the north coast? Much is said about them, but little is certain. Some call them vagabonds and pirates. Others say they are wizards. I want you to visit them at a base they're building near the sea, at Chira. Get to know their leaders. Tell them I send you as my ambassador. Invite them to come and pay me homage. But take your time. Linger. Spy on them, play with them, induce them to lower their guard, as you do so well. Yet be sure you overawe them with my power. And tell them as little as possible, especially about my brother Waskhar and the recent troubles—"

"No fear of that, Atawallpa. They won't understand a word. Nor I."

"Don't interrupt! You will be able to speak with them through their interpreter—a Tallan boy they took away with them some years ago. I want to know everything. What they fear. What angers them. What they wear. What they eat. How they are led and disciplined. The smell of their sweat and the colour of their shit. Why they have no women of their kind. And all the obvious things: their animals, their weapons, their plans, their prisoners. Take them food—dry meat, corn, beer, baskets of guavas, avocados. Also, I'll send a royal gift. Fine cloth and emeralds for their leaders, mummified ducks for their gods, and a pair of stone vessels shaped like the Sun House at Tumipampa. Have your men pick all this up from the stores on your way out.

"One other thing. Be sure to ask the locals what became of a man these barbarians left in Tumbes five years ago. That is all."

Francisco Pizarro is equally keen to learn Molina's fate but has been unable to do so until now. After withdrawing from Tumbes and losing several men in skirmishes, his priority has been to set up his base in Chira, where he found an abandoned town his men could repair and fortify.

This turned out to be less than two days' march beyond Little River. It took all of Waman's self-control to keep outwardly calm while they passed so near his old home by the *tupa ñan*, the royal highway. Throughout the weeks in Chira, Waman has watched for a chance to flee. Once, after relieving himself outside one moonless night, he began to steal away, following the bank of a canal he thought would lead to the main road. But he did not get far before a heavy bark drummed on the night air, answered immediately by others. Soon the war-dogs' compound was in uproar.

And if he *had* got away, he has asked himself often since that night, what then? From what he's seen of Tumbes, Chira, and other places on the Spaniards' march, Little River will not have escaped the smallpox. Nor the wars. It may well be utterly forsaken. Always he arrives at this: that he will never find his family. That at worst they're dead, all of them. That at best one or two may have survived the pox, as he did in Seville, only to have been killed or scattered by the war of succession, itself a consequence of the Great Death.

As Waman comes to accept these conclusions, he decides two things. He *must* find out what happened—and soon—before his captors move on. And since it's unlikely his family will still be in Little River, he can go there openly without putting them at risk. Or can he? The dilemma is a pain within him, like a growth.

To be so near is unbearable. This may be his only chance. He must go now.

So he tells the Old One of his parting words to Molina on the caravel in Tumbes. How he begged him to go to Little River. The Commander bends his head and studies the floor. He casts his eyes up at Waman, an ironic smile under whiskered brows.

"Suddenly so keen to help, Felipe. Why is that?"

"Why would I not be, sir? This is my only chance to find my people. Or at least seek word of them."

"You think I'm daft, boy? Suppose we do find Molina. Then I'll have two interpreters, and one of them a Spaniard. Your worth to me will be halved. Are you trying to trick me? Or is your family so dear to you they're worth risking your life for?"

"Yes, sir." The words come out in a squeak. Waman clears his throat. "Yes"—more manfully—"they are." Again he fears what he might bring down upon their heads. But his plan is to make enquiries without giving anything away. Only *he* knows Little River—and Tallan, the local tongue.

Pizarro acts at once, sending two men with Waman and the Greek. "Keep Felipe roped to his saddle. If Molina's there bring him back—in chains if he won't come quietly."

They ride all day, sleeping that night by the roadside. The highways are empty, not only from plague and civil war but because the invaders' reputation runs before them, the burnings, the enslavements. Travellers hide in the desert at the first sound of hoofbeats, the first plume of dust.

About noon the next day they come to the imperial barracks near Little River and some outlying houses. All roofless. Bush has grown up along canals and streets. Everything looks smaller. Nothing fits with Waman's memories. This desolate village might be anywhere. Most houses are still standing, but empty for years, drifts of sand in doorways, rags of awning here and there, overgrown yards, pelicans nesting on roofs, their droppings daubing the walls. Pelicans in town? He's never seen that before. Nothing makes sense until they reach the square and he recognizes the open-fronted hall where he and Tika went to school. The plaza trees have grown tall and wide, shutting out the sky, and the ground is carpeted with leaves and carob pods. Fear roils in Waman's belly. He knows where the old house will be—only blocks away. But can he face the sight of it in ruins? And if anyone *is* there, what might these Spaniards do? Candía he thinks he can trust, but not the others.

"Smoke!" one of them calls. "I smell smoke. Over there." The four dismount and tether the horses. Waman's hands are untied from the pommel of his saddle, retied behind his back. His ankles are hobbled; he can walk but not run. *Sorry,* Candía mouths.

The smoke draws them to a house on the town's edge, beside the dunes. The Spaniards burst in, finding an elderly couple curing fish in a courtyard. Waman does not know who they are.

"Go on, Felipe," the Greek says. "Tell them they've nothing to fear. Then ask about Molina." He taps his nose, unseen by the other two. Waman takes this to mean that anything else will be kept private. Candía has a smattering of Quechua now—not much, but more than any Spaniard—perhaps enough to trace the bones of a conversation. But Waman speaks in Tallan.

The old couple's eyes, clouded with fear, widen at hearing this youth, who seems to be a barbarian and is bound like a criminal, speaking their language, claiming to be Chaska and Mallki's long-lost son. At first they give curt, wary replies. As belief grows that Waman really is the neighbourhood boy who ran away to sea, they begin to open up. The wife does most of the talking, telling Waman that none of his family is here now—there's only a handful left in town, all old like themselves—but as far as she knows his mother and brother are alive.

"My brother?" he says, crushed. They must be thinking of some other family. "I have no brother. Only my cousin, Tika. She lived with us." He wipes a wet eye on his arm. "I am the son of Chaska and Mallki," he says again.

The two speak quickly to each other, voices low. He can't follow this. "Then it must have been after you left," the woman tells him. "Your mother gave birth to a little boy. We don't remember what she called him. But you do have a brother. Lady Chaska took him with her when they went away."

Detecting embarrassment, perhaps evasion in her manner, Waman asks what they know of his father, grandfather, and cousin.

"I'm very sorry to have to tell you that both those good men were taken by the spotted death." The woman's eyes redden; talk of Waman's dead has brought others of her own to mind. "I'm sorry," she says after a while. "You see, Little River lost three in every four." She weeps quietly for a moment. "We ourselves lost our children. But I believe the girl you mentioned may be alive. I didn't know your mother well. I thought that girl was her daughter. I think she became a Chosen. That's right, isn't it, Ni?" Her husband nods.

Waman presses for details, but they can't remember where Tika went, or when. Only that it was some years ago, to a big city in the highlands.

"When did my mother leave here? Do you know why?"

Again a quick, private exchange. The husband speaks.

"I remember your father. Tayta Mallki. A fine man. We fished together sometimes. He was headman for a while. Less than a year. Before . . ." His voice dies in shyness.

The wife resumes. "Widow Chaska stayed on here for some years after your father died. She left when war broke out between Cusco and Quito. So did many others."

She hesitates, glances at her husband. "There's one thing more you should know. By then your mother was no longer alone. She got married again. To a . . . a *stranger* who came here. Can they understand us?" she asks, shooting a fraught glance. He shakes his head. "The stranger looked a bit like one of *them*. Half dead when he got here, he was. Your mother took him in, cared for him. When he got better he worked for her. Later they got married. They all left here together. Those two and the little boy."

"Was the stranger's name Molina?" Waman blurts, instantly biting his tongue. The others must have heard.

"*Mulina?*" The two look baffled. "Turtle, his name was," the husband offers. "That's what folk used to call him. Can't think why."

"Felipe!" Candía cuts in. "What was that? What are they saying about Molina?"

"Only that they've never heard of him."

Candía sends the other two back to fetch the horses. "What news of your kin, Felipe?" he asks, treading carefully, his tone solemn.

"They're not here. I'll tell you the rest later. Not now. I can't . . ."

Candía's large hand falls lightly on his shoulder. "Want to look for your old home?"

"We passed it already. Empty, like the others. They said a few more townsfolk are living by the beach. If we can find any, I should speak to them."

What Waman really longs to do is go to the Town of the Dead in the high desert, mourn quietly there, say words that should be said for his father, his grandfather. But this is impossible. He's seen what Spaniards do at Peruvian cemeteries. Rooting for gold with their swords, cutting up mummies, scattering the dead like trash.

They ride through dunes to the seashore, Waman lost in his old life, his sorrow. And the astonishing tale about his mother and Molina. Can that be true? It is shocking, almost obscene. Yet who is he to judge her, after what she must have suffered here?

A few huts above the foreshore. All empty. But some hearths still warm. The owners hiding.

Waman stands on the long, curving beach where he used to fish, the wind loud with the cries of seabirds.

One man is riding a tiny boat on the horizon, so far out that only Waman sees him. As if seeing himself from years ago. The interpreter breathes a prayer to Mother Sea.

Atawallpa is nearing the highland city of Cajamarca when Maytawillka returns from his assignment, borne swiftly in a travelling hammock by a team of runners. The envoy is bruised about his face and arms. The Inca, on a small throne in his tent, does not look up at him.

"Back so soon? I told you to linger there, Cousin. Not come back in a week."

"Only King, the time I spent among them seemed enough. I thought it best to report quickly—though of course I can go again if you wish."

A nod for Maytawillka to continue.

"The barbarians are two hundred at most. I couldn't make an exact tally because some were away from the camp—at their ships or scouting roads. They have about five hundred prisoners, and auxiliaries from lands beyond the Empire. The bearded ones are lazy. Some never walk more than a few steps, riding instead like children on their beasts. These resemble the big llamas of Qollasuyu, though more heavily built, needing ropes and bridles to stop them bolting. When they run fast the ground shakes. The barbarians also have about thirty fierce hounds, big as pumas. I saw them throw a hotlander to these dogs. He was torn apart in no time."

"Did you see their blowpipes shoot fire? The All-Seer of Tumbes sent my father a description. Like thunder, he said."

"There was no occasion to see fighting. I made a show of friendship, as you said. But I did see their stores. Your knotkeeper has the details. There were only four of the fire-shooters. There could be others with the men who weren't in Chira. But I doubt there are more than seven or eight all told. Their main weapons are long knives that hang from their waists in leather sheaths and trail behind them like tails. Or, as the women say, like giant pricks." Maytawillka stifles a laugh; Atawallpa is unamused. "These knives are of iron, not silver. Their armour too. They spend a lot of time polishing off the rust. What struck me most is how their eyes light up at the sight of gold—like monkeys' seeing fruit. They were always fingering the metal on my clothes. They even tried to tug bits off."

"How did they receive the gifts I sent?"

"I gave them the stuffed ducks without explanation. I wanted to see what they would do. They knew nothing! Some asked if the ducks were good eating. Others feared they might be poisoned. One said they were a threat from you, Sapa Inka, warning them they'd soon be trussed and dried the same way."

"Splendid idea!" Atawallpa laughs, looking his cousin in the eye at last. "Go on."

"The same man said the stone vessels you sent were model castles—to frighten them with all the fortresses that lie in their way."

"How did you follow all this? Is their interpreter any good?"

"He was away when I first got there. He came back to the camp on my third day. If anything, he seems to speak their language better than our own. He has a thick Tallan accent. He told me his name is Waman, though they call him *Pilipi*. He's young, about eighteen, seems bright. Good-looking for a lowlander. Though part of his face is like a peanut shell—from the spotted death, he said, when the barbarians took him away. He dresses like them. Same clothes, same smell. He seems wounded somehow. In his being. A great sorrow within him. Dead eyes."

"The sickness blinded him?"

"No, he sees all right. But he looks like one who has seen too much, too young. He wouldn't speak with me privately. No doubt he was told not to. As you know, he's been their prisoner for years. On their terrible rat-ridden ships, to their land across the Other Sea. Which must also be terrible. Why else would they come so far to get away from it?"

"You're to tell me things, not ask them."

"Forgive me, Sapa Inka. As you ordered, I toyed with them. I drank with them, arm-wrestled, tugged their beards, played a few practical jokes, got them to draw their long blades. They anger quickly. One poked a knife against my chin, another beat me with his fists . . ."

"So that explains your bruises. You look like the hammock men dropped you on the road."

Maytawillka laughs. "Feels like they did. Their leader, whom the interpreter calls the Old One, had a hard time saving my skin. He had to shout at them—imagine, their leader has to shout!—to stop them harming me. They have no self-control. They are careless and wasteful. They slaughter llamas by the hundred but eat only the neck meat and the brain. They piss outside their doors like dogs, shaking their pale pricks at Mother Moon."

"Did they say why they have come?"

"They claim they're sent by the Maker of everything. But this is not our Maker. Despite their strange looks and lofty claims, they are simple men. They eat and drink, dress and undress, stitch their own clothes, fuck their prisoners. Their women told me they can work no magic. When they cross the desert they take water along like anyone else."

"What of their leader. The Old One. How old is he?"

"Between fifty and sixty, I'd guess. Still strong for his years. Taller than most. Hair and beard the colour of smoke. He has a dog's eyes, yellow, shifty. His mouth is a toothless hole like an old woman's sex. He needs a knife to eat."

"How does such a man lead?"

"By his fury and their fear, Sapa Inka," Maytawillka answers, silently adding *not unlike yourself.* "It can't be by birth. There's no great lord among them, for they all dress and behave the same way. Except for their prisoners and blacks. These the bearded ones treat cruelly, as small men do who suddenly have others in their power.

"In short, they are *pumaranra*, *suwa*. Brigands, thieves."

Atawallpa looks away, thinking. After some time he says, "If they have come to attack us, why so few? If they come in peace, why so violent? They're beginning to intrigue me. I look forward to seeing them for myself.

"You've done well, Cousin. Now we'll drink."

The Inca calls for beer. They pour an offering on the ground, the rest down their throats. The helper, a slim beauty in her teens, refills their tankards. Maytawillka smiles at the girl.

"Lovely, isn't she?" Atawallpa says ironically as she retires. "It's high time you found yourself a wife, Maytawillka. If only for appearances. A man without a woman is always a boy."

"But you know me, Ata— Sapa Inka." He risks a wink. "I like being a boy."

Atawallpa darkens. "Did you invite them to visit me?"

"Yes. When I gave your gifts to the Old One."

"Which roads are they scouting? Where will they climb into the mountains?"

"Some of them were on the Qashas highway. Probably while you were encamped at Pukara."

"Qashas! I hear they broke into the House of the Chosen there. Odd way to begin an embassy."

"I heard so too. They lined the girls up in the square. Hundreds. Their captain—not the Old One, another one called Sutu—was picking out the comeliest and handing them to his men. The town lord put a stop to it, telling the bearded ones they'd all be hanged. How dare you do this, he said, when the great Atawallpa is only twenty leagues away with fifty thousand men."

The Inca smiles. He's heard enough of these barbarians. He will do with them as he likes. Take anything worthwhile they have to offer—iron, fire-shooters, their new breed of llama—and humiliate them publicly, an exotic touch to the victory parade he's planning for Cajamarca. Man-drums! With their strange hair and skin they'll make unforgettable man-drums.

❖ 12 ❖

Pizarro musters his troops, leaving some to hold the base camp until Almagro returns with more from Panama. The rest he leads through the desert by the main coast road, southward into unknown territory. The sea lies on their right, silver beyond the dunes. To the east are grey outcrops and purple foothills vibrant in the heat. Above these loom the teeth of the Andes, crowned with ice, veiled in haze yet always *there*. Somewhere beyond those ranges lie the Empire's greatest cities. And its King.

The highway is deserted. The posthouses every two miles are unmanned. As are the *tampu*, the government way stations built one day's travel apart. From some children weeding a canal, Waman learns that the new Inca, Atawallpa, has emptied the land of its men to swell his armies, and of its women to feed and clothe them. There is other, grimmer, evidence of war: bodies strung by the feet from scaffolds, eyes and bellies hollowed by birds, skin made parchment by the desert wind. The Spaniards are unfazed. Such a sight is common enough, whether in Peru or Spain. It is the sight of power.

Here and there the road runs past ancient buildings gone to ruin many centuries ago: wind-eaten walls with fading murals; great pyramids of weathered brick rearing like hills from the sandy plain.

Some days later, about noon, they come to an important crossroad. The Old One calls a halt. The royal highway runs invitingly on towards Cusco, the far-off capital. A secondary road comes from the seashore and runs east into the foothills, its trace visible above the lower slopes, sometimes snaking up mountain flanks, sometimes riding crags head-on. Up there, Pizarro knows, the going will be hard, with risk of ambush at each pass and precipice.

Waman, too, dreads the mountains, which he has never set foot in, though they hovered over every day of his young life. He fears their snows, their earthquakes, and above all the slides of stone and ice they hurl on those who live among them. He thinks of Tika's village, smothered in an instant.

Yet the highlands also lure him with a brittle hope, for the more he thinks on what he learned in Little River the more he believes his family is up there somewhere, deep in the mountains.

While the Commander is halted at the crossroads, Hernando Pizarro (eldest of Francisco's three brothers, though twenty years younger than he) scouts the main road ahead with Waman and a dozen riders. Their way is soon blocked by a wide river and cut bridge, its cables lashing in the flow. Spotting some people fleeing on a raft, Hernando plunges into the shallows and drags a man ashore.

"Where is this man now?" Pizarro demands when his brother returns. "Why didn't you bring him back to me here for questioning?"

"He's already questioned, Francisco. Thoroughly. And in no shape to travel." Hernando laughs darkly, spittle flying from his fleshy lips.

"You've disobeyed orders. No harm to the Indians while we march. You've put our lives at risk."

"They won't find out. What's left of him is on the bottom of the river. With heavy stones for company."

"There'll be no more of that. Not unless I order it." The Old One stares his half brother down until Hernando yields a nod. "Now. What did the man have to say?"

"It wasn't easy. Not a word, Francisco, even with his feet on fire. Nothing till I set the dogs on him. These Indians don't feel pain the way we Christians do." Hernando sighs. "I asked how far it is to Cusco. He said troops on the march would take a month to get there. He said the King is still in Cajamarca, only seven or eight days from here. The army is in two divisions. One stationed at that city, the other at some high pass over there." Hernando lifts the tip of his beard to the road rising from the desert shimmer. "The man said Atawallpa is waiting in great pride, boasting that every one of us will soon be dead." Hernando smirks. "That may have been wishful thinking—by then he was nearly dead himself."

Pizarro scowls and turns away, in jealousy as much as anger. When he sailed for the Indies with Columbus, not one of these brothers had been born. Hernando: what an upstart! Thinks himself the best of us because his mother was the only one our father wed.

"How many troops in these divisions?"

"The main force is at the city. He said the King has fifty thousand there."

"Impossible! The man was raving."

"So I thought too. But nothing I did to him changed his mind. I even made him tell me how Peruvians count, to make sure we understood each other. Felipe confirmed it. They reckon as we do—in tens, hundreds, thousands, and tens of thousands. He said Atawallpa has 'five ten-thousands' at Cajamarca. He didn't know the strength of the other force, but it is smaller."

"You, Brother, and I—and our young friend here"—the Old One fixes Waman with a warning stare—"we keep these numbers to ourselves."

A low buzz of unrest has already arisen from Pizarro's men. Many are for going straight to Cusco. Why bother with Atawallpa at all;

why not sack the Peruvian capital and sail away laden with gold? The more timid are for turning back to Chira, where they were beginning to enjoy the idle life of overlords.

The Commander weighs the risks. God and fortune favour the bold. Atawallpa must not think him hesitant. Nor must he be given time to learn more about the Spaniards. Sacking Cusco has its merits but would take too long. Besides, Atawallpa is said to have another strong army there.

With a mix of dread and awe Pizarro ponders the Peruvian military machine. Roads, garrisons, and warehouses stacked to the roof with weapons, uniforms, footwear, tents, dried food. What organization! Nothing like it has been seen in the Indies, not even in Mexico. Perhaps nowhere on Earth since the Romans.

He takes some heart from the Peruvians' biblical weaponry—maces, pikes, clubs, slings, bows. An armoured horseman is worth a hundred Indians, Hernán Cortés told him in Spain. "Never fight unless you can deploy your horsemen," he said. "That was my worst blunder."

Pizarro recalls the details of Cortés's great mistake: how the Mexicans snared him in the canals of their island city, killing two-thirds of his army at a stroke. He'd had twelve hundred Spaniards—six times Pizarro's strength—yet lost eight hundred in one night. To Indians armed with flint and bronze. Had God not smitten Mexico with smallpox, Cortés would never have recovered.

The Lord has already swept that terrible scythe across Peru. Even so, it will take a miracle to win this land.

The Commander summons Waman and a lowland lord he trusts, a man who hates Atawallpa for things done in the civil war.

"Felipillo, ask this fine fellow if he has the courage to go ahead to Cajamarca as my spy."

The lord laughs and spreads his hands. "No! I do not have the courage. To go as a spy is death." He stares up at the white fangs of the sierra, thinking for some time. "But I might be willing to go as the Old One's ambassador to speak with the Inca, if he'll see me. Perhaps I can learn what he intends."

"Good man!" Pizarro responds, clapping the lord on both shoulders. "In that Indian skin of yours beats the heart of a Spaniard. Here's what you do. First, if you spot any troops on the way send runners back at once. Second, when you speak to Atawallpa, tell him how well we Christians treat everyone who befriends us. Tell him I make war only on those who make war on me. Now pick out your hammock men. Leave right away."

Pizarro mounts the steps of a roadside shrine and looks down on his small army. On battered helmets and rusting mail, on ragged clothes—half Spanish, half Peruvian—on the footwear of man and horse worn down by granite roads. On the crazed, truculent eyes that meet his stare. What a band of rogues! They may not frighten Atawallpa, but at times, by Christ, they frighten him.

He calls Friar Valverde to his side and holds aloft his battle standard—the royal arms on one side, a plumed knight on the other, a crude piece of embroidery done cheaply in Seville, yet good enough to stir these murky souls. He shakes it at the men.

"Listen to me! Never be daunted by any heathen horde. Even if we Christians were fewer and those arrayed against us were much more, the help of God is mightier than all."

Valverde says a blessing. Pizarro announces that Cajamarca—not Cusco—is the goal. Any who wish to return to the base at Chira are free to do so, without shame. Better to cut the rot out now.

To his relief, only a dozen take this offer. The rest—some one hundred and seventy all told, with sixty horse, thirty war-dogs, three hundred Nicaraguan auxiliaries, and a baggage train of slaves and women—march east into the Andes.

Waman leaves the only Peru he knows, the seaboard plain of sand and heat, for a vertical land of rock and mist. The Maker has piled mountains one upon another, each summit merely a crest before a higher summit, and a higher. The Incas have made the only flatness: terraces built anywhere that walls can cling, can hold up strips of earth and corn to the sky. And the road itself: a river of stone flowing against them, carved into cliffs, tunnelled through spurs, raised on viaducts, and often, where steepest, cascading towards them in stairways hewn from living rock. He is thankful when fog blows in, shrouding these terrors, shrinking the giddy landscape to a cocoon of ghostly light.

Nobody rides. Each horseman leads his unwilling mount, the same fear in the eyes of animal and man.

Waman's breath is fast and shallow, overworked lungs fighting to fill his chest. The highlands are so much higher than he'd imagined, steeper and wilder, peaks like colossal beasts lurching above him in the clouds. He feels as foreign here as any Spaniard.

They crest the first pass, unchallenged.

The land opens into a sunny upland roamed by llama herds, the road aimed at another pass, yet higher, beyond a flight of terraces supporting a small town. Above the town stands a fortress, its walls rising from a platform of giant stones. The Old One sends Candía and three others ahead, but they find the fort deserted, eerily still, mist threading through its windows and across a courtyard. *Why?* he asks himself. Why does Atawallpa let us come on?

Pizarro is not much given to doubt or wonder, let alone introspection, but here in this cold, high place with air so thin his heart races even at rest, the unearthliness of Peru strikes him as it never has before. This road, this castle, this kingdom—it all seems impossible, an illusion, a work of enchantment. He thinks of what Candía and Ruiz said after their first sight of Peru: that its wonders and riches were uncanny, as if here in this unknown hemisphere, where winter is summer and north is south, the Devil has built a mockery of Christendom, a kingdom of the Antichrist.

He shudders in the thickening twilight, then chides himself for such light-headedness. He gives orders to spend the night in the great building, and is soon on his folding chair beside a fire of rafters and thatch torn from a nearby roof. Meanwhile some of his men search the town, returning with two elders wrapped in wool against the cold. Atawallpa's troops were here only a week ago, these say, but all men of fighting age are now at Cajamarca.

A young runner arrives shortly afterwards, sent back by Pizarro's spy, who is proceeding to the city. There are no troops on the road.

Cheered by this, safe within the fortress, fed on a stew of dried potatoes and llama jerky, the Spaniards sleep well.

Candía is first up, awakened by cold falling on his pallet from a window. He strides out to warm himself, climbing a terrace in the foredawn mist, treading carefully up corbelled steps that jut from the retaining wall. On the top he finds a stone channel bringing meltwater from a glacier, distributing it to the fort and houses below. He kneels to splash his face and drink from cupped hands, the water thrusting a stiletto of pain into his palate. Mother of God, what cold!

He stands, sees the interpreter has followed.

"Felipe! How do people live here? *Why* do they live here?"

Waman, teeth chattering, gives no answer beyond a sympathetic grin.

"This your first time in the sierra too?"

The boy nods.

"My God, Felipe. Look!"

The mist has fallen below the terrace. They are standing under a deep-blue vault still lit by the last stars. Slowly, Waman turns full circle. The town and the valleys around are smothered by a billowy white surf. He and Candía are alone among volcanoes rising from this sea of cloud like jagged figures wearing icy caps and robes. Among sleeping gods.

The sun leaps from behind a ridge, changing the surf to smoke and fire. Not the gelatinous red sun of the desert, but a blazing sphere of gold in a sky so clear the eye, if it could look, might see the eternal firestorms raging on the solar face.

Both men watch the Andean sunrise in religious awe, the Greek thinking wistfully of Athos and Olympus; the Peruvian understanding, as a transfusion of warmth flows into his body, why the highlanders worship the sun.

The strange creed of the Christians seems to him to have no sway here, no hold upon this land. Or on himself.

While Candía's back is turned, Waman lifts his right arm in prayer and blows a kiss to Tayta Inti, Father Sun. Then another to each peak and glacier. He doesn't know their names, but he knows they are the lords of life in this place, the givers of water, their open veins feeding the land. Apukuna, he whispers, Mountain Lords, I worship you tenfold.

If this is a sin, he will not confess it. Why not have two faiths, as he has two names? One for Christendom. One for Tawantinsuyu.

In late afternoon, at a small pampa with a tarn and stream, Pizarro calls the halt. They camp here, getting into their tents before the sun sets and the frost slinks down from the icefields like a gas.

In the morning two horses are found dead, their bodies frozen to the ground.

On the following day, as they are setting up camp in a somewhat warmer place, a party of uniformed men appears, bearing a palanquin and driving a small llama train. The nearest Spaniards draw their swords, but the newcomers set down the litter and spread their hands to show they are unarmed. The occupant, colourfully dressed and wearing a black fur hat, steps down from his vehicle. Pizarro recognizes him at once: it is Atawallpa's cousin Maytawillka, the envoy who came to Chira.

"Felipe! Bid our friend a hearty welcome. Tell him it gives me much pleasure to see him again. Then have him state his business. Listen well for tricks. Watch out for this one—he's a joker."

Maytawillka gives Waman a nod of recognition. As before, the interpreter strains to follow his speech, formal and guttural, the imperious voice of the Incas. Despite his command of Spanish and the other things he has learnt overseas, Waman feels a yokel here, a mere lowland yokel at that.

"His business, Felipe. What brings him?"

"Maytawillka pays you his respects. He says he comes straight from the great Atawallpa, who sends greetings and these camels for meat. The sacks on their backs are filled with grain, fruit, potatoes. He says the Inca asks what day you will reach Cajamarca, so he can be ready to greet you."

That evening, seated on cushions, they dine in Pizarro's tent,

Maytawillka eating from a golden service brought for his use, aware of the lust—sexual in its intensity—that the metal stirs in the barbarians.

He gives a smoothly evasive account of his cousin's war, emphasizing that the new Inca has routed great armies and killed tens of thousands.

"He would say that, wouldn't he?" Pizarro comments over his shoulder to his brother Hernando.

"Give him this answer, Felipillo. Word for word. Say I have no doubt that Atawallpa is a great lord and a fine soldier." The Old One pauses for Waman to translate. "However, I beg leave to inform him that my lord—His Sacred Catholic Majesty the Emperor Charles—has many greater lords than Atawallpa as his vassals."

"Don Francisco, I beg you. Don't make me say the last bit. It could be the death of us."

Pizarro digs with a little finger in an ear, tugs whiskers on his cheek.

"Very well, then. But you must say King Charles sends me here to bring Atawallpa news of the One True God. If he listens and desires our friendship, it is his! I shall be his ally. I shall help him in his wars and, that done, will leave in peace. For I am merely passing through his kingdom on my way to the Other Sea."

Maytawillka greets the translation with a frozen smile. Perhaps, thinks Waman, he is contriving a clever answer. More likely he's speechless with contempt.

There are sounds of a scuffle outside the tent.

Pizarro's spy—the coastal lord he sent to Cajamarca—bursts in. Without a word, he flies at Maytawillka, seizing the gold discs that cover his ears, trying to break the hidden lobes that hold them.

The Commander springs up and drags his man off, cuffing him hard about the face. "Candía! Get him outside. But keep him by the door." Pizarro returns to his seat, more shaken than the victim. It was bad enough when Maytawillka was attacked in Chira; now it has happened twice.

"Apologise to our guest at once, Felipe. Make a good show of it." He unbuckles the dagger he wears at his waist and presents it, hilt first, to Atawallpa's cousin. "Say that I give him this, my most cherished weapon, to express profound regret for the insult. He may use it with my blessing on that man at dawn."

Once Maytawillka has accepted apology and dagger, the Old One tells Waman to question the offender outside. "Quietly, mind. So our guest won't overhear."

Finding he can talk easily with the coastal lord in Tallan, Waman soon forgets to keep his voice down. He returns to Pizarro's side.

"Don Francisco, your envoy begs forgiveness for losing control of himself. It was because of the danger he saw you in. He says Maytawillka is a liar and scoundrel who is trying to mislead you. He reports that the city of Cajamarca is empty except for troops. All is made ready for war. They wouldn't let him speak with Atawallpa."

"That spy of ours has done more harm than good," Hernando says in his brother's ear. "Let this Peruvian peacock kill the prattler now." He draws a thumb across his throat with a salty laugh.

At this, Maytawillka—who evidently does know some Tallan—rises to his feet and claps his hands. Smiling at Waman and Pizarro, he speaks slowly, pausing between each phrase for Waman to follow.

"This lowlander you sent ahead lacks the wits to know what he saw. Atawallpa was unable to receive him because he is fasting at the hot springs outside Cajamarca. He is secluded there, treating a small wound. He sees nobody. If there are no civilians in the city, it is only because the Inca has cleared the centre for you to lodge there. Of course Atawallpa has an army. How can that be a surprise? He has been at war a long time now. Some of his foes are still at large. This war began long before the bearded ones returned to our country and does not concern them. That is all."

Maytawillka gathers his splendid cloak around him in a womanly way and sits down.

Pizarro runs a finger through a tangle in his beard, catching the eyes of his officers one by one.

"Tell Maytawillka I accept his explanation. Tell him I set far higher value on the word of a fine lord such as he than on the ravings of a courier who can't keep a cool head."

"Surely you didn't believe a word of that?" Hernando says as soon as Maytawillka has left for his own camp.

The Commander lifts an eyebrow in mock surprise that his brother might think him so naive.

Early next morning Maytawillka pays a farewell visit in his curtained palanquin. The roof, shingled with beaten silver to resemble a turtle's back, still wears a fringe of icicles. The breath of the bearers, a dozen sturdy youths in saffron uniform, fogs the air.

"Come and breakfast with me before you go," the Commander says with an obsequious bow. "Afterwards, you can kill the man who insulted you. Or watch us flog him. A Christian flogging is a thing to see!"

Maytawillka declines with a cool smile, saying he must be on his way to Cajamarca. He hands Pizarro a parcel stitched up in an embroidered cloth. "The Inca Atawallpa sends you these as a personal gift. He asks that you wear them the first time you come before him—so he will know which one you are."

A good idea: the barbarians all dress alike. And smell alike too.

He draws the curtains.

"Walk on," he calls to his men.

———

Pizarro goes back to his tent and opens Atawallpa's gift suspiciously, recalling the stuffed ducks. But here are two handsome bracelets of heavy gold. Very well made, as everything is in Peru. And a pair of wooden shoes, lacquered black and red. The bracelets are tight, needing a smear of grease to force over his sinewy hands. The shoes—presumably requisite footwear at the Inca court—are a snug fit.

What Maytawillka knows and Pizarro doesn't is that these are widows' shoes—a private insult—and no good for running, and that Atawallpa intends to shackle the Commander with the bracelets: the gold-eater snared by his desire.

❦ 13 ❧

At last the broad dale of Cajamarca lies below them, an emerald raft troughed in an ocean of stone. The valley opens as they descend, showing itself to be as fully transformed by man as the oases of the coast: an inlay of contoured fields between walls and roads; canals fanning out from a river; terraces climbing foothills; the strips of land blue, purple, and orange with highland crops in bloom. But many fields, Waman sees, are neglected and overgrown—unworked since the Great Death.

In mid-afternoon the city comes in sight: a layered stack of buildings on a rise below the mountains, the highest roofs shining with gold, the whole townscape gilded by a brassy light.

On a slope beyond the city of stone is a greater city of cloth. Thousands of cotton tents pitched in a grid of grassy streets stretching for more than a mile. Here and there are open squares where smoke drifts from cooking fires in long marquees. Llama trains are coming and going, the mess tents thronged with men and women, their voices carried on the wind.

"Ever see such an army in the Indies?" the Old One says quietly, as if to himself.

"The only time I saw such a proud array, Commander," Candía replies, "was when the Turks beset Vienna. And they had fewer tents than those."

Pizarro feels the undertow of fear sucking at his men, sees them crossing themselves, commending their souls to God. Feels fear in his own belly too. He applies the remedy, casting his mind back to Trujillo long ago, to the beggar and his prophecy. *You shall be great.*

"God hasn't brought us here to quail, boys," he shouts. "He has brought us here for victory. Each one of us is worth a hundred of their best. A thousand with Santiago and the Virgin guiding our blades."

Never hesitate. Never give men time to think. Even brave men can flee at the first vacillation. Never give the infidels time to think, either. Or to consult their demons and soothsayers. And don't give yourself too much thinking time, besides. Do now, pray later.

He sends his brother Hernando with a patrol into the city, to see if it's empty as it looks. "Find a good place for us all to spend the night there."

About two miles from the city is a large complex of buildings beneath a tall mushroom of steam. The Inca's baths, where Atawallpa fasts and waits.

"Go ahead to those hot springs," Pizarro tells the other Hernando, Hernando de Soto—perhaps the only man rash enough to follow the order without qualm. "Seek out Atawallpa right away."

Waman loathes Soto, one of the cruellest, a born fighter with an old scar like a centipede up his cheek and the side of his nose. He hopes the Inca's guard will make short work of him. The two Hernandos share more than a Christian name: both delight in bloodshed and rape as much as in valour and gold. It was Soto who raided the Chosen House at Qashas, who beat Maytawillka with his fists at the camp in Chira. He's also the best horseman of all—a skill the Old One envies bitterly. The Commander might not be altogether grief-stricken, Waman suspects, if that hothead got himself killed.

"Take fifteen horse and the interpreter," Pizarro adds, to Waman's dismay. "Speak of friendship, alliance, the love of God. Don't let the Inca provoke you, whatever he does or says. Invite him to visit me tomorrow morning. Tell him we shall carry no weapons when he comes, in token of our friendship. His men should do the same."

Soto leaves at once, Waman riding pillion behind Candía.

Hernando Pizarro returns from the city centre. He dismounts beside his elder brother, the meaty charmless face wearing a look of awe. "Wait till you see it, Francisco! The plaza is bigger than any in Spain." With military thoroughness he gives the details: a main gate and public halls around three sides; rows of doorways opening onto the square like colonnades, tall enough for a horseman to ride through without brushing the crest of his helm. Each hall is more than two hundred yards long, supplied with water piped into stone basins. There is room for thousands. The one weak point, in Hernando's view, is an adobe wall on the fourth side, put up quickly—the mortar still wet—separating the square from a field. In the middle of the plaza is a kind of fort, rising in terraces with a stairway to the top. A larger castle overlooks the city from a height where the houses end.

"Any people? Any troops in these forts?"

"Nobody anywhere. Only some women in a nunnery beside the golden temple. Those buildings are secluded behind high walls. We left them alone. The plaza's the best place for us."

"Why not the castle on the hill?"

"We'd never get horses up there, let alone down. But it's a good spot for a lookout and some guns."

Hernando turns his gaze to the sky. Dark overcast has crept into the valley from the east, hiding all but the skirts of the mountains on that side. The sun, about to set over the western range, appears for a time below the closing lid of cloud, lighting up Cajamarca's buildings against a charcoal sky. Then hail comes, dancing on roofs, catching in shingles and chevrons, revealing the ornamental thatchwork.

"I don't like it, Francisco," Hernando adds, shouting above the din on his helmet. "Those men you sent to the baths are not enough. Some aren't good riders. Some of their horses are lame. If the Indians strike, they could be overwhelmed. Especially in snow."

Francisco tugs at his whiskers unconsciously, a nervous gesture his brother knows well.

"Then pick out more and go yourself. Catch up with Soto before he gets there, if you can."

Hernando calls out a troop, gallops off.

The Commander raises his arm; a trumpet squeals. The weary column—riders, infantry, women, slaves—begins to move with an intestinal, wormlike progress.

The outlanders file into Cajamarca's eerily empty square.

When he comes to Atawallpa's palace at the baths, Soto finds four hundred pikemen formed up along the outer wall. Leaving his squad nearby, he rides in the gate, Candía and Waman close behind.

They are in a long walled garden with a paved patio and shrubs in earthenware pots. Soldiers in check tunics stand along each side, helmets and shoulders scurfed with melting hail. A smell of brimstone wafts from a steaming pool fed by pipes for hot water and cold. The surrounding halls have whitewashed domes, and at the far end is a wooden gallery, massive yet elegant, its posts and beams finished in red lacquer.

There, in the gallery, sits the Only King, on a low golden bench shaped like a puma. He is dressed simply in a fine white cloak with a belt of heraldic squares. His black hair hangs to his jawline, and across his brow is the crimson fringe of vicuña threads—the *maskhapaycha*—which only the Emperor wears. Behind him, in a semicircle, stand lords and ladies.

"You can smell the Devil in here all right!" Soto remarks to Candía, sniffing the sulphurous vapour as they ride past the bath. "And that sultan in white must be Friar Valverde's Antichrist. What rot."

"Best not tempt the Lord God, sir. We may need Him."

The Inca takes no notice of the horsemen as they pull up in front of him, staying in their saddles. Head cocked to one side, he keeps his eyes down, shaded by the royal fringe.

Soto snaps his fingers for Waman to dismount. "Boy! Get down before the King. Then tell him this: I am the Commander's deputy. Our leader sends us here to invite him to visit us tomorrow morning."

Waman climbs down and falls to his knees, using his cloak—now wet and cold—for the symbolic burden. "Sapa Inka—" he begins, stuttering out the curt message.

Atawallpa does not move or give any sign that he has heard. An older man steps up and acts as spokesman: "My lord is fasting and cannot speak with anyone. His fast will end tomorrow. You may go."

Hernando Pizarro now rides in, drawing his roan mare up beside Soto's stallion. The stallion whinnies and tosses his head, nipping her neck, licking the foam at her mouth.

"My Bullyboy's getting frisky. That mare of yours is coming into heat."

"How goes it? What has the Indian said?"

"Not a word. He hasn't even looked at us."

"A sight, isn't he? Sitting there with all the majesty in the world, like the Emperor Charles himself. About the same age too."

"Hard to say. These savages don't age like Christians. Look about you. Not a bald head. And few grey. Valverde says it's because no conscience weighs upon their heathen souls."

"Who is this new one?" asks the Inca's spokesman.

Waman can hardly find voice. Don't these Spaniards know their lives are hanging by a thread? Still on his knees, stifled by his doublet, cold sweat running from his armpits, the interpreter crosses himself, regretting his backsliding prayers in that splendid highland dawn.

"Only King. This is Don Hernando, brother of Don Francisco, the white men's lord."

"His brother?" Atawallpa speaks at last, without looking up. "That's better. Why is he here?"

Hernando Pizarro bends from his saddle and grasps Waman's shoulder hard. "Say my brother sends me to request the pleasure of this Indian's—this King's—company tomorrow in the city square. He wishes to eat and drink with him and become his dearest friend."

"My friend?" Atawallpa returns with a sarcasm the interpreter doesn't miss. "Perhaps my *friend* should be here himself to explain what I've learnt of his brigands' activities. They have been killing my subjects on the coast for months. They've put hundreds in chains. They've fed them to their dogs. They burn people alive. They even boil men down for fat to salve their wounds. I do not need such friends."

Waman softens the Inca's words, substituting *Christians* for *brigands*. Still, Soto reddens furiously.

"This savage will find out what we're made of soon enough. Tell him Maytawillka is a lying rogue. Tell him the men of Tumbes fled like women." He spits on the ground between the horses.

"What is the angry one saying? Is it because my people in Tumbes killed three of them and a horse?"

Hernando Pizarro whispers to Soto, "Those were our losses exactly. The tyrant is well-informed. Let's not waste our breath gainsaying him. I'll give the rest of my brother's message. Then we'll go."

"Now, Felipillo," Hernando resumes, "tell lord Atawallpa that my brother loves him dearly. That we Christians never attack except in self-defence. But if the King has any unquelled enemies we'll crush them for him. My brother will send ten horsemen. Ten will be more than enough. Atawallpa won't need his own troops except to round up those who flee."

Waman translates the boast. Atawallpa looks at the Spaniards for the first time. A scornful smile is his only reply.

"Did you mark that?" Hernando Pizarro says to Soto. "He takes us for nothing!"

The Inca's attention has already left the bearded ones. It is the horses he is watching. Fascinating creatures, a dignity about them. A dignity their owners lack. Meeker than llamas, maybe, but evidently stronger. He will breed them. He wonders if it's true what Maytawillka thought, that the beasts can't run at night. Is that why the barbarians are in such haste to leave?

The interpreter, who is keeping his head down, feels the royal gaze upon him. "You," Atawallpa says. "Who are you? Where are you from?"

"I am Waman, Only King. From Tumbes Province. A small fishing town called Little River."

"Are you their only *chaka*, the only bridge between tongues?"

"Yes, Sapa Inka."

A vile accent. But the boy seems bright. He will be useful.

"Tomorrow you and I will speak. You will tell me everything I want to know. Now tell these barbarians to get down and stand on their own feet. They will dine with me before they go. Their animals may browse the shrubbery in here."

"Tell him it's late," Soto answers. "We must go back, as our leader commands."

The Inca insists they at least have a drink.

"All right. We'll take a quick swallow, Felipe. Just one." The Spaniards nervously dismount.

Two young women of Waman's age, utterly lovely to his eyes, their hair long enough for them to sit on, bring beer, sky-blue dresses swishing about slim ankles. Like Qoyllur, he thinks. And Tika. She'd be like these now.

Lifting his drink in both hands, the Inca smiles thinly at his guests. He tips an offering to Mother Earth.

"Do the same," Hernando Pizarro hisses to Soto. "And pour it all. It may be poisoned."

The Inca drains his tankard in one long, gorgeous, fast-breaking draught. The first drink, besides sulphurous water, that he's taken in five days.

The Spaniards empty theirs on the floor, quickly putting the beakers to their lips, pretending to drink what isn't there. But Atawallpa has seen. He does not mistake the trick for an accident, or for an excess of piety. The bearded ones' deed is unforgivable. They reject his hospitality in front of his women and courtiers. They insult the Earth.

Noting the Inca's anger, Soto slips a jewelled ring from his finger and tries to give it to him. Atawallpa looks away in refusal and whispers to his spokesman. Waman catches a phrase: *the behaviour of these people makes no sense.*

"They may go now," the spokesman says. "The Sapa Inka will visit their leader tomorrow. Tell them to spend the night in the public halls around the square. But they are forbidden to climb the *usnu*."

Waman ponders this word, recalling the raised fountain in the square of Tumbes where he ate his meagre lunch so long ago. It was called the usnu, he thinks; people said the Emperor's men would make long speeches there. "In the city plaza," he tells the Spaniards, "there will be some kind of platform. You are not to use it."

It is nearly dark. Women are lighting lamps in niches along the walls and braziers on the courtyard. Atawallpa's anger seems to subside. Another hushed exchange with his spokesman, who passes on this afterthought:

"Sapa Inka Atawallpa asks one last thing. He would like very much to see your animals run."

The two Hernandos remount and glance at one another. "This one's yours, Soto. You're the better man for it."

Soto nods—the compliment is no more than the truth—and almost before his nod has ended he is standing in the stirrups, hauling on the reins, making his stallion rear and turn on its heels. Leaning into the horse's neck, he brings it down and gallops past the bath towards the gate and the Inca's guard. Most of the guardsmen stand their ground, but a handful shrink from the onrushing beast. Wheeling suddenly, horseshoes sparking on stone, Soto canters back along the courtyard—straight towards the Emperor, emerging like a demon from a nimbus of firelit steam.

Lords spring forward to interpose themselves; a few draw back. At the last moment Soto rears his steed, holds it aloft, then lets its forefeet hammer the paving. So near that the horse's breath stirs the royal fringe on Atawallpa's brow.

Seated and still throughout, the Inca shows no emotion. But he hasn't been this angry since his brother's general took him prisoner. First these barbarians insult him by spilling their drinks; now some of his men show fear—fear of a big black llama with a stinking thief on its back! His wrath is hard to tame. Beer on an empty belly has gone straight to his head.

He inclines the befuddled head so the maskhapaycha eaves his eyes. A strange smell is lingering in the crimson fringe: the grassy breath of Soto's horse.

As soon as the Spaniards have left, Atawallpa calls his highest official, the earl of the Empire's western quarter, a trusted friend. "Apu Chincha, some flinched from the barbarian's display. Did you note them?"

The Apu is alarmed by Atawallpa's icy tone.

"It was only a few, Sapa Inka. A handful. Regrettable, yet understandable. Who could know what that barbarian—"

"Find all who flinched and execute them."

"Execute them?"

"Behead them right away."

"All, Sapa Inka? Even the lords?"

"Especially the lords."

The morning is half gone when Atawallpa awakes in a shaft of sunlight between two concubines on the richly woven chaos of his bed. His head throbs and his heart is racing. It takes some time for a dream to ebb—a recurring nightmare of captivity in Tumipampa, of his brother Waskhar's short-lived triumph. Relief washes over him as reality returns. The events of the evening begin to play before his eyes. The barbarians! And a discussion with his advisers until dawn. Much talk, much drink, little sleep.

His hand strokes a breast, the nipple firm under his palm. The girl murmurs but stays lost in sleep. So does the other. He can't even remember what fun they had, if any. Drinking wasn't the wisest way to break his fast. Atawallpa shakes them awake. "Bring me guava juice and beer, mixed half-and-half. With salt and avocado. A dish of cherries." They take up their gowns and flee.

Today he will kill the barbarians. Though it might be amusing to castrate a few, keep them unsexed to guard his women. Especially that cocky blackbeard on the rearing beast.

At noon, feeling somewhat better, Atawallpa sends his cousin into Cajamarca to tell the Spaniards he will visit them later.

When Maytawillka returns from this errand, he is reassured to find the Inca conferring with Wayta Yupanki and the other advisers. He gives them a message from Pizarro: the Inca should come as soon as possible to enjoy a feast in his honour, which the women are preparing.

"What women? Have they taken Chosen women again?"

"I believe not, Sapa Inka. The ones I saw seem to be slaves and camp followers picked up along their way to cook and share their beds. There are also some townsfolk drifting about in curiosity."

"What are the barbarians doing?" Wayta Yupanki asks his son.

"Lurking in the public halls. Every one of them. The locals are jeering at them, calling them cowards, saying they'll all be dead by nightfall. The barbarians are deeply afraid. I saw some pissing themselves in terror."

"Let them wait and fear," says Atawallpa. "Meanwhile send runners to clear the streets. All citizens must leave until it's over."

"Do you still propose to go today?" asks Wayta Yupanki.

"The sun is high. It's time to put an end to them."

"But why go yourself? Why not send in General Rumiñawi? His men can seize the leaders and bring them to you. You can deal with them when you're . . . rested."

Wayta Yupanki does not trust Atawallpa's judgment, and not only because of his drinking on top of a fast. In his nephew's heart is the rat that gnaws at the sons of all great men: the fear he's not the equal of his father. This makes him rash. And cruel, as he was last night with those who flinched. Not that Waskhar would be any better, the uncle reflects sadly. The Empire's in unsteady hands. If only Wayna Qhapaq were alive!

"Why hurry?" the old man adds. "Time is with you. It weakens them. I think my brother—your late father—would wait for a new day."

"I'm the Sapa Inka now!" Atawallpa glares round the room with bloodshot eyes. "The Inca doesn't hesitate. Nor does he lead from behind. I shall squash them in their nest today like wasps." He rubs his left shoulder to remind his advisers of the wound he's been treating in the baths—a wound from the spear of Hanku, the Cusco general whose head he keeps. The head has now been unfleshed and lined with gold to make a drinking cup. It came back this morning, nicely done.

At length Apu Chinchaysuyu speaks. "No one in this room or in this Empire doubts your courage, Only King. But you could be entering a trap. The barbarians could run you down with their animals. Or shoot you with their blowpipes."

"My dear Chincha, do you think I haven't foreseen all that? We know they have only a handful of the fire-shooters, which are little better than a sling and take much longer to reload. I shall enter the city amid five thousand: enough to fill the square and shield me. The open side has been walled up. The barbarian llamas will have no room to run. We—all of you are coming with me—we shall be on the usnu, high above harm's way. Then Rumiñawi will move in with his troops and round them up."

If we *get* to the usnu, thinks Apu Chincha.

"The barbarians aren't fools," Atawallpa adds, after another draught. (How well beer helps him think!) "They know I have fifty thousand men outside the city. If they attack us they will die. We'll go this afternoon. And"—the Inca pauses for effect—"and to show how little we fear them, we'll go unarmed."

"Unarmed?" Wayta Yupanki gives his nephew a shocked, imploring look.

"That is all."

The Spaniards, too, have had a restless night. Pizarro was not cheered by his brother's report of the meeting at the Inca's baths. Such discipline in native troops? Troops who have never seen a Spaniard or a horse before? To say nothing of the King himself, seated calm as a milkmaid before an oncoming warhorse in full cry.

Waman, also sleepless, saw the Commander walking the halls all night, handing out words of encouragement to his men. Meanwhile, on hills above the city, the myriad lights and campfires of the Inca army sparkled like a star-filled sky.

The bleary men have been at the ready since first light; horsemen in the saddle, the rest standing, fidgeting, whispering, scratching at lice roaming scrotums tight with fear. Townsfolk come by to mock and gloat on their way out of the city, which already feels besieged. Even the Spaniards' women seem to be melting away, as if warned of things to come.

Who has the initiative now? Pizarro asks himself. Not I! We wait on this dog to stir from his kennel.

It is mid-afternoon before Atawallpa and his entourage at last draw near, halting briefly on the road while squads of men and courtiers take their places in the line. Waman and Pizarro watch for a while from the hilltop fort where Candía has set up the guns: six arquebuses and a small brass cannon loaded with grapeshot. Not enough, the Greek knows, to kill more than a few—and only if the rain holds off. As it is, his matchcords smoulder feebly in the highland air. He shrugs. Old soldiers have often lectured him in taverns, saying guns are newfangled toys, for cowards, and the battles of their youth were all the better for not having them.

Pizarro knows his one hope is surprise. It must be soon, before the men lose their edge.

He clutches Candía in a sudden embrace, startling the gunner, who does not expect such intimacy from the old, cold man. "Keep out of sight, Candía, until the King is in the square. Then watch me closely." He draws a scarlet kerchief from his sleeve. "Fire the moment I wave this flag. And not before."

The Commander takes Waman back to the plaza. There they find Friar Valverde gliding among the men in his long robes, sprinkling holy water, holy words. What is in that priest's sour soul? the interpreter wonders. Is he driven by greed like the others? Or is it power: King Charles's promise to make him Bishop of Peru?

Again the Old One walks the echoing halls, cheering his troops with rough eloquence, telling them all are one, there's no gulf between great and small, between the most blue-blooded hidalgo and the duskiest son of a Moor. On this day every man is a knight. A knight of Christ and Santiago!

"Now hear this and remember: take good care not to harm the King. He's mine alone. I must take him alive. If he dies, so will we all. Make no move until you hear the gun. That's your signal. Then you burst out and mow the Indians down like hay."

Candía, in his nest, sees Atawallpa's vanguard start to move: a squadron in red-and-white checkered uniforms, sweeping the road and singing a lilting song. Then other squadrons, each with a different livery, singing and swaying in a graceful dance to flutes and drums. The music floats towards him on the crystalline air. Strange and lovely.

Waiting where he's told—in the gloom at the back of a hall behind the Spanish foot—Waman catches the spraint of fear, an acid sharpness on the usual stench of the unwashed men. That and the smell of the mastiffs, big as pumas and as fierce, fitted with steel jackets and spiked collars, their handlers barely able to restrain them. The interpreter prays his shell of Christian clothes and grime will be enough to save him from their taste for Indian flesh.

The Inca's vanguard comes, marching through the gate, forming up around the square in squadrons. Then two columns of lords in blue tunics—eighty all told—shouldering the Inca's great palanquin with its silver poles, sides of gold, and iridescent canopy fledged with the plumage of hummingbirds. Smaller litters, carrying lords and ladies—even some highborn children—bring up the rear.

Hearing a ripple of surprise and relief among the Spaniards, Waman stands on a bench for a better look. It is true: the Inca's men have brought no weapons; nothing but ceremonial knives of gold with little half-moon blades.

The great square of Cajamarca is filled but by no means crowded. The middle is open. There the Inca sits aloft in his throne at the foot of the usnu steps. This platform is much grander than the one where Waman ate his lunch in Tumbes. It is a tiered stone pyramid, some thirty feet high, with a single flight of stairs to the top, where twin seats are hewn from a single block of stone.

The litter curtains are drawn back, revealing the Intiq Churin, Son of the Sun. All in the square look down, as if afraid to burn their eyes. Waman does not observe this rule. Atawallpa, he sees, is wearing a purple tunic. Around his neck is a collar of emeralds. The crimson fringe hangs at his brow beneath a plain gold band.

The plaza falls still but for the susurration of five thousand breaths. The halls, too, are quiet. Waman hears only a few sharp whispers, the snort of a horse, low growls and whimpers from the war-dogs as their handlers make ready to let slip.

In the square, nobody moves except four men in orange uniforms, who run up the usnu stairs to raise the imperial standard: the rainbow and twin serpents of Tawantinsuyu, United Quarters of the World.

"Where are the bearded ones?" Atawallpa calls out in a loud voice.

"They are hiding, Only King," comes a chorused reply.

He stands up in the palanquin—the effect marred by his unsteadiness—and beams at the assembly. Triumph lights his face.

"Then the barbarians are my prisoners!"

Atawallpa is about to step from his vehicle to the usnu stairs. But at this moment Pizarro approaches on foot with Waman, doffs his feathered helmet, and makes a sweeping bow. "Felipe, beg the Inca to come down so we may embrace and speak together."

For a moment Atawallpa acts as if they are not there. Then he resumes his seat in the palanquin and speaks up without looking at Waman or Pizarro.

"Tell the Old One I shall not stir from here until he has made good all the damage he has done in my Empire. Until he has compensated the families of everyone killed, everyone maimed, everyone raped. Until he has returned everything stolen, right down to the last pair of shoes. The records are exact. I know all."

Having made this demand—a good one, he thinks, for how can

these bandits ever fulfill it?—Atawallpa takes a fortifying swig from Hanku's gilded skull. His attention then turns to a strange figure emerging from a doorway. Short-bearded, yet dressed more like a widow than a man. A black cloak and white undergarment flowing to its feet. A shaved patch on its crown, red with sunburn.

Friar Valverde glides to Pizarro's side, Bible and a document in hand.

"I must read this heathen the Requirement now. Then you may strike with a conscience spotless in the sight of God."

Waman wishes Candía was beside him. The Old One and the priest unnerve him, make him feel callow and vulnerable, as indeed he is. Which should he fear more: Atawallpa or Pizarro? He looks at the rows of lords bearing the litter on their shoulders, sees Maytawillka among them, just below the Inca's throne.

Valverde begins to read:

> *I, Commander Francisco Pizarro, vassal and envoy of the high and mighty Kings of Castile and León, conquerors of barbarous nations, hereby inform you that God Our Lord . . .*

The interpreter's voice is reedy, faltering, as he struggles to translate the untranslatable.

Atawallpa barely listens, drumming his fingers on the litter's sill; then stopping Waman with a raised hand. He leans and speaks to Maytawillka. "The youth is ill-spoken. His accent gets thicker with each word. Make out what he's saying as best you can. Give me the gist of it." He pirouettes his hand for Waman to continue.

"The interpreter is indeed floundering, Sapa Inka," says Maytawillka after hearing more. "But it isn't all his fault. The blackgown is babbling—barbarian fables and nonsense. He speaks of 'one true god' yet says this god is three—a father, a son, and a ghost. Or maybe that makes four."

"Have you seen this god of theirs?"

"I have, my lord. They carry it around with them. An evil thing. A dead man nailed to a piece of wood."

Atawallpa hears the rest of Valverde's speech in growing amazement.

"Imagine, Maytawillka, a holy father called the Papa—the great Potato!" The Inca chuckles at his joke, a weak one in his cousin's view, but Maytawillka gives a flattering smile. "And an emperor who lays claim to the whole Earth," Atawallpa goes on, "because this Papa *gave* it to him? If such a ruler existed, would he send brigands like these as his ambassadors?"

The Inca turns to Waman: "Tell him that the high priest of which he speaks has indeed been generous with others' property. Only a madman gives away lands across the sea of which he knows nothing and that are not his.

"As for the gods the black-gown speaks of, I shall repay his kindness by telling him of mine. Tell him I worship Pachakamaq, Maker of all Space and Time. And the living Sun who never dies, whose power I feel on my face each day. And the Sun's sister and wife, the Moon. And the Earth, who is the mother of all living things. And all other gods and shrines throughout this land."

The Inca folds his arms and looks away; then, as he often does, he has an afterthought.

"Ask the black-gown who told him such things. Where does he get such notions?"

Valverde answers that they are written in the book of God.

"These things are in the *qillqa* of their god," Waman explains shakily. "That sh-sheaf of drawings he has in his hand. The outlanders draw their knots instead of tying them."

"I will see this."

Valverde holds out the Bible. It is taken respectfully by May-tawillka, who hands it up to the Inca.

"This is the thing they value most, is it not?"

"I believe so, my lord. Aside from gold."

Atawallpa smiles. Now is the time to repay the barbarians for their insult of last night. Then he will proceed to the top of the usnu and order Rumiñawi's troops to come and seize them. He opens the book and riffles through it. The sheets are like other barbarian drawings Maytawillka brought from the coast. Sheets covered with marching ants.

"How should I know what this says?" Atawallpa demands loudly, for all to hear. "This tells me nothing!"

He slings the Bible high in the air.

The book flutters like a shot pigeon and drops at the Spaniards' feet.

"Antichrist!" Valverde yells. "Lucifer! Antichrist! Christians, avenge the insult to our Holy Faith. I absolve you all. Santiago!"

Pizarro waves the red kerchief and repeats the war cry: *Santiago!* A thunderclap sounds from the fort above the city.

Several men in an Inca squadron fall to the ground, some writhing, others killed by grapeshot. A few of the wounded keep to their feet, clutching themselves in disbelief where roses of blood blossom on their uniforms. Already the horsemen are charging from the halls, slashing at the Peruvians with long blades, laying open bellies, severing arms and hands raised in hopeless defence. For a time the unarmed Peruvians hold formation as Spaniards scythe them down and war-dogs lunge at their throats. But soon the swaths are wide enough for the cavalry to manoeuvre, wheeling, hacking, trampling.

Then panic is upon the square. Hundreds rush to the main gate, others to a narrow door in the new wall on the far side. So many pile up against the fresh adobe that it falls outward under their weight. Those who flee into the field beyond find no escape: horsemen vault bodies and rubble, spearing Peruvians as if hunting boar.

The cannon sounds again, now aimed beyond the square at the army outside, which is streaming towards the main entrance. But Rumiñawi's troops cannot get in. The great stone gate through which the Inca's litter passed not an hour ago is choked to the lintel by a crush of living and dead.

Amid the sea of chaos is a shrinking island of calm. The nobles around Atawallpa are standing their ground. As the Spaniards cut away those holding the Inca's throne, other bearers step forward to take their place. Some even heft the poles on gushing shoulders without arms. Francisco Pizarro is on foot at the front of this slaughter, slashing at a thicket of flesh and bone that seems to grow back as soon as it is felled, his old body tiring from the work. But he is not alone. Christians are cutting towards the Inca on all sides. It is only a matter of time.

At length, the thinning stand of nobles cannot hold. The palanquin sways and topples. Pizarro leaps upon Atawallpa and drags him out by his hair.

An earspool falls, revealing the misshapen band of flesh.

One man, in frenzy, lunges at the Inca with a knife. Pizarro parries the blow just in time, taking a cut to his left hand.

It is the only wound suffered by a Spaniard.

❖ 14 ❖

There were faces, voices. Waman can't recall the words or even the language. There is a veil between him and everything around. He is dead, his throat torn away by the great hounds, and this misty world he wanders is the land the dead must walk. An underworld of ice and darkness, with nothing to eat but stones.

Felipe! Waman!

Faces. Worried eyes.

Who are you?

You must drink. You must eat.

I can't eat stones.

He's still raving. Or possessed.

Many days and nights have passed. He is no longer in the public hall but in a house, a room with a fresh smell of new thatch, with warmth and sunlight streaming in the door. Beneath him is a sheet, a cotton mattress. Above him a soft alpaca blanket. A real bed. Like long ago in Little River.

Where am I? Is this death?

Not a scratch on you. You must eat. Drink.

When water is put to his mouth it tastes of gore.

Candía brings a local woman, a matronly sort, to nurse him. Sometimes the Old One comes, pacing and wittering. Shaking him awake, the sunken yellow eyes, the lamprey mouth, calling on him to speak to Atawallpa. How can Atawallpa be alive? How can anyone?

Waman walks the room on Candía's arm. His body strengthens. Even when strong enough he will not go outside.

The streets are swept and washed. Palm oil lamps burn in the niches, incense wafts from braziers. But nothing can drive the fetor of spilt blood and bowels from Cajamarca. The dead are gone, they say. Waman does not believe this. He knows the dead are all around, for every night they come to him—men, women, children—walking on stumps without feet, reaching for him with handless arms. Some have no jaws or heads, yet still they speak. *We are the dead.* He murdered them, betrayed them. He is the chaka, the bridge by which bearded demons crossed into the World.

You were only the *lengua*, Candía says. You wielded only a tongue. Besides, you helped overthrow a tyrant who'd already spilt more blood than we did. Why such shock at what Christians do in war? You saw us fight in Tumbes. You know what we do. And you gave the Inca the Requirement. He was fairly warned. He was a fool. Undone by his own pride.

Waman cannot find answers for his friend. Nor for himself. Yes, he knew what could happen. But to know is not the same as to see. Atawallpa, perhaps, had a choice, a moment of decision. His people did not. And this was no battlefield. It was a slaughterhouse. And he, Waman, the Judas goat.

The Commander at the door again, left hand still wrapped in bloody cotton. "Enough is enough, Little Philip. To work! I need you. Every Christian needs you. Without you, we may yet all die. Do as I say, or I'll compel you. You know I can."

Oh, yes. Waman knows how men are made to talk. With fire and iron. With man-eating dogs.

He walks out slowly into the sun, into a city where only some stained walls and paving show that anything has happened. But everywhere he smells death. He sees the oily smoke rising from a gully beyond the town, the stacked gyre of vultures overhead. He hears the madding flies.

The Old One brings the Inca to dine with him and his officers at the royal palace in the city, now the Spaniards' barracks. The banquet is set out in the Inca way, low dining boards on the stone floor of a lamplit hall, dishes and settings arrayed on a long fawn cloth with a red hem. The diners are sitting on rows of cushions. The two leaders, Commander and Inca, preside at the head on golden stools, as if both were hosts—which in a way they are, since the food and service are from the Inca's headquarters at the hot springs. Waman is kneeling behind them, at the ready.

"How much longer must we squat like savages?" Soto blusters as he takes his place. "Those carpenters are idling." He jerks his thumb towards the sound of sawing and chiselling in a back courtyard—the servants' yard, where Waman is kept.

"Have patience, Don Hernando," says Valverde. "With patience one gets to Heaven. God's house must have its furnishings before we do. The cross is done. The altar won't take much longer. Besides, Our Lord Himself dined as we do now."

"Nonsense, Father. Look at any painting of the Supper. The apostles ate like Christians, not Moors. Tables and chairs, man!"

"Those paintings are wrong. Any scholar will tell you."

"Scholars, my arse!" Soto spits on the floor behind him. A girl appears, discreetly wipes the polished stone.

Pizarro claps his hands. "Father Valverde, say grace."

All this time Atawallpa has been sitting quietly, his eyes downcast, his head to one side as always. He still wears the imperial fringe, but his neck is bruised by the iron collar he wears in his prison each night. The Inca does not look up until the Spaniards bow their heads and shut their eyes for the blessing. He watches their priest with a cat-like stare.

Pizarro pours a round of wine, precious stuff brought all the way from Spain. Then: "Christians! Tonight our royal guest does us the honour of dining in our company. Raise your cups and let's hear you. Atawallpa!"

"Atawallpa."

The Inca takes no notice. He seems far away, as if thinking over his mistake.

"Why so sad and silent?" the Commander asks. "Have no fear for your life, Lord Inca. In every land where we Christians have overthrown great kings they soon become our friends. We kill only in the heat of battle, never in cold blood."

"A battle!" Atawallpa replies. "You call that a battle? Spare me your jokes." He gazes bleakly over golden salvers, jugs, dishes, the steaming piles of food, the wild, bearded men. Then, as if to himself: "You were to be my prisoner, Old One. Now I am yours. This is a *pachakuti*, the world thrown upside down."

"What was that?" Pizarro demands. "Did you catch it, boy?"

"He says things have turned out the reverse of what he expected. That you should be the prisoner here, not he."

"Don't shorten his words, boy. And don't embroider them either. I want to know exactly what he says."

"That was all. I swear."

The Spaniard grunts. The Inca sinks back into stillness, eating nothing, not even touching the wine. He sees what Maytawillka noted. (Poor cousin, cut to shreds!) How the Spaniards fondle his dinner service; how they tap the metal and bite it to gauge its purity, rolling their eyes, grinning and whistling.

The first thing they did when they chained him up in the Sun's House after the massacre was begin stripping the temple of its gold. Now they have the gold from his field camp, too—not least this banqueting service.

"Tell me, Old One," he says, the interpreter rendering every word, along with the Inca's mocking tone. "Tell me this. Like all men you seek power over others. I know that if a man lacks power, he may risk his life to get it. I have done so myself. But why gamble your lives for *gold*?"

Pizarro twirls an end of his moustache, unseating a few grains of quinoa and a louse.

"Because, Lord Inca, amongst us, gold *is* power. Gold makes the small man great, the ugly handsome, the old young. It takes away hunger. It takes away fear—even the fear of Hell. Why, with gold the worst of sinners can buy their way to Heaven."

"There's already enough gold in Heaven. It shines on us each day. The metal we find is merely the sweat of Father Sun, the drops that fall to Earth. Why would Heaven need gold?"

"You will understand, Lord Inca, when you become a Christian. Gold pays for charity, for prayers to save our souls. Charity washes away our sins . . . our misdeeds. It frees us from the chains of death. Ask Friar Valverde. He will gladly enlighten you on all matters of our Holy Faith."

As always, Waman has trouble conveying spiritual talk. What Atawallpa hears is this: *Gold is swapped for love and good deeds and chanting to set spirits free. Love washes away misdeeds. Therefore gold undoes the bonds of death. Ask the black-gown. His name is* Walwirti. *He will teach you holy things.*

The Inca falls still, thinking. Then: "You say gold frees men from death?"

Pizarro nods. "If we remember God and the poor when we die we go to Heaven and eternal life. Instead of Hell and everlasting fire."

"Why don't Christians remember their god and the poor while they're alive?"

"Some do, Lord Inca. Friars mostly."

"Can gold buy freedom from the bonds of men?"

"Indeed. The poor man rots in jail for his crimes. The rich man pays the King and walks away. He pays a lawyer too."

"Then I shall give you more gold than your horses can carry to your ships. And you shall give me freedom in return."

Again Pizarro toys with his moustache.

"How much? How soon?"

"The room in the Sun's House where you keep me. That room filled to the niche-line on the walls. It will take about two months."

"Two *months*?" The same thought is in both heads: enough time to escape, to raise a counterstrike.

"My kingdom is far greater than you know. The cities are many and the roads are long. Across deserts, jungles, ranges. From the Blue River in Quito to the Mauli River in Chile is more than three thousand of your miles. So, two months. But I'll fill two further rooms with silver."

Commander and Inca study each other, Pizarro's expression changing like weather from desire to menace under the sparse wool of his beard. Why not? Why not have the Inca do the looting for them?

"You must send your armies far from here. If they kill one Christian you die."

"Agreed, Old One. Rumiñawi will strike camp tomorrow and pull back to the far north. My other generals are weeks away, in Huanuco, Xauxa, and Cusco. I shall tell them to stay put and do anything you command."

"Done!" cries Pizarro, wiping his right hand on his whiskers and holding it out. Atawallpa has seen this white men's custom. He takes the hand, still slick with fat despite its cleansing on the beard.

"Check." It is the endgame. A hint of triumph flits like the shadow of a bird across the Inca's face. He has been Pizarro's captive for more than a month now, and in this time has become the strongest player in Peru, better than Candía, Valverde, Hernando Pizarro. Even a little better than Waman, the former champion, against whom he takes two games in three; though sometimes, when the Inca is more downcast than usual, the interpreter lets him win. Today is one of those days—for the Commander has boasted that ships will soon be landing at Tumbes, bringing his partner Almagro back from Panama with hundreds of fresh troops.

Waman makes a weak move, though he has seen a way to slip from the Inca's check.

"Don't humour me, Waman . . . Pilipi . . . whichever you call yourself today. Take that back and think again. Play like a man. Like an Inca!" Atawallpa lets out a bitter laugh.

The Inca is clever, for all that he made one great mistake. He calls the game *taptana*, which means ambush, and has named the chessmen: *inka* for king, *qoya* for queen, *pukara* for castle, *runa* for pawn, *willaq* for bishop, after the head priests in Cusco. For the knights he says *hatun llama*, big llama, or sometimes *kawallu*, his pronunciation of the Spanish word for horse. He is learning his captors' language quickly. Others, meanwhile, are picking up a bit of Quechua. If things drag on too long the Inca won't need him, Waman fears. And neither will Pizarro. What then?

"Yes," the interpreter says faintly, withdrawing his hasty pawn, advancing a knight.

"Yes what?"

"*Arí, Sapa Inka.* Yes, Only King."

"Do not forget, Waman. This . . . all this"—Atawallpa sweeps his hand around the room, a hand soft as a woman's, with long, buffed nails which tap the pondered chessmen with a dry clacking that at times makes Waman want to scream—"all this will change. I shall get out of here. Out of these . . ." The Inca gestures at his shackled feet. "The World will then be as it was. So you'd be wise to treat me with respect. In your words and in your games. Play straight with me and I shall make you a great man."

Waman cannot help pitying the fallen Inca—his Empire shrunk to this board, these tiny men, tiny castles. He guesses that Atawallpa dislikes him. Why wouldn't he? But he likes the game. Moreover, despite Pizarro's precautions (there is always a Spaniard who has some Quechua within earshot), the Inca uses the games to learn of Spanish ways, Spanish plans, and the land of Spain from which his troubles flow.

As agreed with Pizarro, the Inca's prison is also his treasury, his strongrooms for the gold and silver. The heap of gold has nearly reached the line—the dark painted band that rings all the great halls of the Incas, running through the niches at the height of a man's eye. But the ransom is taking longer to gather than Atawallpa expected, for as the hoard grows—vessels, jewellery, architectural plates and finials, a dozen life-size statues of the dynasty's queens—Pizarro has everything hollow pounded flat.

The Inca is wearing his velvety robe of bat skins, sewn into a

225

single fabric like the night. A cloud of spice surrounds him and at his forehead hangs the crimson fringe. He still has the trappings of kingship, perhaps even of divinity. He is allowed wives and concubines, his blind musicians, his dwarves and jugglers, his personal staff—the women who dress and feed him. But no men save the young postmen who bring delicacies: smoked fowl and rare fruit from the jungle, seafood from the coast. More dangerously, they also bring the Inca reports and carry away his orders, though these are always vetted by Pizarro, using a captive knotkeeper and Waman. This risk must be run, for only through the Inca can the Spaniard wield his brittle power.

Rings within rings. In the middle, Atawallpa. Around him the barbarians. Around them the Empire, little of which they have seen, much less of which they understand. Peru is frozen. And so is the conquest of Peru. It did not end on that bloody afternoon in the plaza. It has only begun.

Atawallpa's armies could still overwhelm the invaders, but if he orders an attack the Old One will burn him alive. The Inca dreads fire above all deaths, and not only for the pain. A Sapa Inka's afterlife is lived in Cusco, where—like all previous kings and queens enthroned in their palaces—he presides, embalmed, over his royal house forever. The Inca can save his kingdom or himself.

Atawallpa's dilemma, it seems to Waman, is like their Christ's. He must give his life to save his World.

The Inca's broad face lifts from the chessboard to the piled gold and the light—the face of a man much older than his thirty years. For a long time he sits like a royal mummy, regal yet lifeless, gazing on things to come. Then his hand lifts to his cheek as if to brush aside a hair. The hand falls wet.

"Your move," he says at last.

"With respect, Sapa Inka, I believe it may be yours. My horse . . ."

"Such shame . . ." the Inca mutters, regarding the youth with sudden revulsion, as if surprised to find him here.

Atawallpa overthrows the board.

One morning the Old One visits the Inca after breakfast and blithely orders him to send for his imprisoned brother Waskhar and have him brought from Huanuco right away. A good move, the Inca admits to himself. I would do the same thing if I were Pizarro. Waskhar will welcome the bearded ones as his deliverers. The Old One will then kill me like a bug and march in triumph to the capital.

He calls for his women to bring beer and coca. He must think.

Waskhar is coming, everyone hears. But shortly before he is expected in Cajamarca they hear that he is dead, slain on the road. How did Atawallpa do it? Waman wonders. How did he send out word for Waskhar to be murdered?

The Spaniards do not understand the quipus and pay less attention to them than they should. But the Commander's own knotkeeper inspected the orders sent to Huanuco, reading them out to Waman, who followed the man's fingers playing slowly over every knot and thread.

Pizarro burns with rage for days, accusing the interpreter of incompetence, even collusion. Again Waman feels the Old One's blows, his hand twisting his ear. "You're much luckier than you deserve, boy." He hisses, a vein in his neck pulsing and writhing like a snake. "Lucky I have need of you. There'll be no visits to the Inca except when I want you there. I should have you flogged to death in the stocks. The knotkeeper too. I'll brook no treason. One more slip and you die."

Alone in his room, Waman soothes his anger as he often does—by thinking of the Spaniard he felled on Gallo Island years ago. If he could do it then, he can do it again now. The fire in his mind lights up the different ways: a sling, a bludgeon, a stolen knife or sword, poison, fire. If the Old One thinks me a traitor, I shall be one. If he plans to kill me, I shall kill him first.

The pack trains of gold arrive less often now, and the pieces they bring are less fine. Fear, boredom, and rumour take root in the Spanish camp. Why is the flow of treasure faltering? Has Peru been stripped of its best? Or are the highways choked with soldiers, massing for attack?

"You must be joking," Atawallpa says when the Old One confronts him with these accusations. "Why are you always making fun of me? Look at me here! How can I and my people be any threat to you?" He gestures theatrically at his new cell, smaller and darker than the last. His punishment for Waskhar's death is separation from his ransom. No longer can he see what is added—and what spirited away. "If you think I'm assembling troops, send out scouts to look. If you think I'm running out of gold and silver, send men to the capital. Let them see the metal in Cusco. Let them oversee its transport here. What's stopping you?"

"There's no time for that. I know how long it would take. A month each way."

"Doubtless you need every man you have to guard me," the Inca taunts. "You have so few. But why not send two or three by hammock? What harm in that? If something happens to them, your loss is small. And it will be fast—faster than your horses." Twenty runners, he explains, go with each hammock, taking turns on the pole day and night. "They'll get there almost as quickly as the post. They could be back in a week."

The Commander lifts a doubting eyebrow, runs a fingernail through prawn-like whiskers.

"A week?"

"Our week. Ten days. Five each way."

The stalemate draws on. The tension grows. Pizarro sends three men to Cusco as Atawallpa suggested. One comes back right away to say all is quiet. The others linger in the capital, protected by Atawallpa's occupying army while they sack the Empire's richest temple, Qorikancha, the Golden Court. This they have to do themselves, with ladders and crowbars, for no Peruvian will raise a hand against the Sun's greatest house on Earth.

It takes three hundred llamas to carry the metal to Cajamarca.

Atawallpa's ransom is now fulfilled.

But as the Cusco gold arrives in Cajamarca, so does Pizarro's partner. Almagro marches into the city at the head of a fresh army, more than doubling the occupiers' strength. The Spaniards rejoice wildly. Waman watches with foreboding as One-Eye reins up in the square, doffs his helmet, exposes his bald scalp and ice-blue stare.

Pizarro gives the order for the melting to begin. Llama trains come from the jungle, unloading mounds of charcoal. Smiths brought from the Empire's mines and workshops build furnaces on a hillside, placed to catch the wind.

The furnaces burn round the clock for weeks, lighting the cold, clear nights of the Andean winter like fiery volcanoes. Day by day, the goldsmiths reduce their lives' work to ingots. Pizarro and Almagro oversee everything together, united by mistrust as much as partnership. At the end there are seven tons of gold and thirteen tons of silver, each bar weighed and stamped by the royal taxman who assays the whole and levies King Charles's fifth. More than once the taxman shakes his head in disbelief: Atawallpa's ransom is worth more than all the treasuries in Christendom.

The Inca himself is half forgotten, his value leaking away as the hot metal of his bargain runs into the moulds. The tension now is between the Old One and Almagro, who argue daily over how much each partner and his men should get. Waman hears their anger rumbling like thunder in the palace halls. The men, too, are uneasy, dissecting each rumour of what a horseman, a foot soldier, an armourer—even a tailor—will receive.

At last the distribution is made. From dawn until dusk in the palace courtyard, men file past a table where the royal taxman and his notaries sit behind ledgers and pots of ink. Waman watches from the shadows for a while. It is hard to read faces behind beards, but the eyes say much: alight with anticipation, greed, impatience. As each man signs or makes his rough mark, chests of wood and rawhide are brought out and handed over.

Each footman receives a man's weight in precious metal: ninety pounds of silver, forty-five pounds of gold. Horsemen get a double share, and officers more according to their rank. The Old One awards himself thirteen. On top of that he claims a "gift"—the Inca's palanquin—worth another two shares or more. The beggar's prophecy has come true: Francisco Pizarro is the richest conqueror on Earth.

That night Waman and Candía climb to the summit of the usnu. They sit side by side in its twin seats high above the torchlit crowd in the square, where men are gambling at dice and cards, paying losses on the spot with bars of gold.

"Already it glides from their hands," Waman remarks. The sight disgusts him.

Candía pours cups of beer from a jug. "Cheer up, my friend," he says, wagging his great beard. "To health and wealth."

"And time to enjoy them."

"Time to go where we can spend it! We're like men without arse-holes at a feast." The gunner reveals he earned a horseman's share, and a bit extra for his guns. "But what can I do with it here? The more gold we have, the less it buys. I just saw a horse change hands for the cost of a castle in Spain."

"I don't have to worry about that," Waman says. "The Old One gave me nothing, not even a tailor's share."

"You're not the only one he bilked. Almagro and his men got nothing too! Only repayment for their outlay in coming here and more promises: whatever treasure may lie far ahead in the south. Pizarro can get away with cheating you, Felipe. But he's mad to cheat Almagro."

"Because I'm a gunner," the Greek adds after a silence, "people think I'm deaf. But I'm not too deaf to hear angry soldiers. Almagro's lot want revenge. They want a fight."

The jug is empty. The night deepens as the torches below them die one by one and Pizarro's delirious men drift away to beds and women. Waman hears a metallic chime on the arm of the stone seat. "Take this, Felipe," Candía says softly, sliding an ingot against his hand. Waman slides it back, unsure whether he does so from pride or because the metal is made of blood.

"Go on, Felipe, take it. Are you wary of Greeks bearing gifts?"

"No," says the interpreter, missing the joke.

"Take it," Candía insists. "Now that Peru's awash with gold, anyone without it will starve. Like they do in every other land I've seen. One day that little bar might save your life. Anyway, I'm rich as Croesus. I have a hundred more."

Again he says no, but the Greek will not be refused. Candía tucks the bar into Waman's jerkin, holds it there with a firm hand.

"If you won't keep it for yourself, Felipe, then keep it for me. So I don't gamble it away."

Trusted again (or allowed, at least) to visit Atawallpa now the Spaniards' fortunes have brightened so dramatically, Waman resumes his chess games with the prisoner. One afternoon he finds the Inca cross-legged on the floor, bent over a square of red cloth with coca leaves arrayed in patterns. In his right palm are other leaves, on which he blows a prayer then casts like dice.

Beside him is a young woman who gathers up each throw and prepares a new fan of leaves for Atawallpa's hand. She is young, slim, like the girls who served beer at the Inca's baths on the night before the slaughter. Months ago now, and they feel like years. The light is low, the windows screened. He can't see her face well. Yet she seems familiar. Maybe she was one of those at the baths. Or one who came in and gathered up the pieces when Atawallpa overthrew the chessboard.

Her poise, her straight back as she kneels, reminds him of Tika. But then so does every woman of her age and build. Often he has seen her—in doorways and fields; in shops, markets; crossing streets—the wishful foolishness of a lover whose love is lost, his cousin dissolving into a stranger whenever he gets near. He thinks of how his people all seemed alike when he came back from Spain. Same skin, same hair, same almond eyes. If, one day, he does see

Tika, would he know her? And would she know him, especially now, his face a ruin? *I believe the girl you mentioned may be alive.* He clings to this, spoken haltingly by that woman he questioned in Little River. Yet more than half the World has died. And there must be scores of cities like Cajamarca. Scores of Chosen Houses. Tika could be in any of them. Or none. The odds are against him; against her.

He has seen coca leaves read before, but never by the Inca. He should not be intruding on this ritual. It seems Atawallpa has not yet felt his presence, and Waman begins to catfoot from the room. The girl glances up, lowers her eyes quickly, makes a patting motion with a hand. He gets the impression that to slink out would be unwise, riskier than to stay. Besides, what can Atawallpa do to him—to any-body—now that One-Eye and his men are here?

He sinks to the floor behind them, catching some of the Inca's whispered words: *Mama Kuka, kuka kintu, kananchiktapas yachanki . . .* Lady Coca, choice coca, you know the destiny of all . . .

While Atawallpa scries the leaves, the girl stretches an arm be-hind her towards Waman, beckoning him with fluttered fingers. He approaches softly, crouching, until their fingers touch. She pushes something into his palm. She folds his hand shut and pats it away. Now he should go.

He walks briskly down the street, hears the brass-bound door slammed shut by Pizarro's sentries. As soon as he's out of their sight, he opens his fist and looks. A thread. No knots, no encoded words. Only a plain blue thread plucked from the hem of her dress. A mes-sage; yet no message. Like a blank scrap of paper.

That night he can't sleep, the afternoon at the Inca's prison cir-cling in his mind. She *must* be Tika. Who else would do such a thing, take such a risk? Or is it simply that the girl is desperate, seek-ing a new protector in case something happens to Atawallpa. As well it may.

The next morning goes by with agonising slowness. He paces in his room, wanders courtyards and halls, walks the city streets for miles, mind roiling, hardly aware where he is or where he's been. He returns to Atawallpa's quarters when the sun, well past the zenith, is touching a certain stone on the curved wall of the temple, the usual time for their games. The girl is not there. Only the Inca. And Pizarro's guards at the door.

Atawallpa takes the first game. Soon after they begin a second— a rapid slaughter of pawns—the same girl comes in with cups and a jug. She waits in a corner. Waman feels her gaze upon him. He tries to return it sidelong, when the Inca's eyes are on the board, but again she's in shadow and he can't see clearly. Just the glint of a silver brooch pinning her shawl.

"You have my permission to look at *me*, Waman," Atawallpa says coldly, studying the chessboard. "But that does not extend to making eyes at my women. Luckily for you, things are not normal now. But soon they will be. Reflect on what I've said before. I can make you a great man. Or I can squash you. As for her"—Atawallpa nods at the girl—"she has no guardian but me. You risk her life with your eyes."

Before Waman can recover and beg forgiveness, the Inca changes the subject to Pizarro and Almagro.

"I hear," he says in a probing tone, "that the Machu Apu and One-Eye are fighting. So far only with words. But will it come to war between them, I ask myself, as it did with Waskhar and me? You know those men, Waman. What do you say?"

"I can't say, Only King."

"Can't or won't?"

"I hear nothing beyond what everyone hears. Since Waskhar's death I've been mistrusted, kept away from weighty matters."

"Then tell me what 'everyone' is hearing."

"Just what you know. That the two have fallen out over the metal."

"What else?"

Waman's mind is on the girl, who must be Tika. He is certain now. But how to reach her?

He struggles to recall any news or gossip for the Inca. "Some say the Old One has persuaded Almagro that there's more gold in Cusco—much more than was brought here. Also, Hernando Pizarro is getting ready to leave for Spain."

"He alone? Why not all?"

"I don't know, Sapa Inka."

"What are they saying about me?"

"Most say you have fulfilled your promise and should be freed. Some say you can't be released safely until all the Christians reach their ships."

"Do any want me dead?"

"I . . . I have heard one or two say this. Only a few."

"Who?"

"I don't know them—men of Almagro's. With respect, I beg you, my lord, to bear in mind that everything I've heard is mere rumour and low gossip. Except Hernando Pizarro's preparations for going to Spain, which are plain to see. He's taking gold for their King."

Atawallpa falls still. Only his eyelids move, nervously batting the lashes in an oddly girlish way. Waman has not seen this tic since the first days of the Inca's overthrow.

"You've spoken plainly," the Inca says at last. "Come back tomorrow. We'll finish the game then. Keep your ears open."

As Waman gets up, bowing and backing to the door, his head strays towards the girl. He reins it just in time.

"You needn't worry about her," Atawallpa adds, undeceived. "She won't talk. She can't. She is *upa*."

"She is simple, my lord?"

"Not simple. Struck dumb. This makes her useful. My women say no word has passed her lips since the night the barbarians attacked. She was a novice in the House of the Chosen.

"That is all."

The sun is slipping behind the mountains when Waman returns to his room on the back courtyard. Carpenters are sweeping up and armourers dousing their forge for the night. The place, he thinks, is starting to resemble a barrio of some Spanish town. Men are playing cards in doorways. Others are drinking, laughing. A fellow from Seville with faraway eyes and a mysterious air has set up shop as an astrologer. He tells fortunes, makes horoscopes, conjures messages from home, speaks with angels in a crystal. Waman has noticed Pizarro himself go in there. Also, at other times, Almagro. Atawallpa isn't the only leader scrying the future.

He lingers by the warm bricks of the forge, thinking over the afternoon. How can he contrive to pick up another message, if there is one? How can they talk? How can he even get a good look at her? Since hearing Atawallpa's parting words, half of him hopes she is *not* Tika. He has heard what happened when the Spaniards broke into the Chosen House after the massacre.

Waman can learn nothing more. There are no more chess games with the Inca. Atawallpa's confinement is now solitary. The Commander and One-Eye have made up their minds. They will not leave Peru. Pizarro won't abandon his prize for hollow honours, like his cousin Cortés. Almagro is in a rush to advance south, where his fortune beckons from the city of Cusco and whatever lies beyond. Atawallpa is no longer needed; he must die. They will rid themselves of this northern tyrant now, and thereby befriend the southern side in the Empire's civil war. In Cusco they'll find a new Inca to set in Atawallpa's place.

At the bottom of the usnu glides the vulturine figure of Valverde, flesh wattled by the highland sun, clutching a silver cross and breviary, overseeing the preparation of firewood around a stake at the foot of the stairway. Here he will burn the Antichrist alive.

It is late afternoon when Atawallpa is brought into the plaza. Pizarro, Almagro, and their officers form an avenue of dignitaries leading to the stake. Behind them stand hundreds more Spaniards, under arms, jostling for a view. The rest of the square is thronged by slaves, townsfolk, and Atawallpa's wives and courtiers, many weeping.

Waman, made to stand beside Pizarro, searches the crowd for Tika, eyes darting like a hummingbird, alighting on each likely face. If she is here he cannot see her. Or, rather, he sees a dozen Tikas everywhere he looks.

Late rays of sunlight are gilding the great square. The last act in the tragedy that began at this hour and place eight months ago is about to be played out.

The Inca, ankles hobbled, is brought up to the Old One and Waman. He is blinking in the glare, his skin almost as pale as a Spaniard's from being locked indoors so long.

"Where is your charity now?" Atawallpa demands, pointing his lower lip at Valverde. "If you burn me, will you not burn forever in your own god's house of fire?"

"Not if I offer you mercy, Lord Inca," the Old One answers. "Mercy is an everlasting gift. Repent and become a Christian."

"And if I do?"

"We won't burn you."

Atawallpa brightens, though only for an instant.

"You will die by the garrotte instead—by throttling—a merciful end. And you'll go straight to Heaven and eternal life. These are the mercies I can give you."

The Inca has foreseen something like this. "To understand your beliefs," he says thoughtfully, "will take time. They must enter my mind. My heart. There is much to learn."

"Ah, no." Pizarro stifles a smirk. "There you're mistaken, Lord Inca. Father Valverde has spoken to you many times of our True Faith. All that remains is baptism. He'll baptise you now."

The Inca is bareheaded, dressed in a simple white tunic and plain sandals, without any trappings of kingship except his bearing. He stands arms folded, stoic, rigid with outrage. And with dread, Waman thinks, seeing the eyelashes flutter again.

"If I do this—if I receive your god—you must promise me one thing. You must look after my wives, my children. There are seven little ones—four girls, three boys. They are in Tumipampa." The Inca recites their names, showing the height of each one with his hand. At this a great surge of pity washes through Waman. He has not loved this man, but he has come to know him as much as any outsider could. He is filled with sorrow and disbelief at this injustice, and with fear—fear of what it may unleash upon the World. Water runs from his eyes. For Atawallpa, for Tika, for the times to come.

"Tell him to forget his brats and whores," Valverde hisses at Pizarro, "and think instead of his immortal soul."

"That I shall do, and do gladly, Lord Inca," the Commander answers Atawallpa, ignoring the priest.

The Inca consents to be baptised—not to escape the flames, or to live forever in the Christians' heaven, but so his body will endure on Earth along with all the kings and queens before him.

Valverde approaches at once, pouring holy water on his head, scattering a pinch of salt and drops of chrism, hastening through the service, afraid his victim may yet change his mind. To convert this heathen monarch is a fine moment in the priest's career. And when reports of the doings in Cajamarca reach King Charles in Spain, the crime of regicide is more likely to be overlooked if the deed was merciful and pious.

Do you renounce Satan and all his works? the priest intones, barely pausing for Waman to translate. Then: *Ego te baptizo in nomine Patris, et Filii, et Spiritus Sancti. Amen.*

The Inca is tied in a wooden chair against the stake.

"My own name!" Pizarro says grandly. "I give the Inca my own Christian name."

Sapa Inka Atawallpa Q'aqcha Yupanki becomes, for these few moments, Don Francisco de Atahuallpa.

The last earthly sound Atawallpa hears is the creak of the strangling cord and the cracking of his neck.

❧ 15 ❧

Atawallpa . . . Atawallpa . . . Atawallpa. A woman's voice deep in the royal palace, calling for the Inca as one calls a lost child. No guard at the door, no one in sight. Only a few lamps burning in niches, their light soaking into grey stonework and red tapestry. *Atawallpa . . .*

He follows the voice through dim halls until he sees her. A royal lady, perhaps a wife or sister—stumbling more than walking—steadying herself with a hand against the wall, twitching aside tapestries and door curtains, searching behind them. She gives a start as Waman comes up, turns with a triumphant smile. "Ah," she says, brushing his forehead with her fingertips, "you are here! I knew you were."

Even in the gloom Waman can see the grief-madness in her eyes, the clawed cheeks, the wild cascade of wet and bloody hair. She has torn clumps from her scalp.

"Come, now. Come with me," says a soothing voice. An older woman enters and settles her arm across the other's shoulders. "Come, now, Ñaña. We'll get some rest, shall we? There's nobody here."

"He is here! Our mighty brother. Look!"

The older one glares at Waman. "How dare you come in," she hisses, her whisper like a curse. He apologises meekly. "I'm the inter-

240

preter," he adds, to explain his Spanish clothes. "I'm looking for someone. The girl who can't speak. Have you seen her?"

Without a word, the lady turns her back. Waman makes his way out into cold night filled with howls and weeping. Everyone else has gone to the square, swelling the dark whirlpool of mourners slowly circling the Inca's body slumped in its chair at the foot of the usnu steps. All are cowled like monks in black shawls. He examines every face he can for Tika, until night drowns the dismal scene.

Tika is looking for Waman. She couldn't find him in the square, nor in the palace. Where else might he be? She sees a wedge of light spilling from the door of the Sun's hall, which the barbarians have made their church. It is crowded and noisy inside, chaotic. She does not go in. Keeping to one side, in shadow, she scans the faces in the temple. The barbarian priest is directing workers to prise up the stone floor and dig Atawallpa's grave. Women are shrieking at him, tugging his robes, saying the Inca must be mummified, not buried. Others are demanding the tomb be much wider, so they can fling themselves in beside their lord. Some are openly mocking, their grief turned to anger. *That's your own grave you're digging. Show us your resurrection! Make your dead god bring our Inca back to life!*

If Valverde understands any of this, he gives no sign. He and his workers are the only men within. Waman is not there. Tika is about to walk on when she spies the outline of a Spaniard coming down the street. She shrinks back into the doorway, ready to mingle with the women inside if the barbarian comes too near. The man stops, looks in. That scarry face. Waman!

She comes up behind him, grabs the tuft on his chin and puts her mouth to his ear. "If you and I are to become friends again, Cousin," she says, "the first thing we do is pluck this out."

She releases the goatee and he whirls around to wrap her in his arms. They lean back, still clasped, study each other in the glow, wonder and joy on both faces. Only then does he realize she has spoken.

"*Achachaw*, Tika! You can speak! Mother Earth!" He buries his fingers in her hair, pulls her face to his chest. "What—" he begins.

"Not here," she whispers, breaking free. "No talking here."

Her hand takes his. She pulls him down the street into the night, away from public buildings, from people. Waman follows like a child, too elated to care where they are going. There are stars between black walls, a breath of fog. Soon he hears the rush of water. She stops here, sits down on a low wall. His eyes make out a pearly glow. The water is loud; they are beside the river.

"Tika. You're all right! Your voice. When did it come back? I thought you were *upa*. I want—"

Her hand finds his face. She rests a finger on his lips.

"Not here," she whispers again. "We'll go somewhere warm. Safe. I know where. Nobody will be there now."

Gripping his hand fiercely, she tows him back towards the centre, the only light a scatter of weak stars between black eaves. He recognizes a back entrance to the palace and takes the lead, treading softly into the familiar courtyard with its smells of sawdust, hoof glue, quenched iron. No light. No sound.

He kindles a flame with flint and steel in his small room, lights the lamp and sets it in a niche, and she comes up to him again, taking his hands in hers, searching his face. She sees him flinch from the light. "You needn't be shy about this," she says softly, stroking the rough skin with a finger. "Half the people in the World have that, or worse. It makes you look . . . lived. Someone who's seen a thing or two. A survivor."

She shrugs off her mourning cowl, lets it drop to the floor. She is dressed as she was in Atawallpa's rooms: blue skirt sweeping to her

feet, dark-red belt at her thin waist, spoon-shaped brooch fastening
her embroidered shawl. Waman takes her chin in his hand, turns her
to the lamp. His gaze roams over the strong cheekbones, the fetching underbite, the spirit and resolve in the set of her jaw. Her lower
lip is full and flushed, her beauty etched by cares, by fine lines on her
forehead and beneath her eyes, by the tiny scar above an eyebrow, the
one visible trace of her burial alive as a child.

Still the same Tika. Or is she? He feels giddy, as if looking down
on her from a height, the piled years since they lived in Little River.
Are the Tika who was, and the Tika who is, the same person? Of
course they are, he tells himself, then doubting. What has she seen
and suffered?

She returns his gaze, looking into one eye, then the other. She
kisses his ruined cheek.

"Here," she says at last, patting his ridiculous beard as if bidding
it farewell, "I've been waiting a long time to give you this." From a
small bag at her waist she draws out a knotted string.

"You'll have to read it out to me," Waman says. "I was never much
good with quipus." Ashamed of this, and keen to impress her, he
adds, "But I'm learning the bearded ones' letters. I . . ." Her face has
frozen. What a foolish thing to say. How she must hate them. His
mind casts back to his capture, those first days on the barbarian ship,
when he feared they might be cannibals or demons. To her they're
still beings from nightmare. And it's all too likely, as Atawallpa im-
plied, that they attacked her.

She puts the string in his hand, closes his fingers around it as she
did with the thread from her hem. "I think even you, Waman, will
be able to read this one." She folds her arms, leans back with a chal-
lenging smile.

Yes. He does know these childish knots. Tied by his own hand
and given to Molina all those years ago in Tumbes.

"How did—"

She stops him with a tap on his lips. "I'll tell you all I can, Waman. But first I must think where to begin. Is there anything to eat or drink in here?"

He glances in the corners, the niches, rummages in a leather chest. "I did have. Must have finished it the other day."

"I'll fetch some from the kitchens."

"No you won't, Tika. We'll fetch it together. I'm not letting you out of my sight. Never again. Not after waiting . . . what? Six years?"

"Six and a half. Since I kicked you on your foolish way." They start laughing and can't stop, embracing like drunks, a shattering cloudburst of laughter, from relief and remembrance, and at the un-fathomable luck of finding each other, of feeling the unknown years between them drop away.

The great halls are deserted, though a light still burns here and there. "If we meet anyone," she warns in a whisper, "you do the talk-ing. Don't forget, I'm dumb. I want to stay that way. Same around your bearded friends."

In the kitchens they find beer and bread, take it back to his room and eat hungrily. They talk most of the night. He is careful not to ask about her time in Cajamarca, how she came to the Inca's house-hold. All that is for her to tell when—and if—she chooses. She says only that she did lose her voice for a while, for a week or two after the massacre, and that the Mother of the Chosen brought her to the palace along with other girls saved from the barbarians.

"I remember you wanting to join the Chosen," Waman says. "After I left I hoped you wouldn't. I hoped you'd stay in Little River with my parents. At least for a year or so."

"You could hardly expect me to make up for you! Not after you just . . . ran off like that. I thought you'd be back soon, a few months at most. We all did. Your grandfather was wonderful. He told us not to worry, that one voyage to the hotlands would be enough to cure you. He was proud of having done that himself, running to sea as a boy. Anyway, I did wait half a year. Then I got the chance to go to Huanuco. It was too good to miss. That's where my people were from. And your mother's. Aunt Chaska backed me. She came with me. And when we said goodbye at the door of the House there, she told me a secret—that she thought she was going to have another child. And she did! I haven't met him, but I know he's lovely and his name is Atuq." She stops suddenly. "Waman, I'm not thinking. How much do you know? About your father and grandfather, I mean."

He tells her what he heard at Little River. She takes a hand in hers. "What you heard is true. I'm so sorry, Waman. Your father was a father to me too." She waits, holding his eye. Then: "Atuq was born just before the sickness struck. Somehow he and your mother didn't catch it. At least your father and granddad lived to see the baby."

Waman says nothing, still in the ruins of Little River. She pauses, looks round the room as if baffled to find herself there.

"That all happened after I went to Huanuco. Chaska didn't know what had become of you until that barbarian turned up. The one your mother married. Turtle, she calls him. I call him Monkey. Her monkey-man. They're all so hairy. I still can't believe she did it. What's he like, really?"

"You mean you haven't met him? How did you get the quipu? When I heard they left Little River for the highlands, I assumed they must have gone to be near you."

"That was their plan. Aunt Chaska sent me a message saying they'd be coming soon—she sent your quipu with it. Then the war between the Incas broke out." Tika stops herself, hands him her empty cup. "Time for another round. And time I let you do the talking. I'm like a broken dam. All those months of silence."

They pour Mother Earth her share, hoist their cups, look at

each other without speaking. She must watch what she says, she warns herself. Best to keep quiet about where Chaska, Atuq, and the monkey-man might be. The less Waman knows, the safer for everyone. She must throw him off the scent, at least for now.

"To our dead," says Tika.

"To Father and Grandfather," Waman answers. "All our lost, wherever they are."

"I doubt they ever made it to Huanuco Pampa," she says after a while. "Not with the war. If they did, they wouldn't have found me. The Chosen House was evacuated when war broke out and we were taken to Cajamarca. No one told us why. Or who ordered it. There weren't many of us left by then anyway."

"Because of the Great Death?"

"Not directly. It never got into my House. We were cut off for a long time. They walled up the door. By the end of it we had nothing but *chuñu* to eat. Disgusting stuff. Hope I never have to live on that again. But we lived, all thousand of us. Other Houses weren't so lucky. Afterwards many of our girls were reassigned to the ones that had been hit hardest—to Cusco, Xauxa . . ." She sighs deeply, puts her head in her hands. "It feels so long ago." Waman nods, thinking of the World he left behind him. Populous, orderly, ruled by Wayna Qhapaq, the great Emperor his father admired.

"Now," Tika says, "tell me what you've been through, whatever you can—it must have been terrible. But first I have to hear about this Turtle your mother took on. The monkey-man."

Waman explains that his knowledge of the barbarian tongue was still weak when Molina was left behind at Tumbes; he can't say he knew him very well. "He was young then, twenty or so. About our age now. The others used to call him a hothead. But they're all hotheads, every one! He helped me learn their language. He was quick to anger—they all are—but kind to me in a rough way. He laughed a lot. My friend Candía—he's the one I've got to know best—he liked Molina too."

"*Mulina?*"

"Turtle's real name."

"What is it, some kind of animal?"

"Don't think so. It's just a town in their land. Most of them are known that way, by where they come from. Or say they do—quite a few have things to hide. The bearded ones aren't all alike. Candía's a Greek, not a Spaniard. A different nation with their own language. No one seemed to know what Molina was. He wouldn't talk about it. Some said he was a Moor or half a Moor, a people conquered by the Spaniards. He's darker than most, almost our colour. Black hair. Good-looking. So if my mother's keeping him clean and plucked, he won't be such a monkey after all."

Tika laughs. They're both tipsy now, with emotion as much as beer. "Aunt Chaska always had good taste in men. Your father was a handsome man. And you're not bad-looking yourself."

Waman's hand flies to his cheek.

"Don't be silly," she says. "You look distinguished. And you're lucky. A lot went blind. Say it again, my step-uncle's real name. And your friend's."

"Molina. And Candía."

"*Mulina. Kantiya.* I like it. They sound almost human. About as human as you are nowadays. Tomorrow I'm pulling out that beard. And you'll have to get rid of those barbarian clothes. They look awful. And they stink."

Now the invaders pull out of Cajamarca, not westward to their ships but south along the highland road to the capital. The journey takes three months. From time to time they are harried by northern troops, losing men and horses. But not enough to stop them. Atawallpa's forces are drifting away to their homes and his officers are losing heart, wondering whom they are still fighting for, and why. Moreover, Pizarro holds hostages: the dead Inca's lords and ladies who survived the massacre, and one of his top generals, Challkuchima.

As the strange killers of Atawallpa move southward, troops loyal to Waskhar's faction come out of hiding to support them, warning of ambush points, helping fight off each attack. The column swells to thousands, a moving village of bearded men on foot and horse, Nicaraguan auxiliaries, Peruvian and African slaves, Inca troops loyal to Cusco, and an ever-growing number of women and camp followers. The Empire's fine roads and way stations, by which it projected its power, now serve its invaders, supplying food and shelter on the march.

The Old One and his leading men have helped themselves to Atawallpa's wives and concubines, Pizarro taking the Inca's sister Wayllas Yupanki as a mistress, the one Waman saw searching for her brother so pathetically the night he died.

Waman and Tika travel together, sharing a tent, sleeping chastely on separate alpaca skins. He has told the Old One that she is his sister, long lost, rescued from Atawallpa's retinue. Without ever having discussed the matter, this is how they treat each other: as siblings. Tika stays voiceless in public. But when they're sure they can't be overheard, they talk; reliving their shared years in Little River, rehearsing family stories, telling each other more and more of their years apart. In Tawantinsuyu. In Spain.

Waman longs to become more than a brother to her, and sometimes he thinks he sees something in her eyes or her manner that hints she might feel the same. But he makes no move. She has not spoken of what happened in Cajamarca, the thing that made her speechless. He will give her all the time she needs. That kind of love, if it ever comes, must come in its own time, its own way.

About a month south of Cajamarca, the royal road crosses a bald plain between two ranges, a high, cold place where a sea of dry grass runs before the wind in waves, and llamas graze under a wide sky that seems very near the Earth. The Andean winter is bitter here, the ground crisp with frost each morning, the roadside ditches glazed with cat ice. Yet the sun is growing stronger, heralding spring and the months of warmth and rain.

One morning before dawn, while the column is still asleep, Waman and Tika climb a small rise to greet P'unchaw, the Day. Tika seems excited.

"There!" she says, tugging Waman's arm once the first rays are lighting up each feature of the subtly undulating plain. "There. Can you see it?"

"What?" Dull with cold and sleep, Waman sees nothing but the same great pampa stretching onward to a faint loom of hills and the white tips of mountains so far away they might be in another land.

"That hill with towers. Can't you see?" She tilts back her head, points her full lips at the horizon. Waman, hands cupped around his eyes, scans the pitiless landscape. Far ahead, where plain meets sky, he makes out a ridge with a row of dots along the crest, bright in the sun.

"That's my city! Huanuco Pampa. Those are the warehouses. We'll be there tonight."

He nods, gives a stoic smile. It will be interesting to see where Tika lived so many years, to have her show him her old haunts, maybe even the former House of the Chosen, normally forbidden to men. But he hopes the column won't linger in Huanuco Pampa. He's wearing every stitch he has, Castilian clothes under his Tumbes tunic and an alpaca poncho. Even his chin, deprived of its tuft, feels chilled. Who would build a city on such a wind-scoured heath? Only the Incas, of course, who can build anything anywhere.

Guessing his thoughts, Tika tries to picture the place through his lowland eyes. What seems bleak and stark to him is to her magnificent. This is her homeland, the province she was born in, where she lived more than half her girlhood, and where she came back as a young Aklla, a Chosen One. True, she found the Inca city colder than her old village of Yaruwillka, which lay in a dale mild enough for corn and fruit and flowers. But it's good to be back in Huanuco Province again. And far from Cajamarca.

They reach the centre in late afternoon. Tika sees that some roofs have burnt in the war, and all are stripped of their golden trim. Yet the buildings still have a fresh-hewn look—unworn, their stone the same colour as the grasslands—the look of a city built by decree where nothing had stood before, so new that parts of the royal compound stand unfinished. Stopped dead by the Great Death.

The excitement she felt that morning curdles to sorrow among these walls. As they make their way across the great square, she sees only hundreds of citizens where before there were tens of thousands. She feels how Waman must have felt when he found Little River an empty shell. What is missing from Huanuco Pampa is its life—townsfolk in deep-red woollens, soldiers and workers in bright uniforms, farmers from surrounding towns, each town with its distinctive headgear, and the splendid palanquins of Inca officials coming and going on the Empire's business.

The Old One assigns billets: Almagro, himself, his mistress, his brothers, and other leading officers within the stone gates of the royal palace; horsemen and their mounts in the public halls looking onto the plaza; the rest in the city's barracks, workshops, and empty compounds.

Tika and Waman are assigned a room in the empty House of the Chosen, along with kitchen staff, other women from the column, and prisoners of particular value. Built to keep men out, it serves equally well to keep them in. This town within a town—some forty halls enclosed by a high perimeter wall pierced by a single gate—is guarded now by Spaniards, as it was by imperial sentries when Tika lived here.

She passes through the narrow entrance in a welter of memory and apprehension. It was this door, bricked up for weeks, that saved the House from the Great Death. Perhaps she owes her life to it. And it was here that she and Chaska said their last goodbye, the sadness leavened by her aunt's surprising news: *I wasn't quite sure, Tika. At my age one can't be. But now I am. There've been three of us on this journey. You and me, and a little one in here. A good traveller.* She took Tika's hand and placed it on her belly, promising to come back with the youngster as soon as they could make the long trek from Little River. And that was that. Neither knew those would be the last days of safe roads, sound bridges, well-kept way stations: the last days of the World that was.

Will she ever see her aunt again? And might she, perhaps, see her *soon*? If Chaska did come to Huanuco with Atuq and Turtle, as her message promised, they would likely have gone on to Puma Hill, the hamlet in the eastern foothills where they had kin. That would have been about two years ago. They may still be there. The only certainty is that they never returned to Little River.

Tika remembers the way well enough. On her first leave from Huanuco Pampa, just before the Great Death, she visited there with two friends from her House. It was only a few days' walk, a bit longer coming back because of a stiff climb into the highlands. She recalls her cousins' welcome, the evening meals spread out on bright cloths above the coca terraces, the jungle far below them, fireflies pricking the night. A warm place with warm folk who helped make the cloistered simplicity of her life in Huanuco easier to bear.

While the column rests and resupplies itself, she must decide what she will do. It wouldn't be hard to slip away while Waman is busy working for the Old One or playing that silly board game with his bearded friend. The guards on the gate wouldn't stop her, wouldn't even know who she is.

The dilemma tears her, splits her in two. How far can she trust Waman? How much of a barbarian has he become? Will he be able to change, abandon his bearded friends, fight them if need be? His longing for her—always obvious, sometimes oppressive—makes her uneasy. How much is it really a longing for his past, for his old home and innocence, a second beginning? If she leaves him now in Huanuco Pampa, she can't tell him why or where she is going. No matter how trustworthy he may be, the barbarians might suspect some plot, might torture him. And if he told them, they would rake the district—not for her, but for Molina.

She could go. But only in silence. Only alone.

And her plan, to call it that, is made of nothing but guesswork and wishful thinking. She might well find Puma Hill deserted like so many towns and villages they've seen along the way. She can't be sure its remoteness will have saved it from the Great Death or the war. Again she thinks of the peace and plenty of the hamlet as she saw it. Yet it's just as easy to imagine Puma Hill forsaken, its roofs rotted, its fields gone to the wild.

She sleeps badly that night, her dreams filled with obstacles she struggles to overcome, only to be confronted by another, and another. Several times she wakes adrift, not knowing where she is, or thinking she is back in the past, a student here in the Akllawasi, and everything since is merely nightmare, an illusory future.

In the morning, after the two of them have eaten in the kitchen, she shows Waman round the buildings where she lived and worked. It's clear from the state of the House that it was used as a barracks in the civil war. And there's more recent damage: barbarians riding ahead of the main column have ransacked the compound for anything of value. The buildings are intact but the contents scattered—the brewery strewn with potsherds and overturned vats—the weaving halls littered with broken spindles and shuttles, tangled skeins, trodden rags. Waman seems to find some detached fascination in these forlorn discoveries. Tika, remembering the House as her home—clean, cheerful, scholastic, orderly—burns with sad anger at the wrecking of this women's sanctuary by the wrath of men.

She falls silent, goes back to her bed for the afternoon but gets little rest. Reality has fallen on her like a net. She feels pinned, inert, drained of will and possibility, her mind racing. Waman is not a free man, and is unlikely to become one until . . . Until what? What will happen when the invaders reach the capital, if they ever do? Another Cajamarca? His fate is tied to the barbarians' fate. And hers to his.

Unless she flees now. But if she abandons him—the one member of her kindred she can be certain is alive—she might find nothing, might become lost in a world destroyed, as she was when the earthquake smothered her young life. It comes to her now that maybe that's why she wanted to join the Chosen in the first place: to belong to a family so big she would never again be alone.

While his cousin is resting, Waman seeks out Candía, feeling eyes upon him—guards' eyes—as he walks the city centre. It's been a while since they had a chess game. The Greek has been busy with military duties, and Waman spends most of his time with Tika, who avoids all the invaders, acting as if she cannot see or hear them.

It is nearly sundown when he spots his friend's bulky figure on the usnu. They embrace at the head of the stairs in the Spanish way, patting backs. "Any idea how long we'll be here?" Waman says. "This city's too cold for me."

"Me too," the Greek answers, bending over the cannon he's placed to command the square. Candía's black mane is shaggier than ever, a single pelt from head to belly, his liquid eyes shining above sunburnt cheeks. "This thing's mainly for show," he says, tapping the bronze barrel. "Never seen such a huge plaza. I'd be lucky to hit the nearest house." He draws himself up to his full height, stares over the city roofs to the darkening pampa. "So flat. So big. If your horse ran away here you could watch him leaving for a week."

Waman laughs, arches an eyebrow. "Time for a game?"

"I'll fetch the set." Candía strides through the twilight to the royal compound.

Waman feels the wind dropping, as it often does at sundown. But the usnu is exposed to every whim of the chill air. He goes to the rear of the unusually large stone platform—a raised plaza itself—where a small open-fronted building offers a sheltered spot. Candía is soon back with board, candles, and beer.

"How are things with your sister, Felipe? Has she got her voice back?"

Waman shakes his head, sorry he must lie to his friend. Candía gives a sympathetic grunt, sets up the board. He pours them a drink. "To Pachamama!" he says brightly, tipping a few drops. It cheers the lad when he acts Peruvian.

"What are they saying about her?" Waman asks. "Almagro's men are always teasing. 'You're a sly one, Felipillo. A girl who can't talk. Lucky dog.' That kind of thing. And they leer at her. I hate it. She fears them enough as it is."

Candía nods. "We'll be out of here soon, day after tomorrow. On to Hatun Xauxa. Pizarro wants me to find iron. The horses' shoes are wearing out. What are the chances, Felipe—is there any in Peru? There must be. How could they build so well without it?"

Waman says there's a word for iron in the language, but he has never seen any. After the next game, which the interpreter wins, he returns to the matter of his 'sister,' sensing Candía is withholding something.

"Well, yes," the Greek admits gloomily, "there's worse than jokes. Worse and more . . . dangerous. I was wondering whether I should tell you. If anyone asks, I haven't." He taps the side of his nose. "They're saying Tika isn't your kin at all. That she was one of Atawallpa's wives. You fell in love with her and did what it took to get her."

Was she a wife or just a helper? Only Tika can answer that. All Waman knows is that she doesn't seem to miss the dead Inca. He picks up a pebble and hurls it into the night. "It's Pizarro and his men who got Atawallpa's wives."

"They're saying you plotted to get Tika by seeding the rumours that Atawallpa was planning an attack. Rumours that sent him to his death." Candía lifts his hands theatrically, puts them around his throat with a gargling sound. "Inca garrotted. Interpreter takes the girl."

"They're trying to blame me for their own treachery!"

"Of course they are. They need a scapegoat. In case King Charles ever charges them with regicide. Almagro's likely the one behind it. Watch out for him."

The Spaniards press on towards the south. Finding no iron in Xauxa, they have Inca smiths make horseshoes out of silver.

In early November they approach the Apurimaq canyon, a deep

gash through the Andes crossed by the greatest suspension bridge in the World, the last obstacle before the capital. The rains have just begun. Without this crossing—a span of two hundred feet stretched high above the river—the way will be impassable. Hernando de Soto is leading the vanguard, one-third of the whole army, rushing onward to the bridge before it can be cut.

The highway approaches the structure by a tunnel hewn through the canyon wall. Soto enters its dark mouth on foot, drawn by a promise of light and the Apurimaq's voice at the far end. Beyond this is a massive buttress, like a ledge, supporting the stone pylons. He is too late. The cables have been burnt. Their stumps, thicker than a stout man's body, are still smouldering like giant cigars.

Soto pulls back, searches the canyon for another way across. The rains have been light so far; he finds one place shallow enough to ford.

Late that day the remnant of Atawallpa's southern army makes a last stand in the hills, killing enough Spaniards and horses that Soto is forced to retreat. But in the small hours after midnight comes the sound of trumpets. Almagro has broken through with reinforcements.

The road to the capital lies open.

FOUR

Cusco and Chile

1533-35

{ 16 }

A pair of young eyes, watchful, long in hiding, observes the
strange procession straggling for leagues along the highway. At
the head are armed barbarian riders, four abreast; then foot soldiers,
hundreds more bearded ones, thousands of auxiliaries; in the rear
come women, chained prisoners and slaves, a pack of hounds, a long
llama train carrying supplies. The watcher notes several palanquins
of Inca lords, their colours and banners, the bearers' uniforms: members of his own kindred and others who opposed Atawallpa. Friends.

The column is nearing the causeway across the Anta marshes.
Cusco is only hours away. Now is the time to end his exile and an-
nounce himself. Now or not at all.

Waman sees the lone figure walking down a grassy hillside on a
course to intercept the Old One and One-Eye at the column's head.
The Spanish leaders also notice the visitor. Though he seems young
and slight, wearing the dress of Indian farmers in these parts—a
simple tunic and yellow cotton cloak—there is something in his
bearing and the boldness of his approach which makes the Commander call a halt.

Always more at ease on his own feet, Pizarro gets down from his
horse and calls for the interpreter. The visitor can be no threat. His
hands are open and empty, and when the wind presses his clothing
to his body there's no trace of hidden weapons; only the slim build of

a youth in his teens. But a youth who seems to have something of importance to say.

By now two other men are coming down the hill—older, judging by their gait; though dressed as plainly as the first, they too have the bearing of lords. "Stay in your saddles," Pizarro tells his officers. "Keep your eyes on that ridge." He signals Candía to ready a musket. The young stranger, now only yards away, is unfazed by these preparations, though he knows very well what they are. He watched the fighting above the Apurimaq two days ago; he saw how these barbarians use their weapons.

"Ah, Felipe. There you are!" the Old One says. "Find out what this Indian wants."

Waman looks at the youth. A few years younger than himself, perhaps seventeen. The sun brightens from behind thin cloud, lighting their faces, and as their eyes meet a spark of empathy passes between them, an unspoken *you too*. Both are marked by smallpox, and in much the same way: each has a light drift of pitting on one cheek, a deeper roughness on the other. Waman is about to speak when he recognizes something else. In the broad highland face, strong-boned and handsome but for its scars, there is a look of Atawallpa.

"Get on with it, Felipillo!" The Old One hisses. But Waman deems it unwise to speak first. This is no lowly farmer. It is an Inca; likely a prince.

"I see you understand their tongue," the visitor says, looking the interpreter up and down. In deference to Tika, and not expecting to have any duties until Cusco, Waman is dressed as the northern lowlander he is, with the unhappy addition of a threadbare velvet cap. "Do you understand me also?" the youth asks.

Waman nods, unsure how to address him. He adds a hesitant *Arí, qhapaq Inka*, Yes, mighty Inca, lowering his eyes.

"Good. I am Manku Yupanki, son of Inka Wayna Qhapaq and Qoya Mama Runtu. I am the brother of Inka Waskhar, half brother to the rebel Atawallpa." He pauses while Waman relays this to Pizarro, going on to say he has lived in hiding for more than a year, ever since Atawallpa's army occupied the capital and began slaughtering potential rivals for the throne. "This is why I am disguised as you see. Tell the Machu Apu here that I have heard great things of him, that I would have preferred to welcome him to my city more fittingly. This will be done in due course. All in Cusco are grateful to the bearded ones for killing the usurper. We shall honour and reward them well. That is all."

By this time the two elders who shared Manku's exile have joined the group. They summon Inca lords with the barbarian column. All give the same answer to the Old One's eager questions. This young Manku is the highest-born prince in the Empire. He will be crowned Sapa Inka in Cusco's great square as soon as members of the royal clans who fled the northern occupation have returned.

Waman hears excited chatter among the Spanish leaders. Broad grins on hairy faces show their delight. Here is the puppet king they need! Better still, this new Inca is a boy. It will be easy to tug his strings.

"Felipe, tell Lord Manku this. That I have come here not for my own ends, but for the express purpose of freeing him and his people from the tyranny of Atawallpa. Those are my Emperor Charles's orders."

Suppressing a skeptical smile (a smile, Waman thinks, much like Atawallpa's when Hernando Pizarro boasted so windily at the Cajamarca baths), Manku steps forward and embraces the Old One in the way he has seen them do amongst themselves. The coarse wool of the beard brushes his cheek; the barbarian's foul smell invades

261

his nostrils. But Manku, too, is delighted. Drawing back, he turns to his nearest kinsman. "They mean to use us," he whispers. "We shall use them."

Waman and Tika have heard many tales of the capital's splendour. Cusco, they expect, will be like Cajamarca and Huanuco Pampa, only more so. A vast city rearing from the land on some height or rise where its buildings can impress from afar. They are up at the front now, walking beside the Old One's dapple mare. Manku leads the way, riding in a double palanquin with one of the Inca lords from the column, dressed now in borrowed finery: a vicuña tunic of brightly coloured squares; gold earspools with emerald inlay; a gilt-bronze helmet framed by a short arc of crimson plumes.

The city itself is not in sight, though outlying towns already climb the hills on either side of the highway. These suburbs are as dense as any Waman saw around Spanish cities, though better laid out, with paved streets and water channels. The road is sloping downward, beside a small river in a conduit, and the steepening hills are contoured with terraces.

Manku calls a halt and steps down from his palanquin. He beckons Waman and the leading Spaniards, bidding them follow him a few yards to a rock outcrop carved like a dais. From here, with outstretched arm, the Inca blows a prayer to the Sun, to snowpeaks on the horizon, and to Qosqo Llaqta, the City of Cusco, at his feet.

Waman feels a light touch on his elbow. Tika has come up silently behind him, lifting herself on tiptoe to rest her chin on his shoulder. They look down on an extraordinary sight, one neither of them could have imagined, or will ever forget. The Empire's capital, Navel of the World and City of the Sun, lies hundreds of feet below. It fills the head of a long valley sunk among mountains on three sides. The fourth side is open to the south, widening out to distant fields and icy ranges. Nearest them is the heart of the royal city, steep roofs and bannered towers laid out between two rivers. One of these is the Watanay, the same stream that runs by the highway, water and road descending to a broad square in the midst of great halls with elaborate thatches and dazzling crests of gold.

The only building Waman thinks he can identify—from descriptions brought back to Cajamarca by the two Spaniards who looted it on Atawallpa's behalf—is a high structure commanding the far end of the city, where the two rivers seem to meet. That must be Qorikancha, the Golden Court, the Empire's greatest temple to the Sun and heavenly powers.

Manku stands on the carved rock as if in trance. He says nothing, takes no notice of the throng behind him, the gleeful backslapping, the greedy laughter, the din of the barbarian tongue. After a year of flight, hardship, and fear for his life, he has returned at last, ready to rule the United Quarters of the World.

The Inca beckons the Old One and an ugly one-eyed man, also old, who is with him. The column moves down into the city, drawing up in the great square, which Waman now sees is two squares divided by the Watanay yet joined by a row of three stone bridges. A large crowd has gathered, cheering, singing, waving banners. The Inca orders his palanquin to halt on the middle bridge. He stands up, raising his hand and letting it fall slowly until there is silence, even among the Spaniards.

A herald announces who he is, though this news has already been brought by runners sent ahead.

"All hear me," Manku begins. "I stand here today on the bridge between the squares of War and Peace. Beneath me runs the River of Years. These outlanders from across the sea are my guests and allies. They have killed the killer of my brother Waskhar. Young though I am, in due course I shall offer myself for election by the royal clans to take my worthy brother's place. In the meantime I ask you to treat these people as our friends. Do anything they ask of you, as you would if I asked it myself. The times of war are ending. A new peace begins.

"That is all."

A month goes by. The Inca kindreds—all those who have survived the plague and civil war—return to the city and declare their support for Manku, their new Sapa Inka. His coronation is about to be held, coinciding with the solstice.

Alone at dawn some days beforehand the young Inca leaves his palace on Granary Terrace, halfway up the escarpment crowned by Cusco's hilltop citadel. Dressed once again as a simple farmer, though for humility now, not disguise, Manku climbs a road that runs beside a stretch of the megalithic ramparts above the city. From here he will walk all day without food or drink, making his way by nightfall to a small mountain shrine where each new Sapa Inka must fast three days, mourning his predecessor, calling on all his forerunners to guide his hand and mind.

The path is in deep shadow, the air cool, Cusco's other river, the Tullumayu, plunging behind him in its conduit. Manku takes a last look at his waking capital, its rooftops draped with scarves of mist. He turns to the huge stones beside him, some big as a house, all flawlessly cut and fitted, a masterwork that took thirty thousand men fifty years to build. He remembers when his father brought him up here as a boy, showed him every feature—the tiered ramparts, the water supplied to the heights by pressure, the towers' tall windows watching over the city. At the top of the middle tower, his father traced out for him the schematic puma in the city's plan, explaining that the fortress is the head of the great cat, with the zigzagging bastions its teeth.

Manku lingers, draws strength from the building: the Empire's might proclaimed in stone. *We did this once; we will do such things again.* He gazes up at the walls sailing against a pink-flecked sky. As sunrise touches the highest tower, he utters a prayer to the Day.

The new Inca hastens on, his slight figure soon swallowed by the hills beyond.

Notwithstanding his outward poise, his youthful sense of invulnerability heightened by surviving the Great Death and Atawallpa's purge, Manku knows he is the youngest ever to become the Only King. Yet there is no one else. All elder brothers by his father's Queen are dead, along with most of his uncles and senior advisers. His half brother Pawllu, now living with him in Waskhar's former palace, will be a help. Born to an Aymara noblewoman from Lake Titicaca, Pawllu is well connected in the southern quarters of the Empire. But even younger, barely sixteen. Together they must deal with these barbarians led by a pair of old men. Old yet strong, shrewd, seasoned by long lives of fighting and intrigue. How to control them? How to rid the World of them when they're no longer needed?

Manku is not seen until the morning of the ceremony, when he returns on a rich palanquin, dressed in full regalia, lacking only the imperial sceptre and the crimson fringe that is Tawantinsuyu's crown. These will be conferred on him later by the high priest, Willaq Uma. That morning, the new King visits eleven previous kings and queens, kneeling before them in their palaces, where they preside everlastingly over the lives of their descendant clans.

In the afternoon these ancestors repay Manku's homage. To the amazement of the Spaniards and the wrath of Friar Valverde, the royal forebears are carried solemnly into the square on canopied thrones like a grand procession of Christian saints. They are set down by their bearers, who stand aside while Chosen women fan the ancient faces and lay out food and drink for them. The royal mummies indeed look lifelike to Waman, their faces and limbs unwithered. Only the eyes give them away: pupils of polished obsidian in whites of sea-ivory.

To Manku's right sits his father, the great Wayna Qhapaq, face pitted and half his nose destroyed by smallpox. On Manku's left is his dead mother, Mama Runtu, at the head of all the queens. A hush falls on the eerie scene.

Waman is trembling, racked with belly pains and fear, despite the Spanish army camped behind him in the other square. Or rather because of it. He will have to translate the Requirement yet again, when the Old One chooses. It could all end in blood.

Although Cusco, like its Empire, has lost more than half its people, the plaza is thronged by royal kindreds and other high-ranking onlookers from across the World. Every window, doorway, and terrace is filled with faces. The best outlook (and the safest, Waman thinks) is enjoyed by those high up on two flat-roofed towers flanking the gate of Wayna Qhapaq's palace.

There begins a heartbeat of big drums, a hooting of pan-pipes, a shrilling of flutes and women's voices. The serpents-and-rainbow flag swishes at the tip of the Roundhouse, the highest tower on the square, roofed by a cone of lacquered wood with a mahogany spire like a mast. Scars where Atawallpa's ransom was torn from the walls are hidden by bunting and flowers, and it is almost possible to believe that everything is as it should be in the City of the Sun.

"Look there, Commander," Valverde says to the Old One. The

friar has just arrived from the Christians' camp after saying a mass to counteract the heathen rites. "Here comes their pagan pope!" A procession is emerging from the mouth of Sun Street, which runs into the square from the Golden Court at the far end of the city. Leading on foot, dressed simply in white cotton, comes the high priest, Willaq Uma. In his hands are staves, one topped with a silver moon, the other with a golden sunburst. Borne in a litter behind him is the Day, a gold statue of a seated boy, recalling the first Inca's descent from the Sun.

Valverde can barely contain his outrage at what seems to him a demonic parody of his own faith. These sights would not be out of place in Rome: the golden image might be Our Lord in youth; the sun-headed stave a monstrance for the consecrated Host. "How the Devil mocks us!" he says for all to hear. "Our sacred duty is to ensure this young Antichrist's reign will be a short one."

Willaq Uma, a sturdy man in middle years, walks up to Manku and makes a short speech. Waman strives to follow. It is an oath in an old form of the language, adjuring the new Sapa Inka to rule for the good of all; to treat the Empire's citizens as one great family; to feed, shelter, and care for them, never neglecting their needs, nor failing to protect them. Once Manku has answered, the older man places the royal sceptre in the smooth young hands and fastens the crimson fringe across the forehead of the Only King.

At this Valverde and the Old One step forward, Waman between them, sweating heavily. Although Manku has agreed in advance to accept the Requirement, forestalling any *casus belli*, Waman's mind is back in Cajamarca. The tossed Bible, the five thousand butchered in an hour.

It is Manku who brings the interpreter back to here and now. Before Waman remembers to lower his head in respect, the Inca meets his gaze for an instant. Again that flow of empathy. *You too.*

War Square now rings with the sound of Castilian as Valverde reads out his rival claim to heavenly and earthly powers. If the new Inca listens to Waman's stumbling translation, he gives no sign. He stares through the three men as if they were not there, still as the dead monarchs around him. At the end he says simply, *Kusan*. It is well.

For Manku this formality is a mere courtesy to the foreigners whose intervention brings a welcome end to the Inca war of succession. It proclaims nothing more than an alliance. Once they have helped him mop up Atawallpa's forces, he will load them with all the treasure they can carry and send them to their ships. Gold is easily replaced. Tawantinsuyu will then enjoy a fresh beginning, united under himself—a new King named for the very first, Manku Qhapaq, the ancient Sunchild looking on through obsidian eyes.

The Inca stands, holding a beaker aloft. He tips the Earth her drink, toasts the mountains and people on all four sides, drains it in one long draught.

A joyful shout from the crowd: *Kawsachun Sapa Inka!* Long live the Emperor!

The Old One lifts his hand, not to signal a massacre this time but in salute. *¡Viva el rey!* he shouts. *¡Viva el rey del Perú!*

And who is that? Waman asks himself. Manku Yupanki? Or Carlos Habsburg?

The usnu in the middle of Cusco's square is a round stone fountain with a golden bowl representing the navel of the World. This begins to fill, as if by magic, with an endless flow of beer.

The celebrations go on for a whole month. So many are the drinkers, and so great their thirst, that the city drains brim with urine where they empty downstream into the Watanay.

It is Tika who points out this remarkable sight to Waman while they are strolling beside the river arm in arm; a little unsteadily, having contributed their share. Like everyone in Cusco, they are divinely drunk. Not the private drinking of Spaniards but a communal drunkenness hosted by the state in honour of its gods and institutions. The Inca's generosity flows to and from the people, repaying them for their duties to the Empire, affirming the Empire's duties to them. Waman is swept up in the collective mood; he feels welcomed home at last. His part in the invasion, which has weighed on him so long, has been lifted, washed away. If Peru and Spain are now at peace, then the war within himself can end.

Standing here with Tika at the riverside, watching the yellow spate of plenty and happiness begin its journey to the sea, he feels she is drawing closer to him, day by day, in her own time, like the returning sun.

Until Cusco, until that moment when she rested her chin on his shoulder, he had felt the reverse. After their reunion in Cajamarca the easy conversations had all been had; the hard ones, unspoken, were a wall between them. He feared he was losing her; that instead of growing towards him, accepting his life as a bridge between worlds, she was withdrawing into herself, shrinking not only from the invaders but from him, from the past they shared.

Now, by the river, in a capital at peace filled with music and song, the barrier between them seems to be crumbling away. That night, they sleep together—not as lovers, but side by side in the same bed like the children they used to be.

The new Inca's first task is to assign lodging to his allies from across the sea. Pizarro is given the Qasana, the largest palace on the square, with a great hall that can seat four thousand under one roof. Manku thought all the bearded ones and their auxiliaries might fit into this comfortably, but the Old One—fearing a trap and keen to assert his standing—keeps it for himself and his retainers, demanding another palace for One-Eye, and a third for his brother Hernando when he gets back from Spain. Friar Valverde (whose application to become Bishop of Cusco is already on its way to Rome) demands the Sunturwasi, the Roundhouse tower, at the eastern corner of the square, for a church.

Manku assents with good grace. The clans affected will grumble, but the palaces are half empty nowadays, and no one lives in the Roundhouse anyway. Besides, it is only for the time being, a small price for peace. Manku also assigns the bearded ones most of the remaining gold and silver from public buildings. The sooner they satisfy that curious hunger, the sooner they can leave.

The Cusco treasure is melted—as much again as Atawallpa's ransom—and shared more fairly with Almagro and his men.

The Inca's priority is to put his alliance with the barbarians to work, to crush all pockets of resistance to his rule. To this end he raises an army and marches north for many months, pursuing the rump of Atawallpa's forces with Almagro, Soto, Candía, and sometimes Pizarro himself. Cusco he leaves in the untried hands of his half brother Pawllu, given the office of Inkaq Rantin, Inca's Deputy.

To their relief, Waman and Tika are also left in Cusco, with a room each on a back courtyard of the Old One's ample billet. There are other interpreters now, both Peruvian and Spanish; none nearly as fluent as Waman, but several good enough for military duties. Only he can handle the work in Cusco, which includes religious translations for Valverde, matters of law and custom, and communications with sixteen-year-old Pawllu.

A brittle calm falls over the city. The two worlds, Inca and Spanish, run on in parallel, largely unaware of each other's workings. Pizarro's conquest has been thwarted by Manku's acceptance of the Requirement. The Peruvian King is now, by Spanish law, a vassal of Emperor Charles. Yet Charles is far away. The young Inca still rules his World.

Manku and Pizarro: each thinks himself master of the Empire. And each has doubts.

The Commander decides to build a city of his own on the coast, far from the Inca capital. The sea is his lifeline and, if need be, his escape. He chooses the irrigated valley of Rimaq, which the locals pronounce as *Lima*.

Several mornings a week Waman has the pleasant task of giving lessons at the Yachaywasi, or House of Learning, the imperial college near Cusco's square. This is interesting work in itself and an honour, for it puts him among the *amawta*, Tawantinsuyu's leading scholars, who train sons and daughters of the royal clans and officials from across the Empire. Waman teaches Spanish to these pupils— who sit cross-legged in rows, heads bent, fingers busy over their quipus—and Quechua to any Spaniards wishing to learn. The latter, who bring folding chairs and sheets of paper, are mainly notaries and friars.

The Empire rewards Waman for this work with food, beer, fine cloth. His bearded students—wealthy men now—sometimes offer to pay him in silver and gold. But he never takes it. The metals have no worth as currency. In the highlands everything is by government issue and reciprocal exchange; even the copper money of the coast is seldom used. Instead, he asks for help with reading and writing. He has the alphabet already but is still baffled by the spelling. Sometimes more than one sign is used for a single sound, while other signs have several sounds within them. And his informants do not always agree on which to use, even when writing their own names. Is it Xéres or Jérez, Valencia or Balenzia? Then there are numerals of two different kinds, Roman and Arabic. Besides these hurdles there's his own clumsiness with quill and ink.

Still, after a couple of months Waman can write Castilian. He finds he can also make the letters work for Quechua. These accomplishments he keeps to himself. It would be unwise to flaunt a skill lacked by the Commander.

Best about his mornings at the House of Learning is that Tika often comes too. With the departure of so many barbarians to the north and the seaboard, her confidence has returned. She is no longer silent in public. And things are easier between them. Although they still treat each other as siblings, Tika is warmer, more trusting; sometimes (it seems to Waman) even a little flirtatious. Yet if he is rash enough to flirt back she withdraws, stiffly polite. At first he wondered why she came to the college—he can teach her all the Spanish she wants at home—but she is there mainly to polish her Quechua, to mingle with other students and pick up the fine speech of the capital.

Tika does not tell Waman this—it would only get his hopes up—but since coming to Cusco she has found new respect for her cousin. During their months on the road she saw him as a prisoner. She pitied him. And pity left no room for admiration. But here at the House of Learning, Waman has become a somebody, an expert on the foreigners with whom the new Inca has chosen to cooperate.

She likes the imperial school, its cloistered atmosphere reminiscent of her years with the Chosen. And when she found out that some of the women who came to study were from the great Akllawasi, the Chosen House on the south side of the square, she befriended them. She spoke of her life in Huanuco, and asked if any Chosen in Cusco might have come from there. The Mothers were reticent at first, perhaps leery of her link with the barbarians through her "brother." The mass rapes in the north have not been forgotten. But once they get to know Tika better, they invite her to visit them. Though well below full strength, the capital's Akllawasi holds thousands. It takes several visits before Tika finds girls—young women now—whom she used to know. After that she becomes a regular guest, often spending her mornings at the school and afternoons in the House, where she takes up a loom beside her old friends or helps with brewing the beer consumed in the city's many feasts and rituals.

One evening Tika and Waman walk up to the fortress, as they often do. They sit on a terrace below the ramparts, gazing down on Cusco's beautiful roofs and, beyond, the grey-green hillsides darkening to purple. He has brought a bag of toasted corn, a flask of beer. They sip and munch, both drowsy from the climb. Her head tilts against his. The first stars show above the icy mountains; night settles on the city below, its darkness broken by braziers in the squares and pools of light from doors and windows. Smells of woodsmoke and cooking drift towards them. Their fingers interlace.

"You know, Tika," he says after a while, "all that time I was in Spain, and at sea, not a day went by when I didn't think of you. I wanted time to roll back, to live that morning over again—the morning I left home. To respond like a man when you kissed me. Not the silly boy I was. I swore I'd come back all grown up and win you. Make you my wife." He pauses, tries to feel her reaction in her touch.

"Oh, Waman." Her chest falls in a sigh. She looks away, sighs again. "We were children! I can't remember what I said. Or did. I suppose I may have thought of you that way—for a moment. Perhaps only to make you stay. Or because I was starting to think about boys, and you were the one within reach. We didn't know what we were doing. Neither of us. We were thirteen."

Crestfallen, he ponders the cruelties of time and space, how two lives can tear apart. How hard it is to stitch them back together.

"Of course I missed you, worried about you," Tika adds more softly. "We all did, terribly. When we heard of the barbarians for the first time—their attack on a trading ship soon after you left—we were beside ourselves. Your parents went to Tumbes many times, searching for any word. Your mother even went to priests and sooth-sayers. They told her you were all right—far away, happy, safe. That's what they always say, isn't it? Chaska's not the kind to be consoled by that for long."

It's still light enough to see her press the heel of her hand to an eye. She misses Chaska, as does he. Finding no words, he offers the bag of corn. He becomes aware of evening sounds rising from the city. A flute on the air, mournful and pure; a horse's whinny; the Angelus tolling from Valverde's makeshift church in the Sunturwasi. She may not have known what she felt for him when he ran away to sea, he thinks, but she seems to know now. And it's not what he has longed for all these years.

"We must go and look for her," he says. "For my mother and the others. We'll start in Huanuco. What about that village you and she both came from?"

"There's nothing there," Tika answers quickly. "I already told you. We saw Yaruwillka, Chaska and I. Nothing but the dead."

"There must be others. Other villages around there where she might be."

"Perhaps, but how can we go? Huanuco's shattered by war. Worse than we saw. I've heard things. At the House."

"We have to see for ourselves. We could leave tonight. Or tomorrow. I'll always protect you, Tika."

"Oh, Waman," she says again, in a tone that makes him feel like a boy. "How can you? You can't protect yourself." She pats his hand. "There's nothing I want more than to find Chaska. To get away from these barbarians. To be gone with you. Someday we will do it. But not now. We're safer here—at the eye, in Manku's city. If they're alive, they'll be safe too. In hiding. But getting there, even if we knew where . . . No. Not until we see how things are going. Or war breaks out in Cusco and we have no choice."

Late that night, sleepless, his mind runs over everything awakened by their talk. Little River. His parents. His desertion. The need to find his mother, the little brother he's never met. As for Tika, he will always love her. He doesn't doubt that she loves him, though not in the same way. Perhaps nothing he can do or become will change her feelings, ever. Perhaps she will never want any man.

He must learn to love her in a way she can accept. And he asks himself whether he too is caged by the things that have happened since he ran away. Whether wanting Tika as his wife has all along been something else: a way into the past, a way home.

{ 17 }

The Inca Manku returns at last to his capital, as do many of the bearded allies who have helped him overcome his foes. The Old One stays in Lima, leaving his interests in Cusco to his brothers Gonzalo and Juan, both young, both bastards, and both troublemakers; Gonzalo the worse. Almagro reappears, deepening the tensions. The rains are beginning: sudden downpours that turn streets into waterfalls, fill drains to the brim, set the twin rivers raging and bucking under their bridges of corbelled stone.

Candía is back in Cusco too, though it's some time before he and Waman are sitting across a chessboard in the great Qasana hall. Milky daylight is spilling through the door from the plaza, where figures hurry by, bent against wind and rain.

"Health and wealth, Felipe!" The Greek tips some beer on the floor.

"And time," Waman says, more cheerily than he feels. His friend has aged: grey strands in the glossy beard, cheeks withered by the highland sun; even, it seems, a measure of sadness or resignation in the dark pools of his large eyes.

"Time. Yes," Candía replies sagely with a wag of his head, nudging a pawn onto the field. "I think time is running out."

With the return of armed men, horses, war-dogs, the capital's months of calm have ended. And many more barbarians are arriving, new would-be conquerors drawn by the fame of Peruvian gold. At night the streets echo with shouts and singing in Castilian. There are scuffles, especially between newcomers seeking their fortune and the first cohort with their hoards of treasure. Treasure they are willing to gamble but not to share. Waman feels thunder building in the city, as it did in Cajamarca during Atawallpa's captivity. When wealth sticks to a few hands, peace can't hold for long.

"I think the Inca Manku would agree with you," Waman says. "Have you seen him lately? He's looking haunted. Like a man who can't sleep. He feels time flowing against him too." Waman refills their cups, goes on. "The other day—I was interpreting for Almagro—Manku asked me why his Christian guests have put up that gallows right beside the usnu fountain. The square may be called War, he said, but it's a place of nourishment not death. I could see how angry he was, though he hid it well. One-Eye said it was merely to remind the Christians to behave themselves."

"A good answer."

"When Manku finds out what it really means, anything could happen."

"How so?" says Candía, thoughts elsewhere. He brings a knight into play.

"They've 'founded' Cusco as a Spanish city—Santiago del Cusco. They've formed a town council. And it seems the first thing every Spanish city has to have is a gallows! They've also been discussing how to cut up the royal halls into houses and shops. That's on the quiet. But I thought you might have heard."

Candía looks up from the board to the window, lets out a low whistle. "Those Pizarros! They don't waste time, do they?" He pours another round, changes the subject. "How's your sister doing?"

"Last time I saw Manku," Waman continues, "he had me stay behind. He said his knotkeepers are counting the bearded ones. A year ago they were hundreds, now they're thousands."

"He's right. Look around you, Felipe. All the new men here. Countless more on the coast. As soon as Hernando Pizarro reached the Isthmus with the gold for Spain, everyone rushed here like flies. Santo Domingo is empty of Spaniards. So's Guatemala. Yucatán. All they do in Panama is throw ships together for Peru. Flimsy as you like—built to last one way. They're landing in droves. A year ago I was the only Greek. There's a dozen of us now."

"So that's what you've been doing since you came back. Greeking with Greeks."

"It's good to speak my own tongue again! You know how that is, Felipe. And one can have enough of Spaniards. I needn't tell you that either. Anyhow, you've been scarce yourself. I hear you've become a scholar."

Waman nods, falls silent. His thoughts are on Tika. The new men are dangerous enough. But worse are the unseen killers they bring with them: smallpox, measles, influenza. She survived the Great Death by isolation. The next outbreak could take her.

"Felipe! You're in check."

Waman glances at the board. He could win, but the need for it has left him. He topples his king. Candía shoots a worried look, says nothing.

"The Inca also asked me this," Waman says. "How much gold and silver would he have to send the King of Spain to make his people stop coming. To make all the barbarians go home. I didn't know what to say. I told him the King of Spain was the least of it, because he takes only a fifth. Then Manku ordered a helper to pour a big jar of corn on the floor and he picked up one kernel. All the gold the bearded ones have taken so far, Manku said, is like this one grain compared with what there is in the World. Answer me as best you can."

Candía makes a wry smile, pours the last of their beer. "What answer did you give? Did you tell him wealth is nothing without health and time to enjoy it?"

"What Spaniard truly thinks so? I said all the gold in all the mountains of Peru would never be enough. Because their King couldn't stop them coming if he tried."

❧ 18 ❧

The rains end, the harvest ripens, filling granaries and silos; the highland winter brings its sunny days and freezing nights. It is the season for campaigns. Troubles in Cusco have worsened. More infighting among the barbarians; more plundering of the people, their homes, their tombs, their shrines. The Inca kindreds are restless, doubting the wisdom of Manku's policy, fearing the barbarians will never go.

Down in Lima, the Commander has had no news of when his brother Hernando will get back from Spain. But plenty of news from Cusco has reached his ears, none of it good. He decides he must leave his beloved new city and make the long trek to the Inca capital.

Within a month he is walking the polished floor of the Qasana. The solution is obvious: Diego de Almagro must leave the city and take most of the new men with him. Now is the time for One-Eye to claim his great prize: the whole southern half of the Empire, still untrodden by a horse's hoof. All of Qollasuyu and Kuntisuyu, including the province of Chile.

Pizarro finds it easier than expected to persuade his turbulent partner. Control of the Inca capital is moot until King Charles's wishes are known. There is little more gold in Cusco anyway. Almagro is keen to move on, to seize his own kingdom at last. Pizarro hopes his partner will indeed find great cities and treasures. Enough to keep him there.

"Take all the men you want, Don Diego," the Commander is saying by the Qasana's main door, where a crowd of Spaniards has gathered. "Lots of fine fellows here." He doffs his plumed helmet and flourishes it at the hopefuls. They raise a cheer. "And Manku's brother Pawllu has offered to escort you to Chile himself."

Waman is in earshot but unseen, he thinks, in the shadows of the hall. "Furthermore," the Old One adds expansively, "I will give you the best interpreter." He turns on Waman like a hound. "Felipillo! Stop your eavesdropping and come here. You'll be leaving with Don Diego soon as Pawllu's ready. Until then you stay in town where we can find you. No wandering in the hills with your whore."

Waman bites his cheek till he tastes blood. *Why me?* He knew Pawllu would be going—he was at Manku's palace when it was agreed—but nothing was said about himself. If the Old One hadn't caught him listening, would this be happening at all? It seems cruel, arbitrary. And foolish. How will the Pizarros deal with Manku without him?

He spends the rest of the afternoon looking for Tika. She is not in her room, nor at the school. She must be in the Akllawasi, but no man sets foot in there. He leaves a message with the sentries on the gate—to meet him behind the Roundhouse as soon as she comes out. He waits on a stone bench in the shade of a cherry tree.

How will Tika take it? Will she agree to flee with him tonight? Could that succeed, with so many Spaniards in Cusco? Or will she want to come to Chile with him? Not likely, not in the midst of the biggest barbarian army yet assembled in Peru. It would be wrong to put her through that, even if she asks. Even if everything goes well. And how can it? This will end in blood and fire.

Tika sees the dejected figure of her cousin slumped on the bench, elbows on knees, head in hands. She touches his shoulder gently, yet he starts. That dead look in Waman's eyes, a look she hasn't seen for some time. She puts an arm around his shoulders. "What's happened?"

The news tumbles from him. She is as shocked as he.

"How long will you be gone?"

"Months! All winter at least. It could be a year."

She sits quietly for a while, gazing at the high walls of the Aklla-wasi as the setting sun creeps up them, lighting the bright colours of the mural on the top storey, under the eaves. Chevrons, frets, flying geese, hummingbirds, pumas. Weaving motifs writ large.

Her cousin is again what he was when they first found each other: a prisoner of the bearded ones.

"There's only one thing to do, Waman. I'll join the House until you get back. I'm sure they'll have me. One of the Mothers already asked. I'll be safe among friends in there."

She gets up, takes Waman's hands, pulls him to his feet. She hugs him fiercely, feeling the knot within. "Tomorrow. I'll join first thing tomorrow. Then it's settled. Then only one of us has to worry. Only me."

Next morning they say tearful goodbyes at the Akllawasi door. He hands over her things. A plan for escaping the Spaniards is already forming in his mind. He knows that much of Chile Province lies along the sea, beyond the highest ranges in the World. Once Almagro's army gets down near the coast he will run, find a trading ship, make his way north by sail. After that . . . he doesn't know.

That night he and Candía get drunk. Waman nearly blurts his

escape plan but reminds himself just in time that while the Greek may be his closest friend, he is also a conquistador.

"I don't much like the smell of this, Felipe. My guess is Almagro wanted you as part of his price for going quietly. But why? He got along fine without you on campaign last winter. And I doubt he'll be needing you to translate any psalms. Walk carefully there. The Commander's a dangerous dog. Almagro is a mad one."

Almost as if he has guessed the turn of Waman's thoughts, Candía adds, "Don't forget that little ingot. Did you get it cut up yet, like I told you?"

"I did. In ten bits. Neatly done by a goldsmith on Peace Square. The old fellow looked wretched—said he'd melted his life's work into bars like that." Waman pats his doublet. Six gold squares sewn into the padding, the other four swapped for small items easier to exchange: copper axe coins, steel blades, a few emeralds.

"Good lad. Mind you don't lose it."

Almagro musters five hundred Spaniards in War Square, himself on a tall grey horse by the gallows, helmet hanging from pommel, his bald head shining in the sun almost as brightly as his breastplate. The lone blue eye sweeps coldly over the scene. Waman, given a bay mare too old for war, is also mounted and in Spanish attire, his Peruvian clothes in a swag fastened behind him.

Two silver-roofed battle palanquins are coming into the square from Manku's palace. The first brings young Pawllu. The other holds a man in his forties dressed as an Inca general. To Waman's surprise, this is the high priest, Willaq Uma. Why would he be coming, and as a field commander?

A further surprise has been the arrival in Cusco of One-Eye's son, named Diego like his father. Most call him simply the Boy. Waman recalls seeing him years ago in Panama, a little boy then, one of the first mestizos of that place. Now he looks about fifteen, with the colouring and features of an Indian, easy on his horse, though too slim to fill his armour.

Within a week, after crossing a cold plain, they reach an inland sea lifted high between ice-fanged ranges. Lake Titicaca. Here, in the land of his mother's kindred, Pawllu and his guests are received with feasts and dances. Even so, Almagro's men raid public buildings along the shore, and neither the young prince nor Willaq Uma tries to stop them, despite the thousands of Inca troops under their command. Evidently Manku has told them to let the barbarians take what they want, as in Cusco. The most Willaq Uma can do is save the shrines at Copacabana and on the holy islands of the Sun and Moon, where the first Inca pair came down from the heavens to bring order to the World.

The soldier-priest keeps aloof from the barbarians. Waman is sure he loathes them—has hated them, no doubt, since the very first reached Cusco and jimmied the gold off his finest temple. Pawllu is harder to read. For a while he seemed to fear One-Eye. At times, while interpreting between them, Waman saw the same nervous flutter of eyelashes that Atawallpa had. He wondered if their father, Wayna Qhapaq, also had the tic. Hard to imagine that great Emperor fearing anything. But maybe he did when young. In other respects Pawllu does not resemble Atawallpa or Manku much at all. He is shorter and more thickly set, like many in this region, with a doughy face, broad nose, and heavy-lidded eyes.

Whatever Pawllu may think of One-Eye, he has warmed to the

man's son, Almagro the Boy, who has been showing him what he knows of riding and swordplay. In return, the prince is teaching the Boy how to catch vicuña alive with an *ayllu*: three weights at the end of stout cords which are whirled above the head and thrown to entangle the animals' legs. Pawllu is clearly enjoying the role of local expert; for once, he isn't the younger, the lesser, as he has been in Cusco. That role now falls to the Boy.

Almagro encourages this friendship, sometimes demonstrating Spanish warcraft to the two teenagers himself.

In haste to reach Chile after tarrying by the lake, One-Eye insists on taking the shortest route—across salt flats and bald ranges between Titicaca and the coastal desert. Pawllu and Willaq Uma warn against it. "Tell Sapa Ñawi," they instruct Waman (adopting the nickname he coined), "that the road he favours runs over the harshest country in the World. At this time of year the cold is extreme. We will guide him to a better way, by lower passes and green valleys further south."

Almagro laughs in their faces. "Why should I follow a heathen priest and an Indian barely older than my son?" Waman does not translate the remark, but the two Incas exchange a look that suggests he didn't need to.

One-Eye presses on compulsively, towards icefields and passes far higher than anything Waman or the Spaniards have yet seen. Range after range, with nothing but treeless plains, salt pans, and bitter lakes between them. The fingers of great glaciers claw at the road, and the air is so thin on the passes that Waman's mind loses power over speech, unable to summon any language except a few words of his native Tallan. Only his body still functions at these heights, slow and ponderous as the body of an ox.

Horses go lame and die of frostbite. So do men, beginning with slaves in the baggage train. As each one drops, the Spaniards cut off his head to save themselves unbolting the iron collar. The two Almagros now share a curtained litter warmed by a charcoal brazier, a suggestion from Pawllu they did not disdain. Waman wears all his clothes, Spanish under Peruvian, and his thick alpaca poncho; he drapes a blanket over the saddle to spare his old horse. The Inca squadrons are equipped with heavy cloaks and ear-flapped hats of wool or fur. But many Spaniards, who have little to wear besides armour, see their flesh turn to marble. Some, pulling off their boots, watch in horror as toes come away as well.

With the cold is noise: glaciers cracking like bones; wind keening in frozen weeds and cactus spines. Hail stings like grapeshot in the face. Nobody lives on these high plains but a few herders following llamas and alpacas. As supplies run low, Almagro's horsemen ride out and steal the flocks, killing anyone in their way.

The worst comes at the first outlying hamlets of Chile Province— not far below the snow line on the western wall of the mountains— small oases of huts and grass at the bottom of gravelly ravines stained ochre and green with ore. The Spaniards fall on these settlements, killing men and livestock, tearing down roofs to make campfires, taking the women.

Riding at the rear of the cavalry through wind-carved dunes of snow, Waman comes upon a dozen Spaniards thawing their feet in the disembowelled bodies of people they have slain. He sees others, not far ahead, butchering three stout women merely for this purpose.

Then nothing.

He feels himself being helped to his feet. A Spaniard he doesn't know. "You dropped from your horse, lengua. Like you'd been shot." Waman looks around. The gruesome scene is still there. Bloody snow, war-dogs at the corpses, others lapping vomit where he fell. His own.

He climbs back into his saddle, shaking, avoiding the barbarians' eyes, not answering when they call, *Are you all right?* He rides off a short way, lets his mare drink where a spring breaks from the ice. He cannot watch more, cannot wait until One-Eye nears the sea. He must flee soon, at the first chance, no matter what risk. He must get down to the coast, return in disguise by some roundabout way to Cusco, to Tika. The barbarians appear to him now as they must to her: as demons, creatures of nightmare.

On the following afternoon the vanguard spies a terraced hillside of corn and potato fields, and the first town of any size in Chile.

The houses are empty of people and supplies. Forewarned of what is coming, the townsfolk have barricaded themselves behind some ancient ramparts on a crag, which Pawllu's men call Mawk'a Pukara, the Ruined Fort. Almagro sends Waman up alone with the usual message: that the people have nothing to fear if they will surrender and become the Christians' friends.

At the foot of the ragged walls the interpreter unbuttons his doublet, bares his chest, and spreads his hands to show he is an Indian and unarmed. After a short delay, he is allowed through the gate and taken to a roofless building near the top of the stronghold. From the woollens of those around him comes a smell of smoke and cold sweat, a taint of fear. He is given water and a bowl of potato stew—the best meal he's eaten in weeks.

Waman relays Almagro's message to some leading men who understand the Empire's language. He then tells them it is a lie, that if they leave the fort they will all be killed, even women and children. Their only hope is to stay where they are.

For some time they give no answer. He sees them speaking in their own tongue, looking him up and down, inspecting his strange clothes. Why should they trust him?

"If you wish," he says, "I will stay with you. I will help you hold this place. I'll tell you all I know about the strangers. How best to fight them. They are many. Their beasts run like the wind. Their swords can cut a head off in one blow. They have pipes that shoot fire with a sound of thunder. And they are well armoured, very hard to kill. I am not saying that if you listen to me you will win. The choice may be bleak: to die fighting up here or be slaughtered like llamas down there. The decision must be yours."

Again, the people confer in their own tongue.

"Tell us who you are," an elder woman asks. "If they are as you say—and you are as you say—why haven't they killed you? Why are you with them? Why do you claim to be our friend."

Why indeed? Waman gives the quickest summary he can. "I am their prisoner," he concludes. "I have chosen this moment to escape. Escape or die." In the discussion that follows he hears them saying *Atawallpa, Cusco, Manku* several times. A man takes Waman to a high vantage point on the walls. They can see the Cusco squadrons forming up behind the Spaniards, pikes flying the serpents-and-rainbow.

"Why so many troops of the Inca with those barbarians?"

Waman begins to elaborate, then stops. How to answer them? How much does he truly know? Nothing in the World is what it seems. Is Pawllu here as a hostage? Or are he and Willaq Uma feigning, waiting for the best time to throw their troops against Almagro's? "I am not sure," he admits. "There was discord in Cusco. Among the barbarians and among the Incas. All may be playing hidden games."

It is just possible, he thinks, that if these Chileans put up a good fight, Willaq Uma might attack the Spaniards here. He keeps it to himself: he mustn't tempt these folk with his own hopes.

"Whether you want me with you or not," he adds, "here's what I can tell you. The bearded ones are most dangerous in open country, where they fight from their animals' backs and spear anyone who walks or runs. But you have this crag, these walls, many boulders and sling stones. And I see you have food and water. Do not leave the fort, even if they turn and flee. That's a favourite trick of theirs, to draw you out. Stay behind your walls. Hurl everything you've got when they're in range."

All that day and the next, the fighting raged. On the second evening Spaniards swarmed over the weakest points with ladders. Waman heard the war cries—*Santiago!*—and the wounded invaders calling on their god, or cursing him. He climbed a broken parapet above the breach, threw rocks at glinting helmets until it was too dark to see. Several times he heard that sound from Gallo Island: the low crunch of stone on skull. Spanish losses were heavy, but not enough to stop them cutting down the defenders, room by room. *The interpreter!* He heard. *Find the interpreter! Take him alive.*

But the sky had clouded over and darkness pooled thick in the warrens of the ancient fort. Waman lost his footing on the wall, knocked his head, blacked out. He came round sticky with blood, pinned under fallen men, unsure if he was badly hurt. He could hear Spaniards elsewhere in the ruins—congratulating one another, readying to leave, carrying out their wounded—a shouted order to leave the dead till morning.

Waman lay still, heart pumping. When there were no more voices and the attackers seemed to have gone, he wriggled free. His limbs worked; the blood on him was mostly others'. He took the clothes off a headless Chilean and dressed the body in his own. Remembering the gold and other valuables sewn into his doublet, he searched the quilting still warm with his old life.

He stayed where he was for what seemed two hours, until sure the Spaniards had gone. A thick fog descended, with freezing drizzle. A few survivors began to groan and stir.

A man and girl, perhaps father and daughter—both wounded but walking—led him away through the night into the hills.

FIVE

THE AFTERMATH
Cusco and Vitcos
1544

{ 19 }

Waman greets the Day, then sinks onto the doorstep of his one-room farmhouse, elbows on knees, head thrust out towards the risen sun. He feels like an old man at the end of a long, hard life. How old *am* I? he wonders, totting up the years since Chile.

When he fled One-Eye he thought he'd get back to Cusco and Tika within a year at most. But it has taken eight. Two of them at sea. He remembers making his way down through the Chilean mountains to the desert coast, finding a small port and a ship bound for the north—a two-master like the one on which he sailed as a boy. When the ship reached Chincha, a small craft came alongside with news that the Empire was again at war. After enduring many outrages, Waman learned, and being held prisoner in his own palace, the young Inca Manku had escaped from Cusco, repudiated his alliance with the bearded ones, and attacked them throughout Tawantinsuyu. Manku's armies had killed all the barbarians except for the Old One's force at Lima, which was under siege. Some reports said Cusco was also besieged, others that the city had been burnt along with its Spanish occupiers. The fate of Almagro and Pawllu was unknown.

The ship's master changed plans at once, sailing on north beyond the Empire's border. He picked up provisions in the hotlands, then struck west across the ocean many weeks without sight of land.

Waman gazes vacantly at a snowpeak ruddy with dawn, his mind's eye on very different landscapes: ocean fogs and the smoking cone of a volcano; the scrub hills of the Tortoise Islands, roamed by giants of that kind, prized for their meat and shells; lava-rock headlands where great lizards swam like seals in the surf. Then there were gales that carried them far south to other islands—these high and lush—inhabited by wild men tattooed from head to foot. He sighs at the irony: his childhood dream of a great voyage to the faraway lands his grandfather knew was unexpectedly fulfilled. Yet now he has no family he can tell. Perhaps no living kin at all.

Twenty-two when he fled Chile. So he must be thirty now. Eight years. And they seem like eighty.

His eyes stray wearily over the familiar landscape of his refuge, Pukamarka. Its houses of red clay. A dale green with alders at the foot of the hillside. Stepped fields. Coppery grass marching in waves on the uplands. His home for six months now; if a wanderer like him can have a home. He was lucky to find such a place—only three hours' walk from Cusco, yet far enough to have escaped the wars. The people, much reduced by plagues, were glad to take him on as a helper, to plant and weed, clean sluices and canals.

Twice a month he goes into the capital, disguised as a simple hill farmer—hardly a disguise, for that is what he is. At last it seems safe, more or less. Those who knew him years ago in Cusco are all dead or gone away. All except Pawllu, and Waman takes care to avoid that turncoat Inca. He seeks travellers and traders, shifting beggars, healers, helpers—anyone who might have got wind of his family on the lonely, broken highways of the Empire. For though the capital is burnt and half in ruins now, all roads still lead there: Cusco is still the centre of the World.

Always he asks the same questions, questions he's asked from

Tumbes to Huanuco to Tinta, everywhere he's roamed since returning from the sea. And in the capital—the heart of the wars that raged while he was gone—he is trying to find out what became of the Chosen when Manku fell on the invaders. Did the women escape before the city was unroofed by flames? Has anyone seen an Aklla, or former Aklla—a Chosen One—of his own age and with something of his looks, though unmarked by the spotted death?

A shape is moving in the distance, lurching through mist snagged like wool on the alders at the foot of the hill. A llama? A deer? The shape becomes human, a running figure. As the runner comes nearer, Waman makes out the checkered uniform of the imperial post. Not a common sight these days, especially so far from a main road. He watches from his threshold, interest turning to unease as the postman heads his way. The *chaski* is soon standing before him, fogging the air with heavy breaths, retrieving a letter from a shoulder bag as patched and faded as his uniform.

"Are you Felipe Waman, formerly of Tumbes Province?"

Still sleepy, he is too surprised to deny it, though he doesn't admit it either. His first thought is that the message could be word from Tika or his mother. Word at last.

"I'm instructed to await a reply," the postman adds with self-importance. Waman bids him sit down and brings water. The youth peers into the cup fastidiously, then drinks.

The letter is on fine Valencia paper, folded and sealed. He holds the scab of wax at an angle to the sunlight and makes out the imprint of the Bishop's ring. But there hasn't been a Bishop of Cusco since Valverde fled—to a well-earned death in the hotlands. Eaten by cannibals, they say.

"Who wrote this?"

"I only know who sent it."

The runner has indeed come from the Bishop's palace, where he was summoned by a servant at first light.

Waman hesitates. Over the years he has heard more than once that the Spaniards think their old interpreter Felipillo is long dead. Death suits him; the dead have little to fear.

Now he is uncovered. But how? Who could have recognized him? He looks so different: humble, ragged, his Spanish dress and ways all gone. His youth too. He considers dismissing the postman and fleeing at once to the no man's land along the border.

The World is now partitioned: half of it occupied, half free. Pizarro's cavalry broke the siege of Lima when the Inca troops came down onto the fields for a final assault. Almagro did the same in Cusco, after an outbreak of smallpox crippled the Inca army. In this he was also helped by Pawllu, who betrayed his elder brother and took One-Eye's side. Pawllu's reward was to be crowned puppet Emperor by Almagro. A reward he still enjoys—though the Old One and both Almagros have been dead for years, killed in a string of wars and assassinations as the Spaniards began fighting amongst themselves, more divided than the Incas.

An uneasy stalemate has taken hold. The invaders control the seaboard and parts of the highlands, including Cusco. But the invasion has stalled at the high ranges east and north of the capital, where roads are blocked and bridges all thrown down. Beyond this mountain wall the defiant Manku is the Only King, waging guerrilla warfare from the Empire's eastern quarter, planning to retake the whole.

Waman looks at the postman, thinks again of fleeing. But it's too late. Soldiers on horseback could catch him easily this near the city. And if they failed they'd vent their anger on the farm folk who have sheltered him.

He breaks the Bishop's seal.

To the esteemed royal interpreter, Don Felipe
Waman of Tumbes, greetings

First, it cheers my heart to learn you are alive. Many had
given you up for lost, saying you died in Chile or perhaps
in the wars for this city when the Inca Manku rebelled
and the traitor Almagro made war upon his fellow
Christians.

I write with good news. Our Sacred Catholic Majesty
has sent this kingdom the blessing of a Viceroy, Don Blasco
Núñez Vela, recently arrived at Lima. He brings New Laws
for the protection and welfare of all Indians. In light of this
I have every confidence that this realm will soon be restored
to the order and good government it enjoyed in the days of
its own sovereigns.

You may therefore return to Cusco in full trust and safety,
as have many other displaced persons. Here there is much
need of your services. In particular, the Inca Pawllu, a great
friend and bulwark to us Christians, was recently baptised
into the Holy Faith. We expect that a general conversion of
his subjects will soon follow.

The letter goes on to say that although there are now several interpreters in royal service, none is the equal of Felipe. Only he can be
entrusted with so delicate a task as the translation of liturgy and
scripture.

I therefore have the honour of requesting your help in this holy
work and, God willing, some other matters which I shall set
before you. You may find the latter to be of personal interest
and advantage.

I need hardly add that your cooperation will wipe away all stains with which, during your long absence, some have unjustly besmirched your name.

The Viceroy will learn of your services and, in due course, reward your worthiness and loyalty.

From this city of Santiago del Cusco,
Day 14 of July, year of Our Lord 1544,
Luis de Morales, Vicar-General

Curiosity satisfied, disappointment follows. The letter brings no news of his family. Not unless *personal interest* refers to them somehow.

Waman reads it through more closely. Flattery ("Don Felipe"); a threat (thinly veiled); a hint of sympathy for the plight of Indians; promises of reward. Sometimes Spaniards keep their promises, but only to those who stay useful; like the treacherous Pawllu, who changes loyalties as easily as shirts—forgiven even for taking the Almagros' side against the Pizarros.

He becomes aware of the young postman staring wide-eyed at the sight of a lowly rustic reading the foreigners' tongue. Waman smiles.

"You may tell the sender that I look forward to seeing him next time I'm in Cusco. In half a month."

"With respect," the youth answers, "I am instructed to say that someone will come tomorrow to escort you. He will bring horses."

Waman agrees. To do otherwise would stir suspicion. Once the runner has left, he looks at the letter again and finds a postscript overleaf. This explains that the writer is fulfilling the Bishop's duties for the time being, because "the long troubles of this realm" have hindered the arrival from Spain of a replacement for Bishop Valverde, "that good servant of God, so savagely martyred in the hotlands."

Waman smiles at this old news.

They are mules, not horses, and the escort is merely a helper from the Bishop's palace, an elderly fellow, unforthcoming and none too clean. Waman finds this reassuring. He had expected a guard, a Spaniard.

On his undercover visits to Cusco he has avoided authorities of every kind, swimming among the little fish, haunting travellers' camps and markets, drinking dens frequented by servants, the shanties where ruined people live like spiders in the ruined city. And the dismal hospices where friars tend the sick and wounded—many maimed or burnt in the wars, others punished by mutilation for taking Inca Manku's side: men without ears or hands; women with breasts and noses cut away.

Waman hasn't been in a saddle since Chile. After riding a while he dismounts and walks beside the mule, preferring his own legs.

They come at last to Cusco's fortress on the brow of the city. Its three towers are broken now, but the citadel's colossal ramparts show little trace of war, so massive they seem a rock formation rather than a work of man.

Some way below, on Granary Terrace, stands one of the few palaces still roofed in Inca style, though its ridges are clad with copper instead of gold. Formerly Waskhar's, then Manku's, it is now the seat of Pawllu.

He hurries by, down into shattered streets, past blackened walls.

Luis de Morales, Vicar-General, leans against the leather back of his cross-framed chair and snaps his fingers. A boy refills their goblets with a musty wine.

Still tired from the road, Waman sips slowly, saying little. He examines the churchman in the lamplight. Short, plump, with the face of an old baby. Might be any Christian priest. But disarming, jovial, keen to please and be pleased. A good man, then. Or perhaps merely a good actor, since the truly good tend to be ineffectual. It's the ruthless who get things done.

Either way, the Vicar-General is not the dry stick Waman expected from the letter's tone. His welcome to the Bishop's palace has been warm: his mule unloaded, his bag carried, a good suit of Spanish clothes—shirt, doublet, hose, cape—awaiting him in the guest quarters. Even a hot bath before supper, a rare thing among Spaniards, especially priests, for whom cleanliness smacks of ungodliness. Of course, the building was already fitted with this luxury, being the palace of an Inca king from long ago.

"Perhaps chess, Don Felipe?"

"Chess?" Waman says, doubting his ears.

"Why, yes. The king of games. The game of kings!" Grinning, the Vicar-General rubs his palms together quickly, as if making fire with a drill. "Come now, Don Felipe. Nothing like chess to soothe the aches of the road. And I've been longing to play the famous interpreter. I hear you're the best in the land." Without waiting for a reply, Morales fetches a board and set of pieces.

"The best in Peru," Waman says, "was Atawallpa."

"It was you taught him—isn't that so?"

"I and others, my lord." (How should one address a Vicar-

General?) "The gunner Candía—who taught me in Spain—and Hernando Pizarro. Occasionally the late Commander too."

The Vicar-General stares at the ceiling for a moment. "What a tragedy, no? The great Marquis Pizarro cut down like Caesar by assassins." He shakes his head. "I didn't know he played."

"He was better known for other things."

So many ghosts around the chessboard. Atawallpa had named the game *taptana*. Ambush. Perhaps in ironic reference to his circumstances. What a chain of murder and misfortune! Atawallpa garrotted by Almagro and the Old One. Juan Pizarro slain in battle by Manku. Almagro garrotted by Hernando Pizarro (now jailed for that in Spain). Soto dead in a northern land called Florida, seeking a new Empire of his own. Manku's Queen tortured and burnt by Pizarro, along with Willaq Uma. Pizarro cut down in Lima by Almagro the Boy's cabal. Candía murdered by the Boy's own hand. And the Boy beheaded.

All within ten years of the massacre in Cajamarca.

He mourns none of those men but one: his old friend Candía. Dead two years now, though Waman didn't learn what happened until recently. It seems Almagro the Boy made the gunner fight on his side at Chupas against Spanish forces loyal to the Crown. But the Greek used his guns so badly that the Boy accused him of treachery and knifed him on the spot. He thinks of Candía's great beard and glossy eyes, his friendship, his guidance, his generosity. To Candía he owes his life; once certainly, maybe more. Waman sees the Greek by his bedside when he had smallpox in Seville, whittling chessmen, coaxing out the will in him to live. And the gift of the gold ingot, which did indeed save his life in Chile, buying food, buying silences. And passage on that ship bound for Chincha, which saved him from the wars. Where could his friend be buried? Was he buried at all?

The Vicar-General coughs expectantly. "Don Felipe, are you all right? You seem . . . far away. Shall we at least make a start? We can always finish tomorrow, when you're rested."

"It would be an honour," Waman manages, "to share a game before retiring." Morales's doughy face lights up. He sets out the pieces swiftly, humming to himself, squirming in his chair like a small boy.

The interpreter lets him win, and quickly.

Enough of the games of kings.

When Waman comes down next morning he finds another priest with Morales.

"Ah," says the Vicar-General, "here's our interpreter! Allow me, Don Felipe, to present you to Friar Juan Pérez—the very one who baptised the Inca Pawllu—our senior priest in Cusco and a soldier for Christ who has done great things."

Morales explains that Friar Pérez is a Knight of Saint John, one who fought the infidel Turks. And lost presumably, adds Waman to himself, recalling Candía's tales of the holy wars in the Middle Sea.

This warrior-priest is lean, tall, past his best years but strongly made. He is clean-shaven, the skin of his face hanging like old drapes from sharp bones. He has Valverde's knack of gliding silently about the room in his robes; the same dour mien.

"You are aware, perhaps, *Don* Felipe," Friar Pérez begins, a note of mockery in the title Morales flatteringly conferred, "that our Holy Mother Church requires everyone, however virtuous, to make confession no less than once a year?"

"Yes, Father." (Was he aware of that?) "I think so."

"Be that as it may, the Vicar-General"—a nod to Morales—"has already told me of your tribulations, your long captivity among the heathen."

Captivity! A good word, that. Better than *displaced*; much better than *hiding*.

"Moreover, the Church allows leniency with New Christians. Especially those whose deeds speak of their good faith and loyalty. Such as yourself, so I'm told. How long has it been? When did you last confess?"

"It's been . . . more than a year."

"Let us proceed at once, then. Have the goodness to follow me."

Friar Pérez takes Waman to a small chapel within the ancient palace, the room's perfect stonework daubed with whitewash, hung with holy pictures and an effigy of the Christians' tortured god. The confessor sits in a high oak chair, its legs and arms ending in claws. Waman kneels on a cushion at his feet. He catches the priest's smell: damp wool, beeswax, incense, unwashed skin.

"First, do you heartily repent of all your sins and renounce the Devil and his works?"

"I do, Father."

"Have you at any time since your last confession worshipped false gods and failed to keep the Sabbath?"

"If . . . if I may ask your guidance, Father?"

A curt nod.

"Is it sinful to miss the Sabbath when one has no Christian calendar and cannot keep track of the week?"

"Circumstances will be weighed in due course. Sins committed without will and consent are not mortal. They are, however, still sins. You must tell me everything."

There was a time, Waman recalls—as if thinking of somebody else—when he *might* have done this thing, might have given in to the unburdening of his soul by this invasive rite. But not after Caja-marca and Chile. Not after what the Christians did in Cusco to young Manku and his Queen Kura Uqllu. Humiliations, beatings, torture; her rape and burning alive.

He sees that now for what it was. Not mere greed and cruelty. No. The Pizarros were provoking Manku to an end. By then they had thousands of new men. If the Inca "rebelled," the terms of the Re-quirement would be broken. They could then conquer Peru deci-sively and make its people slaves.

He will give this priest little things. More than he wants to hear. He will bore him.

"Have you taken the Lord's name in vain? Have you sworn blas-phemously?"

"No, Father. Never." True enough: he's never sworn by the new gods, only the old.

Soon tiring of Waman's drawn-out account of wanderings and petty idolatries—a kiss to a mountain here, a wad of coca left on a cairn there, visits to native healers, oaths calling on Mother Earth— Friar Pérez moves on to matters of the flesh.

"Have you committed adultery?"

"I am unwed."

"Why so?"

"I'm . . . not sure." His mind fills with Tika. They would have married if she'd been willing. They still might, if he can find her. But he won't sully her name by speaking it here. "Maybe it's because I've never led a life I could ask a woman to share. I was a child when I went to Spain. Since then I've never spent more than a few months in one place. Except in Cajamarca. The Commander was eight or nine months there. I can't remember how long in the lowlands before that. Several months anyway. And after, on the road—"

"That will do. Fornication, then?"

Waman looks up, having composed a mask of bewilderment.

"Fornication! Come on, man. Surely you know what fornication is? To lie with whores and loose women."

He admits to a few adventures over the years, beginning with the one in Toledo, arranged by Candía. Another gift. He winces at his jealous and ungrateful outburst.

"Sodomy, then? I know you Indians are great sodomites, even with women. What of sodomy? It's not enough to say you've sinned—you must tell me how. In what ways. How many times." The priest is leaning forward now, his robes gathered in his lap, his breath washing sourly over Waman, gusts of stale wine, sharp cheese, the dunghill odour of bad teeth.

Sodomy? They have so many distinctions between lawful and unlawful ways of love. Does their god not grow weary of these priests?

"It's no good holding shameful things back. Nothing will shock me. I've heard them all."

"No, Father. I know only one way to lie with a woman."

"And what way is that? Go on."

"Always the same way."

"The way of begetting, face to face?"

"Yes."

"Have you sired bastards?"

"Not to my knowledge."

What if he had? What if Tika had taken him and they'd had little ones—would their children have lived? So many miscarried or stillborn since the Christians brought sickness and hunger to this land. And of those that are born, so few who live beyond a year. He has heard some churchmen say these must be the last days, the coming of the Doom—for God is taking New Christians to heaven straightaway, to spare them his terrible wrath when he destroys the Earth.

Maybe they're right, Waman thinks. Maybe the new plagues are their god's will. I shall not worship a god who kills us so.

Outwardly contrite for the sins he has admitted, Waman is shriven. His penance is light: little more than service to the Vicar-General, whatever Morales may require. And on the following Sunday he must come to mass in the city church and take communion.

The sky is unblemished, the violet blue of high altitude, yet a pall seems to shadow Waman on his way to Friar Pérez's church, now called the Church of the Triumph. It is still in the Roundhouse, the Sunturwasi, taken by Valverde after Manku's coronation. But the high spire with the Empire's flag has been ousted by a wooden belfry and the gonfalon of Santiago. And the doorway, he sees, is overlaid with a Spanish architrave, carved by sculptors who did not quite grasp what their new masters had in mind. A mismatch. Straddling two worlds.

Like me, he thinks. Like me.

Waman walks sadly, memories welling at each step. Of the Cusco he and Tika used to know, only the bones remain, a colossal skeleton of stone. Bridges are fallen, paving torn up, streets blocked by rubble and charred beams. Palaces lie open to the sky, their thick walls running above him like causeways in the air. The imperial college is being diced into houses, done roughly with rubble and adobe, the newcomers making muddy nests like swallows in its mighty ruins. Here and there a dull tang of old fire under weeds and rubbish: the reek of war. And things which were never smelt in Cusco before: ripe hams, cheeses, a billy goat. Smells of Spain.

It's as if centuries have passed, not years.

And there is the House of the Chosen: the first place he went when he came back to Cusco. It still wrenches him every time. He feels himself sway, stumbles on, turns behind the Roundhouse. Steadying himself with a hand against a wall, he sinks down onto a stone, part of a broken bench. The old cherry tree is gone, but it is here he waited for Tika that last day they were together. Waman remembers the sentries on the Akllawasi door, the illusion they gave of permanence and safety. He's heard the Spaniards used the great building as a stronghold against Manku's army. But he still doesn't know what happened to the women there. Some say they were scattered or slaughtered. Others believe that the Inca had the House evacuated on the eve of his attack. It is this that Waman clings to.

He makes himself get up and join the worshippers inside the church. Friar Pérez's sermon dwells on the deliverance of the Christians in this tower when Manku burnt the city. How the Virgin herself came down from Heaven and smothered the flames with her skirts. How thousands saw her, on both sides. And Santiago too, riding a white horse in the sky. "A holy miracle," the friar exults. "The Miracle of the Triumph!"

A snort escapes Waman—the sort of sound his grandfather used to make. He hopes it hasn't been noticed. Over the years he's heard many tales of the war, some from people who fought in it. Nobody, neither Spaniard nor Peruvian, has mentioned this miracle before.

He walks from the candled gloom into hard sunlight, the taste of communion acid in his mouth.

The Vicar-General summons Waman the next day, in late afternoon. The first item of business is another chess game. This time Waman decides it will be quicker not to let him win. "Check," he warns mildly after a few minutes.

"Oh," Morales says, hand hovering as he lowers a knight and unwisely slays a pawn. Then, leaning back with satisfaction at his move: "As I mentioned in my letter, Don Felipe—"

The knight falls to Waman's bishop, a fate unforeseen by the churchman. Morales breaks off in mid-sentence, glumly scans the board. "Alas! I see it's checkmate. Or soon will be." He topples his king. "I resign."

Friar Pérez pads in like a tall black cat and lowers himself into a leather chair, its creak the only sound.

Morales coughs. "This brings me to the task before us. The Inca Pawllu has indicated that certain prayers, catechisms, and model sermons rendered into the language of Peru in the late Bishop's time might benefit from some corr—some revision. The wording, he suggested, might be made . . . more *precise*.

"Here, for example." The Vicar-General leafs through a breviary, wetting the pad of his thumb with a pink tongue. Many of the pages, Waman sees, are in the ancient form of Spanish known as Latin, which is beyond him. "Here," says Morales again. "This is the addendum in the Peruvian language for priests and catechists. Here you see our difficulty. How is a New Christian to grasp the meaning of confession, for example, when it's rendered no better than *confesakuy*?"

Waman studies the page. It is riddled with such terms.

"Since his baptism," the Vicar-General goes on, with a nod to Friar Pérez, "the Inca Pawllu earnestly desires to smooth the way of the True Faith into every Indian soul. Having little Spanish as yet, he cannot work on the texts himself. However he has graciously offered to oversee our efforts, to ensure the results are given a final polish in the best Cusco style. It was he who remembered you, Don Felipe—he heard you'd recently returned to the outskirts of this city. I gather he made use of your services during Almagro's campaign in Chile." Morales lifts a questioning brow.

"Yes, my lord. That's why Commander Pizarro sent me there. At that time the Commander and Almagro were still friends. As were Pawllu and Manku."

"Indeed!" Friar Pérez breaks his silence. "Neither the Vicar-General"—bowing to his superior—"nor I myself was here in those days. But we know how our enemy Satan, the Father of Lies, smarting from the defeats we inflicted on him in this land, took revenge by sowing strife amongst us Christians."

Ah, thinks Waman, so the fight between One-Eye and the Pizarros was all Satan's fault. That Devil has his uses.

Ignoring Friar Pérez's observation, the Vicar-General gives a welcome bit of news. Pawllu is away in Qollasuyu, visiting his lands by Lake Titicaca. They will have to make a start without that Inca's guidance. Waman is much relieved. The Inca Pawllu has grown up to be crafty and devious, the undoing of many better men, beginning with his brother Manku. Had Pawllu thrown his troops against Almagro in some Chilean pass, the Empire might be rid of the invaders now.

The interpreter brightens as the evening meal arrives. Broiled guinea pig on a steaming heap of quinoa. Roast llama, potatoes, cornbread. Passion fruit and pineapple.

The Vicar-General lifts the book from the table and sets it aside. "Would you say the blessing for us, Friar Pérez? In Peruvian."

Yayayku, Hanaq Pachapi kaq,
Willkasqa kachun sutiyki . . .
Sapa p'unchaw
t'antaykuta kunan qowayku . . .

Our Father who art in Heaven,
Hallowed be thy name . . .

Give us this day
our daily bread . . .

The friar sets to, stripping meat from a skewer with his teeth. Waman, nervous in this company, knocks a spoon off the table but is quick enough to catch it on the wing.

"Don Felipe," the Vicar-General says, when the edge has gone from their appetites, "the Inca Pawllu has expressed some reservations about that rendering of the Paternoster, the prayer Friar Pérez recited so beautifully just now at this our board. In particular the title of Our Father, Yayayku. We would value your opinion."

Waman purses his lips as if pondering the matter. What is Pawllu up to? How did he find him in his refuge? Why did he tell Morales to send for him—just to rewrite a few prayers?

"May I ask, my lord, when the translation was made. And by whom."

"No one seems to know. It was done not long after the Christians retook this city. The translator must have been an Indian. No Spaniard had enough of the language at that time. All I know is that the late Bishop Valverde approved this version for use throughout the land."

Yayayku! Waman thinks. An elementary blunder. Spaniards are always mixing up Quechua's two forms of *we.* (Just as Peruvians confuse the two styles of *you* in Castilian. That still baffles him. Why call the Lord God *tú,* like a child, but not the lord Bishop?)

"I shall study the prayer carefully and report to you. But it seems . . . possible . . . that the first word might be better as Yayanchik rather than Yayayku. Both indeed mean Our Father. But the Peruvian tongue has two forms of *our* and *we.* One means everyone in general. The other means the speaker and those in the speaker's group, but not the listener. Yayanchik would say Our Father, Father of all. But Yayayku says *Our* Father, not yours." Composing a naive, almost gormless, expression Waman turns to Friar Pérez. "Am I right in thinking that Our Lord is everyone's lord, always?"

"Of course that's right! His power and love are universal. Only a fool—or a pagan knave—would doubt it."

"Very good!" Morales cuts in nimbly with a smile. "Excellent! This is exactly what we're looking for—isn't it, Friar Pérez? Don Felipe here's our man. The very man. Just as the Inca Pawllu said he would be."

The friar refills his own glass without comment, accustomed to drinking alone. Waman allows himself an inner chuckle. Maybe the unknown translator made no mistake at all. Maybe he was mocking the Spaniards, letting everyone know the new god was *their* father. Not ours.

July gives way to August. It is the height of the sunny Cusco winter. The hills are brown except where green lines of aqueducts link the few terraces not destroyed. Faltering lines, as if drawn on the land by a pen short of ink, trace channels broken in war.

Morales seems in no hurry with the work, spending as much time on chess as anything else. His game improves. Sometimes he passes on news he receives by letter—from Lima, Mexico, Spain. All these places seem far away to Waman, only of faint interest. The Vicar-General also talks of his youth, his days as a scholar at Salamanca. These reminiscences become repetitive; Waman begins to wonder if Morales is waiting for something—for instructions from Lima, perhaps, or the return of Pawllu from Lake Titicaca.

One evening late in August, the interpreter comes down to the main hall to find the Vicar-General unusually distracted, drumming his fingers on the table, fidgeting in his chair, as if bursting with a secret. Neither food nor chess is on the table.

"Do be seated, Don Felipe," he says fulsomely. "Some wine will be along shortly. So will Friar Pérez." He gets up and peers into the courtyard, turns on his heel, drops back into the chair.

"I have a proposal to put before you, one I alluded to in the letter I sent you in . . . that place you were living. Never fear, by the way, that I blame you for choosing to retire incognito as it were. Your steadfastness in searching for your family is commendable."

He summons the city beyond the palace with a pirouette of his hand. "I can imagine how hurtful it must be, to a man of your race and sensibilities, to see this land, once thriving and orderly, in this fallen state. Like a great lady violated and disfigured. Before I left home I'd heard wonderful things. Especially of Cusco. Finer than any city in the Indies, everyone said, and some said even in Spain. Twenty thousand houses! And when I got here . . . Well, it was a wonder to see a roof."

Waman looks up expectantly, readying paper and pen to make notes. He is not reassured when Friar Pérez glides into the room. Where is this going?

Wine arrives, brought in by a young black man. Waman thinks of his old friend Tomás. What became of him? Did he get home to Africa, as he longed? And he thinks of poor Qoyllur in Spain. Treated like a chattel, taken by smallpox.

Morales resumes talking of the wars. Of burnt towns and farms, abandoned way stations, rifled warehouses, rotting suspension bridges. How the conquistadors are becoming tyrants, extorting unbearable tribute from the Indians; even branding them on the face as slaves, against all royal and Church law. How jumped-up cobblers and ostlers are keeping harems like infidel sultans.

"But now we have our Viceroy. A man of integrity. A close

friend of King Charles. I had the honour of meeting him some years ago in Burgos—his brother is Archbishop there. Consider, Don Felipe, what a difference this will make! It's like having our own King in Lima. We can speak to him. He can hand down royal justice. With the New Laws, the Viceroy will bring order. He'll tame the rogue conquistadors. Mend roads, rebuild bridges, restore the posts, restock the warehouses. In short, Peru will soon be safe and prosperous."

He fills their glasses, then: "Men such as yourself, Don Felipe, respected by all—by both Indian and Spaniard—are few. This is a time of great change, great opportunity. You are needed. I don't mean just to interpret. You can achieve great things."

Waman is stroking his ear nervously with his quill. He catches himself, sees he should make some reply. Not everyone is so pleased to have a Viceroy, least of all the conquerors who came in the first wave, who ride about in palanquins like Inca lords. He has heard rumours that Gonzalo—the only Pizarro brother left—is raising an army of such men. That he means to send the Viceroy packing, marry an Inca princess, and make himself King of Peru.

"My lord, I may still be young in years, but I am old in heart. I've had my fill of great things. Allow me to continue with smaller ones, such as the work you have assigned me here. When that is done I must turn to other matters, to finding my kin. As you know, my mother and sister have been lost many years. I must search for them. And if my greatest fear is true and they no longer live, I must find out what befell them and do honour to their memory."

"Commendable indeed, as I've said, Don Felipe. But this new business I ask will not take long. Only three or four weeks. Then you'll be able to apply yourself to the worthy task you speak of. And I give you my word I shall help you in that. When prudent to do so, of course. No kingdom can be safe until it is at peace. By God's grace the fires of war no longer touch this city. But they still smoulder and flare elsewhere throughout the land. First, help us make peace. This is what I ask. Then we shall be able to help you." The Vicar-General refills Waman's glass. "Indeed, the very thing I'm about to propose may well bear fruit in your personal matter. Have you searched yet beyond Christendom's frontier?"

Waman admits that his travels have sometimes taken him into disputed territory, but he has shied away from Manku's stronghold in the Empire's eastern quarter. To go there, he fears, would bring death, revenge for his years with the Spaniards.

"Ah, but things are changing, Don Felipe. The chance for you to go there is now. With our blessing and protection."

Morales explains that by suppressing abuses against the native population, the New Laws will remove just cause for Manku's resistance. The Viceroy believes the time is ripe to approach Manku, to sue for peace.

A loud sniff from the dark figure in the room. "Peace," Friar Pérez declares, "must be both spiritual and temporal. Peace under God and King. Neither can be achieved while the Inca Manku clings to the falsehoods of his fathers. Anyone who doubts this land was Satan's realm has only to see that fortress up there." He shakes an angry finger in the citadel's direction. "There the Devil's hand is plain, for men alone could not have built it!

"Manku's kingdom," he goes on, "may be only the rump of Peru, but it bristles with idols and he lives in those mountains like a god. The Indians everywhere—here in Cusco, even in Lima—still worship him, as the Romans did their Caesars. They won't convert until he does. Peru won't rest until Manku lets Christ into his soul and friars into his lair!"

The Vicar-General seems annoyed by this outburst. "Quite so," is all he says.

Waman says nothing. He knows Manku is the key—and in more ways than one. Not only have the Spaniards, despite many attempts, failed to crush him, but Manku is the fiercest foe of Gonzalo Pizarro—the man who stole his first Queen. If Gonzalo attacks the Viceroy, Manku is again a potential ally for the Crown.

"So, what we ask," Morales goes on, "is that you go there, to Manku's city of Vitcos in the province of Willkapampa, with gifts for the Inca and a letter from myself. An exploratory gesture of goodwill. Nothing more. You'll be back here in no time."

The request—the command, rather—appals Waman. True, it may allow him to search for his family in the forbidden kingdom. But it could easily end in disaster. For himself and for the Inca.

"I'm not the one to send, my lord. Manku will remember me as the Commander's mouthpiece. He will also see me as one of Pawllu's party. I'll be killed as soon as I set foot across the border."

The Vicar-General strokes the soft continuum of his chin and throat, as if pondering these objections. "We have reason to think otherwise." He reminds Waman that the alliance between Manku and Pizarro was still in effect when the interpreter left Cusco for Chile. "As for your connection with Pawllu during Almagro's campaign in the south, didn't you leave those two before they conspired and marched on Cusco?" He gives Waman a searching look. "There's also a report, Don Felipe—doubtless a slur against you spread by ill-wishers of Almagro's party—that you took up arms against them yourself. That you went over to the Chilean natives and helped them hold a fort."

Waman feels the ground opening beneath him. How could they know that?

"Then you must also have heard that I died there. Obviously I didn't."

"Mere lies, of course, as I've said, Don Felipe. Do not allow them to upset you. Even if it *were* true that you fought against Almagro . . . well, he was a traitor. To betray a traitor is no crime."

The Vicar-General holds Waman with his small eyes, bright above puffed cheeks. He gives a sticky smile. "There is a question of timing, though. There are those who say that at that particular time Almagro wasn't *yet* a traitor. He had yet to show his hand."

Morales leans back in his chair, arms folded, watching.

"My point is merely this," he adds, when he judges the implications have sunk in. "However groundless that tale may be, if we have heard it, the Inca Manku will have heard it too. It will serve you well. Manku will welcome you."

And if I refuse, Waman thinks, what I did in Chile will be investigated.

I am caught. Again.

❧ 20 ❧

Waman saddles up in a steely foredawn, his mules' breath hanging like smoke in the dark courtyard.

Followed by three helpers, also mounted and bearing gifts for the Inca Manku in their saddlebags, he rides unsteadily down the street, his eyes following the locked shadows and sunken joints of the palace's cyclopean wall. He would rather be alone, especially at this hour. He would rather be on foot, leading a llama. He would rather not be doing this thing at all.

Might his "mission" (Morales's word) become the trigger of another war? He wonders whether Manku, as some say, is raising an army to retake the city. What then, if the Sun were to rule again in Cusco? The new faith, the new power, squat uneasily in the capital, flimsy as the new belfries and terra-cotta roofs, awaiting the next earthquake, whether sent by gods or men.

The four riders cross the Tullumayu, the Bone River, spine of the puma in the city's layout. The bridge is whole, though the channel below is more sewer now than stream. They climb from the valley by the eastern highway—towards Antisuyu, the unconquered quarter of the Empire.

The top of the sun's fire appears, welling up like molten lava. After a glance over his shoulder Waman stretches out his hand to greet it, asking for help with this fool's errand in which he is ensnared. He stops and looks back on the capital. Sacked by invaders, burnt by its own, burnt again when the invaders fought one another, Cusco is still the holy city, the axis of the World. Dawn is blooding the puma's fangs, the citadel's great sawtooth ramparts, where Manku's troops killed Juan Pizarro.

They reach an upland where the wind plays over a sea of grass and the sun burns their faces, though every boulder shades a frosty outpost of the night. Hawks and condors ride the sky. The llama herds whose land this was were slaughtered in the wars. Only a few still graze, lifting watchful heads from time to time as if searching for their dead.

Waman's mood brightens as the road at last winds down towards the Willkamayu, the Holy River. Its valley comes into sight, a corridor of warmth and order in the sunlight, towns and contoured fields, the river running straight between embankment walls.

They spend the night at Tampu, last town in occupied Peru. If Tampu can be called occupied at all. There are no Spaniards here, and the few locals are wary and tight-lipped. They lodge in a public hall on the plaza, silent but for the hiss of fast water nearby. Above them in the twilight hangs a hilltop temple as fine as any in Cusco, though still only half built when Manku made it into a fortress, adding embrasures for his captured guns. It was here he fought the conquest to a standstill, miring the invaders' cavalry by opening sluices and flooding the valley floor. While the Spaniards stumbled and drowned, the Inca watched from the temple on a tall white horse, a pike in his hand.

Beyond Tampu, precipitous mountains pinch the valley to a gorge. The river runs wild and fierce to Manku's free kingdom and the rainforest beyond. Not even the Incas carved a road through there. The way to Willkapampa makes a long roundabout climb to a high pass below the eastern snowfields. For a while they can ride this fading track, but as it steepens they have to dismount and tow the unwilling mules, who protest with bared teeth and flattened ears. Not long ago, when the World was one, this was a *road*, Waman reflects. Now it's an obstacle course, its flags torn up and piled in barricades when Manku sealed the border between Spanish and free Peru. Yet the seal is not absolute. Like the waist of an hourglass, the way becomes slow and narrow, yet open just enough for his party to slip through.

No line, no gate, no garrison. Not even a manned watchtower. None in sight, anyway. Yet with each step and turn Waman feels the world of the Christians withering behind him, while another is ripening ahead. Unmarked, unfixed, the shift between realms has no definition; it is, rather, an ordeal through which the traveller passes and is changed. Like winter and summer, Waman thinks. Like his years of wandering. Only with time, with hindsight, can a person know that one season—or one life—has ended and the next begun. Time and space. Castilian needs two words: *tiempo* and *espacio*. Quechua has one: *pacha*. Pacha is space, and pacha is time, for neither exists without the other. With time, every place becomes another place. And any journey in space is also a journey in time.

He steps aside to piss. An emerald hummingbird, drawn by the glint of moisture, hangs in the air above his stream. They are near the high pass, in a noon light bleached by snowfields. No clouds, no shadows. Nothing stirs. Waman feels as if time has stalled, as if the sun has ceased to roll across the sky. A bird, a man, a kingdom, a universe. All are pacha.

He buttons his britches—he is still in Spanish garb—and blows a prayer to the mountain lords above in their white gowns. Once again he is the chaka, the bridge between worlds.

He thinks of what he saw that morning as they left Tampu—great stones on ramps and rollers, waiting for the temple-building to resume.

So one world ends and another begins. Or has it? Does it?

A night of cold and starlight, some way beyond the pass but still in highlands. They huddle under blankets against a comb of broken wall. Then down and down all morning, sinking into a quilt of overcast and a cloud forest of giant ferns, writhen trees, shaggy beards of dripping moss.

"Ever seen anything like it?" the interpreter remarks to the helper called Kunturi when they stop for lunch. Oldest of the Vicar-General's men, Kunturi is the only one at ease in Quechua, though with a heavy accent. Among themselves the three all speak Aymara. Are they just levies from the south serving their work-tax, as the Empire's machinery rolls on by sheer momentum? Or could they be Pawllu's men, from Lake Titicaca? Not only Waman's helpers but his guards? Certainly they eat like lakers—salt fish and freeze-dried potato.

"Like what, *siñu*?" Unsure what to call Waman, Kunturi mangles *señor*.

"This heat, these woods. Hail up there this morning"—Waman nods at the pass over which they came—"now rain as warm as blood."

"Never, siñu." The old helper shakes his head. "I don't like it. So gloomy. Father Sun's face is veiled here, yet he still steams us like cobs in a pot." The man shrugs off his woollen tunic, revealing the wrinkled hide of a stocky highland chest. "If you don't mind, siñu?"

"Wear what you like. But watch for snakes. The deadliest, I'm told, are green. They look like vines."

The tunic goes back on.

They are nearing the Holy River again, many thousands of feet below Tampu, its voice raging in the woods, punctuated by the low boom of stones bowled headlong in the flow. The road is better here, undamaged though overgrown. Several times they've had a hard time scrambling across downed trees alive with ants and spiky plants like pineapples. Waman examines the moss on the paving: thick, untramped. Nobody can have come this way for months, maybe years. He wonders how the Vicar-General and Viceroy know anything of affairs inside Willkapampa. But of course there are other ways out of the Inca's stronghold—secret passes, known only to the Inca Manku and his generals, by which their troops appear without warning, strike the invaders, and vanish. Perhaps, Waman muses, he is invited as well as sent?

The road ends abruptly at a rock face above seething water. Two stone pylons and a great pier in the middle of the stream are all that remain of Chuqichaka, the Golden Bridge, whose name seemed to promise a grand crossing to Manku's kingdom. The river is not wide here but deep and angry. Amid the bush on the far bank Waman can make out an answering pair of towers for the missing suspension cables. Perhaps they are still there, coiled like anacondas in a shed, awaiting the Inca's command to open the way. The interpreter calls out, just in case a bridgekeeper is on duty. His shouts die on the water's roar.

So, this ends before it can begin. A relief. Yet also a disappointment, the shutting of a door that might have led him to his family.

Kunturi comes up in a hurry, takes him to see the sag of a thin line spanning the chasm, hidden among trailing roots and vines. The helpers haul on the rope, which is tied to a stronger one that unspools from one of the far pylons. This they pull taut and belay. So, a missing bridge that is not quite missing; a bridge like the road it serves, enough for a few to cross like monkeys, nothing more. Waman orders an *uraya* made from a saddle and pack threads—a hanging basket on which he can pull himself hand over hand along the cable. In this undignified way he and the younger helpers reach the far bank. Kunturi he sends back to Cusco with the mules.

In Manku's kingdom now, Waman sheds his foreign garb and dons a fawn vicuña tunic with a black-and-red checkered belt—fine Cusco wear given him by the Vicar-General. He runs his hands down the silky weave, feels easier in these clothes.

They spend the night in the bridgekeeper's empty house, which smells of mice and bats, setting off again at sunrise. The morning is hot and muggy, but as they leave the wooded lowlands the air slowly dries and cools, though the sun does not relent. The road to Vitcos peels away from the main river to climb alongside the Willkapampa, a tributary flowing from the mountain wall that defends the free state on the west and south. Unrefreshed by new snow for months, the peaks are yellowed teeth in the afternoon light, cracked with ridges of dark rock, smirched by drifts of scree. Then the sun drops behind the icy claw of Pumasillu, casting shadow and chill in the walkers' path. Dusk is upon them quickly. The way steepens into a step-road, its granite slabs glowing palely in the twilight as if lit from within.

Cloud settles on them, more felt than seen, wetting Waman's face and hands. The darkness is thicker now, and once or twice his feet nearly stray from the road into nothing.

A figure appears, almost runs into him, yells out a startled greeting. Head wrapped against the cold, the man, who has no lantern, will say only that the Inca Manku has sent him to greet and guide the visitors. Placing a woollen rope in their hands, he leads them the rest of the way like little children. Not until they reach a house can Waman examine his escort: near forty, vigorous, with a blue sunburst on one cheek and a spiral on the other—or so it looks by the glow of a brazier warming the room. He has never seen tattoos like these, not even in the islands. Yet there seems something familiar about their owner, a man of few words, which he speaks oddly.

"Hamuy, Waman. Wasiykipim kanki." Welcome, Waman. You are in your own house.

In my own house? A fine courtesy but a Spanish one. The interpreter has never heard a Peruvian say it. The fellow is a puzzle. So is this Vitcos, or Witkhus, a name for something hidden, something enfolded. A place of mystery, and all the more so because he has come by night. He feels unsettled, unmoored. He goes to the door and looks out, aware for the first time of scattered lights and sounds. Vitcos is around him, but all he knows of it is this room, a moonless night, a scrim of cloud brushing the stars.

Waman sleeps fitfully, fighting for breath. This place must be high as Cusco. A dream of heaving up and down as he runs and takes off through the air in flying strides (why doesn't he move like this always?). He awakes in darkness and the dream dies like a flame. He surfaces briefly, sinks back into rippled sleep. His father comes to him, speaks to him. Brings news of Little River, where all is as it was. The Great Death spared him. He never died! How, Waman asks himself, has he been so mistaken? Then he is in Seville, in the cathedral, his father beside him. Outside he can hear a rattle of hooves and wheels, the cries of beggars by the door.

Adrift between dream and wakefulness, he opens his eyes. Not Spain. Peru. The Bishop's palace? Has he been in Cusco all along?

Daylight is seeping through oiled parchment screens in the windows. He looks around at stone walls and red-lacquered roof beams, the pattern of the ceiling panels. His room in Cusco has no panels. And only one window. And a desk, a chair, a crucifix. Here the niches are empty except for a white marble lamp in the shape of an alpaca.

Thunder outside. No, the rolling beat of running hooves. War-horses laden with armour and armoured men. A sound he fears. He is wide awake now.

Psst! A hiss at the door. A door of stretched cloth, of gentler times, unlike the heavy ones studded with iron that are spreading through Cusco as if every home is to become a jail. He gets up, throws on his tunic; unties the door warily, twitching it aside. The hoofbeats are louder.

That man again, the odd tattoos, sitting on the step in the morning sun as if he owned the place. The man looks up over his shoulder, blue cheek creased in something between amusement and mistrust. He stands, puckering his brow, motioning with his eyes that they should go in. Waman feels a spread hand in the small of his back, urging him inside. Once the door is fastened, the stranger lowers his voice and speaks in Spanish.

"Excellent! If you can't see through me, nobody can. I bring us breakfast, Felipe. With coca tea—to rouse you—and new bread." He takes these items from a carrying cloth, handling the tea jug carefully, setting them on the floor. The room has no furniture beyond cushions, mats, and the stuffed cotton mattress on a platform at the end. The man sits down, unwinds his turban slowly, turning his profile to the window. Waman has heard talk that a few Spanish renegades—foes of the Pizarros—might be sheltering in Vitcos. But this fellow is dark, beardless, tattooed like a cannibal. He's also wearing native clothes, though in a mix of styles. He regards the interpreter teasingly, a knavish lizard eye.

And with that Waman knows him.

"Molina? Alonso de Molina?"

The man shakes with laughter till his cheeks are wet. "For my sins, Felipillo. For my sins!" His face cracks open like a scallop, a gap-toothed grin from ear to ear.

The old shipmates embrace warmly. Then they pull apart, still clutching forearms, studying faces.

"Molina! I should have known you'd be all right. The Devil looks after his own. How *are* you?"

"Above ground, Felipe. Above ground."

"Mother and Tika. Are they with you?"

"Neither, sorry to say. But your mother was alive and well last I heard, though that's some time ago. And her boy, Fox—he'll have turned sixteen by now. Tika I never knew. She'd left for a nunnery before I got to Little River. The first thing I thought when I saw you was, Felipe will have news. It was all I could do to go off home last night and let you rest."

"How did you know who I was?"

"More on that later. Well? Let's hear your news."

Waman tells how he found Tika in Cajamarca, and what she told him of his mother, Atuq, and Molina. He passes over the circumstances, the time with Atawallpa, her loss of voice. "We had more than a year together in Cusco. Then Pizarro sent me to Chile with Almagro." Waman stops. He wipes an eye. "So many years ago now. I've been looking for her—for them—ever since. All over Peru."

Molina pats Waman's shoulder. "People are in hiding everywhere . . ." His voice trails off, as if to avoid something. "What Tika told you is right," he goes on. "Your mother and I and your little brother, we took good care to avoid Pizarro's lot. Much better to live with Chaska, I says to myself, than die with that old bastard." He stops with a sheepish laugh, realizing what he's said is hardly praise. "Your mother was . . . *is* . . . a wonder. The best woman I've known in all my life. The best person, woman or man. You don't need me to tell you that. I miss her. Atuq too—he's like my own son."

Waman nods quickly, urges Molina on, and listens rapt to a rambling account full of oaths, digressions, low opinions of man and God. When it looked like war would break out between the Incas they went to Huanuco Pampa, to find Tika. But the city was full of soldiers. Nobody knew, or would say, where the Chosen had been taken. Travel on the main roads was impossible by then anyway. "But Chaska knew a place in Lower Huanuco where she had kin. Coca fields. Out of the way, near the jungle. We thought we'd hide there till the fighting was over. Ended up staying—"

"Where?" Waman cuts in. "Where in Lower Huanuco? I must go there."

"Chaska made me swear never to tell anyone, not even you if I found you. For your own good. Not until it's safe. That whole province keeps changing hands. That's why I'm not there myself." Molina's eyes drift away, as if he's wondering whether to say more.

How much is he *not* saying, Waman thinks. How much is even true?

"Your mother always knows best, eh?" Molina laughs, embraces Waman again. "Christ, Felipillo! All grown up. How old are you now?"

"Please don't call me that. I'm Waman. Felipe if you must. And I'm over thirty."

Molina whistles, leans back and looks at him, shakes his head.

"Well?" says Waman. "How did you fetch up here?"

Molina scratches under his headcloth, examines his nails for nits. "Long story, Felipe. The bones of it will have to do for now. When the Spaniards took Huanuco Province, Chaska made me hide with the Sacha Runa, the jungle folk. Then Manku's men took Huanuco back, and they found me. They worked out I was a barbarian deserter and brought me here. To be an interpreter, like you! Your mother made me an Indian."

"You may look like one. But you don't sound like one. That accent wouldn't fool a baby."

"Oh, I'm not a Peruvian. I'm a Mexican! Came with those native troops of Alvarado's. Most of them froze to death in Quito. None got down here. Nobody speaks their language. So it's perfect. And Peruvians are afraid of Mexicans. They think they're berserkers."

"Who does the Inca Manku think you are?"

"The Inca knows everything. The only one who does. He's very glad to have me. Treats me well. Good house. Even a good woman to keep me warm." He winks. "Just for the time being, of course. She's from the jungle too. Did my tattoos." He puffs out his cheeks. "Mexican style, near enough. Becoming, no?"

Molina stops and the good humour drains from his face. He looks up at the window, turns back disconsolate.

"*Ananaw*, Waman! It hurts to be away from Chaska and Atuq. We'll find them one day. I'll take you there. That's what we'll do."

Waman is deep in thought, going over all he's heard. He doesn't touch the breakfast. Wonderful news! Yet nothing of Tika. Molina is slurping tea and chewing cornbread noisily. Still a ruffian. And now this ruffian is his stepfather—what a thought! But there was something about him Waman liked when he was young. And maybe he still does.

"You heard Candía died?"

"I did, Felipe. A sad end to a good man." He sighs. "God, so many dead! Gambled their lives on Peru. Won it—more or less. And having won, lost all."

"What do you think will happen to us if Manku wins? Can Manku win?"

"You know more than I do about the state of things beyond these mountains. I may be safe here, but I'm stuck. Hideouts are always traps."

Waman nods. "Sometimes I think I've spent my whole life falling into traps."

Molina gets up and fiddles with the windows, taking down the night screens. A shaft of sunlight strikes the unmade bed. "Sail with the wind, Waman, wherever it takes you. That's my advice. Who can foresee next week? If Manku does win, stay with him. The lords of Peru are as good as any. And so are the gods—better, I say, because they don't mind what others you have." He blows a kiss to the Sun and winks. "Badluck Molina worships anything that keeps him in one piece.

"Even if Manku wins back his whole Empire," he adds, "he'll still need people like us. If only to help him keep the rest of us away."

"Is that why he keeps you?"

"I do certain things for him that no one else can." Molina lowers his voice, sweeps his eyes from side to side. "From now on, you and I speak only Peruvian. Even in private. My name is Coyotl, if anyone asks. And we never met before last night. If I'm overheard talking Castilian I'm done for. There are some other Spaniards here. To them I'm just a lowly *indio* from New Spain. They treat me like a shitarse. Load my back like a mule. *Hey, Mexicano! Son of a whore. Fetch this, carry that!* That's all they ever say to me. But I listen. I hear. I am the Inca Manku's ears."

Waman smiles. Molina always was a braggart.

"Is that what I'm hearing out there—these other Spaniards?"

"War games. Come and watch."

Once outside, Waman sees that his room is in a long block of apartments on a terrace, with the small city spread before him on a sunny spur. The day is bright and clear, a scarf of mist sailing down the valley below. There are other buildings on either hand, roofed with steep thatches in the usual Inca style. And an open square or parade ground with an usnu making one side. On the right, to the east, fields drop away in flights of terraces to the step-road he climbed in the dark. The Willkapampa can't be seen under its white shroud, though its voice echoes from steep crags on the far bank. Beyond these green walls are other walls, darker, more jagged, and above them peaks and icefields.

Townsfolk are gathered round the edge of the plaza. On the usnu—a broad one in a single tier—lords and ladies are standing under sunshades and banners held by attendants. There's a burr of lazy conversation, outbreaks of laughter, the onlookers relaxing during a break in the show.

The tattooed "Mexican"—what did he say his name was?—leads his stepson through the crowd to the parade ground, a dry lawn studded with the yellow heads of dandelions, one of the new weeds come to Peru. Near the middle the turf is broken up by hooves. A musk of horses hangs in the brittle air.

Conch trumpets sound, rising to a howl like high wind in a ship's rig, dying away. Two files of horsemen enter at a trot, half a dozen riders on each side. They are in full armour with steel helms and visors. Some carry lances, all wear swords. One team has white plumes in their crests, the other red. The horsemen canter and joust, wheeling and rearing their mounts.

Then come two squads of infantry, a hundred men each, some in Spanish mail and leather, others in the quilted armour and wicker or bronze helmets of Inca troops—a mix of this battledress on either side. Several have long pikes, which they stake at an angle in the ground to fend off cavalry. The rest carry Toledo swords—or so it seems. The chime of the blades is of wood, not steel.

A cannon barks from the usnu, followed by a patter of musketry and sulphurous waft of gunsmoke. The fighters take no notice; they are used to the fire-shooters now. In the middle of the square, an imposing figure on a chestnut stallion unhorses a bearded opponent and dominates the fray.

"That one." Molina at Waman's ear. "That's the Inca Manku."

The weapon drill adjourns for lunch. Onlookers are chatting and picnicking nearby. So this is Vitcos. Hardly the reclusive fragment of the Empire he'd imagined, ruled by a broken man living on dreams. Here Peruvians become Spaniards, and Spaniards Peruvians. He regards Molina, seeing how easily he fades into the crowd. Yes, the rogue can pass for some kind of Indian here, so long as he remembers to pluck his beard. But what does *he* think he is?

Neighbours in the crowd—a couple with a lively girl of ten or eleven and two small boys—invite Waman and Molina to share steamed corn and bowls of soup. Who are those bearded fighters? the interpreter asks the wife, accepting a warm cob in a leaf from her hand. Women hear more than men. Sometimes they tell more. But all she says is *pipas pillapas*, whoever. Her daughter is more forthcoming: *Almagrista! Almagrista!* the girl shouts gleefully, as if she's just learnt the word.

Almagro's men?

Molina accompanies Waman back to his room at sundown. Food and drink have been laid out on a dining board, though no one is there when they come in. He fastens the door and fits the screens. He pours beakers of beer. Both men spill the customary drops to the Earth.

"That girl was right, Fel— Waman. There are seven Spaniards here, followers of the Boy. You know he's dead? No more Almagros, thank Christ!" Molina explains that after the Boy's defeat and execution, these seven were jailed in Cusco. Somehow they broke out and fled to Manku, begging asylum. "Watch out for the lot of them, but especially Méndez. The leader. Diego Méndez. Heard of him?"

Waman shakes his head. "I haven't been following public affairs. Though they seem to follow me."

"He's the one stabbed Pizarro down in Lima. The others all had a hand in it. But Méndez's blade was first in the Old One's back."

Waman is astonished. He studies Molina for any trace of a lie. He gets up and lights the lamp with a spill from the brazier, returns and again looks at him intently.

"You think I'm making this up?" Molina says.

"No. But it makes no sense. I can see why the Inca might want Spaniards here to train his men. But the very ones who murdered the Commander . . . It's madness. Those aren't soldiers. They're murderers."

"Tell me the difference, Waman. Who here's not a killer? Maybe you. But not me. Not Manku. He likes to boast he's killed two thousand Spaniards. He probably has."

"But in war. Not cold blood."

"He killed three of his own brothers in cold blood. True, that was years ago and they were working for Pizarro." Molina rubs his chin, as if suddenly aware he needs a tweezing.

"Walk carefully here, Waman."

———

That night he lies awake, feverish, blood throbbing in his ears, his thoughts in Spain, Cajamarca, Cusco, Chile. The dead walking in his mind, a repeating play he can't escape, a cycle of mistakes, evils, disasters; an endless tragedy. Have I killed thousands, with my tongue?

The stage behind his eyes does not fall dark until the small hours, when—he can hardly believe it—he hears a cascade of plucked strings far away. The sound of a lute, an Andalusian melody, pure and clear on the night.

❦ 21 ❧

The days go slowly. There's nothing much to do but see the small city with Molina—and not all of it. Manku's royal compound is closed, the gate flanked by sentries. They also avoid the lower ward where Pizarro's assassins live.

Waman asks if there's a Chosen House in the city.

"Not in Vitcos, far as I know. There are holy women at a temple nearby, a shrine called White Rock. But I doubt there are many. You'll have to ask Manku when you get the chance."

Idleness makes him uneasy. Has the Inca no interest in hearing what brings him here? Or is he making him cool his heels to show there are weightier matters in hand than dealing with a barbarian emissary?

Someone has been looking through his things. His clothes, writing materials, the gifts from the Vicar-General—all put back too neatly.

One afternoon, while Waman is napping, Molina brings word that the Inca may at last be ready to receive him.

"We'll watch target practice. After that Manku may summon you. Dress your best. Bring something to carry on your shoulders as you approach him. Get down on your knees and never look him in the eye. To your clergymen pals in Cusco he may be just a rebel Indian. Here he's a god."

"I know how to behave around Incas."

Molina waves a jug. "A beer before we go. Good for the nerves. There's time." He adds that the meeting, if it happens, will be just for show. Nothing of substance will be discussed.

Waman asks about the lute. He's heard it twice now, enough to be sure it's real.

"Francisco Barba, most likely. If it's any good, it'll be him. He plays for the Inca sometimes. It amuses Manku to keep a bearded one called Beard."

"He lets them into his palace?"

"He treats them as guests. They tell him about Spain. Play cards together. Horseshoes—Manku loves to play horseshoes. If he asks you, don't say no."

"Chess too?"

"They're not the sort for chess. Neither am I, come to that." Molina rolls his eyes. "How things change, eh? When they showed up, begging for their lives, all the lords spoke against it. They told Manku to kill them right away. But he decided their use outweighed the risk. He keeps a close watch on them. And he did take away their weapons. They're only allowed toys, like you saw."

Waman nods.

"I've warned him," Molina goes on loftily, shaking his head. "Watch out, Sapa Inka. That's what I tell him. It doesn't take a sword to kill a man. A broken bottle will do. Seen that enough times. Trouble is they've been here so long they seem like friends. And they're showing Manku how to make gunpowder. They found saltpeter up the valley." Molina spits. "I still don't trust them."

"How much can Manku trust them if he has you spy on them?"

"Manku's no fool. When you knew him . . . well, he was just a boy then, wasn't he? Not now. Way he sees it, they've burnt their bridges.

Owe him their lives. They've nowhere else to go." Molina sighs. He reaches for the jug.

"To health and wealth!"

"And time to enjoy them," Waman replies. His face falls, turns bleak.

"What sorrows, lad? Drink up."

"Nothing . . . That toast. Reminds me of Candía. He taught me that in Spain. Candía was a good friend to me."

"And to me, Waman. That Greek was worth all the Spaniards on Ruiz's ship. Here's to his heretic soul."

Several hundred townsfolk have gathered to watch the gunplay. Targets are set up on the far side of the square, where there are no buildings and the land falls away to the river. Four marksmen stand with arquebuses, sighting along the heavy barrels on forked rests. At the first war game Waman saw, the musket reports had seemed a mere patter after the thundering cannon. But today they are deafening, carried to the onlookers on a breeze sharp with brimstone.

After each volley targets are inspected and smoking guns exchanged for loaded ones. The gunners seem to be a bearded Spaniard, two Inca lords, and a third wearing a rich cloak of coloured squares over a steel breastplate. This last is also the best shot. Though who would dare outshoot the Sapa Inka?

"Not many gunners today," Molina says quietly in Waman's ear as the shooting ends and the Inca's party strolls towards the usnu. "And I don't see Pumasupa here, Manku's top general. There's a rumour he's on the move with his crack troops. To Cusco."

"Approach the throne, say who you are, and state your business." It is a herald or spokesman calling from the usnu, beckoning Waman to climb the stairs. The interpreter does so, legs weak with nerves and beer. He draws level with the top, where the court is arrayed in the sloping light of late afternoon. He lowers his eyes, dropping to his knees.

Manku and his Queen, the Qoya Kusi Warqay, are side by side on a twin stone seat, lords and ladies standing in an arc behind them. Above the royal couple is an awning of parrot feathers. Tame pumas crouch on either hand, gold-collared and tethered to stone rings. Waman can smell their meaty breath.

Sweat runs inside his tunic, though the air is cool. The thick bolt of vicuña cloth on his shoulders is more than a symbolic burden: it is heavy with the Vicar-General's gifts.

"Sapa Inka, Sapa Qoya," Waman begins, eyes fixed humbly on the flagstones of the usnu floor, repeating words he first spoke half a lifetime ago to a king and queen in Spain. He gives his name and reason for being here, adding that he is from Little River, near Tumbes, and that his father, Mallki, had the honour of fighting under Manku's father in Quito Province.

The fingers of a royal knotkeeper weave his words onto strings.

"Are you the same Waman, called by the Christians Felipe, who spoke for them at Cajamarca?" asks the herald.

"I am."

"And who spoke for them also when our Sapa Inka Manku Qhapaq Yupanki, here presiding, was crowned in Cusco?"

"Yes, my lord."

"I am told you are sent by the Bishop of Cusco." Manku's own voice, older and deeper than Waman remembers, yet the same. An honour. A sign that all is well.

"Sapa Inka. The late Bishop Valverde has still to be replaced. In the meantime a deputy runs the bishopric. This lord, Vicar-General Luis de Morales, sends his most respectful greetings and these humble gifts, which he begs you will be kind enough to accept."

"You may sit up and offer the gifts," the herald says. Waman unrolls the bundle at the royal feet, revealing a canvas of Virgin and Child, a letter on parchment, two beeswax altar candles thick as bedposts (luckily unbroken), a brocade vest, a Venetian glass goblet (likewise), and two pairs of Flemish hose.

The Inca makes a gesture of acceptance with his hand.

"And what word does the Bishop—the Bishop's stand-in—send with his kind gifts?" Manku's own voice again. "What does that *qillqa* say? Just in short."

Waman takes up the parchment and is alarmed how it amplifies the shaking of his hand.

"Only King. The Vicar-General greets and salutes Your Highness. He longs to kiss your royal hands and feet. He says these gifts are mere tokens of an infinitely greater gift—the gift of the Holy Faith, which he prays you will one day allow into your soul as your brother Pawllu has done, called Don Pablo by the Christians—"

"Don Pablo, indeed?" The Inca chuckles sardonically. "How lucky for my brother!" Answering laughter—some hearty, some sycophantic—sweeps the usnu. At the far end of the crowd Waman spots two or three beards: Almagrists watching from the wings.

He waits until the mirth subsides. Then: "Only King, the Vicar-General humbly begs that Your Highness consider the wisdom of admitting some friars here—kind and godly men who will tend the sick and poor—so that your subjects too may see the mercy of the One True God. This is what is written here, Sapa Inka."

Manku's hand reaches down to the puma beside him. He strokes its back and scratches its head between the rounded ears. The resulting purr, a mighty rumble like the gears of a mill, is for a long moment the only sound in Vitcos.

"You may tell the Bishop's stand-in this: I thank him warmly for his gifts. I accept them in the spirit of friendship he extends. I shall send him gifts in return when you leave us. But kindly remind my friend in Cusco that I have heard these entreaties before. The request has not changed. Neither has my answer."

The Inca stands and turns slowly, casting his gaze on all, who look down as the royal eye sweeps over them.

"*Wawqiypanaykuna, uyariwaychik,*" he resumes formally. "My brothers and sisters, hear me. Many of you have seen for yourselves the new kind of people who have come to our World, the bearded ones who infest this land and for the time being occupy the capital. They gave me their word that they were with me, that we were allies. You will recall that from the first I commanded you to serve them as you serve myself. Since then I have learnt, as have we all, how cheap is their word, and how vilely they repaid me."

The Inca sits, the crowd is still. The pumas are dozing. Only bird sounds now: the far scream of a hawk, the *thrum* of a humming-bird sipping at blooms along the usnu wall.

"No doubt there are some worthy men among the bearded ones," Manku continues, with a glance at the Almagrists. "No doubt the acting Bishop who has sent you is among these few. I'm sure he means well. But if he were to favour us with his presence he would find no work for his friars. Here there are no poor, nor any sick who lack good care. However, we hear that in Cusco there are many poor—many hungry, lacking food and help. Even begging on the streets. These are shameful things, things never seen in this land until the Christians came.

"That is all."

Waman hears nothing more from Manku for some time, though he sees the Inca from a distance: practising new arts of war; playing horseshoes with Pizarro's assassins on a pitch beside the usnu; presiding over the weekend feasts, when all are given a long lunch in the plaza by the state—a custom dying out in occupied Peru.

Meanwhile he is well looked after by Molina and a young woman who brings beer and meals from the Inca's kitchens, and who often busies herself (more than necessary, it seems) in the room when Waman and his stepfather are talking. Is he an honoured diplomat, or simply a valuable prisoner? Either way, Waman concludes, Manku means him to absorb an education: from the good order of Vitcos, a miniature Cusco-in-waiting, its main buildings named after those of the lost capital; and from the weapons drill, designed not only to dispel fear of Spanish tactics but to foster confidence that Incas can do anything Spaniards can do, and do it better.

This, Waman guesses, is why Manku is in no hurry with their business.

For a few days Waman is unwell. Loose bowels, aching bones, a fierce headache. When he is better, Molina comes one evening to lead him through the darkness for an audience in Manku's palace.

"There, Waman, look!" he says excitedly, pointing out stars between the dark shoulders of the mountains—and a deeper darkness within the powdered starlight. "Look there. The Black Llama. A good sign, no? The Llama high in the sky."

Waman wonders about his stepfather's enthusiasm for everything Peruvian. Is Molina a true convert, a Christian gone to the other side? Or is he simply an unbeliever, a man with faith in nothing but himself and what his hands can grasp? That feels more likely.

Sentries admit them at the palace gate and usher Waman to a reception hall, taking Molina to a smaller room across the courtyard.

Manku is standing in the ruddy glow of a heater, arms folded, his back to the yellow lamplight in a wall niche. Waman falls to his knees, a furled cloth on his shoulders.

"Ah, the man from Cusco. Off your knees. You may look at me."

They are alone. No ladies, lords; not even helpers. The Inca pours two beakers of beer, hands him one, motions him to a stool beside the heater—an earthenware brazier shaped like a frog, coals glowing in its maw. "I hope Sisa has been giving you good care. No need for friars, I trust? Who would you rather have at your bedside—a sweet young girl or a smelly old buzzard?"

Waman is taken aback by the informality. With formality there is safety, predictability. Now it seems anything might happen. Without his crimson fringe, Manku's broad face in the firelight reminds him of their first meeting—when the young Inca, alone and dressed as a farmer, strode boldly up to the Commander's column on the road to Cusco. More than ten years ago now. And more than eight since Waman last saw Manku, at the palace on Granary Terrace now occupied by Pawllu. The Sapa Inka is still handsome—strong chin, good teeth—yet worn by the years, which have deepened his resemblance to Atawallpa. Furrows on forehead and below the eyes. The rough etch of smallpox on his cheeks.

Manku regards Waman, similar thoughts in his mind.

"Ah, yes, we share this." The Inca swells a cheek, tapping his scar. "We're lucky men, you and I. The Great Death marked us and moved on. Where did it catch you—in Tumbes?"

"In Spain, Sapa Inka. I nearly died."

"So did I. Very nearly."

Manku falls silent. This interpreter, now envoy, is potentially dangerous. Many have said so. A man of two tongues. And two hearts. At best a go-between; at worst a spy, a betrayer. Yet in their dealings in Cusco years ago, he found that Waman answered his questions plainly, and asked few—only those he was obliged to by the barbarians. Some think well of him. Molina, of course, for what it's worth. Yet also some of Manku's informants in Cusco. And he himself took a liking to the interpreter in those early days. If only because they were both young, both bearing the same scars.

"I'm told you turned against Almagro and my brother Pawllu years ago in Chile. Any truth in that?"

"Yes, Sapa Inka. After witnessing many evils, many killings and cruelties, I got away from him in the mountains beyond the salt lakes."

"Where was that exactly?"

At a small place called Mawk'a Pukara. The local people had fled to an old fort. I tried to help them hold it against One-Eye. We did not succeed. The Spaniards killed almost everyone inside."

"How come you escaped?"

Waman tells how he played dead, swapped clothes. "The body was headless. Nobody could tell it wasn't me. But somehow they've found out. The Vicar-General threatened me with this—so I would agree to come here."

The Inca nods. What the interpreter has said agrees with what he knows.

341

"Why didn't you flee the moment they tracked you down near Cusco?"

"That was my first thought. But it was too sudden. Too late. They would have caught me."

"There are also tales about Cajamarca. Is it true you took one of Atawallpa's wives?"

"Only King, forgive me, but you've been misinformed. One-Eye and others accused me of that to hide their own crimes."

"More than likely. But I don't care what you did in Cajamarca. Atawallpa deserved what he got. Tonight, Waman, we speak as friends, without reserve. But just here, you understand. Between ourselves."

Emboldened by this, Waman admits that he did rescue a woman from Atawallpa's retinue. He tells Manku about his cousin Tika, his long search for her. He asks if the Chosen of Cusco escaped the war.

"We got most of them out in time. They're not all in one place now. There are many towns in Willkapampa besides Vitcos. I'll raise it with the Queen. All things concerning women rest in the Qoya's hands, not mine. She is, as it were, their Sapa Inka."

Manku takes off his russet cloak banded with heraldic symbols. "You may also ask our people here," he adds. "But do not speak to the Almagrists. Keep your distance there."

Beneath the cloak is a Toledo breastplate, which the Inca unstraps, emerging slim and human from the shell of steel. He takes up the brocade vest sent by the Vicar-General, richly embossed with silver and gold thread. He holds it to the light, frowns, lets it drop to the floor. "Their work is always so . . . so overwrought. Or did you grow to like their style in Spain?"

"There's no question, Sapa Inka: our *kumpi* is much finer. In Spain they value it more highly than any cloth of theirs. They deem it equal to the silks of China. They also like our tweezers."

"Ah, yes." Manku laughs. "Barba told me. They send tweezers home to their wives, hoping they'll put them to use. I gather Spanish ladies are almost as hairy as the men." He lifts an eyebrow.

"Now to business. The Vicar-General didn't send you here to speak of faith and friars. I may live deep in these mountains but I have ears throughout Tawantinsuyu. Things are changing. A few months ago a great lord arrived from Spain. They say he comes to leash the wild dogs, especially Gonzalo Pizarro. What do you know of this lord—what support has he? Is he strong enough?"

"I know little, Sapa Inka. I've avoided all Spaniards for years." He tells Manku what Morales told him: that this new lord comes straight from the King of Spain. That he holds the title of Viceroy and brings new laws to curb the conquistadors, who are working the people to death. "The rest is rumour. In Cusco it's being said that Gonzalo is raising an army. That he claims he's doing this to attack you, Sapa Inka. But few believe it. They say he really intends to march on Lima, overthrow this Viceroy, and make himself King of Peru. No one is sure who will win if it comes to war."

"This office—*Viceroy*—how do you translate it?"

"In their language it means a stand-in, a second person to their King. Like an Inkaq Rantin."

"The invaders certainly don't lack ambition." Manku refills the golden beakers. "I assume the Vicar-General sent you here because this half-king told him to?"

"It seems likely. Vicar-General Morales told me this visit is only a first step. An exploratory gesture. He said the Viceroy holds out to you the branch of an *olive*, which is the Christians' tree of peace, like our qantu."

"They might have sent a cask of real olives while they were about it." Manku chuckles, adding charcoal to the brazier. "I'd rather have that than a fancy jacket. Go on."

"He says the Viceroy invites you to send ambassadors to Lima, to seek terms under which peace between yourself and King Charles might be restored. That with peace you might wish to leave Willka-pampa and reside in Cusco. If so, he would settle great lands on you, estates that belonged to your late father and his kindred."

"The Spaniards are always so generous with our property! What do they mean to do about my brother Pawllu?"

"I don't know, Sapa Inka."

Manku lifts his drink and Waman follows his cue. The two toast Pachamama.

The Inca is silent for a while, then: "Let me guess. They'll want me to become a Christian, at least in name. That means I'd have to give up my Qoya, Kusi Warqay. She's already borne me a son. You may have seen him, he just turned three. Tupa Amaru is his name. The Christians don't like our royal marriages. They call it *incest*."

"The Vicar-General spoke several times of your conversion. I don't know if this came from him or the Viceroy, but he said the Pope in Rome—the Holy Father who rules their Church—might be willing to grant a special dispensation. So you and the Qoya can stay wed."

"How big of him. Perhaps he should grant himself a dispensation too. I gather not all his fathering is holy."

Waman laughs. "The word of their god is often unclear to me, Sapa Inka. Translating earthly things is easy enough. But heavenly things are less straightforward. *Sin*, for one. Is it crime? Is it filth? Is it guilt? Is it shame? Or take their word *salvation*. The nearest equivalent we have is freedom."

"Freedom! Is that what Pawllu thought he was getting?" Manku chuckles scornfully. "My brother's a fool. By converting he thought he'd make himself the only true Inca in Christian eyes. And the

Christians thought our people would follow him into church like their sheep into a fold. He couldn't have been more wrong. Nor they."

The Inca takes up a small pouch made of antique cloth with a striking black-and-red design: great staring eyes of a feline god from long ago when the World was young. He reaches inside for leaves and lime.

"We'll chew. You're not so Christian you won't take Lady Coca, are you?"

"Not at all, Only King. But it's too great an honour." Waman retrieves some fine coca from his own bag. He holds it out shyly, the leaves trembling in his hand as if in a breeze. The Inca takes them, fanning out the best from both bags on a cloth, making up two quids with catalytic lime. He blows gently over these, invoking the mountain lords and Mama Kuka, the plant herself. He hands one to his guest.

The men chew in silence for a while, feeling the leaves bestow their mysterious power, numbing their cheeks, sending warmth throughout their being. With warmth comes energy, clarity. And confidence, unbounded confidence. For the first time Waman feels equal to his mission, that all will be well, that he can nimbly sidestep any snare which fate may set in his way.

"What Pawllu achieved by converting," Manku volunteers, "was to make himself less of an Inca. Pawllu is just a man. I am still a god. Now the people look only to me—as much in the occupied provinces as here. I am my people's freedom. Their *salvation*."

The boast is not an empty one, Waman knows. Few have given up the old beliefs and observances. They offer breath each dawn to the Day, to the mountains, and to this Inca who lives defiant in the mountains. There isn't a Peruvian on the road to Cusco who doesn't stretch out a hand and pray at first sight of the City of the Sun, gutted and desecrated though it is. Apart from Pawllu's followers, only the Empire's bitterest foes—those who fought Inca rule and were crushed—have welcomed the new order. And even among these the welcome wears thin as the Spaniards abuse power, take all they want and, unlike the Incas, give nothing in return.

Manku is deep in thought, the strong bright thought of Mother Coca. How the barbarians fight one another—more fiercely than they fight himself! He will bide his time. He will keep the interpreter idling here as long as possible. He will watch how events unfold among the bearded ones. Which will prevail: the half-king sent from Spain, or Gonzalo, last and worst of the Pizarros? If Gonzalo marches on Lima, so much the better. General Pumasupa is poised to retake the capital and cut the great bridge across the Apurimaq as soon as Cusco's Spaniards are gone down to the coast to war.

As always when he thinks of Gonzalo, Manku hungers for revenge on the man who took his first Qoya, whom the Old One later burnt to death. A brave woman, shouting insults at the barbarians to the last. He remembers her poor charred body, sent floating down the river from Tampu in a basket for his people to find. Woe to Gonzalo when he's in my hands!

The Inca's thoughts turn to pleasanter things: rebuilding the capital as it was; ousting the friars from the temples, tearing down their dolls and images of death. And exposing their ridiculous lies. No miracle, no lady from heaven, put out the flames on the Sunturwasi, as they are boasting now. They sent their black slaves up on the roof with buckets of water. He saw it himself.

He knows them, and he knows how to kill them—in highland ravines where armour can't save them from cascades of rock. Soon the World will be rid of the bearded ones. We shall awake from this nightmare and rejoice. *Qosqoman!* On to Cusco!

The brazier dies down. A lamp flickers and winks out. A cold blade of the night slips in beneath the door. But for a long time the coca chewers do not notice the gathering cold and dark.

Manku claps his hands for a helper, awakening the interpreter from reverie. "Send in the Mexican to see my guest home. And bring more charcoal and lamp oil."

The man bows and backs out of the room.

"So. Enough of these matters for now, Waman. You'll have a reply and gifts for the Vicar-General in due course. In the meantime enjoy yourself amongst us. See all you want but say nothing of our talk. And keep mum around Méndez and his friends. If they corner you, give them only the weather and the time of day."

Now Waman is often invited to keep company with Manku and the Inca's inner circle. He stands in the front row at war games. He tries his hand at tossing horseshoes. And he watches the archery— squads of bowmen from the forest who shoot at stuffed targets shaped like men. Men with pink faces and black beards.

"When those are *real* Spaniards," a young voice at his shoulder says one day, "they'll use real arrows. Poison tipped. They paralyse in the time it takes to fry an egg." It is Titu Kusi, the Inca's eldest son.

"I didn't know you cooked, my lord," says Waman. He has met the prince several times at the horseshoe pitch. The boy never tires of the interpreter's tales—his capture at sea, his voyages on both oceans, above all his time in Spain. At thirteen, Titu Kusi carries himself like a man. An outgoing nature makes him older. As does his figure: he has the body of one who will grow stout. He jokes with his father and Molina, fences well with a dulled sword, is a good rider and arquebus shot. Already Titu Kusi drinks beer and has a pair of concubines.

The boy reminds Waman of himself at the same age, of his own unruly spirit and thirst for a wider world. Titu Kusi, too, has been a captive of the invaders—taken when he was five, along with the first Qoya. For several years he was kept in Cusco at the house of a Spaniard, apparently a kind man, who taught him a bit of Castilian and urged him to be baptised.

And were you? Waman once asked. It was the wrong thing to say. The prince snapped that he didn't remember, in both languages: *no recuerdo*; *mana yuyanichu*. But surely he would remember? He was nearly eight when Manku freed him and brought him to Vitcos. Of course—Manku has sworn to oust the Christians and their faith. No son of his can admit any contact with it. Especially after Pawllu's treason and conversion. Not that Titu Kusi seems religious at all, avoiding routine observances of any kind, preferring to stalk deer in the hills or disappear on picnics with his girls.

It is November now and the highland rains have begun. Great thunderheads boil up from the jungle, borne aloft on sultry winds to crash against the glaciers, spending themselves each night in epic lightning storms. Rivers are swollen, red with the gore of landslides. Rocks and trees career down canyons, branches plucking at the bridges.

One afternoon Waman and Molina are invited to the Inca's palace for a meal, to the main hall ringed by a row of niches and the usual dark band at eye level. A red cloth and gold service cover the dining board. The Qoya Kusi Warqay is there, welcoming the guests. On her back, in a shawl, she carries a baby girl, also called Kusi Warqay; at her side is the youngest boy, Tupa Amaru, peeking shyly from behind the Queen's flared skirt. The same reserve seems to affect Manku's middle son, ten-year-old Sayri Tupa, whose mother was seized by Gonzalo Pizarro and burnt by Francisco. Waman wonders what the boy might have seen.

Titu Kusi comes in last—only when his stepmother yells *K'usillu!* at the door. Waman smiles at the nickname: Monkey. To judge from his peeved look, the boy feels he has outgrown it. Hence its effectiveness.

There is fish and meat and jungle fruit, and plenty of young beer, which has a light fizziness Waman likes. Helpers move silently behind the diners. It is a family affair, no other guests, no hurry in the conversation.

At dusk, Manku draws the interpreter aside to a smaller room. "Let's chew," he says. He calls for lamps and makes up quids as before. There follows a companionable silence of working jaws, the leaves numbing the mouth, quickening the mind.

"The Qoya has ordered inquiries," the Inca says. "They may take a little while. But if your cousin is still a Chosen, she will be found."

Waman launches into fulsome thanks, expressing his burning wish to be someday in a position to requite, in his humble way, such kingly kindness.

Manku lifts a hand to stop the flow. "You can repay me now by considering a proposition. You needn't answer right away—take a few days to think it over. You're free to say yes or no." He looks Waman in the eye. "Why not stay with us in Willkapampa? Your cousin too when we find her. I will give you a good house, helpers, everything you need. What better place to further the search for your family? From here you can go anywhere you wish in Antisuyu. I also have many lands beyond this *suyu*. Among them Huanuco Province, which is held by General Illa Tupa. He will help you when you go there. That's the likeliest place, isn't it, from what you said?"

"I believe so, Sapa Inka. I was planning to go there as soon as my business in Cusco is—"

"Why go to Cusco? Why put yourself back in Spanish hands? Perhaps in Spanish irons. Your helpers can take my answer to the Vicar-General. Write him a letter. Tell him you're ill and can't travel. Not ill enough for him to send a friar, though." Manku chuckles. "You could even say I'm keeping you . . . detained."

Maybe that *is* what he's doing, Waman thinks.

"I've seen," the Inca goes on, "that my eldest has taken to you. Titu Kusi has a lively mind. He needs a tutor. So will the others in a few years. We have good teachers here—scholars from the House of Learning. I know you taught there yourself for a while. But they are elderly. They know little of the world beyond Tawantinsuyu.

"Also, the time is coming when I shall need a secretary. My sons certainly will. Someone who can read and write, both Quechua and Castilian. When we retake Cusco this need will be urgent. The state archives all went up in flames. Every year more knotkeepers die. Beyond my borders no new ones are being trained.

"That's all, Waman. Think well."

At the door Manku calls for Titu Kusi. When that fails he bellows the boy's full name with mock formality: "Titu Kusi Yupanki!"

The youth arrives a little dishevelled, as if he has been in bed and not alone.

"Bid good night to our guest, now. Say it in Castilian."

"*Winas nuchis,*" Titu Kusi manages, holding out his hand.

"*Buenas noches, señor mío,*" Waman replies, grasping it.

Waman has slept little, the Inca's offer burning in his mind. Why not take it? Especially if Tika can be found. A new life for the two of them, when they seemed to have lost everything. But what if the Spaniards overrun Willkapampa? He is being asked to foresee the future.

He is delighted to hear Molina at his door, bringing breakfast from the palace. The only person he can turn to for advice. Whatever else his stepfather may be, Molina is shrewd and canny. The older man listens, sipping coca tea.

"I'll say this for it, Waman—you've won Manku's trust, and you can trust him. He will treat you as he's promised. He's treated me well enough. Even those Almagrist rogues." With that Molina falls silent, a deep frown creasing his tattoos. Waman wonders what's wrong, why the hesitation. Molina is usually so forthright, so talkative. Is he jealous? Does he wish he'd mastered the alphabet and been offered this himself?

"Have some more tea, Waman. It'll help us think." He fills their cups slowly, adjusting the level in each one as if playing for time. "I've heard something. And I don't like it. It could affect your decision."

"What?"

"The Almagrists: Méndez, Barba . . ."

Molina drops his voice so low that Waman must strain to hear him above the sounds of the town: dogs and children, roosters, horses nickering on the lawn. "Don't forget I'm still a Spaniard under these clothes. Enough to know those men. I was just like them once. I pick up things. Glances, gestures."

He pauses, takes a bite of bread and honey.

"For some time now I've suspected they're up to something. It's looking worse since you got here, since the Inca received you that day at the usnu. What he said about 'bearded ones' rattled them, even though his words were just for show."

"How would they know what was said? Did they ask?"

"I'm sure they did. Their women. And one or two of them may understand the language better than we think."

Molina springs up and draws a corner of the door aside. Satisfied no one is eavesdropping, he comes back to his breakfast, voice muffled by chewing.

"Barba's woman told my Sallqa that she's noticed a change. She has only a few words of Spanish, but a sharp nose. She says the Almagrists joke around like always when someone's watching, but they're not joking amongst themselves. They're whispering. She thinks they're plotting an escape."

"But they've been here for years. Where would they go? They can't go to Gonzalo—he'd kill them on the spot."

"Oh, they won't go to Gonzalo. That would be suicide. But they may think—even if it's only wishful thinking—that if they inform on the Inca somehow they will be welcomed in Lima, taken back by their own people. The Viceroy is holding out an olive branch. Manku may not be the only one to clutch at it."

"They can't know about that. How do *you* know that?"

"Manku told me himself. I had a word with him late last night, to warn him. He's vulnerable right now—with Pumasupa and the best fighting men not here. But Méndez and Barba could have guessed it anyway. They know there's more to your presence than that letter you read out. They may even have been approached."

"How could they?"

"What about those two helpers who came with you?"

"They're simple fellows. Lakers. They only speak Aymara."

"You sure of that?"

Waman's spirits, brittle at best, shatter in remorse. What Molina suspects is all too likely. "I've been a fool! I should have sent all of them back to Cusco at the bridge. When I had the chance."

Molina pats him on the knee. "Only guesswork. Like I say, the signs go back before that anyway. Don't ride yourself so hard. I never do."

"How did Manku take your warning?"

"Like you did. He thinks they've got too much to lose, beginning with their lives. Where can they go? he says. Where can they live better?"

"What did you say to that?"

"I said Spaniards always think they can live better."

Waman takes two days to give the Inca his decision. He accepts, but asks if he may do so provisionally—until he knows the whereabouts of Tika and his mother. He should consult with them on longer plans. The Inca agrees curtly. Manku is not used to subordinates who dither. Yet he did promise the man a free choice.

That afternoon the sun breaks through a charcoal sky, burnishing the plaza lawn, steaming the town's heavy thatches and the coats of llamas and horses. The Almagrists gather by the usnu for a game of horseshoes. The Inca and Titu Kusi stroll over to join them. Few onlookers turn out. Manku's best men are still away, and most of the townsfolk are indoors. It's already late in the day; a smell of cooking hangs in the streets.

Waman and Molina are there. Sallqa, Molina's woman, arrives with Sisa, the girl who brings the interpreter his meals. The women talk gaily between themselves, offering the men guavas and tamales, a dish which has caught on in Vitcos since the "Mexican" introduced it.

"She's soft on you, lad," Molina whispers, with a sidelong glance at Sisa. "Your type, I reckon. Time you made a move. A single man's always a boy in Peru, no matter how old he grows. Why haven't you got a wife by now anyway?"

The women settle on cushions near the pitch, spreading their skirts around them.

"You know very well."

"Ah, yes. Your cousin. You like to keep it in the family. Cousins, sisters—if you ask me, the Incas don't set the best example. Mind you, I doubt they're as inbred as the Habsburgs. I hear King Charles is one of the lucky ones. Some of his cousins can't even wipe their own arses."

The two have not been paying attention to the game, which ends in scattered applause. An Almagrist win. Waman's ear is plucked by a lovely sound, a lute's arpeggio, reeling him back to the Moorish alleys of Seville. The tones fan out in the thin air, each note the heart of a ripple, as if from coins dropped in a pool. The lute player is the bearded one called Beard—Francisco Barba. A brash, disagreeable man. A master on the strings.

Méndez and the others crowd around Barba admiringly, hiding player and instrument from view. Manku, eager for another game to wipe out his loss, is walking up the pitch, gathering horseshoes, bending to right the hob—little tasks he enjoys.

They are on him so fast that nobody, not even Molina, understands what is happening until the Inca slumps over the hob with three or four stilettoes in his back. Then they are gone like cats—before the onlookers' shock turns to panic, to fury, and the women let out a fearful wail. Only Titu Kusi matches their speed, snatching up his father's lance and hurling it at Méndez. The lance misses narrowly, ploughs the turf. The assassin uproots it, hurls it back, cutting the boy's thigh.

"Get the boy!" Méndez yells at Barba. "Finish the boy. I'll hold your horse."

The lutenist, dagger in hand, runs after the wounded prince. Though limping and bloody, Titu Kusi reaches the square's open side and plunges down terracing into bushes below. By this time

Waman and Molina have armed themselves, Molina with the lance, the interpreter with stones. They throw them at the fleeing Almagrists. No hits, but at least they stop the hunt for Titu Kusi.

The assassins are soon away, galloping bareback down the step-road, clinging like ticks to their horses' necks.

Manku is on his side, the daggers left in his back for a healer to remove. His eyes are glassy. There is much blood on the ground and his clothing. He dressed in Inca cloth today. If only he had worn his armour, Waman thinks. But doubtless they'd have found a way. Most likely they'd have slit his throat.

"My son . . ." the Inca's voice is faint. Pink foam appears at a corner of his mouth. "Titu Kusi . . ."

"Safe, Only King," Waman answers. "We saw him get away. The Mexican has gone to find him."

Manku looks up at the interpreter unsteadily. His head slumps. A gasp from all who see. More wails from the women. At that moment the healer arrives. He plucks out the daggers one by one, applies dressings. He leans in and listens to the Inca's chest through a silver tube. The old man's competent manner reassures the crowd. *Sapa Inka kawsanmi,* is all he says. The Inca lives.

Against a wall is Barba's lute, its belly crushed to matchwood. The signal for attack. The weapons' hiding place.

As soon as Titu Kusi limped out of the bush, the royal buildings were sealed. Nobody has entered or left the Inca's household for two days. There are rumours: that he is dead but a successor is not yet agreed; that he is sleeping in the Sun's House beside the mummy of Wayna Qhapaq, so that both his heavenly and earthly fathers heal him; that he has already left Vitcos, flying like a condor in pursuit of his assailants.

On the third day, at mid-morning, conches sound and the gate of the compound is thrown open. Runners go down streets, calling people to the square. Three palanquins emerge. Side by side in the first sit the Inca and Qoya with their baby girl. The second holds Titu Kusi. The other princes, Sayri Tupa and Tupa Amaru, ride together in the last. All are carried gently up the usnu, where Manku is lifted out and seated in the great stone chair beneath a feather sunshade and a banner of the Empire. The Queen is beside him, her face drawn. The two small boys sit on stools to the right. Titu Kusi stays in his litter on the left, smiling and waving at the crowd, evidently much restored, though his thigh is tightly bandaged.

Manku is still. So still that Waman fears he may be dead, a fact easily hidden by a little makeup and the kingly fringe.

"All hear," the herald calls. "Our Only King Manku Qhapaq Yupanki lives. He will address you himself in a few days." Manku raises his right hand slowly, face taut with pain and determination. He does not look like a man who will be well enough to make a speech in a few days.

The herald continues with news. The bearded ones who attacked the Inca with such treachery have all been killed. Runners were sent over the secret passes to Pumasupa. The general turned from his march and intercepted the attackers. Two were dragged from their horses, others tried to barricade themselves inside a house. The house was set alight. Those who fled the blaze were shot as they emerged. The rest died in the flames.

A great shout of vengeance greets this news. Manku manages a shaky salute to the Sun with outstretched hand. The family is borne back into the palace.

On the evening of the fourth day Molina takes Waman to the Inca's bedside, telling him to bring pen and paper.

Manku is much worse, his breathing shallow and fast. His knees are drawn up to ease his belly, hideously swollen under the bed-clothes. He is shivering, yet his face is dewy with sweat. The Qoya Kusi Warqay bends over him, fanning her husband with a goose wing. Behind the bed a priest holds up a silver staff topped by a golden sunburst. A knotkeeper sits beside the Inca on a stool.

The royal children and a small group of lords and ladies stand around the walls. General Pumasupa—just back from catching the attackers—comes up to Waman, grasping his arm, guiding him to a seat beside the knotkeeper. He hands him a board on which to rest his papers.

"The Inca wishes you to write his words," he whispers. "You are to take them with you when you leave."

"Take them to whom?" Waman asks, but the general hushes him.

"My children," Manku begins. His voice is weak, with an odd clicking sound after each breath and a gurgling deep within. The Qoya protests. Her husband must rest, not speak. Others in the room murmur agreement. Some are weeping. The Inca silences them with a small wag of his head.

"My children. Brothers and sisters. All listen. I do not believe I shall escape from this. You see me in this state because, for the second time in my life, I trusted men from Spain. First the Old One and his brothers, with whom I made an alliance. And who betrayed me. Then those who murdered him. The same ones who have now struck me.

"Do not weep. If anyone weeps it should be me. For having

brought this end upon myself and all of you. Now note what I command. Never again have dealings of any kind with the bearded ones. Never again let them into this realm, no matter who they are. Or how sweet their words . . ." Manku's voice fades. The healer brings water to his lips.

The Sapa Inka struggles on. "I commend the people to your care. Never forget how they have followed us, helped us, stood by us in these dreadful times. It rests with you always to be fair, to be just and generous. That is the foundation of our power.

"I name Sayri Tupa my heir. General Pumasupa will rule through a council of regents until Sayri Tupa is of age. Titu Kusi shall sit on this council, and all lords present.

"That is all."

Epilogue

Three people on a raft of logs on water red with silt. They are in the jungle lowlands now. The swollen river has slackened and widened like a sea, its shores indistinct: a green smudge far off where the water meets the sky. Nothing can touch them here but sun and rain and hunger. They have a little deckhouse of palm leaves, a fishing net, some food; an oar and a moon to steer by.

As soon as he had blotted Manku's words, Waman was sent back to his quarters with Molina. "Wait there. Be ready to leave at once," Pumasupa told them. "If the Inca dies, the people will go mad with grief. No outsider will be safe."

Molina paced the room for hours, opening the door, scanning the stars, listening. Neither slept.

After midnight a soldier came, bringing two teams of bearers with travelling hammocks slung from poles.

Waman asked where they were going. No reply. Only the jolt and tilt of the hammocks, and no way to see anything till dawn, when they were borne over a snowy pass and down step-roads into clouds and trees. About noon on the second day they came to the bank of a river in spate. The bearers, still unwilling to talk, began building a raft from logs kept in a shed.

Shortly before the raft was done, a third hammock arrived. In it was Tika.

She climbed out and stood still for a moment, blinking in the hard light of the clearing, lovely in the sky-blue dress of a Chosen. "Waman!" she called, seeing him running towards her from the shade.

They held each other until they felt the stares of the others upon them.

He introduced her to Molina. She was shy with him, even cool. Waman guessed she hadn't seen a man in years, except her bearers. She wouldn't say much until the three of them were aboard and the water was carrying them away between the forest walls.

"The Inca Manku has died," Tika said then.

"Did you see him?"

"They didn't take me into Vitcos. But I knew. I could hear from the road. I've never heard such grief."

"Where have you been living all these years?" Waman asked. "Can you say?"

"No. Not even if I knew. But I don't. There's a hidden city, in the clouds, between two mountains. They took us there from Cusco. All women. We travelled at night. Many nights. They said we'd be safe there forever, that they'd torn up the road behind. You would never have found me, Waman. Not without the Qoya's help."

Later she asks if they know where they're going.

"No more than you do," says Molina. "They put us on this raft without a word and shoved us off."

"Well, I do know a little more than you. In a few days we must be sure to keep to the left bank. There's a riverside town called Red

Earth. From there a road runs up into the foothills of Lower Huanuco. They gave me this."

She hands Waman a small quipu, sees his surprise.

"It's a safe-conduct—to show Manku's officials when we get there."

It's as if they are standing still, for they move at the speed of the river, so wide and deep it seems not to flow at all.

Molina makes a notch in a timber each dawn. He is getting sunburnt, his lips cracked, the skin moulting from his shoulders.

Waman tells him to go into the palm-leaf deckhouse, but he doesn't move. Perhaps he is shy of Tika, who is dozing there.

"Now I'll tell you," he says.

"Tell me what?"

"Where Chaska and I were living."

"Puma Hill!" Tika's voice from the shelter. "Was it Puma Hill?"

"Yes," he says. "It's been more than two years since I left. But I think she'll still be there. She and Atuq."

They question Molina until the sun is fierce and he agrees to go into the shade.

In this emptiness, this heat, this seeming stillness—and this anticipation—a man might lose his mind. Waman withdraws to the stern, throws the net. The fishing is bad in the soupy water. Only three small fish in five days.

On the ninth day, about noon, they reach Red Earth.

"First we eat," Tika says to Waman. "Then we walk. Up into the mountains."

The free Inca state lived on almost thirty years after Manku's death, ruled by his sons from a new capital nearer the jungle, less easily reached than Vitcos.

Meanwhile, Gonzalo Pizarro overthrew the Lima Viceroy and killed him in 1546. Gonzalo's conquistador regime, brutal even for its day, ended with his hanging by the Spanish Crown in 1548. But the revolt caused repeal of the benevolent New Laws, worsening the plight of Peruvians.

The quisling Pawllu died in 1549, perhaps of foul play, during negotiations with the Inca state. His son, Carlos Inca, married a Spanish noblewoman and presided over collaborationist Inca aristocrats in Cusco.

In the late 1550s, Sayri Tupa travelled to Lima and made a short-lived peace, building a palace near Cusco, where he was poisoned three years later. The Pope had approved Sayri Tupa's marriage to his sister Kusi Warqay, and their daughter later married into Jesuit nobility. Ironically, their granddaughter would marry a Borgia, kin to the pope who had given the New World to Spain and Portugal long before the mainland was invaded.

Titu Kusi now took over in Willkapampa, ruling until his death in 1571 (perhaps of natural causes). Shrewd and resourceful, he fended off Spanish attack with drawn-out negotiations while secretly continuing his father's policy of supporting uprisings in occupied Peru. Titu Kusi also became the author of an important history of the Spanish invasion and his father's resistance (see the Afterword). This he sent to Spain, hoping to convince King Philip II of the justice of the Inca cause.

He was succeeded by Manku's youngest son, Tupa Amaru (or Tupac Amaru), who ruled Willkapampa only a year. After yet another smallpox outbreak ravaged the independent state, the ruthless Viceroy Toledo pursued this last Sapa Inka into the jungle and, despite strong protest from both Incas and moderate Spaniards, beheaded him in Cusco.

With resistance crushed and the native population still collapsing—by the early 1600s it would fall to less than a tenth of what it had been in Wayna Qhapaq's day—Toledo felt secure enough to convert the old Inca work-tax into grinding slavery. Over the following two centuries, more than a million would die in the silver mines of Potosí and the toxic mercury workings at Huancavelica, used for refining silver and gold.

Even so, the history of the Incas did not end. The Spaniards had killed Tupa Amaru's son, but not his daughter. In 1780, by which time the population had begun to recover and nationalist feelings were stirring among the native aristocracy, a direct descendant proclaimed himself Inca Tupa Amaru II and came close to overthrowing Spanish rule. Joined by the Aymara under Tupac Katari, the convulsion shook the Andes. The second Tupa Amaru, like the first, was executed in Cusco's great square, but his rebellion exposed the weakness of the Spanish Empire, hastening its breakup in the 1820s.

Although the republics that replaced Spanish rule were founded by small white elites intent on exploiting indigenous people and erasing their culture, the ancient civilization of the Andes lives on in the twenty-first century. Quechua is the most widespread native language of the Americas, with some ten million speakers in Peru and other parts of the old Tawantinsuyu; Aymara is spoken by three million, mostly in Bolivia. Despite centuries of persecution, native religious traditions thrive both openly and under a Christian veneer. In recent years a political transformation has begun as white elites lose some of their power through the ballot box. Peru and Bolivia currently have presidents of indigenous background: Ollanta Humala and Evo Morales Ayma. Morales, who is Aymara, has been the more radical and effective, implementing policies to redress five hundred years of colonization.

Afterword

How much of *The Gold Eaters* is true—insofar as truth can be deduced from a patchy, complex, and sometimes contradictory historical record? I have kept to the skeleton of fact, adding flesh where fiction demands. The main events happened, and most of my characters are based on people known to have taken part in them. Inca and Spanish leaders are much better documented than ordinary folk, of course. After the raid on the Inca ship, a young Peruvian (perhaps several) was kidnapped and taken to Spain. The Spaniards dubbed him Felipe or Felipillo. Meanwhile a Spaniard named Molina was left ashore at Tumbes, his subsequent fate uncertain. Most sources agree that Felipe was the interpreter at Cajamarca six years later, and in Cusco.

Felipe's life after that is less clear, but accounts have him rebelling against the Spaniards during Almagro's invasion of Chile. There is no evidence he ended up in the Inca Manku's kingdom, though it's not impossible; other go-betweens and fugitives certainly did, not least Manku's assassins. Felipe's own name and family are unknown. I've called him Waman in honour of Felipe Waman Puma, the indigenous writer and artist whose work so brilliantly illuminates the Peruvian experience of those tragic times.

Specialists will know the freedoms I've taken. The definitive modern history is John Hemming's superb *The Conquest of the Incas*

(1970). James Lockhart's *The Men of Cajamarca* (1972) is indispensable for details of Pizarro's army and the melting of Atawallpa's ransom. William H. Prescott's classic *History of the Conquest of Peru* (1847) still repays the reader. Kim MacQuarrie's *The Last Days of the Incas* (2007) also gives a good account, especially on events after Cajamarca.

Many Spanish chronicles are available in various English editions. The best, and most fair-minded, is widely agreed to be Pedro de Cieza de León's *The Discovery and Conquest of Peru*, first published in part in 1553, now available in full from Duke University Press (1998).

Of histories written by indigenous Peruvians, David Frye (2006) has made a well-abridged translation of the massive *First New Chronicle and Good Government* by Felipe Waman Puma (or Guaman Poma), written in the 1590s and early 1600s, though unknown until 1908.

The work of Manku's son Titu Kusi Yupanki (or Titu Cusi Yupanqui) has recently been translated twice, by Ralph Bauer (2005), and in a bilingual edition with the original on facing pages by Catherine Julien (2006).

The most famous history with an Inca perspective is the *Royal Commentaries of the Incas*, by Garcilaso de la Vega, El Inca, whose mother was Ñusta Chimpu Ocllo, a niece of Emperor Wayna Qhapaq, and whose father was a conquistador. First published in 1609, the work became a seventeenth-century bestseller which did much to establish a Utopian view of the Inca Empire. It was later deemed subversive and banned by Spanish authorities, though not before it helped inspire the great revolt led by Tupa Amaru II. The best translation is by Harold V. Livermore (1966).

I have modernized spelling of Quechua words and Inca names (Wayna Qhapaq for Huayna Capac, etc.) but have kept traditional spelling for words and place names commonly used in English, such as Cusco (Qosqo or Qusqu), Cajamarca (Qashamarka), Huanuco (Wanuku), and quipu (khipu).

Some eyebrows may be raised by my assumption that quipus—besides being mathematical in content—were a mature form of writing, but this is supported by recent research, most notably the work of Gary Urton. It is in any case hard to see how lengthy messages could have been sent thousands of miles, with hundreds of fast relays, if they needed spoken commentary.

Readers curious about the Inca language (also called Runasimi) can get started with Lonely Planet's Quechua phrasebook by Serafín Coronel-Molina (2008), much expanded and improved since a slim first edition done by me in 1989 with the help of Nilda Callañaupa.

Acknowledgments

First thanks to the book's first readers, to whom I owe many helpful suggestions: above all Deborah Campbell, who read several drafts; also Anthony Weller, Denis Smith, Michael Wall, and my agents Jackie Kaiser and Henry Dunow. I am very grateful to Nicole Winstanley at Penguin Canada and Laura Perciasepe at Riverhead in New York, whose editing was all one could wish for; and to Alexander Schultz for his deft copy editing. Flaws that persist are my own.

I'm also indebted to many people for fruitful discussions about this book and historical fiction in general, especially Louise Dennys, George Lovell, Sarah Dunant, Colm Tóibín, Annabel Lyon, Louise Doughty, Karen Robert, and Sarah Tidbury.

My thanks to Robin Vose for his insights and kind loan of early sources, to John Hemming for his inspiring work and conversations over the years, to Persis Clarkson for her knowledge of Chile, to the late Celia Toribia Chávez for the folk song (adapted) in chapter 10, to Shane Hawkins for information on period Greek, to Satva Hall for photography, and to Charles Montgomery, whose portrait of Inca Garcilaso watched wryly over my efforts.

I am deeply grateful to all the Peruvians and *peruanistas*—too many to name—who have been so kind, hospitable, and generous over many years of travel and research in their country.

I thank the Canada Council and the British Columbia Arts Council for their support.